The Blue Mask

MICK BURKE

The Blue Mask

tellwell

Tellwell Talent
www.tellwell.ca

ISBN
978-0-2288-8414-9 (Hardcover)
978-0-2288-8413-2 (Paperback)
978-0-2288-8415-6 (eBook)

To Janet

You are an awesome woman & I am so happy to know you!

Thanks, girl

Mick

To all who have supported my writing over the years.
And especially to Claus, with love and without whom.

"Sticking a needle in your arm is no way to reach a ripe old age. But hey—drugs, sex and rock and roll. That was the name of the game. We hit the golden age of rock after we got through the boy meets girl - boy gets girl thing and we came up with a walk on the wild side. Life is a party. Love anyone and everyone and have a good time. It was an anthem. Live fast and if you happened to die young at least you'd make a beautiful corpse.

"Everyone I know went through it—some still are. The music talked about it and we all jumped in. You did the drugs your favourite musicians were doing if you wanted to be cool—and who didn't? And you slept with everyone. Free love may have started in the sixties but it grew up in the seventies and eighties.

"Yeah, well, the golden age has faded and we're hitting the twilight of that little history lesson. Walking on the wild side doesn't cut it. Not even with the musicians. Drugs, sex and rock and roll. Somehow that anthem doesn't work anymore. It's payback time."

The interview tape had been done some time ago as part of a concerted effort by several agencies who wanted to carry the message of no drugs and safe sex to teenagers. The face of the person watching the screen was a smooth mask as the interview continued. Short, black curling hair framed the pale skin with its sharp features, thin mouth and eyes so dark they looked black. The comments carried on, muted now, a background to memory.

None of them had ever thought things would end up quite this way. The Blue Mask started out in such a spirit of fun, much like the age that was being described on the tape. Drugs had almost destroyed them but a year and a half of silence had not dulled fan support. When the band regrouped and started touring, people hadn't forgotten. Despite haphazard gigs and uneven management, interest was fired rather than quelled. The two long years of hard work that followed culminated in an early morning phone call. Hidden tides were turning but it was like a blip on the radar screen, something seen through the wrong end of a telescope.

Then.

It turned into something quite different later.

CHAPTER 1

Spring 1990

Alix Lane drove quickly through the late night streets on a warm spring evening, as she did after every gig they played at home. It was her safe way of coming down when the blood was still pounding through her veins, pushed by the tremendous rush of adrenaline that accompanied her through shows, even after all these years. She liked the long partying that could do the same thing but now restricted it closing nights of extended gigs. In the early years that wearing down had led to more insidious ways of keeping up with the gruelling schedule, long runs on alcohol and speed. Cruising in a car was a much easier way to get old and, at twenty-six, she still had a way to go.

A soft rain penetrated the Vancouver night, glinting silver in the street lights and misting its way through the open window to settle gently on her hair. Eventually, she pulled into the West End – her haven – the place where the weirdos, artists, layabouts and outcasts of the mainstream made their homes in an atmosphere both secretive and tolerant. It was an old world mix of three and four story walk-ups and highrises where boarding houses sat alongside single family residences. She slid her car into a space near the Arlington Terrace, a grand, old crumbling matron where both she and Joel lived. Grabbing her leathers, she locked up and treaded the familiar path to the oak front door with the tarnished lion's head knocker on it and passed through it up to her room. Joel wouldn't be home for hours yet. The lovely lady who had been draping herself all over him like a dying swan would see to that.

Once inside she tossed her possessions on the bed, lit a cigarette and poured a glass of Scotch, adding a handful of ice from the fridge. Though both she and Joel could afford to live in more sumptuous surroundings they resisted any pressure to leave the Arlington. She loved this bohemian place. Shut the door and the world went away to be recreated in a kind of twilight. She switched off the overhead light and turned on the neon on the wall – a martini glass with an olive it in that Robin had found for her in one of the many second-hand stores around Commercial.

The elegant, airy quality that the twelve foot ceilings gave the long, large loft disappeared and became intimate, caressing. A small kitchen occupied one corner, with a bathroom tucked off to the side. At the other end her bed and desk lay in shadow; a corner closet on the far wall contained her stage clothes and the black jeans and shirts she favoured. The central area had been left mostly empty. She dragged an armchair across the polished hardwood to one of two floor-to-ceiling windows that rose unencumbered to the rococo trim and sat quietly, drinking and smoking as she watched the desultory parade of people go by on the street below. When her body had slowed down sufficiently she would crawl into bed to recharge. It had been a long week. The level in the bottle dwindled and the ashtray was overflowing when she finally stumbled to bed.

The phone rang early the next morning. Alix groaned as she rolled over and reached for it. "Yeah?"

"Nice mood, babe. You got a hangover?"

"As a matter of fact, yes," she answered, smiling. "How you doing, Brad?"

"I'm groovin'."

"And honouring me with a long distance call at some ungodly hour of the morning. What's up?"

"Ever heard of a guy goes by the by the name Geoffrey Davis?"

"Yeah, he owns Dome Records. Their office has been in touch with us."

"I know him personal. Some of my bands have signed contracts. He was in Toronto yesterday and I ran into him."

"And?"

"He's hot for the Mask, babe. He heard the album you did back in ancient times and he's talking rerelease and more. He is very, very into doing something for you."

"I know but we've been busy for the last while touring. So why'd he tell you this?"

He laughed. "Don't blow up on me; I told him I was negotiating to manage you. Actually, I told him it was in the bag."

"What, from Toronto," she sneered in sarcastic disbelief. "Come on, Brad. We're managing ourselves – everyone around here knows that."

"Yeah, and making a balls-up of it. I'm flying out tonight, Alix. Can you find me a place to crash for a few days?"

"Sure but what the hell is this all about?"

"The Blue Mask got anything on for a day or four?"

"No but we're off at the end of the week, touring south."

"Get them together at your place tomorrow morning and I'll do my pitch."

"Can I see you before then?"

"Plane gets in kinda late. I'll come to the Arlington so you can take me to my crash pad. Let me catch up on some zzz's and I promise we'll gab later. We on?"

"Sure. See you later."

The line went dead.

Alix got up to brush the fur off her tongue and swallow some aspirin, her mind churning. Brad was often given to spur of the moment actions but even those were backed up by well thought-out planning. She'd met him years ago in Toronto through a mutual friend when he was a struggling manager trying to put together a stable of bands and he was a renegade even then. Long dark hair framed a squarish face with no hint of weakness and regular workouts kept his muscular body in shape. He always reminded her of a 'he-man' out of some old time Western and he had the attitude: male chauvinist straight through and proud of it.

She had fought tooth and nail to win his respect and be treated like an equal in those early days and out of it had come a friendship that meant a great deal to them both. Under the hip talk and cool exterior lay a razor-sharp intelligence and a manipulative cunning that had raised him in the ranks of management to hotshot status before he hit thirty. He'd gotten his stable. The bands trusted him implicitly and all did very well out of it.

She grinned. Joel was going to love him.

Despite the early hour, she took a chance and, armed with two cold beers, walked across the hall to bang loudly on his door. "Hey, asshole, you alone?"

"Yeah," came the answering groan, "so leave me in peace."

"No chance." She already had the key ready and inserted it into the lock.

The singer and front-person for the band, Alix got a lot of unwanted attention, as did Joel Stark, their high profile lead guitarist. Though not the only two surviving members of the original Blue Mask – their bassist Leo Sutcliffe was still with them – they were its voice and, as the group ascended, both found new focus on themselves. The Arlington had a good security system but fans soon infiltrated and gone were the days when the two could merely waltz into one another's rooms. Keys were exchanged and doors kept dead-bolted from groupies, well-wishers and hangers-on. This arrangement gave the pair enough freedom to write whenever the whim hit them, which was often, and at any time, which was all hours. So far it had worked well.

The large loft was dim and smelled of stale smoke and sweat. Joel was doing up the fly of a pair of tight black jeans and smiled when she handed him a beer. "You know me so well," he said, leaning over to kiss her and tug on the short black hair.

"Especially at the end of a gig. How long did the party go on?"

"Public or private?"

"Both."

"Most of the night. I went home with the delectable lady, did what she wanted, then split, as usual."

She turned away with a look of disgust. "Yuk."

Joel lit a cigarette and popped the cap on the beer, his features contorting as the first sharp taste went smoothly down his throat. "I don't know if it feels good or hurts." He put the bottle on the counter in the corner where a kitchen unit sat against the wall. "Let me clean up before I listen. Something awesome must be going on to get you up this early."

He disappeared into the bathroom and Alix opened the long black curtains that shaded the windows. Spring sunshine spilled into the room, highlighting the dust motes dancing in the air.

Joel emerged a few minutes later. Although not conventionally handsome, he was arresting and it assured him of a succession of women and a never empty bed. With the added popularity of the band this had only increased. For his part he was always honest with them and made no promises. Alix remained his partner, close friend and confidant.

Clad in the usual black t-shirt and jeans, he was tall and well-built, wiry rather than muscular. His face was angular, cut sharply and reminded her of a wolf, lean and hungry-looking, full of a mischief that had a dangerous edge. His hair was a blonde sheen, combed sleekly back and, though there was intelligence in the features, there was also cruelty. It was a hard face that softened only when he grinned. Eyes of a deep sea green were bracketed by fine lines reflecting twenty-six hard earned years.

Lighting another cigarette, he picked up his beer and indicated two chairs by the long window. "Sit down and talk to me, girl."

"Remember my friend Brad?"

"The hotshot manager back east?"

"He's on his way out here and he wants to manage us. It seems he's had a chat with Dome's Mr. Davis and they want us badly."

"That shouldn't surprise you. Their office has been calling."

"But this is the man himself. I don't know any more. Brad's doing his clam imitation until he sees all of us tomorrow at my place."

"Dome's big, Alix. Shit, they're international. I thought we wanted to stay low key."

"We haven't been low key for months. We've got so much work we don't know whether we're coming or going. Besides, Brad can have all the headaches."

"We don't want to move too fast. Why spoil the fun?"

"It's not all fun now and we might as well move a little faster in the direction we're already headed. We've got a lot of material and it would sure beat having to pay for the studio ourselves."

He reached over to smooth the frown cutting into her pale features. "'Kay, girl, I'll get the others there and you take care of the hotshot's appearance. We'll listen. If we like it, he's in." The lop-sided grin was pronounced. "Now, seeing as we're up, let's go Downtown and get beer and breakfast – in that order."

Alix secured Brad a room at the Crossfield, a boarding establishment down the street and was waiting, key in hand, when he hammered on her door late that night.

Exhausted, he stumbled into her room begging for beer. She opened two and propelled him into an armchair by the long windows.

"Nice pad," he said, looking about him with undisguised interest.

"Yeah, yeah. Now sit down and answer some questions or I'll push you through the glass."

"Let me eye you first, babe. You looking healthy." He smacked his lips and she hit him. But she did look better. No longer skeletally thin, her body ravaged by alcohol and the lasting effects of kicking speed, she had fleshed out. Her eyes were clear and her face had lost the pinched whiteness that he remembered. He shook his head mockingly, taking in the old black jeans, turtleneck and low-heeled leather boots. "You still wearing the same threads I met you in."

"I have a whole wardrobe of this stuff. I replace it when needed."

"You look good, Alix; I'm glad."

"Wish I could say the same for you." The blue silk shirt was wrinkled from the flight and his jeans were soiled at the hem, as were the tooled cowboy boots. "You could've cleaned up at least."

He laughed. "Still a charmer."

"Come on, Brad, now that we have the fashion commentary finished, tell me what the hell's going on."

"Hold on, babe, I'll come clean." He took a long drink and when he turned to face her all the jocularity had gone out of his face. "Stuff in Toronto is running so smooth I don't even have to be present and accounted for. I wanna change and I wanna expand and you guys need me more than you know."

"We're doing just fine, thanks," she retorted. "We're making money and we've got people making offers left, right and center."

"You're not on top of the ladder yet."

"We're headlining our own tours."

He sighed and shook his head. "But you ain't in the big league."

"Get off your high horse."

"Not on one. I get to hear a lot of stuff on the grapevine and I get around in places that count. In a few months, you guys managed to turn a lot of people around who wrote you off a couple years ago. So why not take the leap?"

"Into what?"

"Don't be stupid. You need management and I need stars."

"Stars. You're joking."

"You selling yourself too cheap. Man, that Davis cat likes to get around and see who's going on his label. He takes a real personal interest and I ain't seen him this excited in a long time. Don't forget – I been dealing with him years. Dome ain't EMI but you ain't the Stones either. It's a good label and it does fairly big bucks in the US of A as well as Europe. They got a base in Britain that's earning, which is something in this recession. I know he's contacted you but if you handle it wrong you could get screwed, get below your worth. You got to trust someone some time, Alix. This is my job; I'm good at it."

"What do you get out of it?"

"My percentage." He grinned. "And more stars on my dance card."

"You think you can do that much for us?"

"I got a solid rep and a nose for talent and I know what to do with it. Usually I got bands asking me for help. It's rare I offer. Ask Bear."

"Our drummer?"

"Yeah, I know him from way back. When you picked him for Mark's replacement you made a great choice. He's one of the best on the circuit."

"And you think you can push us into this league of yours?"

He winked. "Sign on with me and I'll take you for a hell of a ride. You won't know what hit you."

He left shortly afterwards, pleading the need for sleep. Alix settled in her favourite armchair, gazing out at the dark, empty street. She had already decided she wanted to sign with him. Experience told her that if he was driving it would indeed be one hell of a ride and if things got a little bumpy, well, she'd been on rocky ground before and come through alive.

Little did she know just how wild that ride was going to be.

CHAPTER 2

All were assembled the following morning. Joining Alix and Joel were Bear McNeil (given name Edgar), a thirty-something transplanted Torontonian mountain of a man with a heart to match his size plus Leo, twenty-seven, a Mick Jagger carbon copy with a frank, open face and dark, serious eyes, and Dixie Adler, at twenty-three the youngest member, a large-boned keyboardist with crimped, dark blonde hair surrounding a vixen's face dominated by merry blue eyes.

Much to Alix's surprise, the meeting went smoothly. Joel recognized a soul mate in Brad and shook hands enthusiastically. Bear hugged him so hard he almost choked and Dixie flirted outrageously before settling down to listen. Leo sat quietly absorbed as Brad outlined in detail what he had told Alix the night before.

"That's about it, hombres. My contract is pretty standard so I'll leave it with you. I'm winging back to transfer ops out here and deal with my management in Toronto. If we got a deal then it's business as usual – my way. I'm good at this and there'll be bread for all of us. Make no mistake."

"We have a lawyer we pass all our signables to," Joel said. "We'll run it by us and then him."

"You got some good habits, Durango. Between him and me and the accountant we're gonna hire to deal with your fortunes, you gonna be sitting on top of the heap."

Leo spoke up after Brad departed. "You sure he's not selling us fairy stories, Alix?"

He was a quiet reflection of the man she'd met years ago. The earlier recklessness had given way to a more guarded approach to life since their previous drummer Mark had died of drug complications. Both Joel and Alix had been heavily using drugs and he had feared they would die too, but Mark's death had shocked them all and given the two the jolt they needed to rethink their lifestyle. During that time he had also lost a few close friends to AIDS. Joel no longer made cracks about Leo's gayness and a new respect had grown between them all with the maturity that their shared experiences had wrought. Yet Alix missed the fun she and Leo used to have, missed his lightheartedness. Relations between them were gentle and sometimes tinged with sadness but he trusted her implicitly.

"He's fine as far as I know but ask Bear. He was in the business in Toronto a long time before me."

"Not to worry, little buddy," Bear said enthusiastically. "If anyone can do it, Brad Easton can. I'm sure as hell glad he's transferring out here. He's honest and he gets results. Where his bands are concerned, he's a shark. Dome hasn't a chance in hell of getting us cheap. He'll push for everything but we'll have to work our asses off once we get it."

For the next three days the five tossed ideas back and forth amid discussions and rehearsals in a loft they rented Downtown. Joel had gotten the nod for the contract from their lawyer and there was no hesitation as far as the band members themselves were concerned.

For his part, Brad sat in on the sessions, taping, listening carefully and taking notes as the Blue Mask ran through the song list for their tour along the southern coast of British Columbia. Already deep in negotiations, he promised to have a solid offer hammered out with Dome when they returned. Armed with past records of the band's business, he set off.

The last night before Alix and Joel were to leave the pair arrived home to find two people on their doorstep, clamouring for attention.

David Ashley – Ash to his friends – was sleek and streamlined with a mane of fiery red hair and a face that, though hard like Joel's, had a sculptured simplicity that he lacked. A promising painter at twenty-three, he had blown several art gallery contracts through repeated drunkenness and abuse to his wealthy, conservative clients. In the intervening years he'd managed to turn himself around, with Joel's assistance and Robin's maintenance, and had been making a living designing posters, CD covers and similar artwork. The Blue Mask had been his first assignment and out of it came their logo: five deep blue masks, each a stylized depiction of the members done in a slash of simple lines, over the band's name on a stark black background. Such a rash of contracts had followed from other bands that he now had little time to paint.

Robin Coxx, a talented dancer/choreographer, had branched into videos with some of the groups Ash designed for. Tall, with long blonde hair, she had a delicate, beautifully proportioned face with high cheekbones, a full mouth and large brown eyes. Ash called her his moon goddess who danced in a dark world and, with Alix and Joel, the four comprised a strong friendship/support group that went back years. They kept in close contact and, despite busy careers, still tried to meet regularly.

"Let us in," Ash demanded, producing a bottle of gin. "We brought libations for the meeting."

"We're leaving tomorrow," Joel protested. "You know our rules on touring."

"You'll be on the road all day so you can sleep it off. Go soak your head; you're getting old."

"Yeah, yeah," Alix said, laughing, "we get the point. Come on Joel, the sooner we let them in, the sooner they'll go."

"Don't bet on it."

The four assembled in Alix's room and, after drinks were poured, settled in happily.

"Rumours, rumours, rumours," Ash said slyly.

Joel opened a beer and tossed the cap at his friend. "You sound like some kind of mystic guru with a brain problem. What's your point?"

"I think we should schedule these goddamn sessions every week so we know what's going on in our little family. Me and Robin haven't seen you for ages."

"We've been working," Alix said.

"Tough. I propose weekly meetings."

"Here, here," Robin agreed.

"All in favour raise your arms." Ash went behind Alix and Joel and pulled both their hands skyward. "Motion passed." He laughed and poured himself another gin.

"Kay," Joel said, shaking his head in mock disgust, "on weeks we're out of town we'll arrange a conference call."

"Seriously," Ash said, taking his place in the circle that the four always unconsciously assumed when together, "I hear you have a new manager. Give me details."

"You used to be able to keep a secret in this town."

"Not when you're friendly with the boss of the Crossfield and one manager-type friend of Alix's, recently arrived from Toronto, gets a phone and fax installed because he has just signed a contract with the Blue Mask."

"That'll do it. Alix, the floor's all yours."

She explained the situation, eyes flashing with excitement, a smile lighting the pale features. Ash sat back thoughtfully when she'd finished. "I'll have to find out more about this Bradley person."

"Not for our sake."

"No, for mine. I called this meeting because I too have news. We both do."

Robin cleared her throat. "Mine's typical. Videos."

"What Little Miss Modest isn't telling you is she's been signed by VidWorks to do a series."

Amid congratulations Robin got hold of him and rubbed her fist in his face. Ash brushed himself off with dignity and banged his bottle on the floor, calling for order. "Does this Bradley person do more than manage bands?"

"Brad," Alix said pointedly, "is far too cool to be called a Bradley person to his face and if you're prepared to risk it, I'm warning you he'll probably rearrange your beautiful mug."

"So I've heard. No chance for me there, I guess." Ash pouted campily but a snort of disgust from Joel quickly wiped the expression off of his face. "Seriously, I need a manager or agent or someone called Friday."

"To what, organize your social schedule," Joel asked with a touch of sharpness. He had little tolerance for references to Ash's lifestyle. It had long been an understanding between the two that those discussions be conducted along certain well-established lines.

"Remember the first poster I did for you for that gig at The Street?"

"Yeah," Alix said. "I couldn't believe the response. People stole them all out of the club. You became a star then."

"I never would've guessed it would net me so much goddamn attention. I got half the bands on the West Coast banging on my door trying to get stuff done. I figured charging them the moon would slow things down but no luck. I'm supposed to be a fucking painter, working on my art and trying to convince the stuck-up bastards at the Western Canadian Gallery they can trust me enough to give me another showing, but I can't see them for the line-ups at the studio. I had to set me up a smart little office so I could find the time to actually work."

"It makes sense."

"It didn't to me. At least not until a couple days ago. It was paying my rent and keeping me in gin and leather, don't get me wrong, but I didn't look at it as art."

"So what happened," Joel asked.

Robin laughed and gave Ash a conspiratorial wink. He nodded sagely. "My moon goddess has been doing a bit of PR on my behalf and showed some of my stuff to a certain agent-type who went to a certain band and the whole thing brought this phone call from Scott Tyler. Name ring a bell?"

"Hades' lead singer." Hades was Dome Records' premier Canadian band. Their current album had debuted at number five on Billboard. It was a triumph for any Canadian band to enter the U.S. charts at such a high spot and the group was even more popular in Europe. Dome's English company reported that it had taken the number one spot in less than four weeks.

Ash sat back smugly. "Hades goes into the studio next week to work on their new album. Any guesses who just signed the contract to design it?"

With a whoop, Alix and Joel dived on him, hollering and cheering.

"It does look like our family stars are on the rise again," Robin said, now serious and somber as she recalled the last time their fortunes were spiralling upward. "Do you think we can hold onto ourselves this time?"

Joel shook his head sadly. "We're not young and stupid anymore, Robin. Me and Alix haven't done drugs in almost four years and Ash isn't seeing life from the bottom of a bottle. You were the most together out of all of us but even we can give you a run for your money now."

"That all only came about because Mark died. What's left to stop us this time?" She could still see his body, sprawled across the bed, the cord from a table lamp tied around his arm and the morning light flashing silver on the syringe lying among the loose wire. Dead because they had driven him too far and he thought that trying Alix and Joel's drug would help him understand. "Only old age, girl." He reached over and tugged her hair. "Stop worrying, 'kay? We won't self-destruct."

Alix poured Scotch into her glass and moved around the circle, refilling everyone's glass with their particular poison. When she'd finished, she cleared her throat and raised her glass. "A toast. To Mark."

All four acknowledged, drank and retreated into private thought. Alix, Joel and Leo had found him first, and then called Ash and Robin. Death – the ultimate kick, the one she and Joel had written songs about, lauding it and the pursuits that could cause it. When they found Mark, they realized that it was a kick, but a cold and empty one.

"He'd be pleased, you know," Robin said finally. "He really believed the band could get somewhere. He loved that first album, even though you thought it was too commercial."

"I listened to it the other day. I hate to admit it, but our producer Jack's instincts were good. I liked it."

"Me too," Joel agreed. "I think we were wrong to attack Apache for selling us out." Apache, their first manager, had demanded the changes to the record.

"Only Mark thought she did the right thing and we attacked him too."

"That's water under the bridge, girl."

Alix felt the familiar rush of guilt wash over her. Apache had blamed her for Mark's death and she still felt a responsibility that she admitted to no one but herself. If she hadn't been so savage he might never have gone near their supplier. He'd done speed for the first time in a drunken haze with some idea that it would help him understand her addiction to it. His death had dragged her out of the pit.

She pushed the ghost away and changed the subject abruptly. "So this office set up is for real? You want to consult Brad?"

"I was only joking about that. But the rest is a go. I'm hiring someone full-time. I have a feeling this Hades thing is ready to explode. I found myself a two-room space I can use as an office/studio and got a phone, answering machine and fax. I guess I've officially gone into business."

The sheepish look on his face made her laugh. "That's one for the record books: David Ashley goes legit." She clinked her glass against his. "Here's to success."

He inclined his head grandly. "Now, if you don't mind, me and Robin have plans to send you on tour with a massive hangover. If there's no other business or smart remarks, can we please get down to it?"

CHAPTER 3

When the Blue Mask returned the following week Brad was pacing impatiently at Alix's door. "Can't it wait till tomorrow," she asked wearily. "I just got in and I need a hot shower and some sleep."

The short black hair hung limply around her small face, emphasizing her pallor. There were dark circles under her eyes and the smell of stale cigarette smoke and Scotch wafted like cheap perfume. "Hungover, babe," he asked casually.

Lighting a cigarette, she nodded. "And before you begin the lecture about my drinking, I don't do it much during gigs. At the end of a long run, when I have the next day off, I go on a binge and make up for lost time. It's under control."

"I got no prob with that. I know you straightened out."

"Good, then let me get some sleep."

"No go," he said smugly.

She took a long drag, watching him carefully. "Okay, spill it."

"I've been in meetings all week," he said in an offhand way, looking around as if he didn't have a care in the world.

"And?"

"They're offering a three album package that includes reworking your first disc and rereleasing it under their label. There's big bread in the works. No more touring for a while. You gonna be kind of busy in the studio."

She screamed and threw her arms around him, nearly knocking him off his feet. Her hangover and tiredness forgotten, she continued to yell, bringing Joel running from across the hall. The Blue Mask quickly assembled in due time to sign, seal and deliver the contracts.

The band was in the studio a week later.

Prep work consisted of rehearsals in the loft Downtown and early Monday all assembled in Dome's Little Arrow Studio. The session began on a sardonic note. One of Dome's best producers was slotted to work with them. Jack Elgin was also the same man Apache had used when they recorded their first album. Alix could hear the groan he politely tried to suppress when the band was introduced.

"It's been a long time, Jack," she said, patting him on the shoulder. "No need to bring in litres of milk for your ulcer on this one. We have no pills, no needles, no booze and no attitude. Honest, we'll surprise you."

She walked away, leaving him standing with mouth agape in the middle of the room.

Brad was consulting with the other members of the band in the corner. "I'm sticking around, hombres."

"We don't need a babysitter," Dixie said brightly. "Most of us have been in a studio before and we promise not to bite the technicians."

Alix spoke up. "She's right, Brad. We are house-trained."

"I want an intro to the Ash dude you and Joel been talking about. We can do it after this session."

"Fine," Dixie agreed. "Now that we know your social schedule, can we please get some work done?"

Alix laughed as she saw Brad's spine stiffen. "See, asshole, I'm not the only one who orders you around."

He shook his head. "Some manager. I get no respect and now it's come to this: the babes think they can boss me. I thought you were supposed to eat lotus leaves for breakfast in Van, not razor blades."

"I think you'll be safer in the booth, little buddy," Bear advised.

"You got a point, Durango."

Jack came over to join them, his bald pate shining under the bright lights. His ruddy, pock-marked features had relaxed and the smile he wore was genuine. "I thought we'd go over the procedure and discuss what lines we'll take on this."

Joel reached over to tug gently on the long pony-tail that plunged down his back. "Over the shell-shock?"

"Sure as hell hope so. We've got work to do."

The sound-proofed studio was cavernous, strewn with instruments, cables, headsets and microphones. Jack's booth was upstairs, behind a glass partition. Speakers were hooked up so that he could communicate with the band through an intercom. Bear's drum kit and Dixie's keyboard were in the corner; technicians had already miked them and tested them for balance, as they had the guitars up front. Everyone would be separated by partitions.

They would start with the bed tapes, laying down basic drums and bass tracks. The guitars would be added, then solos, the main vocals, back-ups and any touches that were to finish the song and flesh out each track. Jack would do the mixing to balance instruments, vocals and highlights. It entailed listening to a song countless times, adjusting levels until the mix was exactly right. Jack's reputation was well-deserved. His skill in a mix-down was what had made his name synonymous with excellence. They were lucky to have him.

Brad joined him in the sound booth and the band got started. It was a long process, without glamour, and the bedrock of any band worth its salt. Enthusiasm gave way to frustration and back as the music, solos and vocals were flubbed, redone and repeated. No one ever got it right in one take. Afterwards, Brad accompanied Joel and Alix to Ash's studio/office where discussions took place for the new album. He was contracted to design it. Business concluded, their manager departed.

Ash whistled as the door closed and his footsteps faded down the stairs to the street. "I can see why I can't call him the Bradley person to his face. That is one manly hunk of man."

"Drop it," Joel bit out. "Your hormones are showing."

"What is your problem?"

"I'm tired, I guess. Things went good today; I just hope to hell the hassles don't bust us."

"Why would they?"

"After that last fiasco in the studio I decided I would never let a dream get me by the balls again."

"Things are going to work out," Alix said.

"Like last time? I don't know if I'm ready for this trip. We've been cruising along fine without a mess of contracts, lawyers and that whole business barrel of shit."

"This means a lot to us, Joel. We've been shooting for another album for a long time and we're not going to fail. Trust Brad; he won't let us down."

"And what if we do? What if we let us down? Maybe we don't have anything to say that anybody wants to hear anymore. Ever think of that?" He shook his head and abruptly left the office.

"What in the hell was that all about," Ash asked. "He seemed so excited about finally getting a move on."

"I'm not sure. He gets like this when things are about to happen for us. Remember that first gig at The Street? He couldn't believe people were still into the band. He wants it to be a success real bad but he won't admit that to anyone. The thought of failing freaks him out and he sees it as a kind of weakness. And we both know how Joel feels about weakness."

Ash gave her a brief hug. "Keep an eye on him and let me know. Once the album's done and out selling and you guys are touring his silly superstitions should disappear. You watch - he'll be back breaking hearts and leaving notch marks on lucky ladies' bed posts."

"I know."

"Does it ever bother you, his sleeping around?"

"Not in the way you mean. Not anymore. It did once but now he just worries me 'cos I don't think it's healthy."

"He's protecting himself. Joel's not stupid; he knows the facts. Hell, he saw what happened when Vince got AIDS. And now the heteros are getting infected."

"I don't mean that. It just seems like a pretty empty way to live."

"You're a good friend, Alix. He's lucky to have you and he knows it."

She frowned. "What brought that out?"

"I don't know. Guess I've been doing a lot of thinking about all of us lately. I used to not like you much. I couldn't see what Joel saw in you. Sure, you have talent, but you were a real pain in the ass."

"We've all changed, Ash; we had to. It was grow up time or die. You've come a long way too. We couldn't have had this conversation once. I didn't think much of you at first, either. Now maybe we should have lunch or something."

He laughed. "You got it. But I haven't lost my edge so I'm still going to bad mouth you on Johnny Carson."

"He's not on TV anymore, moron."

"I know but I've used that line for so many years I just can't give it up."

"I've got to go. This conversation is messing up my head."

Ash opened the door, his face serious again. "Thanks for the vote of approval and the design work. Don't think it's not appreciated."

"You've got a lot of talent. Don't do the modest thing; I know you too well. Soon we'll have to come crawling on our knees for your attention, the line-up will be so long."

"Get out," he said good-naturedly.

"Eat ratshit."

He watched her descend to the street door and waved, his thoughts miles away.

Alix hopped in her car and headed for the West End. She knew Joel wouldn't be home; he would go out on the prowl and burn off a little hysteria. She breezed past the Arlington and headed for Stanley Park. This and the sea wall along English Bay were her favourite places to go when she needed time to herself – good or bad. And if a part of her stood back and cocked a mental eyebrow at her nature-loving rambles, she ignored it. It was better than trying to lose her problems in a sea of drugs and alcohol.

She parked and headed on foot to the tree-shaded paths and the green silence that shadowed her steps. She made her way to the concrete pylons of Lion's Gate Bridge, settled down and lit a cigarette, watching the water lapping.

Joel was always happier in a crisis. It made him nervous when things went too well for too long.

He had tried to follow when she started her solitary wandering but found impatience in it. He preferred bright lights and lots of people. He sought the company of other musicians to bounce ideas off but his way of forgetting and winding down had been like hers in their early days. Like her, he had stopped the drugs and curbed in his alcohol intake but, unlike her, he could sit and nurse a drink. The binges they still indulged in together but for Alix, the thought of going into a bar and partying with a drink or two left her wanting more, so she found other ways to deal and water seemed to be it. She loved to sit by the ocean, watching its movement and its moods.

Never one to actively pursue sex for the sake of sex itself, she had little interest in conquesting the way Joel did. The death of a man she had loved left her alone and unwilling to replace him and an earlier rape had mostly stifled her interest. Joel was another story altogether. She knew he'd be out searching for someone to take the loneliness away and distance him from whatever problems his mind had conjured up. A few hours would do.

Oh well, as Ash had said, she'd keep an eye on him. She was sure that this was just cold feet, a blip in the now smooth running of their careers. She was glad they had Brad.

Calm and serene, she got up and headed back to life.

CHAPTER 4

Summer 1990

Work on the debut album for Dome went at a steady pace. Alix and Joel took to spending their free time pouring over the mixer board, devouring information on the technical side of their creation and Jack was more than happy to play educator. It was light years away from their last working experience together, when keeping the pair straight enough to play had been a mad dance.

"Why the interest," he asked one day. "You never showed this kind of response when Apache and I were doing your first album."

Alix grimaced. "We weren't in any kind of shape to ask anything, especially me."

"No kidding."

"I was pretty messed up then, Jack. I never said anything at the time and I know it's been four years but, for the record, I'm sorry."

He waved off the apology. "I damn near shit when Geoffrey told me he wanted me on this project. I refused at first but he gave me his word things would be different."

Bear and Dixie laughed at their fervour but Leo drew Alix aside on day, knowing how obsessed both of them could get once something caught their attention. "What are you up to," he asked quietly.

Her eyes softened and she lowered her voice. "You okay, Leo?"

He nodded. Another one of his friends had gotten sick and it broke Alix's heart to see his liveliness dimmed by continuing sorrow. AIDS may have started in the eighties but it was still surging as they hit the nineties. He sought solace in work and insisted on being present for every session.

"We're going to take this as far as we can," she explained. "We want to learn the how, what, where, and all that stuff. The more we know the easier things are to understand."

"You're not getting paranoid again, are you?"

"No, Leo. No tricks, I promise." Reaching out to put an arm around him, she said, "How's Mike? Anything I can do to help?"

"He's holding. Thanks, but everything that can be done is being done. We have a wonderful support group at the AIDS Centre and we're not alone."

"If you need anything, just call. Got it?"

"Sure."

Brad showed up pounding on Alix's door the evening after the band finished their last session in the studio, making enough noise to wake the dead.

"How the hell did you get through the security door," she railed. "You scared the hell out of me! Pissing myself wasn't that great but you made me spill my drink."

"Joel was going out and he let me in. Christ, babe, this place is locked up tighter than Fort Knox."

"We paid for extra security last year 'cos people were getting in using credit cards to jimmy the locks. They wanted a go at me or Joel. We've got no privacy anymore."

"It's gonna get worse." He sauntered over to the fridge and pulled out a beer. "You mind?"

"I don't know why you bother asking."

"Good manners, as my old mom taught me." He tossed a business card on the counter next to her and went over to sit in one of the armchairs by the window.

"What's this?"

"Can't you read?"

The white card was simply headed 'Brad Easton Management' with an address underneath it that was not the Crossfield and a telephone number that was not Brad's. "What the hell's going on?"

A smug smile flickered across the hard face. "I'm in business officially. Just signed my next band and did a deal. Got two more lined up."

"Who'd you sign?"

"Slash Burn & Poison."

"You must be joking."

"They're right on and there's still a lot of demand for good punk. It ain't dead."

"What about us?"

"That's another story. 'Fraid I was gonna forget about you?"

"Spit it out, scum."

"I called a meeting in my office in half an hour. If we leave now you won't be late." He drained the bottle. "I'm done my beer."

"You creep," she said, tossing back the contents of her Scotch in one swallow. "I'm your friend and I'm the last to know."

"Don't be that way. At least I came in person."

He directed her along into Kitsilano and they laughed, watching the array of people strolling the streets. The last haven of Flower Power with brilliantly painted houses, smart condos and everything else in between, it was dotted with shops and restaurants from hippy to trendy to yuppie to ethnic. They pulled up in front of an unassuming three story walk-up and he gestured towards the huge ground floor window that fronted the right half of the building. "My office."

The other members of the band were waiting on the sidewalk. Brad unlocked the door and they crowded into the front room, sorting out seats while he went around an old battered wooden desk to sit in a leather executive chair.

"I had a talk with Geoffrey Davis after your last session. He's pleased with the results. Thinks you dudes are almost as much the cat's ass as me. He wants you back in the studio next week to remix your first album 'Out on the Street Again'."

Joel lit a cigarette. "We all discussed this and we'll agree to some remixing but we don't want to add Dix's keyboards and we probably won't need Bear for drums. The original band was on that disc and we want to let it stand, with Mark included. After all, that's where we started and that's what the fans were first true to."

"Any probs," Brad asked, looking at Dixie and Bear.

"None."

"Bear is right," Dixie agreed. "We talked about this when you first brought up the album being included in the deal."

"Good. We'll get Ash to redesign. He's almost done with 'Graffiti'. For the record, Davis agrees with leaving 'Street' as is. Matter of fact, he's into booking you in the Neon for a big launch for it. He figures the fans know it, many of 'em still got the original, and that should be the first one to hit the boards. Once the hype starts he gonna release 'Graffiti' with twice the hoopla: radio play, promo, the works.'

The Neon was one of the prestigious clubs in the city. Set amidst the cobblestone streets of Gastown, it was the queen that dominated the kingdom. Most major groups on the big labels, when wanting to do something more intimate than an arena booked the Neon.

Brad laughed. "I told you he was hot for the Mask. And you wondered how I got so much bread out of him. The dude knows his stuff and he's willing to pay. Now, can we get on with business?"

This was hollered into the midst of the group, who were laughing and back slapping each other. "I ain't done yet. You got the next two days to live it up then you gotta chill right out 'cos you gonna be one busy group of hombres for the next couple years."

"Years," Alix echoed.

"Got it all mapped out."

"Mapped out?"

"Alix, shut up, you sound like a demented parrot. I figured you'd get in trouble between mixing and the Neon date so I organized a little something to keep you occupied."

"Occupied how," Joel asked, a grin tugging at the corner of his mouth. He and Brad were already on the same wavelength.

"The western half of a cross Canada tour opening for Hades. That sound like a summer holiday?" He held up his hand. "And before you screech, you got a couple days off after the Neon and then it's on the bus to do the eastern half. That should keep you busy for the fall."

He waited patiently until the noise abated. "Now you had the good news, it's time for the bad."

"What do you mean?"

"It ain't gruesome, Durango. Dome just wants to make some changes in your look."

"What," Alix demanded.

"Come on, babe, you ain't stupid. Some record execs are rigid – these dudes are at least giving you some leeway. Now, you first. You wear lots of makeup on stage, right? Now it's for all public things too – promos, photo shoots, the whole package. Leather on stage..."

"I wear leather onstage."

"Not this kind. They dig leather jumpsuits with lots of zippers, also bodysuits in electric blue or red with leather stud belts."

"What are they trying to turn me into, some kind of metal queen?"

"It ain't so bad. It's almost your style anyway."

"I won't do it."

"Shut up. There's no negotiation here so grow up and deal. Joel, you're basically okay. Leather, jeans and black muscle shirts. The babes want to see your biceps."

He grinned.

"Leo, jeans are all right, but add primary colours for the shirts and a Nehru-type jacket. It's sixties time for you."

The bassist shrugged. "I don't mind; I like that period."

"Good. Bear, keep the jeans, add Hawaiian-type shirts, lots of colour."

"I mostly do that anyway, little buddy."

"Dixie, they like the gypsy look. The gauzy, drapey things are feminine and that's their focus. Any probs?"

"Like Bear said, I dress like that anyway."

"This is bullshit," Alix said furiously. "Everyone else gets to stay normal and I have to parade around like a clown."

"Not many clowns are wearing leather these days," Joel teased.

She turned on him. "Fuck off, Stark. You got off easy. I'm not being a metal chick."

Brad sighed wearily. He'd known he was going to have a fight on his hands but he suspected it was just on principle. She'd always had a problem with authority. "You'll look great. You got the body for this so why not flaunt it?"

"Come on, girl," Joel said softly. "It's not as radical as you think and it's a small price to pay for what we're getting."

"Last month you were bitching about being mainstream. You selling out now?"

"No and neither are you. We'll see how it works and if you hate it that much I'll stand by you and protest too. Pact?"

Black eyes searched green, probing for traces of mockery. He held her gaze.

"Pact." She turned to Brad. "None of this is written in stone." She left abruptly.

"She gonna be okay, Durango?"

"Yeah, she's just got to get it out of her system."

"Some managements won't hire you unless you fit a size eight dress, no matter how much talent you got. She's getting off lucky."

"A dress would've wrecked it. In all the years I've known her I've never seen her in anything but jeans or leathers. I think she was born in black."

The group laughed.

Joel headed back to the Arlington and let himself into Alix's room. She sat smoking in one of the armchairs. "You all right?"

"I hate this control thing."

He perched beside her. "It'll be fine."

"You think so?"

He tipped her face up. "Have I ever lied to you before?" She shook her head. "I'm not about to start now." He kissed her. "Come on, let's go out. Dinner and drinks are on me."

The excitement and high of the band's fortune quickly dimmed as hard work and reality set in. Studio work completed, they set out in June, on the road with Hades. The first lesson was given before leaving town. Hades was not about to let them jump on their bandwagon. Two separate buses waited, one elaborate and comfortable, the other a customized school bus and the Blue Mask was left in no doubt which one they were to occupy. That didn't bother them. They'd spent many a tour in just such a vehicle and were well used to it.

As the tour wound its way around the west the group realized that their status was to remain second-class. The allotted time for their act was one sixty minute set and in no way were they allowed to run over. Hades' crew started changing the set almost before the last guitar chord sounded and the cheering crowds and excited response the Blue Mask consistently received only irritated the members of Hades. Not invited to share a table with the group in the bar, Alix and Joel found, as their popularity increased, speaking terms with the headliners declined and the two usually met with tight-lipped responses to any questions they asked.

Alix called Brad halfway through. He was sympathetic but adamant. "We got a contract, babe. Just stick with it and ignore 'em. But don't break the rules, you got me? For now we need these dudes."

"What the hell is their problem, anyway? Are they always like this?"

He laughed. "I woulda thought you'd heard about their rep. They are one insecure set of stars. They got no reason – their records sell like wildfire and their fans love 'em but they can be nervous as virgins if they feel threatened. I been doing PR at each of the pit stops. I get in touch with the local stations and the rags and bump you guys and it's worked like a charm. Must be driving Hades nuts."

"It is."

"Ain't you been reading the papers?"

"No time. Me and Joel have been writing and all of us have been partying to wind down and cope."

"Alix," Brad started in on a warning tone but she cut him off.

"Really, we haven't been bad but you can cut the air with a knife some days. We figure the best way to stay out of trouble is to run away from the temptation to screw their show so when we're done we get the hell out. The other night Bear took us bowling."

"Oh shit I gotta get you home. You've lost it. Do I gotta book time in the cookie ward? Now listen. You do what you can to keep a lid on your fuses. We got a contract and it's paying good bread. This high exposure is exactly what you need. So chill out."

"Yeah, yeah, I get it. I don't suppose there's any way of getting out of the fall tour after the Neon, is there?"

"No way. Make sure you stay cool. After your disc comes out things'll really heat up. It's gonna sell like hot cakes and you can bet Hades'll be tuned into that."

"Oh, thanks a bunch, pal. Things get any worse and they'll start rewiring our gear so we get hot-fingered when we turn the power on."

"You're paranoid, Lane. It won't last forever. Hang in there." He hung up with a sigh of relief. Maybe black clouds did have a silver lining. She hadn't said a word about her stage clothes, despite earlier protests when he had brought them to her. Hades was the larger concern now.

Alix hurried back to her room where the rest of the band was waiting. She reported what Brad had said and there was weariness in the sighs of resignation that greeted her.

"That's the price we have to pay," Bear concluded.

The end of the week found Alix and Joel on their own, sitting in a quiet bar after their set.

"I don't know, girl," Joel grumbled. "I can't take much more of this. I'm going to haul off and belt one of those sons of bitches."

"No," she argued. She'd been trying to hold him back for days.

"How do you cope with it?"

"I'm too busy keeping you in line."

"You know, we never treated warm-up acts like this. Is that what happens in the big leagues – you get to be punching bags? I've never seen such a pack of shits. It makes me sick."

Alix reached over and squeezed his arm. "Remember the game plans we used to do for our very last night gigs? The ones where we used to get really bad?"

"Yeah."

"When we do our last show with Hades – I mean the last one of the whole tour – I think we should plan a little something for them."

"I thought you agreed with Brad about keeping cool."

"I do but we don't have to blow our horns about it. Why not something under the table, so to speak?"

"Like not letting their left hand know what our right hand is doing?"

"Yep."

Joel leaned in close. "Got any ideas?"

"Not yet but we have a whole half tour left to think about it."

Laughing, the two toasted each other and, after a couple more drinks, gleefully made their way back to the hotel to get some rest.

CHAPTER 5

The bus brought them home on a bright August morning and the band members went longingly to their own beds for a day before getting ready for their gig at the Neon. Brad summoned them to his office that morning for a briefing.

"I think Hades did you a favour being assholes," he said when they'd settled.

"How do you figure that," Joel asked dryly.

"If you'd been cozy friends round the fire you wouldn't have worked so hard."

"How the hell would you know," Alix asked suspiciously.

"I thought, as you got a little closer to home, maybe I'd have me a little break and take in a gig on the sly. You a lot more fun to watch than Hades. Maybe 'cos you were trying to outdo them. I had some talks with a lot of people to see how you were going over and they were nuts for you guys."

"You sleazeball, you should have told us you were there."

"So I could listen to you bitch? No chance. Besides, I had to find me a bed for the night." He gave Joel a sly wink. "You know what I mean, Durango?"

"Yep."

"You sure didn't help much. Most of the babes had their eye on you and from what I saw you had more than your eye on them. How was the fishing?"

"Outstanding. Hey, I had to do something to fill in my time. Couldn't just write songs, drink, play cards and go bowling."

"Well, pickings were slim but I did manage to find me a little filly who was willing."

"Oh, shut up you two," Alix said in disgust. "If you want to talk about your exploits at least wait until we don't have to listen. I thought this was a meeting, not current events on the lives of two over-sexed idiots with hormones for brains."

The Neon gig that launched the Blue Mask under Dome Records was one Alix would long remember. It seemed that nothing could go wrong. Every move the band made, everything they said, was right. After two short sets, Geoffrey Davis got on stage to make his announcement, the band was presented amid champagne and shenanigans and the party went on for hours. The media attended in droves, drawn by free booze and food and went away in the band's collective pocket. The group waited until the Davis entourage departed, followed by the financial shirt and tie brigade and, like children who have suddenly found themselves free of chaperones, they let loose. Ash and Robin were at a table with the band and Brad and all were having a private party, oblivious to the noise around them.

"Did you see that," Ash wailed mockingly. "Alix being nice to some suit? Honest, she was smiling and answering questions and I don't think she even swore." He turned to her. "How much did it hurt?"

"I'm still bleeding. Now I have to make up for it."

"Aah," Joel cried, pointing at her drunkenly. "The singer from hell!" He fell, writhing, onto the floor.

"Please, Mr. Manager," she pleaded to Brad, "please, can I kick his face in?"

"Not the face – it's got a rep. As a fellow macho stud, I can't see one of my brothers mashed so leave the crotch alone too. Not the hands either; we need 'em. Other than that, feel free but I want him better in the next couple days. You got a tour to finish."

Joel groaned and rolled over. "Kill me now! Don't send me to Hades!" Laughing, he got up and brushed himself off. "Seriously, I am not looking forward to that bullshit again."

"Can it, Durango," Brad said flatly. "Everyone got to pay their dues in the big league and this be yours. You'll deal." He took a long drink of his beer. "I got some planning to do. I want to get a video shot when you get back. You guys were the house band in that Alley View club before. Think the owner'll let us shoot in there? I like the vibes."

Robin cut in. "No problem, I should think. Let me talk to him. We're good friends."

"You got it, babe. I'll call you."

More guffaws started after this announcement and, when Brad's attention was sufficiently diverted, Alix picked up her beer and made her way over to Robin's side. "This is interesting. I haven't seen you since before the tour. What's the gossip?"

"Gossip?"

"You barely knew Brad when we left. Now he's going to call you and he doesn't need the number? Come on, it's me. Start spilling."

To her surprise, Robin blushed. "He got my number from Ash and called one night. We went out for drinks and talked about you and Joel and band history. He wanted to be filled in."

"Ash gave him your number?"

"He's not my keeper."

"Yeah, but he's pretty protective. What about Brad? I've known him a long time, Robin, and I can't believe he just wanted band info. He goes for beautiful women and you fit that category. If he didn't make a pass that has to be one for the record books 'cos it'll be the first time since he went through puberty."

She rolled her eyes. "We've dated a few times and it's been fun. I have to admit, the goodnight kisses have been pretty hot and heavy but so far he's been a good boy."

"I wonder what he's up to."

"I don't know but I sure don't mind."

Alix's eyes narrowed. "You be very careful with your heart, lady. I mean it. Brad is a great friend and I love him but he's a Casanova and I don't want to see you get hurt."

"I'm a big girl; I can take care of myself, you know."

"Yeah, yeah, and pigs fly."

"Don't worry," Robin said quietly. "Really, I'll be careful. I promise."

"What are you little demons whispering about over there," Ash yelled, waving his drink around to get their attention.

"Nothing we're telling you about," Alix retorted with a grin.

"The boys are talking about running over to the Afterhours so we can finish this wingding," Dixie said, sitting down beside Alix. "What do you think? Shall we go elsewhere and let our hair down?"

Alix put her arm around her and laughed. "I knew the first day I met you we'd get along. We think alike."

The Afterhours Club was an old haunt of the Blue Mask's from their early days, an upgraded affair Downtown that specialized in late night partying for the early morning crowd. Like children following the Pied Piper, the troupe filed out after Ash and made their way, amid much frivolity, to their new location. And, in the tradition that they always reserved for celebrations, it was a long, hilarious and drunken party.

After a couple days of rest, the band hit the road for the second leg of the Canadian tour. Brad hauled them into his office before they left, his focus on Alix and Joel.

"The night we all partied it up I did a little eavesdropping and overheard a plot about some practical joke you planned for Hades."

Joel turned a bland face to their manager. "You'd do the same thing. It's a piss off being treated like slime. We'll wait till work's done and then we'll fix them. This isn't open to discussion."

"That's dead on, Durango. It ain't open to discussion and it ain't gonna happen. You got that?"

"What's it to you anyway? We have to take the flak and you just sit here collecting your percent."

"I did the work so you could have the bread to pay that percent. This revenge trip is out. Grow up. Life ain't fair and you can't just react like a put out brat."

"It's one little prank. What's your problem?"

"It's childish I agree," Bear cut in, "but not something you'd get upset about without a reason, is it, little buddy? Why don't you just give us the bad news?"

"What makes you think I got bad news?"

"You're nervous and I haven't seen you that way very often."

Alix glared at him. "You holding out on us?"

"I knew it was something," Joel snapped. "We usually get along, don't we, pal? We're so often on the same wavelength. What the fuck have you done?"

"I made an arrangement with Hades' manager while you were on the road."

Alix groaned. "You didn't, did you, asshole? You didn't book us on another pleasure cruise you've been afraid to tell us about?"

"I did. I know you hate them. Believe me, the feeling seems mutual. But face facts. For some reason you two bands click with audiences. Keep in mind, hombres, you're seasoned but you're babes in the woods in the big league. We're gonna expose the shit out of you come the 'Graffiti' release at Christmas but you still need an intro by a big band to the general people and Hades fits the bill."

"Where do we go," Leo asked.

"The US of A." Brad grinned, sensing a break in the tension. "I told you I was gonna push you and we gotta break into the American market if you're gonna be more than an A-circuit bar band. Hades is madder than hell having to put up with you but they see the sense in it. So, after Christmas, you gonna be busy for a couple months but the exposure'll be worth it."

"So we get to start off the goddamn new year in hell," Alix said. "Oh well. Just promise us no more tours with them."

"According to the plan, you headline from then on."

"We sure are paying our dues now."

"All part of the game. You'll come out winners. Don't worry, it ain't long till Christmas."

It was only when his office door was closed that Brad relaxed and let out a long, tense sigh. He was afraid he would have all out rebellion on his hands with that last little piece of manipulation but the band had taken it surprisingly well. He reached over and drew the phone to him.

Robin answered on the third ring.

"It went off all right, like you said. They gave me some bad moments but they didn't bitch much. You were dead right about Joel."

"He wants big success from this; he just won't admit it. That's what you have to count on when you feed him bad medicine."

"Things'll get a lot easier when their next album comes out. I got people at work in the east and I'm putting out a lot more PR for that tour. With the hoopla coming on, they should get well known."

"I have no doubt they'll worm their way into people's heads one way or the other. Even at the worst of their speeding, Alix and Joel still had something. No matter how vicious they were, the fans never let them down."

"That's 'cos there's something there." His voice dropped, became softer, a caress. "Dinner tonight, Robin? As a thanks?

"I'd love to."

"I'll be over about six."

She put the phone down carefully, tingling with anticipation. She knew Alix was right: Brad was a womanizer. But it had been so long since she'd been really interested in someone that she just couldn't help herself. The thought of being with him excited her. If she was another moth that ventured too close to the flame, then she was just going to have to get burned.

Brad took her to a dark, quiet place in Gastown and they settled back with drinks, content to let the evening drift at a slow pace. She found herself telling him about her career and how she got started choreographing videos, something she now wanted to concentrate on. She was looking to direct them as well.

"You chained by this contract you got with VidWorks or can you freelance too?"

A slow smile spread across her delicate features. "You are some piece of work, Brad Easton. This isn't a thank you dinner, is it? You're setting me up."

"I've seen some of your work and you're amazing."

"You've been checking up on me?"

"I'm good, Robin, 'cos I'm thorough. I know the game and what I want and I want you. Interested in signing on with the Mask? We're on a strict budget for now but our first video has got to be a knockout. That amazing imagination of yours should do it."

"I'd love to," she answered excitedly.

"There's good bread in it. Ash got himself a contract; you get one too. We'll work so there's no probs with VidWorks on time."

"Where is all this money coming from?"

He smiled smugly. "Dome. I got the Mask one hell of a deal and when Davis came through without a fight I knew I was on to a hot thing. We gonna take this band somewhere. Come along, it's gonna be a wild ride."

After dinner the two strolled through Gastown. Music was blaring from the plethora of clubs and bars along the streets and the scene was a mixture of tourists and locals blending without reservation. They made their way slowly back to Robin's. Brad saw her safely inside and when he hesitated, she offered him a drink. He accepted immediately and she went rooting through the fridge for beer. Her nerves were jangling. She wanted him to stay but was afraid to ask and he seemed so cool and unassuming. When she handed him the open bottle of beer his hand closed around hers and he drew her to him.

"You're shaking. What's up?"

"Nothing."

He placed the bottle on the counter and kissed her. "You been kinda jumpy all night. That mean you finally decided to take a chance on me?"

"How did you know," she blurted out.

He smiled. "You are one confident lady but you keep to yourself. I figured you were weighing me up. You don't seem the type who throws herself into bed with any decent looking dude who comes along. I respect that."

"And I thought you were insensitive."

He kissed her again, deeply. Gently, he drew her into the bedroom. "You got any condoms, Robin?"

Her face fell. "I forgot to buy some. I wasn't exactly sure this was going to happen."

Grinning, he drew a package out of his pocket and laid it on the night table. "I was hoping so I figured I should be prepared." He slowly started to remove her dress, his hands lingering on her skin, caressing and arousing. "You are so beautiful. I been thinking about you since we first met."

"What about your beer?"

"I'll drink it later," he said softly.

CHAPTER 6

Autumn 1990

Ash closed his office after a long day and headed wearily down to his sports car. Business was booming. He had hired an assistant to deal with phone calls, appointments and invoices so he'd have enough time to meet his deadlines and the operation was running smoothly. The Blue Mask's next album cover had been completed on schedule and shipped to the printers. He felt fulfilled but it seemed like weeks since he'd had any real fun.

Once home, he stood under a hot shower, letting the water slide over his body. When he finally stepped out to dry himself off he found that, rather than wanting to tumble into bed, he was refreshed and ready for action. He dialled Robin's number but there was no answer. Pouring a small gin, he contemplated the long stretch of night in front of him. He felt restless and turned on. It had been a long time since he'd ventured into any of the gay clubs that he used to frequent. He'd stayed out of the bars for a year while drying out and, once straight, threw himself into work to avoid the pit again. As the months passed, he found he didn't care much for that scene anymore and restricted his forays to once in a blue moon. But he'd been good lately and deserved a treat.

The jeans and sports-shirt he wore at the office weren't quite the club style. Donning his trademark black leathers, he locked up and headed Downtown.

The Flip Side entrance was lit by a neon sign, a flashing LP turning over endlessly in the night. Subtle this club was not, though Ash didn't care as long as it served its purpose. He waved a membership card under the doorman's nose, got his hand stamped and plunged inside. It was early yet and sparse groups of people mingled in the first room. Beyond lay a dance area replete with strobe lights and a glitter ball and past that was a small room with a stand-up bar. It was the place for cruising – the corners dark and private where the smell of leather was strong and dope cheap. Little conversation was needed here; the flicker of an eyelid was sufficient communication.

Ash ordered a drink from the main bar, content to people watch for a while. Tonight he was in no hurry. The bartender slid his glass across the polished wood with a smile. Ash paid, tipped the man and then turned to survey the crowd. He felt safe and warm. Outside, the September wind howled but here no one could hurt him. He had a job he loved, friends he cherished and a problem that was under firm control. In other words, he had a future.

"Life must be good," said a voice beside him. "You've got the cat who stole the cream look on your gob right now, mate."

Ash glanced over at this sudden companion, the smile still in place. "That's just about what I was thinking. Are you a mind reader?"

"No, but I have been there and I'm feeling about the same way right now. Mind if I join you?"

Ash pointed to a couple of chairs at the end of the bar and they moved to sit. The bartender brought two more drinks over, which the newcomer paid for. He was a dark-haired, diminutive Englishman with a wizened, youngish face and merry blue eyes. He was dressed in a stylish black suit with some kind of old school tie. Ash figured he was a jockey. "You live here or just visiting?"

"I'm here on business. I like Vancouver and I've been in the Flip Side a few times. I like the atmosphere. Yourself?"

"I live here." Ash reached over and held out his hand. "David Ashley. My friends call me Ash."

The man smiled and shook hands. "Morris Stockham. My friends call me Morris."

Both started to laugh; the ice broken.

"There've been some changes since I was last here," Morris said. "Care to give a bloke a tour?"

"I haven't been here in ages either so I guess we'll just have to be explorers together."

"Came in on a whim, then? Well I count it my lucky night."

They strolled around and eventually ended up at a corner table in the front room, content to be in each other's company. No need for the back room tonight, where passion escalated with privacy. The two had many common interests and tastes and at the height of the evening when noise levels were reaching stadium proportions, it seemed natural for them to leave together.

"My car's in the parking lot," Ash said as they exited. "You want to go to your hotel or would you like to see the artist's aerie?"

"Oh definitely the aerie."

"The Savoy it's not, but the building's funky and the gin's plentiful."

Once inside Ash's loft at the Arlington Terrace, Morris' interest turned from curiosity to exploration. He roamed around, stopping in front of each of the several oil paintings that Ash had done, examining them in detail. Ash's personal masterpiece, a portrait of Robin in a dance costume of black leather from one of her early shows, he gasped over. "Mate, you are really fabulous. The work is exquisite. You do this for a living?"

Ash shook his head as he served the drinks. "Not anymore. My smart little business takes up most of my time now."

"It's a crying shame, that's what it is. Can I commission you to do something for me? I'd adore to have one to hang in me house in London."

"I'll have to see."

"I'm coming back through this way in the new year. I'm serious; I mean it."

Ash moved over to the stereo system and thumbed through his compact discs. "We need some tunes. Have you heard Mayday's latest?"

Morris hooted with laughter. "Ash, old son, that's like asking if I've seen a picture of the Queen lately."

Mayday, following in the footsteps of great British bands like the Stones, the Who, Led Zeppelin and Queen, had been together fifteen years, had a dozen albums to their credit and a fan following that numbered in the millions.

"Can you deal with another spin of their CD or would you like to hear something local?"

"Oh definitely something local." He stood beside Ash, watching the titles flashing past. "Whenever I travel I always buy some of the local work to take back with me. I like to see what others are up to in their part of the world. "Oy," he cried suddenly, "stop here. I picked that one up in the shops the other day and I've been playing it ad nauseum. Let's have that, then."

Ash smiled. Morris had chosen the rerelease of the Blue Mask's first album, 'Out on the Street Again'. "You picked my favourite band."

"It's primitive and it's got something elemental I really like. Are they in town?"

"No, they're on tour in eastern Canada. They won't be back till Christmas."

"That's a ruddy shame, that is. Are they any good as a live act?"

"I think they're great but I'm prejudiced. The singer and lead guitarist are two of my best friends."

"Any chance of meeting them after Christmas?"

"They'll be in the States. Why are you interested?"

"Always like to meet new people, old son." He drew the cover out of its plastic casing. "Lovely work, this," he said, pointing to the logo of the band that ran across the top.

Ash smiled. "It's mine."

The man's eyes narrowed assessingly. "That's your business?"

"Pretty much. I sort of stumbled into it." Ash sat down on the couch and indicated the place beside him. Morris fed the CD into the machine, adjusted the volume and joined him. "Alix and Joel asked me to design a poster for one of their first gigs after the band got back together. I was still trying to get commissions for my painting and I did it as a favour but it went over like a house on fire. All these other bands started knocking on my door. Things snowballed after that. Don't get me wrong, I'm not complaining. It pays the rent and nets me a comfortable living but I've got so much work I don't have time for painting.

"The Blue Mask signed with Dome Records and I'm contracted for all their album covers as well as my other stuff. I don't know where the days go sometimes. I just finished their next one; it's due out before Christmas. Want to see it?"

He nodded, face tense with suppressed excitement. Ash moved to the table where he had dumped his work when he'd come home and drew the design out of the pile. Morris took it wordlessly and then, with raised brows, fingered the rest. Ash nodded. Morris was mumbling under his breath, getting more excited by the minute. When he finally turned back his eyes were sparkling.

"You're a veritable gold mine, Ash. I knew there was a reason we met tonight."

Confused, uncomfortable at the scrutiny, Ash said simply, "Who are you?"

"Do you believe in karma?"

"Are you trying to avoid the question?"

Laughing, he shook his head. "Who I am hasn't rung a bell with you, my friend. But it's what I do that will make the penny drop."

"Okay, I'll bite. What the hell do you do?"

"I manage Mayday."

"Yeah, right, and Elvis is alive and living in Gastown."

Unoffended, Morris plodded on. "Oh, I don't blame you for not believing me but it's the truth. I'm over here putting the finishing touches on Mayday's North American tour. I also negotiated with Geoffrey Davis to record in Dome's Little Arrow Studio. The band's doing their next album here." He laughed again, seeing the dawning shock on Ash's face. "Ring up Dome tomorrow and ask Davis himself. We're old mates. We went to school together."

"Holy fuck, I feel like Alice when she went through the looking glass."

"You've got some really original ideas and I can't wait to show them to the boys. We might just have a little work for you."

Ash drained his glass and reached for the bottle but Morris stilled his hand with a gentle touch. "Why don't we have our discussions in the morning, love? Let's go to bed. That is why we're here, isn't it?"

"I think we both forgot about that."

"No, but I think we found a mate neither of us was expecting to so our minds got off the path." He poured a small tot of gin into each of their glasses and raised his in a toast. "Here's to the start of a valued friendship."

The toast completed, he dimmed the lights and turned the volume down on the CD. Alix was crooning away about drug addiction and they both laughed.

"Not quite apropos," Morris said, "but it will do."

CHAPTER 7

Winter 1990

Long tours tend to be gruelling affairs. Once in town, the band checks into their hotel, gets some sleep if they're lucky and then heads off to a sound check in the afternoon. In the early days, the Blue Mask had a skeletal crew and did a lot of the setting up themselves. With a full crew that was no longer necessary but the business of sound still demanded their presence. Instrument levels and vocals have to be coordinated and the whole mixed and balanced so that it doesn't come out muddy and indistinguishable. It is not a short process.

Then there is dinner and a quiet interlude where energy is summoned for the show. Make-up, stage wear, the fine tuning of instruments – all have to be seen to before the group hits the stage. It's here that the mundane chores pay off. An audience can fuel a band and take them to the sky. The adrenaline run can keep them up for hours afterwards, particularly on electric gigs. This is the reward, the high that keeps many bands on the road for years.

After each gig, the crew strikes the stage, winds cables and packs the whole system up. Many musicians take personal responsibility for their own instruments and see them safely loaded. No one gets to bed early. The next morning, everyone boards the bus to head out to the next venue, catching up on sleep during travelling. The cycle repeats until the last stop.

Alix and Joel no longer partied on the road – it made them far too weary too early along the line. Many party bands fell into the drug trap simply to keep pace with the machinery of a tour. There never seemed to be enough energy and it had to be carefully conserved so that the shows didn't fall flat. The glamour of a band on the road is only in the eyes of the fans. For the musicians, it's hard work. Yet those same fans are the reward. The rapport between a band and a live audience is intimate, immediate and fulfilling beyond measure.

There is always a price in stamina to pay and the Blue Mask came tumbling home, exhausted, two days before Christmas. No one bothered to update them on changes that had occurred in their absence. Brad was largely responsible for this. There was a Yuletide party organized for the band and Robin and Ash and he was going to give them announcements as presents.

Joel's was utilized as a kitchen – all were bringing dishes to go with the turkey that was being cooked and serving would occur there before the group trooped across to Alix's to eat, drink and be merry.

She rose early on Christmas morning so that she could get everything ready and be free later to join in the fun. Grabbing a small package wrapped in blood red paper and two bottles of beer from the fridge, she slipped across to Joel's room, knocking loudly on the door before letting herself in with a key.

He was still in bed but a woman stood beside him, looking down at his motionless form as she buttoned the front of her dress. She whirled around as Alix burst into the room, colour rushing up to a face raised defiantly against embarrassment.

"Whoa," Alix said, nearly dropping the beer. "I'm sorry, I thought Joel was up. I mean, I thought he was alone." She shook her head. "Hell, I'll come back later."

The woman's voice stopped her. "I'm just leaving. Joel did warn me that you'd be over early to prepare for the party."

She shifted uncomfortably while the pretty blonde donned her coat. "This is a bad time. I'll come back."

"No, I'm leaving." Even more uncomfortable, the woman pushed past her. "Tell him I said good-bye. Maybe he'll call me later." She closed the door softly behind her.

Alix turned to find Joel grinning at her. "You miserable son of a bitch! You were awake the whole time."

"I really didn't want to get in the middle of that, 'kay? It was awkward enough with me supposedly sleeping." Reaching for his jeans, he sat up and dragged them on. "You were pretty polite."

"It's that time of year – you know good will toward men, and women."

"Even the one-night stands of your best friend?"

"Even that. Besides, I was embarrassed as hell."

"Not as much as she was."

"You got laid enough on the road. Couldn't you have slept alone on Christmas Eve? You knew I was coming over early. Or was this show for my benefit?"

"What does that mean?"

"Sometimes I think you pick these women up just to mess with my head. You know I end up with half of them crying on my shoulder when we're around for any length of time. I felt sorry for that one. You tell her about the party and don't invite her and she tells me hoping I will. Why the hell don't you keep your groupies to yourself?"

He accepted a beer and leaned over to kiss her. "I'm sorry and Merry Christmas." He took a long drink. "I sure need this. We drank a lot of wine here last night. How long did you stay at the Alley View after I left?"

"Me and Leo sat till about midnight. I didn't want an all-nighter. We got too much to do this morning."

"Give me a minute to wash up and I'll give you a hand."

He headed off to the bathroom and Alix pulled the covers up over the rumpled bed, a look of disgust on her thin face. He returned with his damp hair combed neatly and his face freshly shaven. The tangy aroma of his shaving cream lingered as he passed her and went over to open the curtains covering the long windows. The bleak winter light trickled in. For once, the street was devoid of people. A cold rain was falling and he opened one of the windows, letting a gust of fresh air blow through.

"It smells in here," Alix said, opening the loaf of bread on the counter and searching for a large pot.

Joel winked. "I was sweating last night."

"I don't want to hear about it."

He joined her at the counter and watched with interest as she began tearing the bread into chunks and tossing them into the pot. "Do you know what you're doing, girl?"

"Making stuffing."

"Where the hell did you learn to cook?"

Smiling, she reached for more bread. "I have an English mother, you idiot. Cooking is the first thing you learn."

"What's the second?"

"How to snare a husband."

He rolled his eyes.

"I'm lousy at that but I'm not bad at the cooking bit." She tossed the red package to him. "Open that while you're waiting. I don't need help yet."

He ripped the paper off. Inside was a garish, multi-coloured package. "Party pack condoms?"

"They're different colours with shapes and stuff on them."

"Condoms."

"You must go through them like water the way you sleep around," she retorted, leering. "Might as well use the spikey ones and give your girls a good time too."

He shook his head and put them at the end of the counter. "You're a pig, Alix, and you're the last one who should be giving me condoms. Want me to make another pass at you like I did years ago?"

"Fuck off," she answered good-naturedly. "It's a joke. Besides, I just saved you some money."

"Money has not been a problem for quite a while. I don't know what to do with it all." He moved over to the night table, taking a package wrapped in newspaper out of the drawer. "Here, I thought I'd spend a bit on you."

"We said no presents."

"You did."

"Mine was a gag."

"Look, girl, I saw this in Toronto and thought you'd like it so just shut up and take it. If I can't buy my best friend a present then what?"

Alix grinned and worked her way through to a white box containing a thick, polished wristband of black iron. "It's gorgeous." She wrapped her arms around him and hugged him fiercely. "Thanks."

She released him and, slipping it on, went back to the counter, touched. Joel could be so cold at times and then would turn around and do something that told her how much she meant to him. Neither was high on sentiment and words never expressed how much their friendship mattered but once in a while each could surprise the other.

"Come on, get to work. This turkey isn't going to cook itself."

People began to arrive early in the afternoon. Robin brought appetizers and the group sat around munching and drinking their various poisons. Alix and Joel sat side by side, smoking, drinking beer and Scotch and teasing each other unmercifully as the alcohol sifted through their systems. Bear and Dixie were giggling as Leo did impressions of Joel picking up a groupie. Brad and Ash were deep in conversation and Robin watched the group with affection. This was all the family any of them would ever need.

"How often have we done this," she said loudly, getting their attention. She raised her wine glass. "To my friends. I love you bums a lot."

Amid groans of sentimentality, they drank. Brad reached over to gently remove the glass from Robin's hand. "All right, hombres. That's enough for now." He pointed to Alix and Joel. "'Specially you two. You burning our grub?"

"Aw, chill out," Alix cracked. "You'll eat when we're ready."

Catcalls started and Brad rose and signalled for silence. He removed five buff envelopes from his jacket, which he distributed to the band.

"What's this," Joel growled. "Homework on Christmas?"

"These are presents, Durango."

"We said no presents."

"Yeah, well this is a collective one from me and Ash and Robin and before you start bitching give me a listen."

Alix groaned and stretched out on the floor, arms wide. "If it's another Hades tour you might as well kill me now. Saves me doing it."

He grabbed a handful of her hair and tugged. She sat up quickly, punching him. "Shut up, babe. You wanna know?"

"He's right," Bear cut in. "Be quiet or I'll sit on you."

Joel had already opened his envelope. "Hey, this is a passport form."

"Dead on, Durango. Now, any of you got a record – and I'm talking criminal, not vinyl?"

Mutterings of "no" were interspersed with rude comments. Joel's voice rose above the noise. "We don't need passports to get into the U.S."

"You do for the U.K."

"As in United Kingdom," Dixie asked, eyes wide. "What have you done, Brad?"

He strutted around the room, pointing at Robin and Ash. "Not just me; I got help on this one."

"Stop teasing us," Leo said.

Brad blew him a kiss and sat down in Alix's favourite chair. "Ash, tell these streets sluts who you met a few weeks ago."

"I went down to the Flip Side one night..." Joel groaned and Ash gave him a sharp flick of his hand. "Not this time, Stark. I'm telling this story."

"Just leave out the romance."

"Fuck off. Anyway, I started talking to this English guy and brought him back to my place. He was going through my CDs and found yours. He'd already heard it and liked it – and the design on the cover. So I showed him the one for your next album."

Brad cut in. "By the way, in case you haven't noticed, it's selling buckets. We sent this dude a copy."

"You guiding Ash's love life now," Joel asked sarcastically.

Alix drove her elbow into his side. "Leave it."

He glared at her but shut his mouth and nodded to Ash to continue.

"This guy went nuts over my work and then told me who he was."

"Yeah, so who was he?"

"Morris Stockham."

"And who the hell is he when he's at home?"

"He's Mayday's manager, asshole."

Silence followed that comment.

"He phoned me a couple of weeks after he got the CD for 'Graffiti'. Mayday loved it but they're still really impressed with 'Street'. They raved about 'The Fallout', not because they like downer songs about speed, but 'cos they see a few smart variations they can do.

"Morris was here finishing off details of their North American tour. You guys are going into Dome's studio to record your next album in the spring. Guess who else will be recording their next album at Little Arrow about that time."

Bear started to laugh. "I'll guess Mayday."

"I got me a smart contract to do Mayday's next cover and Morris has been dealing with Brad for the right to record 'The Fallout' on their next disc."

Joel crawled over to Ash and hugged him. "I'm sorry, pal. I know I don't get your lifestyle and I'm pretty hard on you but you mean the world to me and it's just my way of coping. Still friends?"

"Sure." He turned to Brad while trying to disengage himself. "Will you tell him the rest, please? Talk about coping – if he hugs me again I'll slug him."

"Back to your seat, Durango. Alix, keep a grip on him. Now, you two sign permission over yesterday and I'll take care of the rest. Morris and me went over schedules and both of you are in Spokane early in January. The band wants to meet you." Cheering broke out but he held up his hand. "Not done yet.

"Mayday wants Joel to guest on the track and Alix to do those screechy high back-ups you end with. They got a rep of being perfectionists but look where it's got them. Your choice, but I'd say go for it."

"Now," Joel asked. "Can we yell now?"

"Guess so. Then let's eat – I'm starving."

It was quite a while before the excitement died down. Dixie waited until things were at a dull roar. "Brad, you still haven't explained the passports."

"Geoffrey Davis is ahead of the game as usual. Both albums are selling real fine and the exposure we got planned in the States should help things take right off. Your third disc comes out about the same time as Mayday's and Davis has the London office working PR now. The Mayday tie will sell us like hotcakes and, if plans work out, you'll be doing a gig with them. So we're booking a European tour."

"Shit," Joel said quietly. "I don't believe this."

"As long as you work I don't care if you believe in the Easter Bunny."

"What a year!"

"You ain't seen nothing yet. Next year you ain't gonna have time to breathe. Now, before we chow down, we got a video shoot at the Alley View at the end of the week and I found you one great choreographer."

Robin laughed. "And I'm going to work your asses off."

More merriment erupted. The group filed in to Joel's room to get food and spent the night eating, drinking and carrying on. No one mentioned the plans for the rest of the night. Talk turned to the general and then the ridiculous as the participants celebrated.

For the band, it was a case of shell shock. It seemed as though all the hard work of years was finally paying off.

CHAPTER 8

The party continued until the wee hours of the morning. When everyone else had gone, Alix and Joel sat in her room, toasting each other, old friends and anything else they could come up with, bathed by the neon glow of the martini glass that hung on the wall. Finally, exhausted, she crawled into bed, telling Joel to lock up behind him when he left.

Alix was on a beach. She could feel the cool sand beneath her cheek and the lick of the waves as they lapped up against her. John lay beside her, his curling hair damp at the ends from the water. Smiling, she rolled over, reaching for him. Her mouth opened under his as she felt his probing tongue and groaned softly. The weight of him was so comforting. Panic lit through her and she tensed suddenly. This wasn't real. John had been dead for a long time.

She opened her eyes to find Joel staring down at her. Smiling gently, he stroked her mouth. "Who were you kissing, girl? It sure as hell wasn't me."

She tried to move out from under him but he held her more closely. His hand felt cool against her lips. Tears welled up in her eyes. "Sorry, I was having a dream."

"Some dream."

"What are you doing here?"

The lop-sided grin was sheepish. "I was too tired to go across the hall and you looked comfy so I stripped down and crawled in."

Alix suddenly realized that they were both naked. Her actions had aroused him and he was pressing urgently against her, hard and erect. Colour washed up into her face.

"I know. Pretty weird situation, hey?"

"You can say that again."

"Pretty weird situation, hey?" He sobered suddenly. "Do you mind if I take over from whoever started this?" He could see the indecision on her face – good sense warring with desire – and leaned down to kiss her. "Friend to friend, Alix. I won't hurt you and I won't ask for anything you can't give."

She didn't answer but, as his hands continued to stroke her body, she found herself responding, growing wet.

She let him go on until he was ready to enter her. "Get those condoms I gave you off the counter by the sink," she whispered. "Brad was showing them to Robin and he left them there."

"It's only us, Alix. Leave it."

"No", she said harshly. "You know better than that, Joel. There's a scary disease going around, or haven't you heard?"

He bristled. "Thanks a lot for the vote of confidence. You think I'd give you a STD?"

"Don't pull this guilt trip on me," she pleaded, tears stinging again. "Please don't ruin this."

Grumbling, he got out of bed and came back with the box, tearing it open and roughly putting on a condom. But something had gone from their closeness and they climaxed quickly. Alix's tears spilt over.

With a muffled curse, Joel put his arms around her. "I'm sorry, girl. I'm a selfish pig."

"Maybe it just wasn't a good idea."

"Maybe, but we've been circling around for years so I guess it was time we finally did it. Now we can get on with our friendship. 'Kay?"

She nodded.

He kissed her once more and then released her. "Good girl. I'm for a hot shower. I think it would do you the world of good too. First I make us breakfast and then I'll give you a hand cleaning this dump if you give me one cleaning mine."

Joel got up, removed the condom and threw it in the garbage, then pulled his jeans on. Alix lit a cigarette, watching as he plugged in the kettle and took cups and a jar of instant coffee out of the cupboard. Perhaps he was right. Maybe getting this out of their systems would finally settle it.

Grin in place, green eyes glowing, he came back to the bed and sat down, handing her a cup of coffee. She looked like an elf this morning, the elf he first remembered meeting so long ago. The curling hair was tousled around the pale features and big eyes so dark they looked black. There was a shuttered quality to her face and it could look cruel when drawn but a smile always brought the imp back. She took a gulp from the mug and choked on it. "This is awful. What'd you do?"

"It's breakfast. Half coffee and half Scotch."

"Yuk!"

"Hair of the dog, girl. Now drink it up and take a couple of these." He tossed her a bottle of aspirin. "Stark's guaranteed hangover cure. Follow with a hot shower and another breakfast drink and the world will settle down again."

"One thing you are always right about is hangover cures. Thanks."

He patted her cheek. "I'm going to take a shower."

She stopped him as he started to turn away, her face serious. "It's been a long time since I had a man in my bed, Joel. I'm glad it was you."

"I'm always around if you need me, Alix. There's nothing wrong with having a friend to comfort you."

"As long as that's all it is."

He laughed loudly. "Girl, I got a whole ocean of fish to fry. Don't worry, this won't do us any harm." He strode to the door and paused, his hand on the doorknob. "Now get out of bed. We've got work to do."

She threw a pillow at him. "Eat ratshit."

"All the people in the world to choose from and I get you."

"And don't forget these," she added, tossing the box of condoms.

"Why, did you leave a lady in my bed for Christmas?"

"Christmas is over, asshole."

"'Kay, I get the message." He left, locking the door behind him.

That night found Ash, Robin, Joel and Alix sitting around Ash's loft having the private meeting they had organized as soon as the two band members arrived home.

"By the sounds of it," Robin was saying, "Brad is not going to have you around much."

"Tell me about it," Alix sighed. "We were at his office today and you should see the schedule he's got lined up." She lit a cigarette and exhaled in a harsh gust. "He was right. We're not going to have time to breathe."

"He's talking about two albums for next year. Have you got enough material?"

"We've been working pretty steadily while we've been on the road. Let's face it, there isn't that much to do while travelling. Even Joel can't get laid on the bus – it's just us."

"So true," he agreed. "I get stuck with the deadbeats between cities so I have to give in and write songs with Alix." He lit a cigarette. "Seriously, we already got most of the next album done. Dix, Bear and Leo wait till the song is flushed out and then we work on it as a whole. Saves us time that way."

"How did you know about the albums," Alix asked.

Robin shrugged nonchalantly and the other three smiled slyly. "Brad tells me things."

"From what we've figured out," Joel drawled, "that's not all Brad does."

"True," Ash teased. "I like the way he so broadly put those party condoms Alix gave Joel back on the counter in her room. right in front of everyone. Does he have his own supply with spikes?"

Robin's face was red. "I didn't notice anything broad about it."

"You were too busy blushing and not looking at anyone. Like now."

"Shut up."

"What's to be ashamed of?"

"I'm not ashamed. It's just embarrassing. He's close to everyone and it feels a little awkward."

"It wasn't awkward when we slept together," Ash pointed out.

"That's different." A bubble of laughter erupted from inside her. "You're gay."

"That took me a long time to figure out," Alix said.

"It's not hard to understand," Ash replied. "It's just friends comforting friends. That's all it ever was."

Robin nodded. "It's not hard on the relationship because we are friends."

"Oh I understand now."

Beside her, Joel grunted as he reached over to put his cigarette out. "Yeah, well enough of that. Ash, what happened with this Morris guy?"

"You want details?"

"You must be joking. No, I mean has he been in touch?"

He nodded. "It's weird, you know? This is a business thing we've got going but we're becoming friends in addition to it." He gave Joel a side-long glance and added, "And we're both pretty attracted to each other."

"Whatever makes you happy." He got up. "Anyone want more coffee?"

"Tell us about this video shoot," Alix said to Robin.

"Tim Winston is the director Brad hired and we've been working on it together. The plan is that I learn the ropes and then do it all myself. It's another avenue I want to go down. I rented costumes for everyone except you. I had to buy that one." She gave her friend a wicked grin. "You'll probably shoot me."

"It's not a pink fairy dress with polka dots, is it?"

"No, a black bodysuit slashed in dark blue. You can add it to the uniforms Mr. Davis insists on. I think it will look great."

"Just what exactly are you going to make us do," Joel asked suspiciously.

"We're using lights in and around the Alley View, some under Ash's paintings there so that faces float in and out of the shots. We want it surrealistic and the movements will be subtle but varied, sort of moving poses. The lights will do most of the work."

"That's good 'cos we sure as hell aren't dancers. Could you imagine Bear doing some of your pieces?

This brought a burst of laughter from all four.

The Blue Mask assembled the next day at the Alley View. It was an old basement club in the West End where the band first got its start. A series of steps descended to a door from which loud music could usually be heard blaring. The current owner had put a small sign up to designate the place but in the beginning there was nothing. Word of mouth and the superior quality of the bands were its only advertisement.

The ceilings were high; decoration minimal. It was a twilight place where the night could last forever. A bar at one end and a small stage at the other bordered a large expanse holding wooden tables and chairs. Black crepe hid the windows and the walls were broken by a series of paintings Ash had done years ago of the regulars who haunted the place at the time.

Tim and Robin had temporarily changed the atmosphere. Furniture was moved against the walls and the floor was strewn with thick cables running to a variety of sound, lighting and video equipment. Stage lights glared, highlighted in a variety of colours from harsh white to soft, dark blue and three cameramen were placed at various angles on moving tripods. The band would do a series of actions, shot in short clips that Tim and Robin outlined and rehearsed before the actual filming started. It was a process full of repeats and small variations of stance and action. A great deal of film was shot that they would cut to a three and a half minute video. Titles would be added later.

Robin continuously touched up their make-up. This was an essential as the strong lights washed out bare faces. Their features needed to be outlined, highlighted and powdered to achieve a normal effect and they sweated continually in the heat. It was a long and tiring day but the group managed to wrap up by early evening. The video would be edited and spliced during the week until it became a flowing, seamless piece of celluloid running to music. Tim was a well-respected director whose work was worth his costly fee.

The Blue Mask played the Alley View on New Year's Eve. For them it was a homecoming, a party more than a gig, and they had a riot.

Packed up and grumbling, they hit the road two days later for the last leg of their tour with Hades.

CHAPTER 9

As the meeting date for Mayday drew nearer, the band grew more excited. Hades' behaviour had worsened when the Blue Mask's second album started to grab attention. As it climbed up the charts, their treatment at the hands of the headline band became comparatively more abusive.

Alix sat in her room, complaining to Joel. "I think we should rub this Mayday thing in their faces. Maybe it will shut them up."

"No," he snapped. "I mean it. If they know they'll find a way to screw us up. You say nothing. Promise or I'll strangle you. I don't want us looking unprofessional and I don't want this feud behaviour to come off on Mayday."

"I won't," she agreed grudgingly, "but our hands are tied and they know it and they're laughing at us."

"Don't worry. The record sales are driving them nuts. Just keep up the good work and we'll sell more. That'll fix them better than anything we can come up with."

"I get the message, Joel, so leave me alone. I'll behave."

"Pact," he asked, holding out his hand.

She shook it with a grin. "Pact."

The Blue Mask pulled into Spokane on a grey, cold winter morning in late January and checked into their hotel. Brad was waiting. "I flew in this morning with Ash."

"Ash," Joel responded. "What's he doing here, apart from the obvious?"

"He has a contract too, or have you forgotten," Alix put in, elbowing him. "The world doesn't revolve around you, Stark."

"That's enough," Brad said. "You two have a meeting after your set. Their axe man, Roger March, has invited you morons to his suite.

"Mayday's concert is tomorrow night. They came in early just to talk to you. The Mask is invited over later after discussions. I guess they're taking over the bar in the hotel. With their rep for partying, I'm surprised the management lets 'em stay. That is one classy joint."

"I'm sure they pay through the nose for the privilege," Dixie pointed out. "Management probably welcomes them with open arms and charges them a fortune."

"We've got more to discuss than Mayday's finances," Joel said, "so let's get down to it. I'm beat."

Brad was already pulling papers out of his briefcase. Bear, Leo and Dixie headed for the door, tired and happy they weren't needed. Joel smiled as the three filed out. "We'll wake you up in an hour or so. Later."

"It had better be much later," Dixie snorted.

The three got down to work and then grabbed a few hours' sleep.

Alix and Joel left right after their set that night. Brad had arranged for them to have elevator access to Roger March's floor and given them his suite number and, after the two arrived, took over introductions. Morris Stockham was there as well. The two friends felt awkward, faced with suddenly meeting not only a member of the legendary band, but one of their favourites for years, but Roger put them at ease at once. He stepped forward without hesitation, his tall, lanky form topped by a wiry mass of red hair and a big smile splitting his thin face.

"Finally get to meet after all this negotiation trip," he laughed, shaking hands. "I sure am all for leaving this boring business shit to the managers and getting on with the fun. I snuck in for part of your gig tonight. You lot are on the fast track, bells and all. It's going to be a lark working with you."

Drinks were poured and the five sat down at the long dining table that stood against a huge picture window, the lights of the city sparkling below them. Roger plugged his guitar into a small, portable amp and quickly outlined what Mayday wanted to do with 'The Fallout'. Alix and Joel sat back in shock. This interpretation had never crossed their minds and it excited them. They plunged into discussion, Brad and Morris forgotten.

When the smoke cleared, more drinks were poured and Roger sat back, sipping his ale. "We have a problem about time in the studio. We work fast, you know? You lot don't have much time between the studio and your next tour, so your governor here tells us."

"We can work before or after our sessions," Joel offered. "As far as time goes, we're used to long hours and we don't really have much to do while we're on the road between gigs. I know basically what you want as far as guitar work goes. Let's get a quick tape made and I can play with it on the bus."

"I'm that way too, mate. Not much to do on the road but work, right?" He was grinning. Roger had a greater reputation as a playboy than Joel had yet acquired. Stories of his antics on the road were monumental and, if at least half of them were true, it put Joel out of Roger's league.

"I think you can leave us to sort out the details for now," Morris said blandly. "Why not go down to the bar and have your hard-earned party? Your concentration level, I'm sure, old son" – this to Roger – "is on the wane."

"Morris, you old queen, you are so right."

Brad and Morris settled down to business. The two bands met downstairs in the privacy of the reserved bar together with road crews and a few friends.

Later that night, Roger and Joel were sitting in the corner drinking Scotch. The two had a lot in common and were enjoying themselves immensely.

"You know, this big condom push started with AIDS but I've always used them," Roger was saying. "You never know with the birds you pick up on the road. A lot of them will tell you they're on the pill and the next thing you know your wife's getting a ring from your solicitor informing her a paternity suit has been filed against you. That happened to a bunch of me mates. Me, I stuck with the rubbers. All things aside, if I'd brought a dose of the clap home and given it to me missus, she'd have chopped me goolies off and force fed them to me for me tea."

"I don't have that problem and don't intend to."

"She suspected, mind," Roger added, "but over the years we've come to an understanding. As long as it doesn't come into our lives and nothing is flagrant, like, she pretends it isn't going on. Safer that way."

"Some women wouldn't think so."

Roger laughed loudly. "Had a go or two at you, have they? Never mind. As long as you protect yourself, the rest will work out – that's my philosophy. And with bloody AIDS, it became more fatal than a bastard kid. Any bloke who doesn't double bag it these days is mad, right?

"Even the die-hards use them now – the metal pigs who live on the edge. It really hit home for us when Freddie Mercury got AIDS. Only a few of us have been told, though it seems to have gotten well out now. It's one of the family, you know? I mean, there's a little collective group of us that have run into each other in the studios and clubs over the years – we all started around the same time – and it suddenly hit that it could bloody well happen on your doorstep. Man, that did me fucking head in, that did, as well as me heart. I cried like a bloody baby when he told us. Last time I saw him he looked like walking death – so fragile, you know? It's so useless, such a fucking shame. It's not just that we're losing a mate and can't stop it; it's watching that kind of talent and humanity go as well. And the fucking government got it wrong, as bloody usual. It's not a gay epidemic. It's hitting all of us who aren't fucking careful."

"Things changed in the eighties and it's worse now."

"You can say that again, mate. I see rock as part one, two and three, me. One was all innocence and fun, two was psychedelic shit party time and three is payback. You're in rock now and you have to have a bloody conscience when you write. No more free rides at the fun fair."

"Were they ever really free?"

Roger slung an arm around Joel's shoulder and clinked his glass against his new friend's. "Too right. Let's get off this downer. I'm glad we could meet."

"Cheers to that."

"Alix, me little flower," Roger called, seeing her approach, "come barnstorm us. We're having an attack of the morbids."

Management finally insisted that the bar was closed so Roger ordered drinks from room service and invited the band up to his suite. It was four a.m. when the Blue Mask straggled back to their hotel.

"I've got to sleep all day if I'm ever going to get through the gig tonight," Alix groaned. "Hades pulls any crap and I won't even have the energy to get mad."

The gig was uneventful and they trooped over to the Arena to see Mayday's concert. Roger had invited them backstage. Tiredness was quickly forgotten as they were swept up in Mayday's magic. It was an experience not to be missed. In each of their ways they had been following this group since their teens. They met for drinks at the end but no one had the energy to stay long and, early the next morning, it was back to reality on the bus and on the road. At Roger's request, Joel handed him a schedule of where the Blue Mask was headed so that they could talk while on tour.

The weeks sailed by.

Joel found more than his share of amusements. There was always a willing lady to offer entertainment and a bed in each stop. Bear would occasionally walk off with a fan and Leo even took up the occasional offer. Dixie flirted with everyone and Alix never asked where she disappeared to in the early hours. For her part, she was content to sit in company with other musicians or to be by herself. But they were all finding that, as their exposure increased, it was harder to find privacy. On the road they could get away. Home was quite another thing. The band had been besieged by fans over the last couple of years but Alix knew it was only a matter of time before even the fastness of the Arlington would be breached.

At the end of the run Hades and the Blue Mask were only too glad to part ways.

Exhausted but happy, they headed gratefully home.

CHAPTER 10

Spring/Summer 1991

Brad warned the band that the pace for the remainder of the year would be demanding. After a few days' rest he had them back in the studio. Most of the material was well-rehearsed and work went quickly. Mayday was already halfway through their new album and Alix and Joel spent a week after finishing their own work each day sitting in doing their guest spots on 'The Fallout'. Security within the studio had been stepped up but Mayday had long ago learned to cocoon themselves when on the move and they had it down to a fine art. The Blue Mask had nothing approaching that kind of concern and still moved freely but the band members found their privacy in restaurants and bars was being breached. For now, it didn't bother them much but Roger warned Joel that, as their exposure grew, that would change.

Studio work completed, there were three back to back videos planned to promote two more single releases from their previous album and one for the upcoming disc. The Alley View had been booked and Robin was working with Tim. Both liked the club as it could be dressed up and lit in almost any way. After a week's rest, the group was off again on a headline tour of Canada. Life was easier without the continued aggravation of Hades' presence and the tour sat lightly on their shoulders. Brad had hired a public relations firm to do some heavy promotional work and all were confident. The second album was selling well at home. In Britain and Europe figures were surprisingly strong, generating enough interest to more than justify the European jaunt. The United States was harder territory to conquer but small leaps forward were better than none at all and they were content with that.

Though the band continued to write on the road they also found time to play. Not only were they enjoying themselves but each found that they were enjoying their success and confidence rode high in the weeks that followed.

Joel had a ball and was at the height of his adventures as Mr. Hormone, a name Dixie tagged him with because of his ongoing trysts with willing groupies. Alix had no idea how he could keep up the game with so many other things on the go. "I don't know where you get the energy," she said to him one night when they were sitting in a club, trying to unwind after an adrenalin-fuelled gig.

"After that kind of reception, I always have a rush going for a while." He gave her a lewd wink. "It helps bring me down."

But she wondered about that statement. As their success brought them to higher peaks, he grew more nervous. She suspected that Joel's plunges into sex romps were also a way of coping with a fear of failure – the possibility that success could be snatched from them by the fickle nature of fame.

The two were in a bar in northern Ontario, after a particularly trying gig where hecklers disrupted the first half of the evening until being unceremoniously thrown out by bouncers, when he announced that he wanted to go on a tear.

"We're in the middle of a tour," she protested. "You know our rules."

"We've got three days off. You with me or not?"

"You already know the answer to that. Lead the way."

The two went bar hopping, never spending more time than two drinks in each place they stumbled into. It was late and Joel was drunk when a fan approached. Alix was returning from the bathroom and stopped before she got back to the table.

A woman was whispering in his ear. Her hand went to the tight pocket of his leather trousers and she pushed a key down into its depth, her hand lingering on his thigh. Smiling, he nodded and put an arm around her, mouth close to her ear as he replied. The woman moved off to another table to retrieve her jacket and speak to her friends.

Joel spotted Alix and sauntered over. "Mind if I make myself scarce, girl?"

"The old key trick again?"

He pulled the key out of his pocket. On it was a tag with her name and an address. "I said I'd be with her in about twenty minutes."

"I don't get it. Don't these women have any pride?"

"They know the game. I won't remember their names and they don't expect me to. Ash calls it star-fucking. He sees it as a poll indication of our popularity."

"You don't have to justify it to me."

"You okay getting back to the hotel?"

"I'm grateful actually; my head's splitting."

"To each his own and this is what I need. Later."

She watched him move off and was glad to step aside. This kind of release she couldn't give him and he'd need it after the night they had put in. She headed back to the hotel and sleep-filled oblivion.

The band arrived home in the middle of the summer to a city bursting with riotous colour. Brad proudly informed them that advance sales for the next album were promising and 'The Fast Track' was released with another wave of heavy publicity. After a brief rest he was sending them on a short jaunt into the U.S.

Ash, Robin, Brad, Alix and Joel met over dinner. "I've got me a smart announcement to make," Ash called out, tossing his napkin on his now clean plate and smirking with satisfaction.

Robin watched him fondly. He was working out in a gym and he'd recovered fully from those destructive years of too much alcohol and too many drugs. The swollen, bloated features were gone, the lack of appetite likewise and he had put on much needed weight. Pride in his job and a sense of accomplishment in his control on life gave him a glow of satisfaction – no worries in sight. "You're finally going to get to bad mouth all of us on Johnny Carson," she teased.

"He's not on TV anymore," he answered, mimicking Alix.

The singer winked at him as she lit a cigarette. "Took you long enough to figure that one out though, didn't it?"

"Don't encourage him," Joel said. "Spit it out, Mr. Ashley, or we'll beat it out of you."

He sat back happily. "I bought me a smart little house in the West End. Now I got me a smart little garage to park my smart little sports car in."

His mouth dropped. "You bought a house? You? You're leaving the Arlington?"

"So many questions," Ash said airily. "Yes, yes and yes."

"Why?"

"You know, you could be happy for me."

"For all the years I've known you," Robin responded, "the one thing you always avoided like the plague is anything to do with permanence. A house is pretty permanent."

"I was a lot younger then. You're not the same person I met either, my moon goddess, and I've let you grow without bitching."

"I'm not bitching; it's just a shock."

"You should see this place. It's brick, with three bedrooms and this long, empty basement I'm going to turn into a work studio. It's got as much character as the Arlington so I'm not losing anything, just changing locations. I'm still in the hood."

"What brought this on," Joel asked.

"I want to expand. I want to have some place that's a base. I want a life with a bit of structure to it."

"I think it's a great idea," Brad said. "It's a hell of an investment, Durango." He turned to Alix and Joel. "You two are earning pretty heavy bread these days. It wouldn't be a bad idea to put it into something."

Joel sneered. "No thanks. I'm staying put."

"Me too," Alix agreed. "Besides, what the hell would either of us do with a house? We're never home long enough to do anything but laundry."

"You've been bitching about getting invaded a lot, even with the new security you put into the Arlington," Ash pointed out. "Buy close to me and I'll keep an eye on the place for you."

"Think you might get lonely? Is that why you're pushing this? There'll be no more dropping down to our floor when you want some company."

"We're not teenagers anymore, Joel. We're closing in on thirty and it's long past time for us to be living in a boarding house."

"The Arlington isn't a boarding house."

"When you move in," Brad asked, trying to turn down the heat.

"In a month."

"You having one hell of a house warming?"

"It'll be the talk of the town; the party of the year; the bash to end all bashes..."

"Is Morris Stockham invited," Joel asked archly.

"You're a bastard," Ash said. "No, but I'm going to see him soon enough. I'm going to England with you."

"That's not till the end of the year. You planning that far ahead now?"

"Just like you, pal."

"Speaking of which," Alix interrupted, turning to Brad. "We've all been talking and you know that club we end up at?"

"The De Sade."

"Yeah, well we want the crew that did Mayday's live CD in to record it. It'll satisfy one of our album commitments."

"You dudes just did the last disc in your contract. No new deal has been inked."

She smiled slowly, elbowing Joel. "We got him for once."

"What's going on," Ash asked.

"Little Bradley has been busy again, negotiating another three album deal for us that's even sweeter than the first."

"Who told you?"

"Geoffrey Davis. Me and Joel saw him just after we got home. He asked us if we'd had time to go over the contracts with you."

"So much for the fine art of surprise," he grumbled. "Well, babe, you ain't beat me yet. We talked about this live deal at Christmas, remember? We gonna book that crew that did Mayday's gig and the companion video and we gonna record the lot for posterity. Then we gonna release it and make some more bread. It's already in motion. That do you?"

"One of these days, Mr. Easton," Alix threatened happily, "you're going to be the one on the surprise end of the deal and we are going to make it a big one."

CHAPTER 11

Autumn 1991

Joel gave Ash a hand packing up his possessions over the course of the week, laughing and joking the way they had done long before commitments took away so much of their time together. Alix helped occasionally but was mostly content to be on her own or kicking around the Alley View with other musicians.

Leo, Bear and Dixie had each gone their separate ways to recharge. When the five left a week later, they were back in groove and the tour went off without a hitch. Many of the songs for the next album had been written and these were polished on the road. By the time the band returned home near the end of October they were ready to record. After that, they demanded a rest and Brad cleared their calendar. For two years with him, and two before that, it had been nonstop and they needed a break before the machine started up again at the end of the year.

Brad was waiting for them the first morning in the studio. "I got news, hombres."

"You're getting a new line of chat," Dixie asked hopefully.

"No hope of that, babe." He paused, letting them start to fidget and, when he had their full attention, smiled slowly. "I just got word. 'The Fast Track' hit number one here and is sitting at number five in Britain. We're in the fast lane now.

"Mayday released their new album and is available to let you in on one gig when you first hit the U.K. They're winging to Japan after that and you'll be on your own but it'll be a fab start to your tour. They've included 'The Fallout' in their show."

"And we kick off New Year's Eve...," Bear started.

"In London town, Durango."

"All in all, not a bad way to start off the year," Joel added.

"Let's get this year finished first. We get this disc in the can, finish off a couple of videos, then you get a rest before you start bedding down the British birds. God help 'em."

"Somebody has to keep up our stud reputation and since you retired the whole load is on my shoulders."

"Who said I retired?" Brad laughed, heading out the door.

"Trouble in paradise," Alix asked softly. "If he's screwing Robin up I'll shoot the bastard."

"Not while I'm breathing," Joel threatened. "He's the goose laying golden eggs and we're not touching a hair on his head."

Alix nodded vaguely, her thoughts following Brad down the long hall. She'd call Robin as soon as they were done for the day.

It wasn't until the end of the week that she finally ran her friend to ground and what she saw alarmed her. Robin was not only packing her bags, boxes full of her things were scattered around her rapidly emptying room. "Just what the hell is going on here? First Ash packs up and moves, now you."

"I'm not part of the Arlington scene," she replied, throwing a handful of towels into a nearby carton. "And Ash was right. We're getting too old to be hanging out in boarding houses."

Alix laid a hand on her friend's arm, stilling the constant motion. "Is everything all right? You've been avoiding me and Joel lately."

"That's all in your mind. You two have been busy trying to get this album finished. You're the ones with no time." But Robin wouldn't meet her eyes.

"This is me, remember? No bullshit. Are things going bad with Brad?"

She looked up at that. "Why?"

"He made some crack about keeping up his reputation with Joel. He screwing around?"

She laughed. "No, he hasn't spent a night away from me in months. So he's still on the rep thing." Seeing her friend's confusion, she relented. "It's a private joke we have. He told me that he can't give up his precious rep so he's still going to claim he's a slut. His words, not mine. You see..."

"What is it?"

"It's hard to find a way to say it. Brad says it's like trying to propose it to the parents."

"What?"

"We're moving in together. We're finally ready to make a commitment. I'm twenty-eight years old and I want to settle down. I'm not like you anymore – I don't want to be footloose and fancy free."

"Holy shit! Does Ash know?"

"We told him the night we helped him move. He's happy for us."

"What makes you think we wouldn't be?"

"You're so wary of Brad's reputation and he and Joel are so much alike. We were worried."

"Paranoid, more like it." Alix gave her friend a hug. "I'm really happy for you."

"And no worries?"

She swallowed her doubts and smiled. "No worries."

"We were going to tell you tonight at Ash's dinner."

"I'll hunt Joel down and break it to him before then."

Robin kissed her cheek. "You're a gem, do you know that?"

"Yeah, well don't let it get around. You'll ruin *my* reputation. I'll see you tonight."

She left, heading back to the Arlington to find Joel. He banged on her door and let himself in before she had a chance to go look for him. She was pouring a Scotch and took another glass out of the cupboard, filling it.

He accepted with raised brows. "Not like you to be downing the big ones so early in the day."

"We got some time off and I'm thirsty."

"What's up?"

"Robin and Brad are moving in together."

"That's hardly a surprise," he pointed out. "It's been coming for a while."

"I know but it still makes me nervous."

"Why?"

"I don't know."

He leaned against the counter, regarding her with assessing eyes. "Maybe it's all the changes making you nervous."

She shrugged. "Maybe."

He tipped up her face to meet his. "Feeling left out?"

She laughed without humour. "You know me too well, you asshole." Shifting out of reach, she lit a cigarette. "Ash is moving on; Robin's moving on, but it seems like we're just stuck in the same old rut. Things have been wilder than I ever thought and I don't unwish what's going on, don't get me wrong, but life these days seems like one long round of studios, tours and videos. We don't have time for any friends except Leo, Bear and Dix and that's only because we're working together. I feel like I'm in some kind of holding pattern above life. We're heading for thirty and acting like teenagers."

He tugged on the short, black hair. "You're tired, girl, and you need a break. Don't worry, we'll finish this album and have a rest and things'll be back on an even keel when we head over to England."

"I guess so."

She tried hard to shake the feeling that night when the group had dinner with Ash. They walked around his house, exclaiming over clever touches or odd and unusual things that the occupiers had added over the years.

The band went back into the studio to finish the album, took a day to rest and then insisted on getting the videos out of the way before settling into the weeks that would take them to the end of the year and a new beginning.

Alix was exhausted by the end of the shooting and stayed home for most of the next day. Joel banged on her door and barged in. "We're talking about going to the Afterhours. Coming?"

"No thanks."

"You turn down a celebration?"

"I'm beat, Joel, aren't you?"

"I'm coming down with a cold but it's nothing a little excessive drinking won't cure." His green eyes were glittering.

"I think you've already started."

"Yeah, well I needed a little bracer or twelve."

"Go brace somewhere else."

"What you need is to get out in the sun and have some good times."

Her eyes went to the wide window and she gestured outside. A grey day hovered with low clouds threatening rain. "It looks really sunny out there."

"Try here," he retorted, tossing an envelope into her lap.

"What's this?"

"A Christmas present."

"Oh yeah," she said warily.

"I've been thinking about what you said about everything changing and everyone leaving us behind, so I decided we needed a break and we could do with a little leaving behind ourselves."

"We?"

"I want to go on a holiday and I want some company. No strings attached, Alix. Just two pals whooping it up elsewhere."

"Where's elsewhere?"

The lop-sided grin came slowly but it lit up his face with mischief. "How about Mexico?"

Her eyes sparkled as she took two airline tickets out of the envelope. "You mean it?"

"Course."

"Then I say olé, amigo."

Both spent the evening packing, laughing and planning and, early the next morning, took a cab to the airport. Each got on a pay phone, knowing their friends would not be up yet and left gleeful, unrepentant messages on answering machines saying they would be AWOL for a while.

Like two runaways, they boarded the plane and were calling for drinks right after it had taken off.

CHAPTER 12

Winter 1991

For Alix and Joel that time in Mexico stood out sharply as a highlight in their friendship. Joel's suspicions were well-founded and the day after their arrival he came down with a slight fever and a cough, but it did nothing to impair their fun. Needing rest without the tumult of a wild nightlife, they spent days wandering ruins or shaded beneath a huge umbrella on a blanket on the beach, reading, talking and drinking Margaritas, a passion the two discovered in the bar of the hotel that first night.

Night brought a coolness and silence to the beaches and they spent most of them strolling along the edge of the water, the breakers splashing over their bare feet. For both it was a learning time and they felt out each other's secrets, basking in this greater intimacy and taking advantage of it to ask questions neither would have dared pose a few years ago when their protective shells cloaked both their pain and carefully concealed parts of their personalities and pasts. It was during one such session – they were sitting under an umbrella watching the sun set – that Joel finally asked a question that had been bothering him.

"You know when we slept together last Christmas and you were having some dream and crawled all over me?"

She grimaced. "I'm not proud of that. It was a pretty insulting thing to do."

He grinned. "Depends on which angle you look at it from." He paused to light a cigarette. "Who was it you were with?"

"Some memory. As I recall, it was you."

"You know what I mean, Alix."

She sighed. "Remember when I took off to Toronto and came back for a visit? I got a phone call when we were out. Ash gave me the message and I left the next day."

"Yeah. I asked Brad about it, you know. When he first came out here."

"He never said."

"I told him not to."

"He used to be a blabber mouth whether you told him not to or not."

"Well this time he played his cards close and said to ask you. So I'm asking."

She was silent for so long he thought she wasn't going to answer. The sun was almost gone and he could only just see the outline of her face, pale against the fading light. "I met John in Toronto just after I got there. He was a lunatic and a clown and at first he just made me laugh. But things heated up and I finally gave in. He helped me cope with my father's beatings, then his death. He helped me deal with sex after that bastard raped me and he just eased things. I found I didn't need to hide anymore – I was strong enough to deal with things outright. He brought me a long way down the road to getting better." She shook her head. "He also screwed my head up. But I loved him."

"I tried to help you through the rape. How come you let him but you wouldn't let me?"

"You made a pass at me, asshole. John taught me how to like sex again. Or within reason."

"What do you mean?"

"I was never much into it from the first." She turned to him, lifting her t-shirt, exposing the scar across her ribcage. "Remember when you first saw this? You knew the bastard who raped me didn't have a blade. Well the year before I got attacked at a New Year's party. This guy had been stalking me. He decided that if he couldn't have me no one could and cut me up pretty badly. Brad and my friend Rick pulled him off and got me to a hospital. I came out west just after that. Then there was the rape." She let her shirt fall with a harsh laugh. "Is it any wonder I'm not too fond of making out? My track record isn't exactly glowing."

"Is that why you never get into the guys who hang around gigs trying to pick you up?"

She watched the red glow of his cigarette deepen as he inhaled. "I don't know how you do it. I'm just not that interested. Oh I'm tempted once in a while but only when my body lets me know it's hungry. Other than that it doesn't matter. I'd rather do without the hassle."

"That's hard luck." He doused his cigarette in the sand and dug up the bottle of Scotch he had buried in an attempt to keep it cool. "Want a slug?"

Alix took a drink before passing it back and he followed suit, then recapped the bottle. "So where is this paragon now?"

"Dead." She turned away to light a cigarette, her hand cupping the flickering flame and in it he saw her face closed and shuttered. She drew on the butt and continued. "That was what the call was about. It was from Rick. John was in the hospital and he didn't have long, so I had to go right away if I wanted to see him." Her voice cracked. "He looked awful laying there – so helpless and trying not to show how scared he was."

"What killed him?"

"Booze. He was a chronic alcoholic and had cirrhosis when I met him. Of course he didn't tell me till it was way too late. I was already hooked. He was a coward about some things."

"But not about this?"

"No. I wasn't there at the end. He sent me away; said he didn't want me to see him like that. He made me promise not to stick around and, like the coward I am, I kept it." She passed an impatient hand over the tears that were dripping freely down her thin cheeks. "Some little heroine, huh?"

Joel put his arms around her and pulled her to his chest, his hand stroking her hair. "You did what he asked. That took guts too, you know."

"Stop making excuses for me."

"Why, so you can carry guilt around and weigh yourself down even more than you do? Life's too short, Alix. He sent you away – that was his choice. Just 'cos you went doesn't make you a chicken. I know you've got guts. I've seen you down and fucked up as hell and I watched you climb out of that pit. Just have a look at where we're standing, girl. Who would've thought a couple of drugged out drunks could get here?"

A bubble of laughter rose up in her chest. "Drugged out drunks," she repeated, dousing her cigarette in the sand and wrapping both her arms around him. "Good thing I write most of the lyrics, Stark. You'd have us doing bad stand-up comedy if you did."

He wrestled her to the ground and sat on top of her, running his fingers through the sand. "I could make you eat this stuff, you know. Now take that back. Come on, eat your words."

She bucked beneath him, trying to wriggle out. "No way."

He leaned over her, sifting sand into her hair. "This stuff isn't very appetizing."

"Eat ratshit then."

He leaned even closer, trying to open her clamped mouth. Both were giggling hard, each fighting to win, when the mood suddenly changed. Alix grew quiet and still under him. His green eyes darkened perceptively and, slowly, he lowered his head. She rose to meet him, her mouth opening under his. The two remained entwined for a long time and then Joel shifted gently on the blanket to lie beside her, stroking her skin. She sat up quickly. "We can't here on the beach."

"Everyone's gone, and it's dark. No one will see."

"What about protection?"

He patted the beach bag beside him. "Have condoms will travel."

"Did you plan this?"

He had, but there was no way he was owning up to it. "That's a stupid question and you know it. I've been carrying them around in case I meet a choice senorita."

She lay back down beside him. "Will I do?"

"I guess so," he said quietly, kissing her. "I wasn't much fun for you last time. Let me make it up to you, 'kay? Friend to friend?"

She nodded gravely. "Friend to friend."

He took his time, caressing the thin body, arousing her and watching expressions chase each other across her pale face. They made love slowly, savouring each other and, when both were satisfied, he kissed her. "Still friends?"

"Only friends."

He winked. "But close friends."

Smiling, she pulled her shorts and t-shirt back on. She didn't want Joel to think that this would be a regular occurrence but he seemed to take it as the exception that she did. "Let's go back to the hotel. I need some sleep."

In amiable silence, the two packed up their belongings and returned to the room they were sharing. Joel went straight to his bed and, stripping down, tossed himself into it with welcome exhaustion. Seeing the sudden flash of uncertainty in her face, he blew her a kiss and wished her goodnight. The wariness passed and she got into her own bed, throwing a pillow at him before turning out the light.

"See you tomorrow."

"Not if I see you first." He rolled over and went to sleep.

Alix was never certain whether it was done to reassure her or as a shot at her reluctance to dabble in sex but the next night, after a day of learning how to snorkel, Joel made off with their attractive instructor and didn't come back until the following morning. She was just finishing coffee when he walked in and she surveyed him with a rueful shake of the head. "Even on holidays you have to keep up the stud reputation."

He smiled and poured himself a cup. "Even on holidays."

They spent their last night in the town's tourist center, tripping in and out of cantinas, drinking Margaritas and generally whooping it up. It was a festive party and fitting that their quiet, restful holiday finished with a bang.

Joel's cold had persisted yet he looked tanned and healthy. Ignoring Alix's salvos about the hole in the ozone layer, UV rays and skin cancer, he'd paraded about in the sun, basking in its warmth and making fun of the white-skinned waif who trailed along beside him slathered in sun screen and wearing a broad-brimmed straw hat. "I'm sick and you look like you need a vacation," he joked at the airport, pointing at her sun-starved skin.

"Margaritas and strong cigarettes are not exactly recommended cures for the common cold."

"I get a mean one every year."

"Too bad it had to happen on holiday."

He winked. "Didn't put a damper on things though, did it?"

"Does anything where you're concerned?" She gave him a hug and a smacking kiss. "Thanks for the best Christmas present ever."

"You can return it next year."

"You got a deal."

The trip was met with raised brows at Ash's combination house warming/Christmas party. Alcohol-loosened tongues asked more daring and personal questions but neither of them mentioned the night on the beach.

"We go on tour together for months and no one says anything," Alix protested. "We take a couple weeks off and wander around Mexico and everybody freaks."

"We're not freaking, babe," Brad put in, "we just nosy."

Joel brought out the two rolls of film he had taken and pictures were passed around. There were many goofy shots – one in particular of him larking around behind the snorkel instructor.

"Now there's a beauty," Bear said.

Joel, with a wink and a nod, stilled all suspicion. "And a wildcat in the night."

Amid groans, Ash piped up, "You get mad at me when I start so, touché, my friend and shut up. We don't want to hear about your hot sex life."

Alix and Joel wanted to get one more video shoot in before leaving for England and amid accusations of slave-driving they announced that time had already been booked. Everyone was to report two days later, bright and early.

Both had been working closely with Robin and Tim on each successive shoot. Alix's imagination was fired with visual images and concepts and, as response continued to get more positive, she contributed more ideas. Tim liked the storyboard and reserved a kiddies' amusement park.

The band piled into Bear's van and drove to the site. Cameras and crew were already there. Robin assembled the group under a grey sky for make-up and costumes. The theatrical costumers she found for their first video were now used exclusively to provide anything they needed. The track, off their latest album, was called 'Train to Nowhere' and Alix proposed filming it on a kid's train ride. Shooting went well, despite the threatening clouds and the keen wind that blew through the compound. The set was wrapped and gear loaded before the heavens opened.

Cold, driving rain pierced coats and gloves and soon all were soaked to the skin. Leo proposed getting into the van but Joel, grinning conspiratorially at Bear, tripped him, sending him into a sea of mud. A fight ensued and before long all five of them were laughing and throwing mud balls at each other.

The next day found Bear sneezing and Joel coughing and chilled. Alix, Dixie and Leo, who did the singing and back-up vocals, immediately started gulping Vitamin C in an attempt to stave off similar symptoms. They had a New Year's Eve gig in London. If they messed it up because of some childish romps in the rain, Brad would have their heads.

Two days later, with Brad, Robin and Ash in tow, the group boarded the plane.

CHAPTER 13

Seated together and excited, they partied all the way across the Atlantic Ocean. When they landed the following morning, the representative from Dome Records' English office met with a straggled, red-eyed and hungover band.

Joel watched the confident woman making her brisk way over to them with speculation. "This the rep, Brad?"

"You got it, Durango."

"Hmmm."

"Put a lid on your hormones," Dixie advised. "This one means business. I'm sure there are all sorts of other English crumpets you can have for breakfast."

When she stopped unerringly in front of them, her love beads were still clacking. All eyes surveyed her with lively curiosity. She looked like a vision out of the sixties. The slim legs were encased in black suede lace-up boots and lurid yellow tights that travelled up to disappear under a black-fringed, heart-stoppingly short mini skirt. Large firm breasts rose from a small waist, trapped in a dark silk shirt under the wildly coloured necklaces. The bracelets on her arms jangled from wrist to elbow and large hooped earrings nestled in a teased mass of golden blonde hair. The pretty face was carefully painted. A wide grin broke the mask and hazel eyes flashed with humour and intelligence.

The voice that followed was clipped, educated and upper class. "Don't let appearances fool you," she said merrily. "I know I look like something out of a lucky dip but it's all window-dressing." She held her hand out. "I'm from Dome in London and I have the distinct pleasure of coordinating your British and European tour. Eleanor Sebastian."

Laughing, Brad introduced everyone. Eleanor eyed the band with equal curiosity and nodded to herself as each member was presented. "Mayday was quite impressed with you. Roger March went on for ages. By the way, their album is still at number one. I thought you might like to see what they did with 'The Fallout' so I took the liberty of bringing a tape with me. I'll play it when we get to your hotel. Let's get out of this place and into something more comfortable."

She walked away, all brisk efficiency, and the band trailed behind her in shock. "Geoffrey Davis said she was the best," Brad commented quietly.

"I don't think we're going to lack for anything," Leo agreed. "All I can say is wow!"

Eleanor collected baggage tags, handed them to a liveried driver with whispered instructions and ushered the group into two waiting cars. She got in with Alix, Joel, Brad and Robin and signalled to the driver to start. "Your luggage will be brought to your hotel. We might as well get there first and have a drink. I'm sure you're all in after the flight. Some good English ale is the ticket – it will revive you like nothing else."

"Here's a girl I'll follow anywhere," Joel cracked, elbowing Alix.

"Roger did warn me," came the laughing reply. "And I must say, after a long flight the first thing I like when I settle is a large Scotch."

"As you probably gathered, babe," Brad said dryly, "you just found a way to these two greedy little hearts."

"I'm here to make the ride smooth," she answered, winking. "Mr. Davis' orders."

She chatted easily on the ride in, pointing out passing landmarks, keeping the conversation light and free of business. After checking them into the hotel, she gathered them all together in Joel's room, poured drinks and slipped deftly into business mode.

"All your equipment is booked for the tour and a crew has been supplied. A road manager was appointed but he got ill so I am stepping in and my assistant can handle anything that needs to be taken care of from the London end. Mayday are doing a solo tour but have agreed to have you for their last gig in London before they leave for Japan – in fact they absolutely insisted. I'm afraid that means you'll be starting work one day earlier than planned after the New Year's Eve bash at Rainy Day but I'm sure you won't mind" – this said with a lively smile at the rapidly shaking heads – "so it's going to be a rather busy time. There is a break before you get to the Continent and another after you've finished.

"Everything has been set up for your video/album recording at the De Sade and I hope I've ironed out any bugs that I've tried to think might crop up in this lot. We'll just deal with untoward happenings as they occur, shall we?"

"The gods love us," Joel crooned, "they sent us an angel."

Alix smacked him good-naturedly and Eleanor applauded with approval. "It's going to be frightfully hard work but there will be time in the end to play. I can help there too. I know London well and if it's amusement you're looking for I'm sure I can be of assistance." She turned to

Ash and Leo. "Morris Stockham has, I believe, also offered his services as an escort into any areas I might not be familiar with."

"You know him pretty well," Leo asked.

"I should," came the friendly reply. The hazel eyes were sparkling with mischief. "He's my cousin, you see." She dug into a voluminous multi-coloured canvas bag and came up with a video tape in a black case. Moving to the entertainment unit, she turned everything on, inserted the tape and started it. "This is what gave Mayday their current number one single."

Alix and Joel smiled in satisfaction as the familiar opening chords to 'The Fallout' sounded. The smiles soon wavered, then disappeared as the video progressed. Having been in on some of the recording, both knew their song had been changed and had some idea of what to expect but the visual that accompanied it was a surprise.

It was a delicate, sorrowfully haunting version of their song about speed and an addict who was in love with his drug. Alix's screams, originally at the end, were picked up throughout, punctuated by Joel's often strident guitar. The video itself was harrowing, with blatant shots of addicts in their darkest moments. It was an anti-drug message threaded with a warning not to share needles if you do drugs. As the screen went black an emergency number came up, urging anyone who needed help to call.

The screen snowed as the recording came to an end and Eleanor reached over to turn the system off. She replaced the video in its plastic jacket and laid it on top of the television. "You may keep this."

"That's magic," Bear said in an awed voice.

She nodded. "It sure as bloody hell is. That went straight up the charts when it was released. Mayday donated some of the sales to drug abuse centres and some to AIDS societies. The public has been amazingly supportive."

"I never thought it could be turned around like that," Joel said quietly. "We wrote that as a pro-drug song at the time. Tongue in cheek, maybe, but definitely not with the message I just saw."

"Morris played me the original version. It's a smashing song really. Mayday just put a different slant on it."

"I'm glad they did," Alix said. "We were fuck-ups to put a song out with that kind of message. It was a reckless thing to do."

"Young bands make mistakes," Eleanor said simply. "All of them. Mayday set horrendous examples for their fans in the early days. Maturity does count for something, however, and this is the age of information. The audience has grown up with the music and the message is clear all around: protect yourself and don't experiment with drugs. If you do, don't share needles."

"So much for the free-wheeling sixties," Dixie joked. "Man, how things have changed."

"I think it's a case of having to rather than wanting to." Eleanor laughed and spun around. "And who says the sixties are dead!"

Joel interrupted the hilarity. "I hate to be rude and break up the party but if I don't catch some zzz's I'm going to be in big trouble. We just drained the airline's supply of booze on our way across and I, for one, need to sleep it off."

"I'm sorry," Eleanor said quickly. "I've been so looking forward to meeting you that I'm not thinking. Nothing down for me today. You lot get some rest and I'll meet you in the hotel restaurant tomorrow for breakfast. Say eleven o'clock?"

All nodded in agreement. The luggage arrived and was delivered to each of their rooms and the tired travellers settled down to sleep.

Joel woke in the middle of the afternoon, disoriented and groggy. He took a shower, dressed and headed next door, banging until Alix let him in. "Let's go explore."

"I was sleeping," she complained.

He gave her hair a sharp tug. "You sleep all day and you'll be messed tomorrow. We got a show to do in a couple days, you know."

"Happy New Year. Give me ten minutes."

Twenty minutes later the two were winding their way down the Kings Road, goggling at everything in sight. A cold wind blew but the streets were clear and the threatened rainstorm that had been broadcast was still just a threat. The two dashed in and out of stores and pubs, stopping every few blocks to have a drink and absorb the atmosphere of this foreign place.

Joel's eyes lit up with mischief when he spotted a large record shop ahead of them. "Come on, let's see if they have any of our stuff."

They darted in and inquired. The clerk nodded without hesitation and pointed to an aisle. Much to their shock, there were not only copies of their latest album, but of the earlier ones too. Laughing both departed.

"Holy shit," Alix said outside, "we're international."

"Fuck a duck." He grabbed her arm and hauled her off towards the nearest pub. "Come on, let's get drunk. We have to behave starting tomorrow but we're off the hook today."

She held out her hand in the time-honoured tradition that had started the day they met. "Pact?"

"Pact." He shook her hand then leaned over and kissed her. "Welcome to England."

"Yeah, yeah," she said happily, giving him a sharp push. "First round's on me but you buy the cigarettes."

It was still early when they wandered into the hotel to pick up the rest of their friends and drag them out. Bleary-eyed again, the band showed up on time to face breakfast and Eleanor at eleven the next morning. She eyed them with a rueful shake of the head. "Had to sample the ale right away, I see. I should have warned you, I suppose."

"Fat lot of good it would have done," Alix said cheerfully. "You know, I really like this stuff. I feel better than I have any right to."

"Can't say the same for me," Joel complained, coughing as he lit a cigarette. "I feel like I've been steamrollered."

"It's that stinking cold you picked up before Mexico. You should've had it checked out."

"Stop nagging. Getting caught in the rain on your train video didn't exactly help any of us."

"Now kids," Brad interrupted. "Be good or no hooch."

Eleanor laughed. "That's one way to keep order."

"It's the only way."

She turned to the band members. "I hope you've gotten it out of your systems for now. This is your highest profile tour yet and I've set interviews and press shoots up all over the shop. There's been a lot of interest in you since Mayday's cover of 'The Fallout' – that's what really catapulted you into the big time.

"I've read your first press releases and I see that you're not averse to bad publicity. Some of your earlier songs may stir up controversy but bad publicity isn't always a bad thing, as I'm sure you're aware. You are already on your way in Europe – the band is quite popular in Germany right now and has been for the last six months."

"Me and Alix went into a record store yesterday and found copies of all our albums."

Eleanor nodded. "A lot of underground music is very big here and it comes through the oddest channels. Canadian servicemen have been bringing it in for years – there are quite a lot of them stationed in Europe. It gets mixed in with the local population and Bob's your uncle. There are a frightful lot of you Canukies playing ice hockey in the European leagues and such and they bring music in as well. As I said, you have been popular in Germany for quite a while. We have three shows booked there."

A waiter approached with coffee and took their orders. Conversation carried on throughout the meal as she outlined their itinerary for the next few weeks.

"Let me get this straight," Alix said. "We're around Britain for a while, then Europe, then back around Britain again?"

"Exactly. We're going to be pushing 'The Fast Track' – as it is the tour this is for – but halfway through Dome plans on releasing 'Denizens of the City'. So in essence, it's a double play. I believe there was some talk of a video shoot here for one of the songs."

"We wanted to use the East End of London to shoot the title track. It'll give us something moody and broody."

Joel and Bear almost choked on their toast, they laughed so hard. She shot them both a dirty look and raised a threatening fist. Bear engulfed both her hands in one big mitt and shook his head. "Not in your wildest dreams, little one. I am a mountain and you shall remain a molehill."

"Just remember."

"What?"

She smiled wickedly. "Some molehills can kick."

"Joel's got the wandering appendage; I just play drums."

"Not all the time though, huh Bear?"

"Perhaps not. All right, molehill, I shall remember."

"Fighting in the ranks," Eleanor cooed. She rose and gathered paperwork together. "I'll pick you up at two o'clock and take you to my office. There will be a press gathering in Dome's conference room and then interviews et cetera. I've also invited the press to your sound check at Rainy Day tomorrow afternoon. Tomorrow night, troops, it's all yours." A wide smile split her features. "This is going to be a spree. I can't wait." She waggled her fingers and departed.

"Who'd believe she's a hot shot exec at Dome," Brad said, watching her disappear through the outside door.

"We sure hit the jackpot," Dixie said.

"She handled Hades' last European tour for Dome and hated it."

"Was she stuck on the road with them?"

"No, babe, but the road manager she hired walked right after the tour. They drove everyone loco."

"Glad we're not the only ones. There's a lesson here. It never hurts to treat people decently, no matter who you are. Look at Mayday. They should have swelled heads but they don't. Maybe at first, but they sure learned fast."

"Oh no," Joel moaned, "that mean I have to be even nicer to the senoritas than I already have been?" He clapped a hand to his forehead. "I don't know if I can take this but I have to do my part to help the band. I promise not to let you down, even if it kills me."

"Listen to Mr. Hormone here," she said, patting him on the head. "Isn't he a selfless little player?"

Alix tossed a piece of toast in his face. "Selfless as all hell. Pigs fly too. And over here the senoritas are called birds."

"Can it," Brad ordered.

"How long are you staying?"

"Trying to shed me, babe?"

"Course not. Are you sticking around for the whole tour?"

"Love to, but I got so much work waiting I'm gonna get washed over. This business shit is some responsibility trip."

"You just keep it up," Joel put in. "You're gold dust."

"Thanks for the vote of confidence, Durango. You running in the next election or something?"

"So you're deserting us."

"I'm just a phone call away and if there's any hot stuff happening I'll be on the first plane over. You got no worries." He pinched her cheek until he got a smile out of her. "And you better be good for Dome's exec lady or no hooch."

"You're an asshole," she said good-naturedly.

"That's why we're friends, Alix. One knows another one."

The press conference that afternoon was a news fest. No stranger to interviews, the band was nonetheless surprised at the amount of information the media had on them. Eleanor nodded sagely throughout it and Alix suspected that she'd been more than cooperative regarding the band's history and current scandals. This seemed to be their main concentration. They liked the music but were even more interested in the dirt behind the musicians. Joel had a ball cavorting for them. Alix remained more reluctant and, sensing a secret where there was none, they went after her. Eleanor poured a round of drinks after she ushered the last interviewer out and locked the door. "Any comments?"

"What a bunch of barracudas," Leo said. "How the hell did they find out so much?"

"My fault, I'm afraid," she answered without a trace of regret. "I handed out circulars."

"They sure know how to drink," Bear grunted. "They put us to shame."

"We English do like our bevies."

"That one from the New Media Express asked me about Mark," Alix complained. "I didn't think they'd be that well-informed."

"I gave them a brief history. Our Canadian office faxed some of your early press clippings and this is bread and water for you. The old ones were full of venom. These people aren't any different from the reporters you've been handling for years. Don't acquire a case of the jitters – the tour is going to be a success."

"You sound pretty sure."

"I am. I've been in this business for a number of years and I know how to read the signs."

She was right. The press attended the sound check the following day, concentrating wholly on the music. When the crowd filed in that night it was with a determination to have a wild New Year's Eve.

Alix's confidence built steadily after the first roar of approval at their opening song and the show took off. Dressed in a bodysuit of neon blue with two studded leather belts clacking around the thin waist, she prowled the stage, slashing at chords on her guitar or abandoning it to embrace the crowd, taunting, teasing and joking.

"Come on," she shouted, "we heard you people know how to party!" The fans cheered and rose to meet the challenge.

Leo stayed back and watched as she drove them into a frenzy, still amazed at her control after all their years together. When the seething mass seemed about to spin out, she sat on the edge of the stage and soothed them with a soft, lonely ballad. Bear was up and down, attacking his kit and doing stick twirls. Like Leo, Dixie stayed in place, content to dance at her keyboard. When Alix took a break, Joel stepped effortlessly into the spotlight, doing solos, teasing fans and taking up where she had left off. The cycle carried on throughout and the manipulation was a routine that was well-polished.

By the end of the first half hour the motion was fluid and the atmosphere sizzling. When the band stepped off the stage in the early hours of a clean and sparkling new year, dripping with sweat, adrenalin was running high and exhilaration kept it going until long after dawn.

The reviews were glowing.

CHAPTER 14

Spring 1992

After that there were no more doubts. The band had been on the road for the better part of four years; their sound was tight and their shows retained sparkle and spontaneity. Alix and Joel were the two prime entertainers on stage – Alix as the natural front-person for the band and Joel because he was a natural show-off. It worked for both of them. As a high energy act, she would tire without a break and when Joel took over it gave her a chance to take a breather. There was a constant, silent communication between the two, born of a close friendship and the many years they had been writing together and it flowed seamlessly onstage, coordinating their movements without conscious thought. It was one of the things that made the band's live gigs so dynamic.

Mayday arrived back in London on the last stop of their tour. The Blue Mask's booking as the warm-up act for this show had been well publicized by Dome. During the sound check that afternoon, Roger and Joel hung out with each other like old friends, laughing and talking about Mayday's tour.

"Man, we did notice a few things outside of us, you know," Roger said. "We adopted you lot and we take personal credit when you do something gear. You're getting really well known around the U.K. I hear from Eleanor that the reports in from Europe are fab and getting fabber every day." He shook his head and the red, wiry mass of hair danced like a flickering bush fire under the bright lights. "I remember our first real tour here – the one when we knew we'd finally arrived after all the bloody work and all the sweat and small pubs and clubs where half the people liked you and the other half wanted to put the boot in." He smiled and clapped Joel on the shoulder. "You're there, mate – you all are. I think it's bloody marvelous."

"Let's hope you're one accurate fortune teller, Rog. I sure as hell wouldn't mind taking some time off after this. I'm real excited about the tour, don't get me wrong, but we been on a long run and I'm beat. It'd be nice to get known and be able to cruise for a couple of months before the circus starts again."

"I know that feeling. You'll find the wire when you get on stage, old son, you know that yourself. Anyway, we got time for a bevy or two after the gig. Oh, by the way, me missus is throwing me a bash the sixth of May. If you lot are back from the Continent by then I'd sure like to have you there."

Joel nodded enthusiastically. "What's the occasion?"

Roger grimaced. "The fucking four-oh, that's bloody what. Where the hell did the time go, eh mate? Where?"

"You must have missed it when you were on the road."

Roger laughed loudly. "Too bloody right, Joel, me boy, too bloody right."

The venue that night was jammed with ardent fans. Mayday was slotted to do two shows at Wembley Stadium later on in the year and they wanted to finish off their

European tour with a teaser for the home crowd before taking a break. Their next stop was Japan.

The Blue Mask was on top of the world and the show a roaring success. The group hung around backstage to watch Mayday in action and then both bands assembled at Roger's club for drinks and conversation.

Eleanor packed them on the bus early the next day.

The tour was a laff-riot from the start. Everyone found time to get a look around each city they landed in and the British welcomed them with open arms. The press had a field day. Eleanor made sure that the conferences and photo shoots were well-stocked with booze and there was a good turnout every time. Joel became their darling, constantly sought after by reporters and reviewers. With his outrageous statements and photogenic looks, packaged in tight black trousers and muscle shirt, he always guaranteed a good profile. Stories of his conquests already abounded and this side of his personality was played up because it always made good copy.

Interviewers asked pointed questions about his views on promiscuity in an era of the AIDS epidemic and he responded with adamant insistence on the use of condoms and the need for protection. All of them believed in it but none had yet gotten involved with the efforts of rock personalities to promote safe sex. They simply hadn't been asked.

While Joel played belle of the ball to the hilt, Alix found that she too was acquiring a reputation in the press – as a cipher. Her close-mouthed approach to the deeply personal, probing questions asked attracted more people than it repelled. Joel's response was to elaborate on facts already known to cover the questions he didn't want to answer and the blind-siding worked marvellously but Alix hadn't much to elaborate on. As she didn't pursue a wild private life she concluded that she was probably quite boring copy, so she merely made cryptic comments or blanketing, general statements and the press labelled her as a secretive thinker. This drew loud guffaws from the others in private but in public it became a new game to play.

Leo was sincere and open about himself, but would not answer questions about the personal lives of his friends. Bear was a gregarious partier, full of fun and hijinks, and Dixie a lively, joking comic with a wicked sense of humour. Once the reputations were defined the press relaxed and ventured more into the music.

As the group worked their way around counties and countries Alix and Joel started to jot down places the two wanted to revisit when they had time to take a look around. They pestered Eleanor for information and by the middle of the tour already had quite an itinerary. The gang pulled into Liverpool for two shows and a three day rest.

"I can't believe the miles you two are going to put in after a gruelling tour," Eleanor said, shaking her head. "Are you sure you want to go to all of these places?"

"Why not," Joel asked. "You know something you're not telling us?"

"Of course not. I was just thinking that you don't have much time off between one tour and the next and you might want to take it easy instead of dashing all over the shop looking at ruins and history."

"But we like ruins and history," Alix protested.

"I wish I had your energy."

"Yeah, well I'm not too sure about the energy part," Joel commented. "Maybe we should rent a car and hire someone to drive us." Another coughing spasm hit him and he turned away.

"I can take care of that," she said absently, watching him, "but you must go easy. There is still the Continent after this little lot." She looked at Alix, who was also watching Joel, and saw the concern she felt mirrored in the black eyes. "Perhaps we should get you to a clinic during this break. Your cold seems to be quite persistent."

"England in the winter is not the best place to get better in."

"I'll get some information from the hotel and we'll dispatch you to the nearest doctor."

"Leave it till after the gigs."

A subtle change had been altering the band. As receptions grew more positive in each city, they became used to being recognized and actively pursued. Years of handling publicity made them secure but this was a new level. Roger's words kept running through Joel's mind each time he stepped onstage and the cheering broke out. The shows in Liverpool were no different. Liverpudlians were a critical, partying gang who knew how to have a good time and didn't balk at saying what they thought, however unpopular or gushing it might sound, and they threw their whole-hearted support behind the Blue Mask.

Eleanor gathered them together backstage after the last show and locked the dressing room door. The sweating band members watched her tiredly, their eyes glowing.

"This won't take long," she began, bracelets clanking as she paced back and forth. "Roger March said that Mayday always measures the success of any of their British tours in Liverpool because the fans are the hardest to please and the most honest about it. He figured this would be the place and, as usual, he was right."

"What are you talking about," Leo asked.

"'The Fast Track' hit number one today," she said proudly, stopping in front of them. "That makes it official – you've arrived."

Slow, wide smiles of delight spread through the oddly silent group. Bear summed it up in two words. "Holy shit!"

She let them lap the news up and, hearing noises outside the door, turned an enquiring face to her group. "Shall I let the animals in now?"

"Yeah," Alix piped up, "I feel like kissing every one of them!"

"A thank you will do," Leo teased. "You don't want to wear out those thin little lips."

She smacked him and the mock battle started. Under the cover of that and the ensuing rush after the door was opened. Eleanor drifted up to Joel's side. "Make it an early night and meet me first thing at nine o'clock in the hotel lobby. We'll go out the back way and take a taxi to the clinic. I've arranged for you to see a doctor about that cold."

He nodded in silent acknowledgement before the crowd overran and separated them.

Alix was waiting in his hotel room when he and Eleanor got back. "Well?"

"A viral infection in my lungs. I got drugs, an order to rest, and no alcohol for ten days until I finish the pills."

He had expected her to make a smart remark about him not drinking but she merely nodded. "Sounds good to me but how are we going to manage the rest part?"

"No sight-seeing before and after shows and no parties," Eleanor said firmly. "That should be the ticket."

"Oh no," Joel wailed, "one nurse is bad enough but I got two!"

"We're not nurses; we're more like minders. Don't worry about being attended to. We're simply going to lock you up and go about on our merry way. Does that sound right, Alix?"

"You pick the parties and I'll be there."

"By the way, Dome is planning to release 'Denizens of the City' when we finish the British tour up in London. I suppose we can let you out for that party but only because it is promotional."

"You two are a couple of sadists. You're both enjoying this."

She laughed and closed the door firmly behind her. Alix turned to him, serious again. "I'm glad you went to that clinic; I was getting real worried."

"You and me both, girl, if you want the truth. But the doc said a lot of it had to do with the changing weather here and what we're normally used to. I know Vancouver isn't much different but our heating is better and it's not usually this damn cold. Actually, he was surprised I was the only one sick. I think it'd be a good idea for all of us to take it easy; we've a way to go before a break."

"I'll talk to the others."

Joel's symptoms cleared up and when the band arrived back in London his cold was gone, though it had left him tired and he'd lost some weight. Eleanor assembled a crew for the video shoot in the East End and the group showed up after a day's rest. It was market day and film footage was taken of Cockneys calling out their wares with the band in place as sellers, buyers and part of the crowd. As night fell they wandered into the dark, brooding alleys of Whitechapel, lurking among the soot-stained buildings and narrow, cobblestone streets. At one point a rat ran over Alix's foot and she screamed. The director let the camera roll – it would make a great shot. The promotional party that would launch 'Denizens of the City' was slotted next and then a break before they left for the Continent.

Little partying went on as the heavy spring took its toll and the band spent most of their time sleeping, eating hot, solid food and drinking desultorily in pubs within walking distance of the hotel. As a respite, it was exactly what was needed.

Ash had been busy as well, spending most of his time between Morris and work on designing Mayday's next album, which they were booked to record in September. Alix and Joel teased him unmercifully about his relationship and he was glad they were unoffended by his absence. He hadn't wanted to trail along behind them when he could be with Morris. The trio met in the hotel bar one night for dinner and a long gab session.

"This thing with Morris," Joel started but Ash cut him off abruptly.

"That's enough. You've had your fun now leave me alone." Yet, he was relieved that his friend was joking rather than making the usual caustic comments about his lifestyle.

"I wasn't going to make a crack, 'kay? I was going to say it seems to have settled you down and levelled you out. You're straighter, excuse the pun, and calmer than I've ever seen you."

"It's called growing up. You ought to try it sometime."

"Not on your life," Alix commented.

"Well it's happening to all of us whether we like it or not. And don't think I haven't noticed the same in you, my dear."

She stuck her tongue out at him. "When did Brad and Robin leave? They didn't even say good-bye."

"You two have been kind of busy. I had dinner with them the night before they flew out. Brad said he'd phoned you."

"We got a message but it was in the middle of a two day gig and we weren't around to take the call. Did they have a good time?"

"Brad was caught up with business during the day and Robin shopped for the house. They took off by themselves at night mostly, like two little lovebirds."

Joel laughed. "Seems to be contagious."

"Have your fun, Stark, but someday you're going to fall with a bang and I'll get my revenge."

"Fall and disappoint the senoritas? Not a chance in hell."

"It's been known to freeze over from time to time." Ash sipped his wine, eying his friend appraisingly. "You look like shit. What's going on?"

"Don't worry, I went to a doctor. That cold I got before Mexico infected my lungs. I'm fine now but it took a lot out of me. He said it would be a while before I got back to normal. 'Kay?"

Ash nodded. "You can't run flat out for months at a time without something giving so take it easy. Your senoritas can wait."

"Get off my case. I got enough with Alix and Eleanor going all maternal on me; I don't need you at it too."

Ash choked on his drink. "Alix maternal? You must be crazy!"

She lit a cigarette, ignoring their laughter. "I'm not maternal," she said patiently. "I'm just protecting my investment. We're making obscene amounts of money right now and I don't want this goose" – she gave Joel a hearty swipe – "to stop laying golden eggs."

He started to squawk like a chicken and they all cracked up. The evening descended in typical pattern and it was late when they finally made their way to bed, weaving drunkenly.

The party that launched the Blue Mask's next album was a stunning success but Alix and Joel, miserably hungover, found it hard to keep up. Halfway through the night, after numerous interviews and photographs, Eleanor sauntered over with two glasses of Scotch.

'Hair of the dog," she said cheerfully. "You've been good and I appreciate you not indulging until most of the promotional nonsense is over so, as Brad advised, I've brought your reward. Here is the hooch he promised you for being good."

"Up yours," Joel said, toasting, and gulped the contents greedily.

Alix sipped her drink, looking around at the dwindling number of reporters and music press. "We had a good turnout. That had to be your doing."

"My office, yes. It's part of the job, you see."

"You've been great. We don't know what we would've done without you. Thanks."

"I'm not gone yet. You're stuck with me for the tour of the Continent." But she was touched by Alix's comment.

"Can we take you home with us," Joel asked hopefully.

"No but I will be around for the next tour here so hurry back."

"Hot damn. How about the fall?"

"I have a feeling you'll be worn out by then."

"No kidding," Alix said. "Brad phoned this afternoon with the next schedule. We sure as hell are getting around."

"Want to come to Australia," Joel offered.

"Thanks," Eleanor replied, crinkling her nose, "but I've been many times. The colonies are so charming, don't you find?"

"As Alix says, my dear lady," he shot back, grinning, "eat ratshit."

"You Canukies, what a command you have of the English language."

Joel watched her walk away, eyes narrowed. "If I didn't like her so much I'd go after her."

Alix grunted. "Now I know you're better – those hormones are rearing their ugly little heads."

"Just can't keep them down, girl."

"Believe me; we're all aware of that fact."

He smiled and lit a cigarette. How could he tell her that they weren't stirring the way she thought, that he still felt so tired? She and Eleanor had been more concerned than they let on and he'd tried to reassure them with his returning good health. The lung infection scared him and the lingering effects of it made him realize just how much he'd always taken his body for granted. He finished his drink and stood up.

"I'm going to get some zzz's. We got a lot of work ahead of us and you and Ash made me drink way too much last night." He tugged her hair. "Later."

"See you," she said absently, her mind far away. It was going to be a challenging year. Brad promised a rest at the end of it but the band was hot right now and he wanted maximum exposure. Album sales were strong and would get stronger as the group came into greater contact with their growing audience. It made sense but all of them were feeling the effects of the long months on the road.

Alix was a loner by nature. Joel had an almost paranoid fear of being by himself, perhaps because he had been deserted as a child. It was the fundamental difference in the make-up of their characters: Alix needed time alone to recharge; Joel needed people to do the same thing. And because the early hours before dawn were the worst, he rarely spent them in solitude. When he had to, he induced sleep with alcohol until the morning brought light and people and safety. His illness had worried her. While she didn't think it a particularly healthy need, she understood why he took so many women to bed. Lately he had been too tired and though she didn't think his one-night stands were a good thing, she looked for them to start as an indication that everything was back to normal. So far, he'd been sleeping alone.

CHAPTER 15

The overwhelming success of their tour of the Continent confirmed all Roger March's extravagant claims that the Blue Mask had finally hit the big time. The group not only played to sold out houses but were shocked to find some audiences singing along to favourite songs – in English. It knocked them over time and time again. 'The Fast Track' hit number one across Europe and Eleanor heard from the London office that sales were skyrocketing. The release of 'Denizens of the City' sparked another flurry of purchasing and rose up the British charts, chasing its predecessor.

The band returned to London to record their gig at the De Sade, one of the city's most popular clubs. The group had one day off to prepare but no one minded in the least. They were in top form, their skills and timing honed to a razor edge and they didn't want to lose any of their momentum.

Roger showed up at the sound check, all smiles and congratulations. 'The Fast Track' had finally made number one in the U.S. That piece of news seemed to be the last wire needed to plug them right in and the show that night was spectacular. Video and sound recording went off without a hitch and Alix and Joel prowled around the stage whipping the crowd into a partying frenzy. The fans continued screaming after the last song and the band came back for two encores. They trooped into the dressing room drenched to the skin, adrenalin coursing through them.

"That beats any high I ever had on a speed run," Joel shouted, "even a needle rush. Who needs drugs?"

Eleanor was opening one of the dozen bottles of champagne she had ordered for the occasion. "It was absolutely electric."

"Did you catch Ash messing around with that camera," Alix asked, laughing. "He wants a live photo for the album cover and he's got some wild concepts for packaging."

"I feel like I've been on a roller coaster," Dixie giggled, taking a glass of champagne.

Alix's eyes met Joel's as they both remembered Brad's promise to take them on just such a ride. She grabbed a glass and jumped up on a chair. "Toast!" All fell silent. "To Brad and Eleanor and Ash and Robin and the band and everybody else who had a hand in this. We all deserve one massive pat on the back. And to Apache and Mark, without whom."

They drank solemnly but the excitement was too strong for the moment to last and hilarity erupted again as people began to bang on the dressing room door. Eleanor had locked it after the band filed in. Roger was standing there, with Ash and Morris yelling for champagne behind him. The bouncers were having a hard time keeping back the crowd of fans trying to swarm through into the hallway. Eleanor let the trio in and quickly bolted the door.

Roger accepted a glass from Joel, who filled it to overflowing. "You might think about making a quick escape, mate," he advised, laughing loudly. "If that lot get beyond the minders you could have a stampede."

"They're Canukies," Eleanor responded playfully. "They're used to stampedes."

Alix was puffing on a cigarette and swaggering around. "Let 'em come, I say," she intoned in a husky voice. "This town needs cleaning up."

Joel shook the bottle he was holding and aimed it at her. "Oh no, one of the James babes! We're finished!"

The fight was on. Roger suggested a club he knew and they all piled into taxis and headed over.

The next day found the group flat and exhausted. Joel stayed in bed most of the day, drained and hungover. Alix continued drinking, knowing the binge mood would be on her for a couple more days. She kicked around the pubs that had become her haunts, Leo often in tow, occasionally joined by Ash. Dixie and Bear hung around periodically but Joel remained absent. When he did put in an appearance, he looked tired.

She drew him aside, more worried than ever. "What's going on? I thought you were better."

"I am but the doc said to rest and I didn't. He told me this was going to take time. I just need a break and we got a month coming up so relax and shut up. You worry too much."

"Okay, I get the point. But I think you should get a second opinion if things don't even out soon."

"I will, honest. 'Kay?"

"Yeah."

Though on the mend, there were still lingering aftereffects. The cough had returned, likewise his headache, but he put it down to stress and overwork.

As promised, Eleanor arranged for a car and driver for the pair and they got ready to spend a happy two weeks sight-seeing. But first there was Roger's party.

If the De Sade happening was the crown of the tour, the party was the mace that went with it. Everyone who was anyone in rock was there. The band met people that they had listened to in their teens, idols who became influences on their music. While they weren't greeted as peers, they were accepted as Roger's guests and treated with respect as fellow musicians. The bash went on all night and it was with dawn breaking that Roger drew Joel aside with a wicked leer.

"Got a present for you, mate," he whispered conspiratorially. "Little bird over in the corner just can't wait to meet you. Hope you brought the rubbers – this one's so bloody hot she sizzles."

Alix approached during the last part of his speech. "You two are disgusting. What a bunch of macho shit."

Roger winked at her. "Name of the game, love."

"Not for you though, right? I met your wife and I don't think you'll be panting after any hot sizzlers."

"Too bloody right."

"Don't worry," Joel said softly. "I'll return the favour when you're back on our turf."

"I know that, mate. Why else would I present the bird?"

"You're both assholes," Alix said cheerfully, walking away.

"Thanks a million for everything, Rog," Joel said seriously.

"It's a funny old friend you've become, Joel. But then it's a funny old world. Give us a bell when you get back from the Grand Tour."

Alix stood in a corner, watching as Joel approached the waiting woman. He went into action and she breathed a sigh of relief as the two started toward the door. Everything was all right - he wasn't going to be alone and she could stop worrying. She turned happily and plunged back into the party.

Joel conveyed his thanks to his hostess and, spotting Eleanor in conversation with Ash and Morris, asked his date to wait.

She turned an enquiring face to him when he drew her aside but her eyes flickered sideways. "Ah, a conquest, I see. I'm glad you're back to living up to your formidable reputation."

"I take a bit of time off the ladies and everyone sits on the sidelines waiting for me to pounce."

She caught the serious undertone and gave him her full attention. "Whatever is the matter?"

"I just wondered if you could set me up another appointment with a doctor. This thing is still kicking around and I want to get rid of it once and for all."

"I thought you were all cleared up."

"Yeah, well mostly I am. I don't want to worry anyone but I would like to get it double-checked. 'Kay?"

"I'll be in touch tomorrow." She called him as he turned away and winked broadly. "Have a pleasant evening."

He swaggered off, swept his date out of the door and into the lightening world outside.

Eleanor phoned the next afternoon. "Can you be ready in two hours?"

"Sure, but why the rush?"

"I rang my own doctor – I thought you should have the best and he is – but he's frightfully busy and he agreed to see you after surgery hours. I told him you were due to go out of town tomorrow for a fortnight. I'll pick you up in front of the hotel at half four."

"No problem. Thanks, girl. I know this is above and beyond."

"Not for a friend."

She took him to a discreet house in Harley Street, set back from the pavement and tucked between two similar establishments that reeked of money. The doctor proved to be a silver-haired, elegant man who looked more like an aristocrat in an English social drama than a medical practitioner, but he ushered Joel smoothly into his office, professional mask in place.

He listened as Joel outlined his previous visit to the doctor in Liverpool and the cold that had started so long ago. Pointed questions were inserted quietly into the conversation and then he did an examination. When he was finished he indicated the visitor's chair and took up residence behind a massive black walnut desk.

"Have you considered any other possibilities as to the cause of this cold," he asked bluntly.

Joel's heart sunk. "One."

"It is an option we should explore. Although it is a simple blood test there is some red tape attached. You must get counselling before you take it."

"Look, Doc, I'm going on holiday tomorrow. Can I do it when I get back? I'll sign anything you want but now you've brought it up, I need to know. Can we work something out?"

The man considered him briefly and then nodded. "I will set an appointment up with a group I use for other patients." He pulled a form out of his desk and they went through it together.

"I understand that you will be gone a fortnight. Shall we agree to a consultation at this same time the day after your return?"

"Yeah, and I'll go to the morning session. Can I sneak in here again? You know..."

"I have other patients who are in the same line of work as you, Mr. Stark, and I am well-acquainted with the need for discretion." He assembled his tools and instructed Joel to roll up his sleeve while he donned a pair of latex gloves.

When he was finished, Joel thanked him and rose. The doctor accompanied him to the door.

"I do not want you to worry about this. The counsellor will be of great help and we will cross the bridge if, and only if, we come to it. There are other explanations for your symptoms. From what you have told me you have been working at maximum capacity for much longer than a healthy body can tolerate, let alone one that has been exposed to a viral infection. Enjoy your holiday and try to get as much rest as you can."

"Thanks again." He went out into the waiting room to find Eleanor seated in the corner.

"I thought you might like a lift back to the hotel."

"I could've taken a taxi."

"This way you don't have to." She picked up her canvas bag, bracelets rattling, and swept past him. "What did my doctor have to say to you?"

"I knew that's why you stuck around," he said jokingly, but it fell flat. "He took some tests and I have to see him when I get back. Can you smuggle me out again? Alix is worried enough and I don't want her to find out about this."

"Of course. Now let's get back before you're discovered missing. You can buy me a glass of Scotch and no one will be the wiser as to our little escapade."

Alix found them in the hotel bar half an hour later. "I've been banging on your door for ages."

"I'm not there," Joel cracked, finishing his drink and signalling for the waiter to bring three more.

She accepted her Scotch, took a gulp and turned to Eleanor. "Some bash last night, huh?"

The woman winked. "Especially for some of us."

Joel held up both hands. "'Kay, I give up. Have your fun and get it out of your systems."

"What fun," Alix asked, then burst out laughing.

"I don't know why you find this such a novelty. You used to complain about the groupies bothering you. Make up your mind. You want them around or not?"

"Definitely not on holiday."

"That's what Joel and I have been discussing." Eleanor changed the subject smoothly and Alix began to ask questions about their trip.

CHAPTER 16

The two headed out bright and early the next morning, loaded down with cameras, luggage and cigarettes. Their driver proved to be a lively South London lad with a lot of bright chat and an easy way about him. He had driven lorries around Britain for a good many years until he discovered that well-heeled tourists were a better market for private tours. As a source of information and out of the way surprises on the road, he was outstanding.

It was a meandering two weeks, relaxing and easy and both felt the tension and exhaustion drain away. Lonnie took them on some path of his own that seemed aimless but was the result of careful planning with Eleanor.

Joel was strangely quiet at times and Alix would find him lost in thought, staring out at the countryside. She could not draw him out and, frustrated, gave up, knowing he would talk to her in his own good time.

She teased him about his self-imposed celibacy until one night, in a pub in northern Wales, he lost his temper. "Dammit, I'm tired and I don't always think with my prick! You used to pout when I deserted you for a groupie. Now you're on my case 'cos I'm spending time with you. You sick of my company now after all these years? I want to rest and kick this cold and be with you away from work and writing and all you do is bitch!"

"I'm not bitching," she shot back, stung. "I was just joking."

"Well, girl, you've worn this joke thin, so put a lid on it."

"Why are you so touchy lately? You haven't exactly been a barrel of laughs on this little jaunt. Half the time you stare off into space, sulking, and don't even hear me when I talk to you."

"When you go down to the ocean and stare off into space you call it recharging. When I do it, it's sulking. Talk about a double standard!" His voice had risen and, with an effort, he lowered it. "Look, I'm sorry if I'm ignoring you; I don't mean to. It's the first break we've had in a while and I really am beat. I don't feel like yakking all the time; I just want to have a look around and get back to normal."

He reached across to stroke her cheek, seeing tears gathering. "I haven't been much fun, but I need some peace and quiet. I figured you of all people would understand."

"I do but I didn't think you could be like that too."

"Now that's funny. We're alike in so many ways. Friends again. Pact?"

He held out his hand and she took it. "Pact."

"Let's go walk around outside and look at the mountains. I'll sing you John Denver songs."

"Oh please don't sing! Anything but that!"

Back in sync, they headed to Scotland. They had been sharing a room, with two beds, throughout the trip. It was late and Alix was almost asleep when Joel slid under the covers. He was naked and erect, pressing against her. "I need you, Alix. Please. Friend to friend." There was a desperation and loneliness about him and she responded to it instinctively. He already had a condom on; the sex was hard and rough and both came quickly.

They lay quietly afterward. "What's wrong, Joel?"

"Not now, Alix. Later. Just trust me."

He made a move to leave but she stilled him. "Stay please. Let's sleep together."

He kissed her and turned her on her side, pressing her against him, his arm around her waist. They both drifted off.

No mention of the night was made the next day.

When Lonnie dropped them off at the hotel at the end of their holiday, they were well-rested and the friendship had been fully restored. They checked for messages at the desk, only to find that they had been soundly deserted by everyone. Joel called Eleanor.

"What the hell happened," Alix asked when she joined them an hour later in the bar.

"They thought you were leaving a day later than you did. I have news from that lot.

"Now let me see. Ash and Morris went for a romantic jaunt to the south of France. Leo wanted to see Paris. Bear had relatives to visit in Germany. Dixie said she wanted nothing more than to lay on a beach in Spain. The plan is to meet back home at the end of the month."

"We came back too early."

Joel shook his head. "This way we can hang out here. There's lots of stuff to do."

"Roger gave me a message for you. He said he would keep in touch and hoped to be in Vancouver by autumn. Mayday loved Little Arrow Studio and wants to record their next album there."

Alix finished her drink and put her cigarette out. "On that note I think I'll go for a hot bath and some sleep. Since we've got time left in old London town I'm going to put it to good use." She turned to Eleanor. "You are one fabulous lady. That Lonnie guy was a gem. Can I buy you lunch tomorrow?"

"I have appointments all day. How about a late dinner?"

"Only if drinks are included."

"I haven't been on a spree in ages. You're on."

"Want to join us, Joel?"

He shook his head. "I think I'll find me a hot date. After all, I've been good lately."

"And how. Well, you deserve it. Bang on my door if you want company for breakfast."

"You got it, girl."

Eleanor waited until she left the bar. "I must go as well, I'm afraid. Shall I pick you up at half four tomorrow?"

"Thanks. I owe you."

She kissed him. "No, you don't. You are my friend. Perhaps I'll take my holidays late and come over with Mayday to Vancouver. You can squire me around."

"Anytime," he said, grinning.

Alix was off shopping and the coast was clear when she picked him up the next day. Nervously, he went into the doctor's private office, closing the door behind him. Eleanor would wait.

The doctor shook hands and gestured to a chair. "How do you feel after your rest holiday, Mr. Stark?"

"Actually, Doc, I feel fine, like I'm back to normal. Still a bit tired but, as I said before, we've been mostly working the last five years. I can't remember when I had a real break except for two weeks last December."

"How did the counselling session proceed?"

He hadn't gone. He looked the man straight in the eye and lied through his teeth. "It was a lot of help. How did the test come out?"

"I am afraid it was positive."

All the colour drained from Joel's face. "Shit."

"It might not be as bad as you think," the doctor said gently. "Keep attending the sessions; they will help you immeasurably. The test I sent for is the initial one and is not always accurate. False positive results can and do happen. We will go on to the next stage."

"I'm going home at the end of this month."

"Eleanor did inform me of that but..."

"I'll have to take care of it from that end, Doc."

"Please, Mr. Stark, let me assist you."

"You've been a big help but I won't be here so it's pointless. I promise I'll see my doctor when I get home."

There was sympathy in the grey eyes. "There is a second test that is much more reliable and a further one to confirm without doubt. If all are positive, I hasten to inform you that not everyone who is HIV positive contracts AIDS. Some have carried the virus for years without getting ill themselves.

"Please, see your doctor as soon as you reach home. And get as much information as you are able to. I would recommend abstaining from intercourse, but if that proves impossible, then I strongly suggest you withdraw before ejaculation. And, of course, use a latex condom. That should go without saying." He pushed a buff envelope across to his patient. "Your results, along with some reading material about HIV so that you may begin to learn just how far we have come with this. Try not to worry until you have all of the facts."

Joel took the file absently. "Thanks for everything."

"I'm sorry, Mr. Stark. I wish I could do more but your doctor will assist you to the utmost degree. I wish you all the best."

Joel headed into the waiting room. Eleanor came to him quickly, alarmed at his pallor. "What?"

"Get me out of here, please. Not the hotel. Somewhere quiet."

She hustled him outside and drove to St. James's Park. There was a favourite spot she went to whenever she needed a serene place to calm her. Joel said nothing on the way and she did not press him. She guided him to a bench and they sat down in silence, watching the water ripple in the breeze. When he finally stirred, she turned to him.

"You don't have to say anything and I promise not to ask any questions."

He squeezed her shoulder and the ghost of a smile flickered over the harsh features. "You've been great; I don't know how to thank you." He sighed deeply. "I have to get away and think. I can't see Alix right now. I just can't face her."

"We're having dinner tonight and I suspect she'll want to go out on the town. That means she'll have a long kip tomorrow. Why don't you smuggle yourself out of London in the morning? You can tell her you're having a dirty weekend."

"Yeah, that she'll believe. It won't be the first time I've deserted her. 'Kay, I'll hop a train and be off in the a.m. Any recommendations?"

"I know a charming getaway in northern Scotland. It's a long trip but it's beautiful, peaceful and quiet."

"Can you book me in and get me on my way?"

"Absolutely. How long will you need to be gone?"

"We fly home next week. I'll need some time to sort everything out before that. How about four days?"

"I'll arrange it."

Joel enfolded her, smelling the subtle perfume in her hair, burying his face in her soft flesh. She hugged him fiercely. Tears pricked her eyes and he saw them when he let her go. "Do you know what this is about?"

"Dr. Mortimer didn't tell me, if that's what you're asking."

"But you know it's bad?"

"Only from your reaction."

He took a deep breath. "I had an HIV test. It was positive. He says the first one isn't always reliable and could be wrong but I know it's not. I don't want anyone to know."

"You have my word."

He ran a hand through his hair. "How the fuck am I going to tell Alix?"

"You'll find a way."

"Yeah." He kissed her. "You've been a great friend, Eleanor. Someday maybe I can return the favour."

"Someday, I'm sure you will."

The two walked slowly out of the park, arm in arm.

Alix said nothing the next day when Eleanor informed her that Joel had run off with a woman. As he'd pointed out, it wasn't the first time. She spent the week with newfound friends. Joel returned, rested and calm; she teased but didn't ask where he'd been. He would tell her if he wanted to.

The two bade Eleanor heartfelt good-byes at the airport and extracted a promise from her to come over with Roger March and Morris Stockham later in the year. Both had made a friend they cherished.

The flight was uneventful. Alix slept a good portion of the way and Joel was glad. He'd had a lot of time to think and come to terms with the doctor's news but he couldn't deal with anyone's reaction but his own right now. He watched her tenderly, knowing he could relax while she was asleep. When the plane landed, the two made their way home and sought the sanctuary of their rooms.

CHAPTER 17

Summer 1992

The band members found there were changes when they returned home. Long-time fans had often stopped them to chat; now they were being pursued. Their leap onto the international circuit carried with it a downside. The security measures Joel and Alix had installed in the Arlington were breached. Groupies often hovered around the building waiting for a chance at Joel. Normally he didn't mind the attention but he'd been preoccupied of late and, sitting around one night with Ash, Robin and Alix, he complained at length.

"Have you noticed all those people hanging around?"

Ash grinned. "Women people especially."

"I'm sick of the hassle."

"All those ladies are just ripe for the picking."

"I'm tired of the whole scene, to be honest. Sure, it's fine on the road 'cos it gives me something to do to pass the time but I like my privacy too. It's the first time I've been home in months and I can't seem to get a moment's peace. How about you, Alix?"

She shrugged, mystified by his anger. "I don't have the reputation you do. People expect me to be rude or at least standoffish. I've always been hard to approach and it's pretty common knowledge I don't sleep around."

'Yeah, I suppose. Well, I'm not standing for it anymore. I've been thinking and I've made a decision." He turned to his friend, lighting a cigarette. "Ash, you still have the card of that real estate lady who helped you find your house?"

"You taking the plunge?"

"Damn right."

"That's great. Congrats, pal, you sure won't regret it. I'll give her a call in the morning."

"You're really serious about this," Robin said.

"Leave the Arlington," Alix asked. "You said you never would."

Joel responded gently to the hurt in her voice. He knew she saw this move as a desertion but he had a solution to that problem too. The one thing that bothered him about moving was not having her across the hall. "I've been giving this a lot of thought ever since England. I had a long talk with Roger and he warned me that we were going to find a difference when we got home. It's a trade-off. The higher exposure costs and the price is privacy."

"And you figure buying a house is going to fix that?"

"I'm going to do it through one of the holding companies our accountant set up so the title won't be in my name.

"Also," he pressed on, seeing her about to protest, "I want one of those long basements like Ash has. I'll get it soundproofed and stuff it with recording equipment – make it a home studio. Think of the jump it would give us to have something already laid down instead of going in cold. We'd also have a more private place to work. Our rehearsal loft was great once. It's too open and accessible now. Even Bear agrees and you know how outgoing and party-happy he is. This attention is getting to all of us in one way or another."

"Okay, okay, I give up. Go find your dream home. Just don't try to get me into the house shopping mode."

"I want you with me. I'm going to get a fair-sized place and there'll be lots of room for you to move in." Wariness crept into her face. "Friend to friend," he said, trying to reassure her. "No hassles and we'll draw up any contract you want. At least think about it."

"She works fast," Ash pointed out. "I take it you want something in my area?" He nodded. "Good, we'll be neighbours. Robin and Brad live on the corner."

Robin laughed. "Well, kids, we're growing up. Right, Alix?"

"Stop being crafty. I'll think about it."

"Oh you'll come round in the end. I know how much you like your privacy."

"This chick will work extra hard for you, Joel," Ash interjected with a wink. "She's a really big fan."

He groaned. "Is this going to be a problem?"

"Not as far as I can see. She don't sell, she don't make commissions. She don't make commissions, she don't eat. Comprendo?"

The meeting turned to lighter lines and the four started in on stories of their travels.

Ash called the next day to say he'd set up an afternoon meeting with the real estate agent. Joel hesitated as his friend was about to hang up. "You work with some doctors at that AIDS centre, don't you?"

"Sure."

"I don't know any and I need to see one. Someone friendly – you know how I feel about doctors and dentists."

The alarm came clear across the wire. "What's wrong?"

Joel's voice was light. "Nothing. Remember I told you about that lung infection I went to a doctor in Liverpool about? Well, he told me to see my doctor when I got home and make sure my lungs are clear. He said the drugs would work and they did 'cos I'm fine but to make sure just in case. We're heading out on tour in July and I don't want to risk going through that shit again."

Ash relaxed. "If that's all, I'm sure there won't be a problem. I'll talk to Dr. Marlowe. Robin and me have seen him for flu and stuff like that. He comes down to the centre to give talks and volunteer. You'll like him."

"Set me up an appointment in the next couple of days, will you? Things are probably going to get busy after that and I want to get this out of the way."

"Sure. I'll be seeing him today; I'll phone you later."

"Thanks. This is at least a four-drink job for two favours."

"Four drinks for each favour, pal. You're loaded; don't be so cheap."

He laughed. "You're not doing so bad yourself, you slouch. Mayday and the Blue Mask are your biggest clients and the rest are banging down your door trying to get through."

"Maybe, but we all know what an ingrate I am."

"Too bad Johnny Carson retired."

"Why? Would you go on and bad mouth me?"

"No, I wouldn't mention you at all. That'd really piss you off."

"Eat shit, Stark. I'll see you at my place about seven. We'll have some conversation and sustenance."

"'Kay. With the way Brad's lining us up it'll be weeks before we get another chance." Satisfied that he'd raised no suspicions, he hung up.

The meeting that afternoon with the realtor took him completely by surprise. The woman was a striking redhead and he smiled broadly as they shook hands. "Sherri Contrall. It's a real pleasure to meet you, Joel." She indicated chairs and they sat. "I'm a big fan of your music."

"Thanks. Ash did tell me that."

"And you thought I was going to make a nuisance of myself. Don't worry. I know you've been getting a lot of unasked for attention lately."

"Ash has a big mouth."

She smiled. "No, he explained what you wanted and why." She crossed her legs, settled back in her chair and drew out a pad and pencil. "Now tell me exactly what you have in mind and I'll see if I can find it for you."

She took notes as he talked and when the meeting drew to a close, he asked her out to dinner. She shook her head with visible regret. "I'm sorry, I have a showing tonight. Perhaps when I have some houses to show you we can include dinner. That way you're already in my schedule and I don't have to feel guilty." She grinned ruefully. "Dinner with Joel Stark and I have business to do. Life just isn't fair."

"I'll take a rain check but just this once."

"I'll do my best not to let you down."

He departed with a bounce in his step and a satisfied grin on his face.

Ash rubbed his hands with glee when Joel told him about the encounter later that night. "I figured she'd make an impression. You make a pass?"

"Subtlety was never your strong point. I asked the lady out to dinner."

"Getting rather debonair in your old age," Ash whooped. "You slut, you're as bad as I am."

"No one is ever that bad."

"I want to hear more about this but, before I forget, I talked to Dr. Marlowe today and you can go see him at ten a.m. on Friday. That should make Bradley happy, knowing you're healthy for the next tour. He's locked himself into a little gold mine with you guys."

"It's Brad who's the gold mine. He promoted us and has set it all up. Left to me and Alix, we'd still be playing high schools around the West Coast. You know how bad we were at booking and PR."

"What couldn't be done in a bar didn't get done. What a long way we've all come from those days. Who would've guessed any of us would get this far?"

"I wonder how Apache feels. You think she's followed us?"

"If she's anywhere in the rock world she'd have to. You've been a little hard to miss, especially in the last year."

"I hope she's happy," Joel said quietly. "She sure paid for giving us a hand."

"So did Mark, my friend. So did we all in our own way. Here's to both of them." He clinked his glass against his friend's. "Enough of the morbid atmosphere. This is a smart little party for two. Let's drink!"

It had been a long while since they had been alone together and they made the most of it, reminiscing and joking the way they'd done for years. Joel went thankfully to sleep on Ash's couch at the end of the night, too drunk to drive.

He was at Dr. Marlow's office that Friday. The man proved to be all Ash had claimed. A boyish face belied his forty-five years, topped by a mop of unruly black hair lightly dusted with grey. The dark eyes were merry but with a hint of sadness and his manner was open, inviting confidence. Joel settled himself in the consulting chair with relief. Here was a man he instinctively trusted.

"Ash said something about having your lungs examined," he began.

Joel held up a restraining hand and passed across the envelope Eleanor's doctor had given him with the test results. "That's just what I told him. I saw another doctor who assured me that my infection had cleared up. I have a different problem."

Without comment, Dr. Marlowe opened the envelope and drew out the contents. He read them silently, taking his time. When he finished, he looked up with a nod. "I would like to take the initial test again and we'll do a Western Blot."

"And if they are positive we'll cross that bridge when we come to it?"

"That's exactly what we'll do."

He took some blood samples and did an examination and history. "Wait until the tests come back, Joel. I don't want you to worry or go off half-cocked in a panic."

"I've had a lot of time to think about this, Doc."

"Don't think too much until we're sure. Where can I reach you?"

"I'm in and out and I don't want anyone to know about this. Can I call you in a few days?"

"That'll be fine. We'll set up another appointment when the lab results come back."

Joel reached over to shake the other man's hand. "Thanks."

He left the office quickly, pushing his thoughts firmly away. He would not, absolutely not, think about this until he was sure. There was too damn much to do. And the alternative scared him to death.

CHAPTER 18

The week piled up on all of them. Joel spent hours with Sherri looking at homes and by Thursday she had come up trumps. Across from Ash's house she found a treasure in brick and the two went over that afternoon.

He was like a kid with a new toy. "Get it for me, Sherri. I don't care what it costs, it's mine and I won't take no for an answer. This is the one."

She called back that night. The offer had been accepted.

"Get your glad rags on, girl 'cos I'm taking you out on the town!"

The celebration was done in style and both were riding high when they got back to her apartment. The conclusion was a foregone one. His arms went around her and she raised her face to his, mouth opening as he kissed her. He had purchased condoms earlier and, without the need for any dissembling, they went straight to bed.

Lying side by side the next morning, Joel felt no awkwardness or haste to go rushing out before she woke up. He smoked thoughtfully while she made coffee and brought it in. Climbing back into bed she fluffed her pillows and sat up.

"I think you should get an inspection done on your house even though you've already purchased it."

He marveled at her naturalness and leaned over to kiss her. "I don't know much about it. I'll ask Ash."

"I can set it up for you. I have some good reliable contacts."

"That's above the call of duty, isn't it?"

She smiled. "Yes but I don't mind. It isn't duty, nor was this." Her hand swept over the bed.

"I'm honoured," he said gallantly and they both laughed. "I'd bow but it's kind of hard to when you're lying down. Do you know any contractors as well?"

"You want work done already?"

"I want the basement soundproofed. I'm turning it into a studio."

"I can help organize the whole thing if you want and keep an eye on it. I know you're on tour next month. Besides, I feel like I've got a stake in this in a funny kind of way. Like it was karma that we met."

"I sure as hell am glad we did."

"Ash said this house decision was pretty fast."

"I've been thinking about it a while. A friend in England warned me we were going to get intruded on but I didn't think it would be like this. There are people hanging around the Arlington all the time and they get through the security doors. It's some kind of a novelty, I guess. I mean with the kind of money we're earning it's crazy to be living in a loft but I'm never home much anyway. And this is getting beyond ridiculous."

She kissed him. "I'll take care of setting up your dream home and when you get back it'll be ready."

"What's in it for you?"

She snuggled into his arms. "How about you?"

"You got a deal." He reached over to put his cigarette out and pulled her down under the covers.

Brad gave the band a few days to cover their bases before calling a meeting in his office. There was a lot of friendly ribbing when the five musicians trooped in; they hadn't seen each other since the end of the tour.

"You sure high-tailed it out of England fast," Joel accused Dixie, Bear and Leo. "We got back from our sight-seeing trip and you were long gone."

Leo laughed. "We honestly thought you two were leaving the next day. We came down to have breakfast and say good-bye and you'd already hit the road. So you guys deserted us first."

"Right," Bear chipped in. "Bad."

Dixie threw her arms around him. "Did you miss us?"

"Of course we did. Right, Alix?"

"More than life itself."

Brad shook his head ruefully. "Do your sparring later, hombres. We got business."

"You've always got business," Dixie said fondly.

There was a brief knock on the door and it opened to admit their lawyer, an older, well-starched man whose outer casing hid a sharp and clever mind. He nodded at each of them in turn and placed his briefcase on Brad's desk. "Good afternoon."

Alix turned to him, puzzled. "Is there something going on?"

Brad had the grace to look sheepish. "Mr. Grayson wanted to talk to you all a while ago, babe, but he's here now to shoot his line."

"The truth is that I asked Mr. Easton to gather you together before you flew to England and it slipped his mind."

"There was a ton happening. I'm sorry but things were crazy."

"What was it you wanted to see us about," Joel asked.

"You are all making a great deal of money and between your accountant and myself we have managed to set you up rather nicely. But suppose your plane crashes while you are on tour. Have any of you a will?"

"That's morbid," Dixie grimaced.

"No, it's common sense. There are laws in this province as to whom will get the estate if any of you die without a will. You, Joel, should be particularly concerned. You have no living relatives that you know of. If no one can be found the government deals with your estate. Do you really want that?"

"Not particularly."

"My point exactly. I've come to make appointments with each of you so that we can direct the money you have worked so hard for and invested with such success." He opened his briefcase and withdrew a day timer. "Are there any preferences?"

He sat thoughtfully while the others made their arrangements.

"Joel, may we meet in the next two or three days? I'll have some papers for you to sign on the house purchase and we can take care of this while we are at it."

"Sure, any time's fine. You pick."

Dixie piped up as Mr. Grayson handed out cards with their times written down. "House? You bought a house?"

"Yep. I thought word would've gone around by now."

"I've been away. Why are you joining the home-owning set?"

"The Arlington's hardly a fortress and we've been pretty crowded lately. Haven't you noticed an increase in traffic flow around you?"

"The fans? Sure. I'm moving again because they found out where I live. Something in a high-rise with security."

"Well, I'm getting me a house on the hill and my name's not going to be anywhere in sight."

She grinned. "When's the party?"

"Soon as we get back from the tour."

"Speaking of tours, do you think we could get some details settled?" Brad looked across at the lawyer. "You got everything, Mr. Grayson?"

"Yes, thank you. Good day to you all." He nodded at them and left the office.

"Whew, I'm glad he split. I don't have a hassle dealing with the suits and ties but that dude makes me feel like a kid. He was hot when I forgot to get you together before the tour."

"He's good though," Alix commented. "I don't know what we'd do without him. He was the one who found us that accountant and now we're pretty much set."

Brad rolled his eyes. "Good to know your finances are sorted. Now you think we can get some work done?"

"What's to do? You're so organized all we have to know is where to show up."

"Exactomundo. We have a little jaunt into Japan and then wing down to Australia, over to New Zealand and back up north. Two months should do it. You be back in August and in the studio come September. You have all the material you need?"

"Not like you to ask if we need more time," Bear pointed out.

"Just making sure we're covered. We also got your live gig at the De Sade."

"When's the release date," Leo asked.

"Before Christmas."

"You mercenary."

"Don't give me that line, Leo. It comes out in time for present buying, we make bread. And you like that."

"No pulling the wool over your eyes is there, Brad? Quick as lightning."

"That's me, a regular thunderbolt. Any probs?" A chorus of no's sprung up. "Good, then get outa my hair. You bums due for dinner at me and Robin's tonight. See you at six."

The gang filed out, separating once they hit the street. Alix followed Joel to his car and climbed in. He drove home silently and she did not break into his thoughts. After what Grayson had said, she was preoccupied with her own. There was also Joel's house. Now that it was a reality she had a decision to make. Once home, they ducked past a welcoming committee posted at the rear entrance. Safely inside with the heavy door locked, they smiled ruefully at each other and parted company.

Joel called his doctor to set up an appointment and crossed the hall to see Alix, using his key to let himself in. She stood in the middle of the room, her back to him, looking around as if taking stock. He crept up and wrapped his arms around her, hugging the small body. Into her hand he pressed a key.

"Didn't mean to scare you," he said softly in her ear, his hold tightening as she tried to turn around. "I just want to tell you I'm having your room painted white. Is that acceptable or do you want something else?"

He let her go and turned to walk out. She followed him across the room and put her hand against the door before he opened it. Her palm was outstretched; the key nestled in its center.

"Is this for real? You mean it?"

"There are three large bedrooms, two in front of the house with big windows that look out on the street." He grinned. "They're across the hall from each other, so it won't be that different than here, just more private. That room is yours. Do what you want with it."

"I haven't agreed yet."

"Go take a look for yourself. The place might look like a construction zone right now but it should be finished when we get back."

"What's going on?"

"I'm having it all painted and the hardwood redone and the basement soundproofed and redesigned and... the list goes on. Sherri got me the contractors and Ash is overseeing it all while we're gone."

"Sherri who?"

"Sherri, my realtor."

"Sounds pretty cozy. Do all realtors take an interest in fixing up a house once they sell it?"

"No but we got an agreement. She's doing a little extra for me."

"And what are you doing for her? Do I get three guesses?"

"She's not a one-night stand, Alix; I like her. I think you will too. You'll meet soon."

"We're leaving in a few days."

"Well, if not then when we get back. 'Kay?" He waited for an answer and when she nodded, closed her hand on the key. "You go over when you want and have a look. I'm starving. Come on, I'll buy you lunch and a Scotch or ten."

"Not too many. Brad'll have our heads if we show up drunk at the party."

"Wouldn't be the first time."

"Probably won't be the last either."

Laughing, they locked up and went out.

Joel showed up on time for his appointment with Dr. Marlowe, nervous and wary. The man welcomed him in and told him to take a seat.

"I have the test results," he began, lowering himself into the chair behind his desk.

"Positive, right?"

The dark eyes held his own calmly. "Yes."

He sat back wearily. "Where do I go from here?"

"You are in a very early stage, Joel. Also, some people who are HIV positive do not get AIDS. You could be a carrier only."

"What about the cold that wouldn't clear up and being tired for a long time? I've done a lot of reading and those aren't good signs."

"Based on your medical history I understand you've always had a tendency to catch things. The fact that your mother was a drug abuser before you were born – regardless of whether or not she was actively using during the pregnancy – and the malnutrition as a child have given you a low tolerance. Your own early drug and alcohol abuse are also contributing factors to your health and resistance. Given that, I would also like to point out that you have been driving yourself for the last five years. Your current symptoms are not symptomatic HIV infection; they are the signs of a tired body.

"I had a white cell count done and you are well within the normal range. I'm going to repeat that statement until you lose this notion that things are over. You are in good health."

"I'm HIV positive."

"There are the presence of antibodies in your blood. According to the examination I've done, you're healthy."

"So what do I do?"

"I've got an information package for you and you can call me anytime you need something answered but for now I would advise that you practice the general rules of good health. Get a lot of rest, eat properly and exercise. Do I need to add that alcohol is allowed in moderation but that smoking is not?"

"That's typical government hype."

"It's also common sense and damn good advice."

Joel regarded him steadily. "What about this tour? I'm scheduled to leave for Japan in a few days."

"I see no reason why you shouldn't go. Just take it easy and don't overdo things. Given the schedule the group's been on, I'm surprised all of you aren't sick."

"We don't have time." The ghost of a smile crossed the harsh features. "Anything else?"

"Read the information, be acquainted with signs of anything unusual and report it to me immediately. I want to see you on a regular basis. We'll keep an eye on those white cell counts to see what shape your immune system is in and we'll monitor your overall health. We know a lot more than we did five years ago."

"But you don't know enough to stop it."

"We will. Until then, keep your spirits up. Half of healing is in the mind of the patient. If you think you're going to get sick long enough, you will."

"I'll do my best." He rose.

Dr. Marlowe handed him a thick business envelope. "There are some diet suggestions and general health tips included as well." He stood up and came around the desk. "I don't want you to worry about this. Keep your aims high and your outlook bright."

"Yeah."

He walked him to the door. "I have a patient who's had AIDS for four years. He has had PCP – the pneumonia that usually kills – five times and he's been close to death's door more often than that but he refuses to stop fighting. The nurses in the hospital love him; he's always joking and he's very positive. Right now he's busy organizing a fundraiser to help pay for patient care. He's amazing."

"And I have nothing to be worried about or any problems that great. Right?"

"There are a lot of people much worse off than you are. Take care of yourself and be good to you. Life is precious for the well and the sick."

Joel smiled. "You make a lot of sense, Doc. I'll do what I can. Thanks."

"Come and see me when you return."

"Count on it."

Joel said nothing to anyone and spent the remaining days packing, reading and thinking over what Dr. Marlowe had said. He boarded the plane with the rest of the band with a light heart and the Blue Mask set out to conquer new ground.

CHAPTER 19

Autumn 1992

The band was treated with exquisite politeness by the Japanese and their concerts were sold out. The group then moved on to the rowdier Australians and had a riot. Brad had booked rest breaks between gigs and extra days during travelling and the band arrived in New Zealand for two shows in Auckland with time to look around.

Joel had discovered a new interest since acquiring the house: shopping. With the passion of the newly converted, he dragged Alix through markets, stalls, curio shops and anything featuring the unusual, spending money like water. He arranged to have his purchases shipped home and warned Ash that packages addressed to the holding company the house was registered to would be arriving. He agreed to pile them in the spare room.

As the friends roamed around, Joel encouraged Alix to join in on the fun. "You'll like it, girl. Come on, spend some money on our home."

"It's not ours, Joel; it's yours."

"'Kay, then spend some money on your room."

She eventually caved in, bought a few things and asked if he'd ship them with his.

The lop-sided grin set his green eyes dancing. "So you're moving in?"

She smiled sheepishly. "We both knew I would. I couldn't deal with not having you across the hall."

"Good, then you won't mind."

"Mind what?"

"I asked Ash to organize a three a.m. move so the fans wouldn't find out we're leaving the Arlington. I figured you'd say yes in the end so I gave him your keys too. He's going to get it all hauled and store the cars in the garage. Knowing Ash, it's probably done by now."

"You bastard! You've got one hell of a nerve!"

"You said you were going to agree anyway."

"Why the big secret transfer?"

He turned on her. "Why the big hesitation?"

She lowered her voice, the fight going out of her. "It's like a commitment and I was scared."

"What a con artist. It's me, remember? I don't buy your bullshit and I never have. If you don't know me by now..."

"It's not that," she interrupted quickly, "honest. I can't explain what it is."

"You don't have to," he replied gently. "Things have always been like that with us and I already understand what you're trying to say."

"You know, Joel, I really love you. You're about the best friend I've ever had." She turned away to light a cigarette.

He was touched. Alix was a lot of things, but she wasn't sentimental or easily given to statements as revealing as that one. He took her arm and steered her down another line of stalls in the narrow market. "Come on, let's go pick out some trinkets together."

The tour carried on at a refreshingly moderate pace and, for the band, this easy going was like a holiday. They enjoyed one another's company immensely. Where they usually broke off into splinter groups when not playing, now they arranged to meet every day for at least one meal and a new closeness was forged. As the tour wound on they met frequently to map out their new album. All were excited about the richer sound that had come out of this opportunity to experiment without the pressure of trying to squeeze sessions between gigs, travelling and sleeping. The band flew home happy and looking forward to going into the studio the following month.

Ash and Sherri stood in the middle of Joel's room, tiredly eying the things stacked haphazardly wherever there was space. Another package had arrived that morning but there was no room in the spare bedroom. Ash had loaded the remainder of Alix and Joel's belongings in there after he had set up both their beds, figuring rightly that was the last thing they would want to do after the long flight.

Both lofts at the Arlington were large and, over the years, the two had crammed a surprising amount of possessions into each one. Ash shook his head in disbelief. "It didn't really look like that much when we went to pack it up. And what the hell is Joel doing? He warned me that stuff was coming in from abroad but it looks like he's been buying hand over fist."

"I know," Sherri agreed. "This isn't all going to fit."

"Alix is just as bad."

"Joel had her things moved over without her agreement?"

He smiled. "I knew she'd give in the end. Those two are inseparable."

"They're roommates for sure? She won't change her mind?"

"Just what are you trying to ask me?"

"They're not an item or anything, are they? I mean, is he sleeping with her? Are they involved?" She raised her hands impatiently. "I'm putting this the wrong way. My tongue seems to be tied."

"He and Alix are friends," Ash said simply. "Best friends. I gather from the way Joel's willing to trust you with his house that something is going on. You want it to get serious?"

"I've been interested in him for a long time."

"He needs someone permanent in his life. These one-night stands are fine when you're younger but he's closer to thirty than twenty. It's time he put down roots of some kind."

"So you're on my side?"

"Within reason. But I'm going to give you a very valuable piece of advice and you'd better follow it if you are as serious about him as you say you are."

"I just love being told what to do."

"I would advise you to get along with Alix. And don't ever try to come between them. They have a real tight bond and she is of supreme importance to him. If things get rough, don't ever ask him to make a choice. You'd lose. The last girlfriend he had who tried to do that took a walk."

"That was years ago."

"Maybe, but this thing between them keeps getting stronger. Sometimes, it's spooky."

"I think you're overreacting but I get your point," Sherri stated, not in the least worried.

The phone rang and she reached down to grab it off the floor. The conversation was brief and when she hung up she was smiling. "That was Joel calling from the airport."

"What did he want?"

"To tell me he's home."

Ash jumped up. "I'd better go over to the liquor store and get some booze. Knowing those two, they'll be thirsty."

"I brought something over so check the fridge first."

He disappeared without another word and she lay back on the big bed. There was a magnum of champagne downstairs chilling. Perhaps he'd take a hint and make himself scarce. She'd planned a private homecoming for Joel and, though she didn't know quite what to do about Alix, she hoped that he would take care of dispensing his roommate to another part of the house to leave the two of them alone.

The commotion downstairs signalled the return of Ash as well as the two travellers. The greetings were loud and full of revelry. She heard the sound of beer bottles popping open and then, out of the muddle of voices, came Joel's quite distinctly. "Sherri?"

He took the stairs two at a time and found her sitting demurely on his bed. He scooped her up and planted a long kiss on her mouth. His face was lined and tired, his shirt wrinkled. He was also drunk.

"It was a long flight and there wasn't much else to do," he explained, laughing.

"Did you bring me a drink to toast your homecoming?"

"Let's go downstairs and I'll raid the fridge for you. Besides, I want the grand tour. Ash said all the work's done."

"As promised. Did you see the champagne?"

He leaned over and kissed her again. "First thing that caught my eye. We'll celebrate in style."

"I hope so."

"Then your hope will be granted." He stepped back and executed a slightly wavering bow, then took her hand and led her downstairs.

Ash was showing Alix around the living room. "We put those black velvet curtains from the Arlington here and in the two bedrooms upstairs and there's still have some left over. What did you do, hit an estate sale?"

"Joel helped me buy those when I first came here. I guess we overdid it."

"Don't tell me. You were drunk, right?"

She hugged him. "Weren't we all drunk then, Ash, most of the time?"

He pressed her against him. "Pretty much."

"Yeah, yeah, those were the days," Joel interrupted sarcastically, pushing Sherri forward. "Meet Sherri Contrall, the wonder who found this haven of ours."

Sherri pasted a friendly smile on her face and stepped up, her hand outstretched. "I'm really glad to meet you. Joel has told me a lot and, of course, the band profile is hard to miss these days. Your music is great."

"Thanks." She shook the proffered hand and smiled back. "You want a beer?"

"My job," Joel cut in, leaving the room. "A round?"

"Sure," Ash called after him. "I'll help."

Left alone with Sherri, Alix nervously lit a cigarette. "This place looks good. Joel said you and Ash have been great looking out for him while we were away."

"He means a lot to me. It was no problem."

She swallowed the cutting reply that passed through her head. She had an instinctive distrust and dislike for this creature who was trying so hard to enter Joel's life but, with surprising honesty, she knew that she was not being fair. She had to give this woman a chance. But her startling resemblance to Elaine, Joel's former girlfriend, was a mark against her. That woman had seen Alix as a threat to her relationship with and influence on him and it called up an equal threat in her. She had disliked Elaine immensely and been very wary of her. But she'd left in the end, given her walking papers when she became too demanding. She had issued an ultimatum – always a mistake with Joel – and that had heralded her exit.

"How was the tour," Sherri asked.

Alix pulled her attention back to the woman in front of her. "Sorry, I don't mean to be rude but I seem to be drifting. It was a long flight and I'm beat." The harsh face dissolved into an impish grin. "I also had a few drinks. The tour was great. We had a really good time." Joel and Ash came back into the living room and the awkwardness diminished now that they were no longer alone.

Ash turned on his friend. "Hey, I want you to come upstairs and see what you've done. The place is sky high with boxes!"

"The tour first. We can end up there."

They exclaimed over the work that had been done in the basement. "This is perfect," Joel said. "Exactly what I wanted."

"You were very specific," Sherri pointed out. "I told you this firm did good work."

He kissed her. "I'm impressed and in your debt." He turned to Alix. "Now we can get our gear out of storage and put it to good use."

"We'll have to go shopping if you want to turn this into a studio. I know how much you hate doing that."

"Is that a touché or something," he asked, yanking on her hair.

"Maybe."

Sherri sighed quietly. These two were pretty drunk and in a very jocular mood and she saw her planned night with Joel wasn't going to happen. Oh well, it could wait until tomorrow. Maybe by then Alix would have a place to wander that wasn't inside these walls.

The meandering was interrupted in the kitchen as more beer was dispensed and then the four trooped upstairs to the spare room.

"Now," Ash said, his arm sweeping around to indicate the wrapped packages, "what the hell is all this junk?"

Joel grinned. "We've been filling our house with treasures."

The 'our' was not lost on Sherri. "Treasures?"

He gave Alix a drunken hug. "I've been teaching my roommate here how to decorate."

"Oh hell," Ash moaned. "Between the two of you it'll look like a Dali nightmare!"

"You work with what you have." He weaved out and into his room. "By the way, thanks for setting up the beds."

"What are friends for? I knew the state you two would be in by the time you landed. Now you can pass out without having to put in the work. The thought of you trying to use a hammer to pound the frames together just didn't bear thinking about. You would have beat each other black and blue and ended up on the floor anyway."

Joel sat down heavily on the bed. "This I really owe you for, Ash." He looked up at Sherri, eyes red and tired. "Sorry, girl, but our celebration'll have to keep till another day. I've got to crash. Later." He set his beer on the floor and laid down, his eyes closing as soon as his head hit the pillow.

"Me too," Alix said. "Thanks for everything."

She stumbled off and Ash shook his head, laughing. "What a pair. I think I'll head home while I can still drive."

"You go on," Sherri said. "I'll just get sleeping beauty here tucked in and lock up and I'll be right behind you."

Once Ash had gone, she stripped Joel and pulled the covers over him. He hadn't moved once. Shrugging, she gathered up her things and headed downstairs. The doorbell rang and she opened the door to admit one of the road crew.

"I got Alix and Joel's luggage here."

"Just set it down in the hall. They'll deal with it tomorrow."

"Out cold, eh," he said, chuckling. "We had bets those two wouldn't last the night. Boy, I don't know what was going on but all five of them started to party on the plane and they were soused to the gills by the time we landed."

"That's rock and roll."

"Not for them, not usually. But they were toasting their next disc and yukking it up like a bunch of teenagers. Go figure, huh?"

The man headed down to unload the bags from a waiting van. Once everything was scattered around the hall he waved and folded himself back into the vehicle. She shut the door firmly behind her and locked up.

CHAPTER 20

Alix slept through the morning. Joel was still in bed when she got up so she padded around, giving herself another look at the house. She hadn't been in any shape to take much in the night before. They had all missed their meals on the plane, being too interested in partying and she was starving. Grabbing her car keys, she left a note on the kitchen table and let herself out the back door to go get breakfast.

The curtains downstairs were still drawn when she returned. Quietly she took a suitcase out of the hall and treaded softly upstairs to begin unpacking and sorting out her room.

The other bedroom door was open. Joel was on the phone, his back to her and she was about to turn away when she heard who he was calling.

"Yeah, hi, is Dr. Marlowe in...Joel Stark...Hi, Doc, how are you...Pretty beat. I'm feeling that fatigue you described again...No, I tried to go easy...Are we doing a white cell count...Yeah...Tomorrow...Great...Can I come in the back way...Yeah, as usual...Later."

Alix felt panic rising but she fought it down, trying to keep her voice calm. "As usual? What the hell is as usual?"

He jumped, hearing the low, harsh tones and turned slowly, a guilty flush creeping over his features. "Didn't your mother tell you not to eavesdrop?"

"What the fuck is going on?"

"I just have to see my doctor."

"Your doctor? Since when have you had a doctor? Wait, Ash mentioned something about getting your lungs checked after we got back from England. Joel, that was almost four months ago. Your cough and stuff is gone, so how come you have a doctor?" Her voice was rising again and she swallowed forcibly.

He heard the fear and reached for her but she slipped out of his grasp. "I've been trying to tell you but I couldn't find the words and when I did I couldn't find the guts."

Now he was terrifying her. "What's wrong?"

"I went to Eleanor's doctor when I was in London. My cold hadn't gotten better and I was sick of being sick."

"Is that what was bothering you on our holiday? When you would zone out?"

"I got a test done."

"That night in Scotland, when you came to my bed...."

"I was in a bad way. I was having a case of the midnight horrors. I needed you. I never said thanks or how much it meant when you asked me to sleep with you that night. "

"Well your horrors transmitted. I didn't want to be alone either and I didn't even know why."

"I wasn't going to get the results until the day after we got back. Eleanor took me to her doctor again."

"She never said a word."

"Don't be mad. I made her promise to keep it to herself 'cos I wanted to tell you."

"Tell me what?"

"I tested positive for HIV. I lied to Ash about my lungs so I could ask about a doctor here. He said this one treats a lot of patients down at the AIDS Centre and he's good."

She sat down heavily on his bed and he hurried over. "AIDS?"

"No. The doc said I was fine and gave me clearance to go on tour. My blood counts were normal and he told me to take care of myself. Right now I'm just a carrier. Look, he gave me a bunch of information to read. I want you to go through all of it. It explains things better than I could."

Tears welled up in her eyes and she turned to him, all the anger washing out of her. "Are you going to be okay?"

"I don't know. The doc says we take it one day at a time. Some people just carry this and don't get sick themselves. He told me I have to keep an open mind and an up attitude. That's half the battle. I'm not going to die, Alix, if that's what you're trying to ask. Only the good die young, remember? And that's one thing I'm not. I'm bad, girl, and don't you ever forget it."

"Does anyone else know?"

"Just you."

"The band is going to have to be told. That's only fair. And Ash and Robin and Brad. Will you be okay for the next tour?"

"I'll get clearance from the doc before I go anywhere. Also, I want this easy time between gigs. I get a chance to rest and not push myself too hard. We all have a better time, even if we're on the road longer. That's one thing that amazed Doc Marlowe – that we all weren't sick."

"I know. Brad said he was going to arrange for us to take part of next year off after this album and its tour. And he has relaxed things so we cruise rather than do back to back stops."

"That's all I need, time to cruise."

"So you haven't told Sherri?"

"Like I said, only you so far."

"If you're sleeping with her don't you think she has a right to know?"

"Slept, Alix, once. And I took precautions."

"Like a condom?"

"Like getting out before any fluids started flying." He laughed as she grimaced. "And a condom, yeah."

She didn't join in the laughter. "Was it because you weren't wearing them that you got this? I thought you were protecting yourself – all along, I thought you were. I kept telling myself you were."

He looked away from the accusation in her face. "I don't need a lecture."

"Oh, Joel, why?"

"I fucking hate condoms. You can't feel as much and you come all over yourself. I've never used them. And I just didn't think it would happen to me." He took her face in his hands. "I know, stupid – supremely stupid – and I should know better. But there are a lot of idiots out there who are just like me."

"And you're the ones getting sick. It was the gays and drug addicts at first. The drug addicts still have issues but the gays learned. Why not you macho studs?"

"Stop it. I don't need this."

She hugged him. "I'm sorry; I'm just in shock. If anything happened to you I don't know what I'd do."

He held her, letting her cry. His own throat was tight with unshed tears. He felt the same way. They were soul mates, kindred spirits or whatever name was the going rage. He'd be lost without her.

Wrapped up in their misery, neither heard Sherri come up the stairs. She cleared her throat loudly, uncomfortable and unsure how to handle this situation. "I thought I'd come over with groceries and see if I could help with anything. Am I interrupting?"

Alix withdrew from Joel and wiped a hand across her eyes. "No, just news about a friend. I have to go."

"Alix," he called, "I'll leave that stuff on your bed. Go through it when you have a minute." She nodded and left the room.

Sherri turned to him curiously. "I'm really sorry; I guess I should have called first. Is she going to be all right?"

"Yeah." He sat and patted the place beside him. From below came the slam of the back door and the sound of an engine starting. Sherri sat down and turned to him expectantly. "I've got something to tell you."

He carefully repeated what he had just said to Alix. She listened solemnly, eyes on his face. When he had finished, she watched as he lit a cigarette.

"Why didn't you tell me before?"

"The test results hadn't come in and I wasn't sure."

"But you suspected?"

"Yeah, from the initial one done in England. I'm sorry, I was wrong not to say anything."

"Yes, you were. How safe is the condom?"

"The literature says ninety-eight percent. I'll let you have it when Alix is through. I also pulled out, as an added measure."

"I had noticed," she said softly, "and I must admit I did wonder about it at the time."

"I figured better safe than sorry." He took a long drag on his cigarette, not meeting her eyes. "I'll understand if you walk out right now. I shouldn't have kept you in the dark. I'm an asshole."

"And a scared one, I suspect." She leaned over and kissed him. "We'll deal with this together, Joel. Believe it or not, I've waited a long time for you. Do you still want your homecoming present?"

"You sticking around?"

"Sounds like it to me."

He enfolded her gently and they lay back on the bed but his heart wasn't in it and he stopped her after a while. "I'm sorry."

"What's wrong?"

"It's not going to work right now. My mind's on all this and I'm worried about Alix."

"You're tired. Let's get some rest and try again tonight."

He grinned. "I don't need to be told twice."

Sherri left later that afternoon and Joel marvelled at this lady in his life. Her support had been genuine and she was going to be around. That cheered him. He was sick of being lonely.

He called Bear and the two drove over to the storage company to collect their equipment. A handful of their roadies were assembled and the group happily spent the rest of the day shifting everything to Joel's house. Beer and pizza followed and when Alix finally got back a basement party was in progress. She couldn't face them yet so she fled to her room to read through the information Joel had left on her bed.

When he came up the stairs later her door was closed.

She still hadn't put in an appearance by the next morning so he called Bear again and was out before ten o'clock. They met for breakfast and hit the stores in search of recording equipment, happily dragging their purchases back to the basement. Bear disappeared for half an hour and returned with more pizza and two cases of beer.

"What the hell is going on," Joel asked, laughing. "Do you live on this stuff?"

"Only when I'm hauling equipment. I need sustenance to do this kind of work."

"No kidding."

"I called Greg at Little Arrow and he'll be here any minute to help us hook this mess up and fine tune it."

The doorbell rang upstairs. Bear made a move to answer it but Alix called down saying she would. When Greg presented himself, she was right behind him.

Joel eyed her companionably, hiding his concern. "You all right? I haven't seen you all day."

She smiled, answering both his question and the underlying one he hadn't asked. "Yeah. I was tired last night so I went to bed early and read. I thought I'd sleep in today."

"'Kay now?"

"What is it Roger always says? Sound as a pound."

"That's it, girl." He took two beers out of the box, handed one to Greg with his thanks and the other to Alix.

She winked and leaned over to grab a piece of pizza, yanking on Bear's beard by way of greeting.

The four worked steadily until everything was assembled. Greg took his leave when they finished.

"Hey, did Brad get in touch yet," Bear said as they sat on the floor drinking beer. Joel hadn't got around to buying furniture yet.

"No, why," Alix asked.

"He wants to set up a band meeting. Something about the studio and Ash. He's got a plan to put to us. I guess he talked to Brad when we were away."

"I'll call him later," Joel said. "Can you get in touch with Dix and Leo? We might as well have the meeting here tomorrow. That way everyone can get a look at our new set up."

"This is something," Bear said happily. "Maybe get us some chairs though, little buddy. The place may be soundproofed and set up with high-tech gear but the floor's hard."

"Make it late afternoon and Alix and I will go out in the a.m. and pick up some stuff."

He stood up. "I have to split. I'll phone Dix and Leo as soon as I get home."

They accompanied him to the door together. Once he'd gone, she turned to her friend. "What did the doctor say?"

"I got my levels counted yesterday. You understand about that?"

"I read everything you gave me."

"They were low but still in the normal range." He put his arm around her and led her back downstairs.

"You talk to Sherri?"

"Everything's fine."

"She'll be around?"

"Definitely. Is that a problem?"

Her brow creased. "I don't think so. Are you sure she's not just a groupie jumping on your bandwagon?"

"Positive. I think I know what brought this on. She's not Elaine, girl."

Alix had the decency to look uncomfortable. "I never said she was."

"No but you sure as hell thought it. And Elaine was never a groupie."

"No but she was trouble. Is Sherri going to be able to deal with our friendship? I really don't want a fight on my hands."

"I explained that to her yesterday. She told me Ash also had a talk with her about trying to get between us. No problems on the horizon. 'Kay?"

"Sure." Her eyes swept the room. "This really is something."

"You into shopping tomorrow for chairs? I thought we'd pick up a couple of sofas and tables too. We're going to be spending a lot of time here so we might as well be comfortable."

"Sure, just wake me up early and we'll go spend more money." She started towards the stairs.

"Where are you going?"

"To unpack. Not a bad idea for you either, my friend. We've both been wearing these clothes for a couple of days and they're going to walk away on their own soon."

He threw a beer cap at her and she disappeared upstairs. He pulled the phone over and dialled Brad's number. It was answered immediately. "Were you waiting for someone?"

"Durango, I was literally just gonna ring your bell."

"Bear said you want to meet."

"In one."

"He's getting Dix and Leo over here tomorrow about three. Why don't you and Ash come along and we can kill all the birds with one stone."

"You talking about something? Say it in English."

"We set up a recording/rehearsal space I want to show everyone." He paused, taking a deep breath. "Bring Robin too."

"You got a reason?"

"Yeah, but I'll tell you when you get here."

"This sounds kinda mysterious. Everything grooving?"

"Smooth as clockwork. Later." He hung up quickly, not wanting any more grilling. It was going to be a long afternoon.

Alix and Joel were as good as their word and when everyone assembled in the basement the next day there was an assortment of furniture to sit on. A fridge had also been among their purchases and Joel filled every available bit of space in it with beer. A bottle of gin and Scotch sat on top, separated by a bucket of ice and glasses. A house tour had been given and now all sat comfortably, drinking and talking.

Ash stood up to get himself a gin. "I might as well start this meeting off before you empty this smart fridge of joy juice. Me and Robin have been helping the group at the Centre and their hard work has paid off.

"December fifteenth we're doing a free concert to raise money for the Persons Living with AIDS Society and their agencies. There's bands coming in from all over and a space has been donated. This is a big production. Much is broadcasting and it's been picked up by the U.S. I talked to Roger March yesterday. Mayday will be here recording their new album and they've agreed to participate. That's how the U.S. got interested. We got bands phoning up and offering their services so this should be one hell of a gig. I wonder if we can count on you guys."

All agreed immediately.

"This is one fine thing you're doing." Joel said.

"I'm doing piss all. The people who are kicking in are the ones to thank. A lot of time, effort and hard work is being given for free by people who care. This money will go to good use: centres like ours, research, hospices. You get the drift."

Alix caught Joel's eye and he responded with a wink. "We can work out the details later." He cleared his throat nervously. "I got a little something to say myself."

"Figured that much, Durango. You leaving the band?"

He quietly outlined what had been happening since England. They listened in silence. No one spoke after he had finished and he lit a cigarette with shaking hands, waiting for their reaction.

Bear got up to stand in front of his friend. "It's not the end of the world, is it, little buddy?"

"No."

A grin split the furry face and he reached out to hug him. "Then we march forward."

Conversation erupted and Joel held a hand up for silence. "I got one thing to ask, though. No telling. Absolutely not at all. I'm swearing all of you to secrecy and I want your promise this will go no further. Sherri is the only other person who knows. Nobody else is to hear even a rumour."

Ash eyed his friend thoughtfully. "You sure about this?"

"I've had a long time to think about it. Will you promise me?"

He nodded. Joel looked at each of them in turn and got their word.

Brad broke the silence that followed. "Now, dudes, let's get down to work. Studio dates..."

All relaxed. They were on familiar ground again.

CHAPTER 21

Winter 1992

Alix and Joel spent the next few days settling into their new home. Sherri spent her nights with Joel and was over much of the time, trying to help and ingratiate herself with Alix. Tension and awkwardness gradually eased between them.

Sherri marvelled at the way these two lived. Ash had brought their kitchen supplies over from the Arlington but the selection was minimal as both usually ate out. She got agreement to restock the kitchen and Joel handed her money to buy whatever she thought suitable but said to keep it basic.

She approached him one day as they sat on his old sofa, watching television. "When's your birthday?"

"In May. Why?"

"It's already passed. How about Alix?"

"July. What's this all about?"

"I thought we should have a party to celebrate your house and a birthday is always a good excuse."

He laughed. "Not for us, girl. We have a rule about not celebrating b-days. We started it with Ash and Robin when we first met."

"Whatever for?"

"Why celebrate something that makes you a year older and closer to dying?"

"That's morbid."

"Well that's us. Alix would flip if you threw her a bash. But if you want a party we can throw one."

She smiled slyly. "Good. Now we can't have a lot of people over without seats, so why don't we go shopping tomorrow and furnish your place? This old stuff can go to charity. You haven't unpacked much of what you bought abroad but I'm sure none of it is big enough to be serviceable furniture."

"Now I see where you're heading. Thanks for the offer but no can do."

"Why not?"

"Any shopping has to be done by me and Alix."

"I don't understand."

"She lives here," he explained gently. "It's not that we don't appreciate what you've done so far 'cos we do, but Alix has to be able to live with this too. Kitchen stuff is one thing but now we're talking about atmosphere."

"What if she picks something you don't like?"

"Then we argue and compromise."

"But what if she decides she wants her own place sometime soon? She might, you know. She needs her privacy. You're here and I'm around a lot of the time – it might be too much."

"That's not her style. Don't worry, she has lots of places to be alone. I had a hell of a time talking her into moving but we've been across the hall from each other ever since we met and it would take a lot to change that." He rose, pulling her up with him. "You're one hell of a woman and thanks for trying to help but it just wouldn't work. Come on, dinner and then let's find you a present for all your hard work."

The change of subject went smoothly and he was relieved. Sherri was establishing herself in the house but it was snowballing. He knew Alix wasn't ready for that kind of an addition to their lives and he was damn sure he wasn't either.

The phone rang early one morning and Joel struggled out of a deep sleep to reach over and answer it. The voice on the other end blared across the wire. "Payback time! We're booked!"

A slow grin spread across his face. "Rog, you old rocker, you drunk?"

"Only three parts, mate. We're coming your way in a month."

"I know. Ash told me."

"Yeah, we're doing that concert with you lot as well. Morris has been on the blower non-stop since this started. I think the old dear's in love."

"Seems Ash is too. I think it's great, Rog; we'll have a ball. I got your dolly birds lined up already."

"As in plural?"

"The more the merrier."

"Joel, me old mate, you are one good egg. Did I ever tell you that?"

"Only when looped, pal."

"When you lot due in the studio?"

"Next week. Brad's got us on a treadmill."

"Too right. Morris would do the same thing to us but we're sarky when we don't get our hols. Has Eleanor rung you yet?"

"No. She promised she'd be over when you guys are here."

"Well she's keeping her word, mate. She's flying over later after we finish the disc and the party really starts."

"It'll be like homecoming week."

"Too right. If you get finished early maybe we can do some jamming in the studio."

"You got yourself a deal."

"I'll ring when we land."

"I'll have the dollies waiting."

A burst of raucous laughter blasted his eardrum. "Sound as a pound, Joel, me old mate, that's what you are!"

Sherri was wide awake when he hung up. "Who was that screeching this early?"

"Roger March. And it's not early where he is."

Her eyes widened. "Roger March as in Mayday?"

"They're doing their next album at Little Arrow. We're having a party to kick the year out."

"This is going to be some Christmas!"

He rolled over on top of her. "Let's start celebrating now."

The band assembled that day in the basement to begin preparations for their stint in the studio at the end of September. Joel was telling them about Roger's call when Alix interrupted. "That reminds me – Eleanor phoned while you were out. She'll be over in time for the AIDS benefit concert and she's staying a while."

"With Mayday on the boards this promises to be one fine party!"

Dixie groaned. "It'll be baby-sitting time with you and Roger."

Joel leered at her. "And do we need sitting!"

She smacked him playfully. "Go stand in the corner."

"Take your guitar," Alix added, laughing. "We've got work to do."

The band spent days ironing bugs out of the proposed songs for the album and when they entered the studio, all were more than ready to get down to work. Things rolled along smoothly and at an easy pace. October saw the release of the album and video the band had recorded at the De Sade – 'Alive in an Alley' – and sales were rapid, pushing it up the charts. It was earlier than Brad had planned originally but he didn't want to saturate the market as the new album had a spring release tagged to it.

Work finished ahead of schedule, the sound richer and more textured than their previous efforts. Dixie made her writing debut, collaborating with Alix on a ballad that looked to be a promising single.

Mayday arrived in town amid pomp and ceremony and both bands got together in the hotel bar for a night of riotous drinking and equally riotous behaviour. True to his word, Joel invited several winsome females to the bash and, with a wink at Roger, introduced them to the festivities. Mayday went into the studio to record. After a few days off, the Blue Mask met to plan a video for the new project.

Robin assembled them in the Alley View on the first day of the shoot for the title track, 'Raising Hell'. Alix and Joel had cooked up a storyboard set in Satan's domain and she'd pulled the appropriate costumes out of the theatrical suppliers. An assortment of fog machines, fire pits and innovative lighting turned the club into what they needed.

She also did their make-up and it was a motley crew that sat around drinking coffee. Alix looked the part of evil pixie in her blood-streaked bodysuit and Joel, having won the toss of the coin against Bear, sat in splendor as the proprietor of the fiery establishment, complete with horns and vampire teeth. Leo and Dixie were cast as tortured souls, blood awash on their faces and features twisted by the stroke of greasepaint. Bear trudged around as a fallen angel, halo askew, harp trailing broken strings. The others roared with laughter and teased him and he obligingly played the clown, clouting them when he'd had enough. The shoot took a couple of days but the work was lighthearted and full of fun.

Everyone relaxed as the Christmas season approached. Joel's counts remained in the normal range and his health was stable. The band was more relieved than they would admit. Alix had been keeping a close eye on her friend, despite his reassurances that he was fine, and even she was satisfied. He had adjusted his diet, amended his lifestyle and looked better than he had for years. The one continuing battle he was losing was the fight to quit smoking. Alix knew it was largely because he didn't want to.

"I can't picture me without a cigarette sticking out of my face. It'd ruin my image."

Joel ducked in and out of the Mayday sessions, playing occasionally, and he and Roger, with Alix sometimes in tow, met for drinks, conversation and fun. There was little on the agenda for the band and they made the most of it. Alix and Joel set about putting the house in order, buying furniture and unpacking the treasures and curiosities they'd picked up. The oddities were planted haphazardly all over the house, Australian mixing with Japanese, Balinese and Maori carvings, pictures and trinkets. Sherri despaired of the lack of order and consistency but they adamantly refused to let her rearrange anything. Ash was right – it did look like a Dali nightmare.

Eleanor arrived the first week in December and was installed in the spare room. The three had a happy reunion. She took Joel aside one afternoon when they were alone.

"How are you?"

He hugged her. "Everything's fine. I'm fine."

She looked him over closely, hazel eyes serious in the pretty, painted face. His firm body was encased in black muscle shirt and tight jeans, the green eyes clear, the hard face fresh and rested. "You look fabulous."

"I'm taking care of myself – doc's orders. There's absolutely nothing to worry about. I really do feel great."

"I'm so glad. I've thought a lot about you since our visit but I didn't want it to look like I was prying by telephoning to check up on your health."

"You would never be prying. Friends can get away with murder."

"You sure do. Your lady certainly seems proud to be your lady but I'm not so sure she relishes having me installed in your household."

"Sherri's all right; she's just shy. I think she's still kind of nervous about being my lady. Ash read her the riot act about not interfering and said if she did I'd give her walking papers."

"And would you?"

"You never know, girl," he said slyly. "I'm enigmatic after all."

"That's Alix," Eleanor responded impudently. "You're the macho slut."

"Not anymore. You got to be real careful who you take home from a bar these days."

She swatted him, bracelets clanking.

The gang decided to hold an early celebration before the concert and piled into the Alley View. Rather than dampen their enthusiasm, it seemed to charge it and both the Blue Mask and Mayday played blistering sets. The program went on for four hours and a number of stations picked up the satellite feed. Ash was ecstatic, as was Robin. The hard work of the organizers had paid off in ways none of them had dared hope for. Morris flew in for the show and he and Ash disappeared for a few days afterwards. Mayday had finished their recording just before the concert and the week was spent partying and celebrating. Things wound down quickly. With Christmas approaching, the English contingent had to get home to their families. Roger took Alix and Joel out for a drink the day before the band was due to fly out. After an hour, he proposed that the three of them return to the house.

Mystified by the sudden change of plan, they complied. Just inside the entrance hall they bumped into a beautifully carved and painted wooden cigar store Indian that was easily as tall as Roger. He winked at Eleanor and both laughed.

"We found this in a tobacco shop and practically beat the owner up before he'd sell it to us," she explained. "Bear picked it up but we had to get you out so that we could set it up."

"Why?" Alix was floored.

Roger laid a long arm around her and Joel. "Eleanor and me wanted to buy you a little pressie for this twisted hole you call home. You've got more bits and bobs in here than a second-hand barrow boy but it's gear. We wanted to add our bit; make our own little statement."

Alix kissed him. "Thanks." She leaned over to hug Eleanor.

Joel gave Eleanor a smacking kiss and executed a low bow before Roger. Laughing, they filed into the living room for one last bash. Alone later, drunk and giggling, Alix and Joel were congratulating themselves in the kitchen. They had arranged with Morris the week before to deliver a case of cheap champagne, wrapped in a Canadian flag, to both Roger and Eleanor. This, Morris promised, would be followed with a bottle of fine wine every day during the twelve days of Christmas. With fond affection, the Brits returned to Britain.

It had been a fabulous holiday for all involved and, as the day itself approached, the band, Brad, Robin and Ash made plans. They always celebrated together and the group gathered at Joel and Alix's for a feast.

Sherri, due at her parents in Victoria, was upset that Joel refused to join her. But he had explained that this was his family and there was no way he would desert them. Knowing she could not win, she conceded defeat and went alone.

Boxing Day, Alix dragged Joel up to the spare room and ordered him to search behind a black lacquered Japanese screen. He had given her a beautiful pirate's chest on Christmas morning and she had thanked him gravely. She'd been slyly secretive all that day and by the next morning had him crawling the walls.

He disappeared behind the screen and she smiled gloatingly at his silence. "I couldn't get it delivered until today. Is it all right?"

Joel came out with tears in his eyes. "It's beautiful. How did you know?"

"Know what?"

"When I was a kid I used to run away whenever the fair came to town. The merry-go-round was my escape into a magic world and I'd spend the whole day and all my cash going on it. I used to steal my old lady's drug money. What the hell made you buy it?"

"You said you'd always wanted a pony when you were a kid. I figured it was the next best thing."

"It's the best thing," he whispered, holding her close and kissing her.

Alix helped him move the gift into his room, placing it in front of the window so that the sunlight shone on the glossy paintwork. She had found it hidden under a pile of blankets in an old, dusty second-hand shop, one of the many she loved to prowl around in, and had hired someone to refinish it, never suspecting the impact it would have.

It was a carousel horse, head high, mane flying.

CHAPTER 22

Spring 1993

February brought the release of the Blue Mask's next album, 'Raising Hell', two more video shoots for selected singles and the commencement of a North American tour. Joel had been checking in with Dr. Marlowe regularly and, as before, got clearance to go. Brad booked the same way he had for the last tour, leaving blocks of time between gigs. The game plan included a European tour and studio time for another album and then a long break for all concerned. They would take half of the next year off. The schedule was not set in stone; everything revolved around Joel's health.

Brad's mapping was simple - a snaking trek down the west coast of the continent, across and then another wide curve up the east coast, with stops in the American Midwest. It would culminate in a cross-Canada tour that would end nicely in Vancouver.

Sales figures were glowing before the 'Raising Hell' tour started and as it wound on the album topped the charts in Canada, the U.K. and the U.S. The band members were finding it hard to be alone and some of the fans could get quite aggressive.

Things progressed along familiar lines. This path was well-trodden and Brad ran his operation smoothly. Any glitches that occurred were quickly ironed out by the tour manager. Interviews and photo shoots were part and parcel of the job and as the band arrived in the southwestern states, Joel found it harder and harder to keep up. Dr. Marlowe had warned him to get as much rest as he could but some of the extras required were taking energy out of him – he was a high profile member and a popular one with the press.

As the group headed north, up the east coast and ever closer to home, Alix encouraged him to hang on and did her best to make things easy for him. He had lost weight and the hard features were acquiring a drawn, tired set.

"Never again are we going to go away for so long," she said sharply one night as the two sat in his hotel room. "This is too much. Your doctor's right; we're all going to get sick."

He saw through the anger to the fear beneath it. "I'm fine, Alix; stop freaking."

"What makes you think I'm freaking?"

He smiled fondly. "The way you're carrying on. The doc warned me if I did too much my body would let me know. Well, it's talking, girl, but that's all."

She made an effort to relax. "All right, but you let me know as soon as anything unusual starts to happen. I read your info too – no holding out."

"'Kay, now get out of here and let me get some sleep." He leered at her. "Or do you want to stay?"

"Are you nuts? I'd never get any sleep." But as she closed the door behind her she knew that statement was no longer true. Joel's trysts – as the press called them – were nonexistent. He hinted at them in interviews but he'd always been discreet and reporters knew better than to try to get names and details out of him. A nudge and a wink were good enough and so far it had been working marvellously.

He was also pushing another piece of fiction. One reporter remarked on how tired he was looking and the fact that his shirt was hanging on him. The reply had been a cheeky wink and the trademark lop-sided grin. "You know what the road is like: party-time, non-stop."

The truth was that he was usually so exhausted he went straight to his room when he got offstage and fell into bed, letting everyone else think he was out charming the socks (and everything else) off adoring females.

The comment had made him aware of appearances though and the day after he and Alix went shopping. Between them, they picked out looser shirts in soft greens and blues. Joel surveyed himself in the mirror with raised brows.

"I don't know about this new look. I feel funny without my uniform on. Why the shirt colours? Can't we stick with black?"

"It makes your face look more pale. I think you look great. Nice change."

"Now you'll be the only one in trademark black shirt and jeans. We're not a matched set anymore."

"We will be. Just hang on till we're home and you can rest and gain back the weight you lost. For now, this covers it."

"You're a great singer, Alix, but you're no designer."

She smacked him playfully. "Then get Ash to give you a hand. Until then, I'll have to do."

As the band started across Canada, Dixie began to have throat problems. Since she handled all the back-up vocals and the lead on the ballad that she and Alix had written, it was a serious blow to the concerts. Leo helped as best as he could but the songs lost the lushness and weight that they needed. She saw a doctor in Ontario who confirmed that the problem was tonsillitis and she would have to have the infected tonsils removed.

Joel was starting to experience fevers and the fatigue was getting worse. He clamped his mouth shut and refused to bow into his fears. Spare time was spent in bed, desperately trying to get the much needed rest that would restore his strength long enough to get him through the gruelling concerts. His cough had returned and he felt fluish and disconnected. He tried to hide his symptoms but as the tour wound on he got more worried. When they had to cancel at the end of May because of Dixie, he breathed a heartfelt sigh of relief. He knew he wouldn't have made it.

They boarded a plane home. Joel went straight to bed and Dixie to her doctor, who arranged the necessary operation. Brad called a press conference as soon as the band phoned him and announced Dixie's illness, adding an apology from the Blue Mask for the cancelled shows. The explanation was accepted without question – everyone had heard her voice going. No mention was made of Joel.

Alix phoned Dr. Marlowe as soon as the group flew in and he told her to keep Joel in bed and monitor his symptoms. If there was no marked improvement in twenty-four hours, he wanted him admitted to hospital.

Both of them were desperately holding on to the idea that he had simply pushed himself too far and was paying the price. Secretly, both knew they were fooling themselves. That night he took a turn for the worst.

Alix had been sleeping with her door open so that she could hear him call if he needed her. Sherri was dismissed from spending nights until this flu cleared up. Alix woke from a bad, disjointed dream to hear her friend groaning and she rushed to his side.

"Phone the doc," he whispered shakily, "and get me to Emergency." His eyes were wide with fear. "Something's wrong."

She tried to soothe him, hiding her jangling nerves. The call was put through and she helped him change. His sheets were soaked with sweat and the cough had gotten worse. She got him into her car and drove carefully to the hospital, shoving down the reckless need to go hell bent for leather. As promised, Dr. Marlowe was waiting. Joel was whisked away and Alix was left to handle the red tape. Once the paperwork was dealt with, she called the band, Ash, Robin and Brad. Dixie was due in that morning in preparation for her tonsillectomy and came armed with a small suitcase. It was five a.m. when the ragged group assembled in the television room of the pulmonary ward. The time passed in relative silence as each of them withdrew into their thoughts.

Dr. Marlowe finally came out, his features composed, mood calm. "How long has this been going on?"

Alix shrugged. "It's hard to say. He was tired and spent a lot of time in his room but when we checked with him he said he was all right. He was getting lots of rest like you told him to."

The man nodded. Joel had suspected all along and was trying to protect his friends by keeping silent. He cleared his throat and spoke in low, careful tones. "No one could have anticipated this. We know quite a bit more about this disease now but it is unpredictable and each case varies."

Ash drew up sharply at the doctor's use of the word disease. "Is it PCP?"

The dark eyes were steady. "Yes."

"What the hell is that," Bear said.

Leo spoke quietly. "Pneumocystis carinii pneumonia – AIDS-related pneumonia."

The words dropped silently into the group.

"We've caught it early. I've got him on Pentamidine and he's stabilized. There is no reason for him not to make a full recovery. There is the presence of thrush in his mouth. Has he been complaining of a sore throat?"

Leo almost smiled. "Dix, our keyboardist, came down with tonsillitis on tour. She's been the one with the sore throat."

"He didn't want to worry anyone," Alix explained. "I was on him but he kept telling me he was fine." She swallowed the lump of fear in her throat. "You sure he's going to be all right?"

"I see no reason why not. Like I said, we caught it early. We're monitoring him closely to see how he reacts to the Pentamidine but we've had marvelous results with it."

"Can we see him?"

"Not all of you." He regarded Alix with gentle eyes. "Why don't you go in and let him know everyone is here? The reassurance will make all of you feel better, Joel included. But please don't stay too long. He needs rest.

"Does anyone have any questions I can answer right now?" Receiving shakes of the head, he smiled. "I would advise you to go home and get some sleep. Joel will be in one to two weeks. You'll see a marked improvement in the next day or two."

They watched as he moved away to consult with one of the nurses at the station.

"People hear things, asleep or not, and it still gets into the subconscious," Robin pointed out. "Alix, go in and let him know we're here and we're not going away. He must feel pretty frightened right now. It's important for him to be sure he's not alone."

"Thrush is one of the signs of advanced HIV. It usually means AIDS is developing. He knows that," Leo said. "Why the hell didn't he tell us? We could've used Dix's tonsillitis to get him home faster."

"Maybe he was denying it to himself," Ash answered. "It wouldn't be the first time it's happened to someone in that position and it sure as hell won't be the last."

Alix listened to the seemingly calm conversation with shaking disbelief. How could they be so matter-of-fact? She felt the ball of fear and panic in her stomach, sitting like lead and then she felt it shift and rise in her throat, harsh and acrid. "I knew this was going to happen," she cried, her heart pounding. "Things have been going too well for us and we always have to pay. That's how it worked for years. Joel kept saying he was just a carrier but I knew he'd get AIDS! I knew it!"

They could all hear the hysteria in her voice but it was Leo who reacted first. Grabbing her by the shoulders, he spun her around to face him, shaking her roughly. "Stop it," he ground out. "Calm down or I'll slap you! I've been through this more times than I want to remember and I've learned a few things. One is that you have to give full support and try to keep their spirits up. That's the mental half of recovering. If you go in there crying like you're already at his funeral then you might as well start planning it!"

Her tears dried up soon as the tirade started and her mouth dropped in shock. In all the years that she'd known Leo he had always treated her gently. He'd never spoken to her like this before.

The silence gave him a chance to calm down and he pushed his anger firmly away. "Now, you and I are going into that room to cheer him up and encourage him and tell him he's going to get well – whether he hears us or not.

And we're going to keep doing it every time we see him. Absolutely no downer trips – ever. Is that clear?"

The voice had gotten quiet but it was still threaded with steel. She nodded tamely. "I'm sorry, Leo. I won't break down again. I promise."

He turned to Ash. "You'd better get Dix checked in." He smiled at her. "We'll be down to see you settled in. When's the operation?"

"This afternoon."

Taking Alix firmly by the arm, he waited until the group started to disperse and then, with a final levelling glance, steered her into Joel's room.

He lay among the pillows, eyes closed, face grey and lined with pain. An IV unit stood beside the bed, the tube with medicine running down to the needle in his arm. She swallowed her misery and went over to stroke his forehead, whispering to him. He didn't stir and after a few minutes, she kissed his cheek and promised she'd be back later.

She stopped in to see Dixie and then left the hospital for home. There was a message from Sherri on the answering machine, asking how Joel was feeling but Alix could not face telling her yet. She opened a bottle of Scotch and took it upstairs to her room. Undressing, she tipped the bottle to her mouth and drank it straight. Methodically, systematically, she continued to force it down until her mind dulled and her thoughts flattened out into nothing. She needed to wipe out for a few hours, to let her mind recover from the reeling shock she couldn't cope with. Everything could be taken care of later.

She woke up late in the afternoon with a pounding head and a mouth full of fur. She took a quick shower, called Sherri to let her know where Joel was and then hurried back to the hospital. Ash sat alone in Joel's room, reading a book. He led her outside.

"He's still asleep and it'll be a while before he's awake but I didn't want him to be alone."

Alix reached out to stroke the dark circles under his eyes. "You look beat. Why don't you go get some sleep? I'll sit with him."

He nodded wearily. "Sounds like a plan. Don't worry; he's going to be all right."

"I know," she said quietly. At least for a while.

Ash left and she was about to head into Joel's room when Sherri came rushing down the hall, face wet with tears, nerves jangling. Alix sat her down, giving the same lecture Leo had given her, though in a softer voice and with more understanding. You used whatever methods worked.

"I don't know much about this," she cried. "I feel so lost."

"Between us we can give you what info we've managed to get. Just ask me or Leo or Ash. But for now, I think you should go home. You're no help to Joel like this. I should've given you more time to digest the news but things have been crazy since last night."

"I can't face him anyway," Sherri said in a shaking voice. "I'm useless right now, aren't I?"

"Go away and give yourself some time. He'll sleep for a while yet. I'll call you if anything comes up."

She was eventually persuaded to leave without seeing Joel. Alix sat quite still, waiting for the air around her to stop vibrating, then went into her friend's room to sit in the chair beside his bed. Eyes closed, his chest rose and fell in the slow rhythm of a medicated sleep. She stroked his hair, then sat back and relaxed, letting her mind wander while she waited for him to wake up.

CHAPTER 23

Summer 1993

The group remained positive and, wonderfully, Joel got better. Alix was sitting beside him when he woke up, groggy and uncertain. A slow smile spread across his gaunt features when he saw her. "Hi stranger."

"How do you feel?"

"A lot better. Have I been out since I checked in?"

"Pretty much. Dr. Marlowe had you shot up with something to calm you down. You were kind of freaking."

"I panicked. I knew it was coming on the tour and when it hit me I pretty much lost it."

"Why didn't you tell me earlier?"

"Denial," he answered honestly. "I guess I hoped in some kind of warped way that it would all just go away. Stupid, huh?"

"No, typical."

"So how am I doing?"

"Your fever's down and the flu symptoms should be going away."

"To tell you the truth, I feel sick."

"That's your medicine," she replied, pointing to the IV unit. "It's one of the side effects."

"Oh well, no cure without a little side effect."

She ran her hand down his cheek. "You're going to be fine."

"For now."

"We're not going to talk like that, Stark."

"Yes, ma'am." He couldn't be that blatant, not yet, not with Alix. He'd had a long time to think about what was happening and, carrier or not, he had no doubt that he would eventually get to this point. It was tied in with some fatalistic view he'd always harboured about his life. But now was not the time to indulge in cynical philosophy with his best friend, who was teetering on her new plateau and trying hard to dig in. "So what's the plan?"

"You'll be in one or two weeks, depending on how good you are. Dr. Marlowe sees no reason why you shouldn't be back to normal after that."

"So I've got at least a week to kill in this place. You gotta help me or I'll go nuts."

"We'll amuse you the best we can, oh high king, but the doc figures you're probably going to spend a fair amount of time catching zzz's so your body can fight this infection."

"Yeah, well, we'll see, girl. Until then, could you bring me a few things from home?"

A slow, impish grin spread across her face. "Like PJs and a robe?"

"I don't own any."

"You do now. Leo brought some over for you." She reached into the bag beside her and yanked out a pair of white cotton pajamas with teddy bears chasing each other across them.

"Where the hell did he find those?"

She burst out laughing. "I don't know but you should've seen his face when he brought them in."

"I'll kill him."

"That's incentive to get better, if nothing else." She dug in again and out came a long black robe with swirls of blue across it. "He figured this would be acceptable to cover the bears."

"I suppose he wants me to model this to entertain him."

"Not just him – all of us. And don't forget, Dix's in here too. She's going to need cheering up."

"You're a bitch, you know that, Alix?"

"I've been told once or twice, yeah."

"Can you bring me some other stuff?"

She pulled a paper and pen out of the pocket of her jacket and handed them to him. "You make a list while I'm off. Dr. Marlowe said I was to have him paged when you woke up."

The casual banter got Alix over the hump of depression and as Joel got better, everyone relaxed. No one mentioned the changes that were perhaps too deep yet to sense but all knew they would eventually have to deal with the fact that things had gone past the point of no return. With Joel ill, their lives were in another realm. The group struggled to keep everything on an even keel, for themselves as much as for him.

Routine settled in as his body fought the PCP. The Pentamidine made him nauseous but he worked through it, determinedly cheerful. For their part, his friends were as positive around him as he was.

Sherri, with Alix's help, got a grip on her fears. Between them, they became his runners, fetching things and keeping him informed on what was going on. Dr. Marlowe allowed the two to supplement the hospital food to help him regain lost weight. Sherri dreamed up snacks and meals that Alix assisted on. Afternoons Joel and Alix spent together, sometimes talking about things they had to do; sometimes reliving old memories or just rambling. By the end of the first week they were working on songs in between meal discussions, bill paying and buying additional things for the house. The band and Ash, Robin and Brad dropped by when they could and the room became a revolving series of gatherings. Everyone was careful to make sure that they didn't overdo it.

Joel asked Ash to buy a couple of traditional cookbooks and have them elaborately wrapped. Two days before his release, he presented them to the women. He had teased them mercilessly about their culinary skills and the light-hearted insulting banter became a part of the rites of mealtime.

Sherri was delighted with her gift but Alix eyed hers warily.

"I'm trying to thank you for your efforts to fatten me up. You don't have to look at it like it'll explode."

"I wouldn't put it past you to put a stink bomb between the covers."

"Ingrate. Maybe I'll tell the press about it the next time they ask me about the mysterious Alix Lane."

"And maybe I'll tell them you took up knitting while you were in here," she shot back. She kissed him. "Actually this cooking bit has been fun. Maybe I'll quit the band and open a restaurant."

Sherri joined in. "Want a partner?"

"Sure. And if Brad blows up because I've walked out in the middle of a contract, I'll tell him it's Joel's fault."

"I get the hint. Give me back the book and I'll give it to Betty Crocker or someone."

"Not a chance. But I would like you to autograph it before I put in on the bookshelf beside the collection of crochet patterns I'm going to buy and sign your name in."

"'Kay, truce, I won't tell the press." He sobered suddenly. "Speaking of press, what's the word on me being in here?"

"Brad called a conference right after you were admitted and said you'd come down with pneumonia due to stress and overwork. He also said we were rundown and have been ordered to take some time off. Dr. Marlowe will back that statement up the whole way. He figures we all look like shit and need a good few months' rest."

"That should cover us for a while. Can you get everyone in on my secret over here tonight? I need to say a couple of things before I'm released and I want all our stories to match."

That night, despite the restrictions on how many visitors were allowed in a patient's room – even a private one – they all crowded in. The nurses had been letting them get away with it and saw no reason to stand on ceremony the night before they were to lose one of their favourite patients.

Joel eyed them sternly. "I want to remind you about your promise. We all know I have AIDS, even though none of you have used that word yet. I still don't want anyone to get wind of it. Brad, what happened with the press?"

"No worries, Durango, it went just like I told you. I said you were recovering from pneumonia – bottom line. With you and Dixie sick there were no questions asked about why this tour and Europe are cancelled for now. No concern, hombre; no one tumbled."

"Thanks." None of them voiced their thoughts, though a single thread ran through them all. It wasn't a matter of cancelling the tour for now – there would be no tour ever. With one bout of PCP behind him, to go on that kind of gruelling trek would be akin to committing suicide.

The next morning Alix came to drive him home, armed with both Dr. Marlowe's orders and a small battery of drugs that included AZT, an antiviral agent that was designed to help bolster his immune system. The doctor himself walked in just before check out.

"You've been having some irritating side effects from the Pentamidine."

"Yeah. Slight fever and really sick from time to time. It was pretty much what you warned me about."

"I want you in once a week for Pentamidine treatments."

"But I'm better now."

"This is preventative and important and will help to delay recurrence. I dilute the drug with sterile water and you inhale it using a nebulizer. Very little of it is absorbed from the lungs into the bloodstream and we've found that the side effects occur much less frequently. You can expect a cough and fatigue during inhalation but it won't be a constant like it was with the drip.

"Also, I want you on AZT as long as possible. We've found it does affect the white blood count so we'll have to do interrupted treatments. I want those counts taken on a regular basis, like the Pentamidine. I've set up a schedule of appointments for you. Absolutely no phoning to say you'll come in another day."

"Guess things have been kind of low lately," Joel said grinning.

"You can say that again. But you're doing fine now. Keep the jokes up and take it easy."

"I feel almost normal."

"In a couple of weeks you should. Get lots of rest. You need to get some of that weight back too. Also, I wouldn't advise that you resume smoking. Do you think you've kicked it?"

"You never know. I sure as hell won't recommend what I've just been through as a common cure though." He extended his hand and the doctor reached out to shake it. "Thanks, Doc, I..." He shook his head, unable to find the words to say what he felt.

The man pressed his other hand on top of Joel's and smiled. "Just get better. And don't deceive yourself that I'm any kind of pushover. If you don't do as you're told I'll be all over you like ugly on a bear."

"Ugly on a bear?"

"My father says that."

"You need some new material, Doc."

Laughing, he picked up Joel's chart, waved to Alix, and headed for the door. "You write me some. It might keep you out of trouble for a while."

"Sure, and pigs fly."

"Oh, by the way, you probably will find you need to build up your stamina. I believe Alix said something about your liking to walk around the beaches and such. That would be a marvelous way to do it." He winked and left.

Joel turned on her. "You told him I hated that stuff?"

She shrugged, laughing. "We were talking about it when he mentioned you exercising to get your strength back."

He picked up his suitcase. "'Kay, smart ass, lead me to your ocean and show me the damn paths."

"The nurse said to wait for the wheelchair escort."

"You must be fucking joking."

With that, he strolled out of the room, leaving her to follow.

CHAPTER 24

Things settled into a slow routine when Joel got home. He was still tired and the lack of energy frustrated him. Sherri came and went between appointments but the three met for evening meals. She would come in with a new recipe and even Alix found, much to her chagrin and Joel's crowing delight, that she was using the cookbook he had given her. He kept her company while she tried to whip something up to make their eating interesting and, though the main purpose was to fatten him up, the three found great pleasure in breaking bread together. It brought the day into focus and gave them a chance to visit in a way there hadn't been time for before.

Word went around among the friends and two or three nights a week someone would call and announce they were coming around with an appetizer or dessert. It culminated in a regular Sunday brunch where the group would gather for a weekly visit, everyone contributing and spending the early afternoon eating and sipping champagne and orange juice or an array of coffees and teas that got more exotic as the gang started experimenting.

Joel would disappear to lie down if tired but adamantly refused to cancel the Sunday affairs. As he had announced at the first brunch gathering, "I really like this idea. Let's face it, the band can't do public stuff like we used to – too many hassles. Anyway, I'm sick of the club and bar scene. We've been living it non-stop the last few years. A little peace and quiet won't hurt any of us."

That pretty well summed up the Blue Mask's feelings. As for Ash, Robin and Brad, they were all too busy to have much time for late night partying. The morning came too fast and brought too much work with it.

True to his word, Joel also started accompanying Alix on her visits to the ocean. That first week he had decided that early evening walks after dinner were just what the doctor had ordered. Sherri usually went off to an appointment or home to catch up on work after coffee had been consumed. She no longer spent nights with him; Joel had requested it until he got his strength back and to give her an out. It was up to her if she wanted to resume their relationship but sex was now out of the question. She was struggling to cope with his illness and he suspected she had had very little to do with anyone even remotely sick before. When she shame-facedly confessed that he was right, he'd kissed her and assured her he would let her take the lead.

It was during the first week of their walks that Joel approached Alix about something he had long been thinking about. They were strolling along when he found a deserted bench and led her to it. "I want you to go see the doc and get yourself tested for HIV."

It was the last thing she expected him to say. When he got that look on his face it was usually to upbraid her for fussing. "What the hell for?"

"'Cos, girl, we've made it together and I want to make sure you weren't exposed. I know you haven't been with anyone else and it's been a year since Scotland so you won't need a follow-up test."

"I feel fine. Leave it."

"Yeah, well, I felt fine for a long time too. Come on, Alix, don't be stupid. You know better than that."

She shrugged, uncomfortable. "Shouldn't you be bugging Sherri?"

His eyes narrowed. "Haven't you two discussed this?"

"Not a lot."

"Why the hell not?"

"She doesn't seem to want to and I'm not sure how to approach her. Besides, what is there to discuss? We take things as they come, Joel. We all do."

He shook his head impatiently, hearing the thread of anger that she was not aware of. "Sherri's been tested. She's fine and will have the follow-up after six months to make sure. Now, will you promise to go see the doc? There's nothing to be embarrassed about."

Her head shot up. "What makes you think I am?"

"You're squirming," he said, grinning. "You do that when you're embarrassed or when you're trying to lie about something and you don't think you can get away with it."

"That's 'cos I know your bullshit detector is never wrong. Okay, I'll go."

He stood up, pulling her with him. "Well, that was a hell of a lot easier than pulling teeth. Come on, let's make tracks."

The test was negative, taking a weight off his shoulders and prompting a relief Alix had not expected to feel. She hadn't thought about being infected – with Joel ill there were too many other things on her mind – but that relief made her realize that, at least subconsciously, she had been concerned.

Joel took to disappearing into the basement to play guitar and work on riffs, much as he had before. Alix marvelled at the way he could lose himself for hours. Her guitar work was desultory at best and, not being wildly proficient, she was content to use it to structure her lyrics and then let him work on the intricacies of the melody line.

To all intents and purposes, he was recovering his earlier lifestyle and getting back to normal. At the end of the first week he was looking well and no one meeting him would have guessed that he had been hospitalized with PCP. He was tired and a little washed out but that was to be expected after a road trip. All of them came back with that look. The weeks of constant travelling took its toll on everyone. But Alix found herself tensing when he traipsed up the stairs to rest or when she stumbled into the bathroom while he was taking medication. It was little things that kept bringing the whole situation back with renewed force.

Joel came home with a bathroom scale one day and she fled to her room to cover the tears that had suddenly sprung up. Dr. Marlowe had stressed how important it was for him to get back to normal and weight was a big part of that. It would be one of the things they would be fighting later. AIDS, in Africa, was not called the 'slim disease' for nothing. It was this impression of fragility about him, fleeting though it was now, that crept up and smacked her in the back of the head. Joel bore it all with patience, refusing to say anything to Alix or Sherri until one of them felt comfortable enough to bring the subject up. He knew they were confused, angry and lost but he couldn't help without their cooperation. It did get to him though and one day when they had fussed over him and hovered one too many times, he blew up. "That's enough, both of you. I'm all right! Stop treating me like a fucking porcelain piece that might break! I want everything back to normal. If you can't deal get out till you can. Believe me you're not helping. Or are you trying to drive me nuts and into an early grave?"

Sherri fled the house in tears; Alix retreated to her room and, angry and frustrated, Joel blockaded himself in the basement behind a wall of noise.

Alix backed off immediately and tried hard to turn her attitude around, or at least to hide it more effectively from Joel's sharp eyes. It got much easier. As the second week rolled by, Joel's weight crept back up and colour returned to his face. He didn't have the energy he once had but he looked great. He'd also managed to stay away from cigarettes.

The only jarring notes were the Pentamidine treatments. He returned from them coughing and exhausted and retreated to bed for the day, listless and unwilling to eat or have company. Alix gritted her teeth against comment and left him to it and by the next day things were fine. Joel was on what Dr. Marlowe called the 'honeymoon' after the first infection. He felt better than he had in months and they had been told this could last up to a year. It was a hopeful remark, designed to encourage, but for her it was another reminder that they had crossed a now destroyed bridge and were stranded in new territory. There was no going back to the easy days. She had come to think of their lives as before they hit alien land and after. Things had changed unalterably. The anger and madness she reserved for midnight horrors when she was alone. She had to confront these wild thoughts, let them loose, and get them behind her.

Ash visited Joel often and they grew very close, forging new bonds in an old friendship that each cherished. The same thing began to happen with Leo. The experience that these two had acquired from the Centre and through helping their own friends with AIDS made him turn to them gratefully, not so much for comfort but for the understanding they possessed. There was no need to dissemble or choose carefully through the minefield of Alix and the others' emotions. With Ash and Leo he could voice some of his own fears honestly, blatantly, with the black gallows humour he possessed. It kept him sane and gave some relief from morbid thoughts. These he refused to entertain and his search for the light side of things surprised and amused him. Ash and Leo came to dinner frequently but there were other people around and what he enjoyed most was when one or both of them dropped by to settle in the armchairs in the basement, raiding the refrigerator that was kept fully stocked for company.

They appreciated not having to tiptoe around Joel's illness as they often had to with people they counselled but this was the hardest case so far. Ash frequently came home exhausted after a visit in the early days. He'd never helped his best friend through this. Others, yes, but not Joel. And he would never let that friend in on his fears. As Leo had said, positive was the only front to present. There were no other alternatives.

CHAPTER 25

Joel brought things to the forefront one afternoon when Leo and Ash had dropped by. They headed to the basement.

"I got some things to go over so I'm taking the floor. First of all, you guys have been great. It's been a big help being able to talk without watching what I say 'cos I sure can't with any of the others yet. But it's time you took the masks off. This cheerfulness is driving me nuts. I've got it coming from all sides. Whose bright idea was it anyway?"

"Gloves right off, huh, Joel," Leo said smiling. "We were taught that for counselling."

"Yeah, but it's for people you're helping that you don't know. We've been friends for too many years so throw out the guidelines. Deal?"

"Look..." Ash started.

Joel cut him off. "I know it's hard on you but look at where I'm sitting. I'm the one who's sick. Ash, you've been heading off to the bathroom a lot when we get into the nitty gritty of things and I know you're not pissing. If you want to shed a tear it's fine by me. And Leo, give me a break. I don't need smiles all the time; I need honesty.

"I'm going to have a talk with all of you and put a stop to this bullshit. Everyone's had time to think about what's happening and how it affects them. Let's get things out in the open. I want people to start dealing with their feelings so I can deal with them the way I used to. This pretense is sucking up too much energy."

"You can't blame it all on us," Leo pointed out. "You haven't seemed to want to talk. We all have questions, Joel."

"I'm not blaming anyone. It isn't that I don't want to; I`m giving all of you time."

"So you've been planning these little pep talks for a while," Ash said, shaking his head in amusement. "Typical. I gather we're the first."

"Yep. Then Robin, Brad, Dix, Bear and Sherri. I got it all planned."

"What about Alix?"

"That's going to be the hardest so I'm leaving her till last."

"Just don't wait too long," Ash warned. "She'll get wind of something up – she always does – and you know what she's like if she thinks she's being excluded from anything. She'll blow sky high."

"Believe me, I know. I've been on the receiving end before and I'm not going through that if I can help it. Don't worry. Speedy Gonzales, that's me."

"Ariba."

"I have something else to run by you."

"Not another lecture," Leo said.

"No, a game plan. Will you see if Brad can get us back in the studio," he asked casually. There was nothing casual about what he wanted. The basement was ideal - with the door shut it was completely soundproof and Alix usually didn't disturb him. He had been working secretly on this project since his diagnosis. She wasn't ready for the whole picture yet – he knew it would upset her. These two were more equipped to deal with facts and he was going to need Leo's help to get to the next stage.

"I think you should go easy. You haven't been home for long and it would be a mistake to jump into something we both know can get pretty heavy when the fever is on us."

"We were working on songs on the road and I have some stuff already done and recorded. We can take it easy; cruise along."

"Why the rush," Ash quizzed, already suspecting the answer.

"The clock is ticking and I don't know when the buzzer will go off. I still have a lot of songs in me and I want to get them down." Seeing the sudden tightening of Leo's features, he laughed. "Don't worry, they're not all downers. Actually, most of them are pretty light. I have a lot to be thankful for."

'You're talking like it's the end of your life."

"It is, only I have the edge 'cos I got a warning. In some ways it's better than being run over by a bus tomorrow. Though that has its advantages too. Much faster." He grinned.

"What the hell are you being so morbid for?"

"I'm not. Don't go thinking this is some kind of warped denial 'cos you'd be wrong. Say what you think – I don't mind. Actually, I demand it. I'm just being realistic. I admit it's easy to plan right now 'cos I feel good but the doc has a point: keep the jokes up and stay occupied. I refuse to sit around brooding about why this happened to me and how it'll end. I've got work to do. How about it, Leo? Will you talk to Brad?"

"Why not do it yourself?"

"'Cos if he thinks it's a bad move he's more likely to say no to you."

"You're a devious bastard."

"Yeah but you've got to admit it's worked pretty good so far."

"Like a charm. What if Brad nixes this?"

He shrugged. "I'll keep recording on my own anyway."

"What are you talking about?"

"When I fitted out the basement I called Jack beforehand and we had a few brainstorming sessions. I told him what I had in mind and he told me what to buy and how to arrange it. He even recommended Greg for fine-tuning and one afternoon when everyone was out he honoured me with a visit for final approval."

"You mind clarifying this in English," Ash asked.

"I wanted a sound that was studio quality. I've been recording stuff that's good enough to go on a master tape for a final pressing – for commercial use."

"You mean what's coming out of here can finish as a CD?"

Joel grinned. "That's it."

"You can't tell me Jack wasn't a little suspicious," Leo commented.

"Me and Alix have been bugging him for years and he's taught us a lot. He knew I wanted to set up a studio I could work out of. Hell, it makes his job easier. He doesn't have to kick around while we experiment. I do my stuff, record on my own track, and hand it in. He mixes it with the rest of the band and I don't even have to show up. That's an ideal situation, of course."

Leo regarded him with a mixture of shock and awe. "Let me get this straight. If something happens, albums could be completed without you using these master tapes and we could carry on until we ran out of them. Right?"

Joel nodded cheerfully. "Clever old me, huh?"

"How long have you been working on this plan?"

"Probably since he bought the house," Ash said.

Joel looked steadily at his friends. "No, since I got diagnosed in England. That's the reason I bought the house."

"Wasn't that playing with fate?"

"Maybe. I wondered about that particular kind of magic or voodoo or what have you. But it also made good sense. If I got AIDS it was a good thing to record my work. If I didn't, then at least the work got recorded. You think you've got all the time in the world, you put things off. You got a deadline, you work to get done in time. And if you think you're in a position where you won't get extensions, then even a minor delay is out of the question."

"How can you think Alix won't tumble to this," Leo asked. "She's bound to get suspicious when you're down here all the time or pushing for the two of you to collaborate."

"That's the beauty of it. We've always written fast and a lot of the time. You know that. We got a bunch of stuff done when I was in the hospital 'cos she knew I had nothing else to do and I'd go nuts. She's used to me disappearing to play music and the more I do it the more she sees I'm recovering. She's been going right along the whole time."

"You bastard, you're worse that I suspected. When she finds out you've been using her she's going to freak."

"She's a lot easier on me these days. Besides there's more to consider. This is for my own good as well as the band's. The rules have changed whether we like it or not. I'm not going to be around as long as the rest of you. We may have a record contract to fulfill but there's also the artistic satisfaction – or whatever you want to call it – that we get from this career of ours. Why else would we still be doing it? I'd like to keep going while I have the strength and energy. We've been at this more than seven years and it's in our blood. You can take a break and try to fool yourself but you know it gets to you when you're not working. Let's face it; we're all hooked."

Leo nodded. "It was nice at first – time to hang out without any responsibilities – but I'm restless now. I won't snow you."

"You couldn't anyway 'cos we all feel the same way. Have you talked to the others?"

"Poor old Joel, no one has confessed much to you lately have they?"

"You can say that again. But they need time. I understand that. Don't forget, I've had months to deal with this."

"They'll open up. As for the band, they'll agree to this plan in a second. If Brad won't go for it, we'll be over here so much you'll regret setting it up."

"Not a chance. Thanks, pal, I won't forget this. You know, whether or not Brad goes for the studio we can still have jamming sessions here. This place is perfect and if I have to lay down, all I do is close the door. We need to do a lot of solidifying on the material for our next album. We got piss all done on the last tour."

Leo was in agreement. He'd jump at the chance, as he knew the rest of the band would. This positive attitude surprised him. Never a patient man, Joel was intolerant of laziness and illness was never an excuse he accepted when it came to work. But he was also prone to brooding; this sensible, even sunny outlook was quite out of character. If he was prepared to fight for normalcy, they all would.

"I'll talk to Brad today and phone you later. What about the others? You want me to call them too?"

"No. I'm going to invite Dix and Bear over today so we can sort this out. I'll ask them then."

"What about Alix?

"Her and Sherri are both little troopers but this act is wearing them out as well as me." He grinned wickedly. "I think both of them are ready for a change. I'll put Alix out of her misery soon. As for the sessions, I know she'll agree. But I have to get this other thing behind us first."

"She needs to take the bull by the horns and tackle it head on," Leo advised. "The sooner, the better."

"I wanted to give her time to deal. She's real mad at me and she doesn't even know it half the time. I can feel it when she looks at me. It confuses her."

"It confuses us all," Ash said. "Robin put it best. She said we have to take our cue from you. How we deal with you depends on how you want us to."

"I've told you how. Now it's just a matter of telling the others."

He kept his word and quickly went through his friends, using his knowledge of them to determine what each could take and how blatant he could be. Above all, he insisted on truth. He wanted to know how they felt, how much of his illness they could deal with and he promised the same truth in return. Alix accepted the visits as the usual calls and didn't intrude. She needed time away. Trying to keep up a cheerful disposition, as Leo had demanded, was draining her reserves. She spent much of the week joking with Joel and then running off to the ocean to pour out tears of fear, anger and frustration.

She began to get suspicious when he took Sherri downstairs and firmly closed the basement door. It was fine when he was alone; she understood his need to work uninterrupted but lately these sessions had been occurring too often. Her suspicions were confirmed when the woman emerged an hour later, eyes red from crying, and headed straight out the door.

"What's going on," she demanded belligerently. "Did you dump her?"

"No, we just had a talk."

"Seems to me there's been a lot of fucking conferences going on around here lately. You plotting something I'm not allowed in on?"

The tones were harsh and challenging and Joel cringed. "I have to lay down, Alix."

"I want to do this now. If you have something to say to me, I have a right to hear it."

"You will, but not now, girl. I really don't feel up to it."

Her anger dissolved suddenly as she saw the strain in his face. This was another wall she couldn't get by. How could she force Joel's hand when he looked so defeated? "I'm sorry but you know how I hate secrets."

"Especially when you're not in on them."

"You need anything?"

"No, I'll be all right." He turned towards the stairs. "We'll talk later."

As promised, he sat her down that afternoon. "I've watched you clamping your mouth shut and I can see the thought go through your head before you stifle it. This Miss Cheerful stuff is driving both of us nuts. Who read you the riot act?"

"No one."

"Come on, no bullshit."

Her mouth thinned. "Leo."

"I thought so. It's what him and Ash were taught for counselling." He took a deep breath and plunged in. "Look, I've had time to think this out from all angles. I'm only going to say it once and I don't want any interruptions till I'm done.

"I'm going to die." She was about to protest but he leaned over and gently touched her mouth. "AIDS is a disease with a fatality rate of one hundred percent. I'm feeling good now but let's face it, even with highs and lows I'm on a downslide so let's not dance around. I may be dead next month or next year so I need every day to count. Above all, I need honesty between us, like always. If you got something on your mind then say it. If I can't deal I'll let you know and you can tell me when I can. There's been too much between us for you to start censoring your thoughts and feelings and emotions.

"You're mad at me sometimes; I can see that. I can also see when you've been to the ocean crying 'cos you come back with red eyes and this sad, lost look on your face. It's all right to let me know. No more secrets, 'kay?"

She nodded. "Can I talk now?"

"Yeah."

"How long have you been thinking about dying?"

"Since I got the first results in England. I had my share of luck, girl, and it ran out. I took some incredibly stupid chances over the years. You play Russian roulette long enough you lose. I went through all those stages I read about: shock, depression, anger, acceptance, plus a few more."

"When did you accept?"

"On the last tour when I knew I was getting worse."

"How the hell can you be so calm?"

"The doc warned me useless emotion won't do any good. It just burns my strength. I can't make this disease go away, but I can use my energy to stay well and carry on and that's what I'm trying to do. Getting mad is pointless."

"You can't tell me you don't react."

"Sure I do. Good thing the basement is soundproof. Some days I go down there just to yell, scream and throw tantrums. Last week I put a crack in one of my guitars banging it against the wall." He grinned. "Put a hole in the wall too. Good thing I own the joint."

"You idiot." She reached over to hug him. "I love you and I'm behind you one hundred percent. You need anything, you tell me."

He squeezed her tightly. "I'll hold you to that."

"But sometimes I need help. Can I get mad?"

"Yeah, but I can too." He paused. "The end is going to be sticky."

"We'll handle it together." She held out her hand. "Pact?"

"Pact." They shook on it.

"I think of us as living in alien land now. Is that bad?"

He smiled, understanding immediately. "It sounds right to me. You here for good or just visiting?"

"I moved in lock, stock and barrel when you did and I'm not going anywhere. What about Sherri? She just visiting?"

"For now. Does that make a difference?"

"No. Will she be around?"

"For a while. Our relationship in the sack is finished as far as sex goes – only sleeping is fine for now but I don't think that'll last long. She's spooked and I don't blame her."

"You think she'll make it to the end?"

"To be honest, no. But if she doesn't no blame, Alix. No guilt trips or anything else. She's doing the best she can and let's face it – she got a raw deal. She told me she's wanted to be with me for years. Well she waited long enough and she's had piss all time to enjoy it.

"There's something else. By now you know what the conferences were about but there was another thing we took care of. Brad has agreed to rebook the studio so we can do the last album of our contract. A lot of the songs are written but they need work. We're rehearsing downstairs. Everyone's agreed. You in?"

"I'm surprised you'd even ask."

"Just a formality, girl; I know you're chomping at the bit. I heard you working on something new late last night in your room."

"You've been doing some solitary basement time yourself. Don't try to tell me you haven't been doing the same damn thing."

"Guilty."

She looked at him searchingly. "Why did you leave me till last, Joel? For the talks I mean."

He kissed her. "'Cos you are the most important. Don't ever forget that."

CHAPTER 26

Things settled into a sorely missed routine after that. All the members of the Blue Mask had been feeling unattached to anything concrete during their enforced two month break. They were used to hard work and creative activity and though composing and working on songs was far from glamourous, it was one of the bedrocks of their careers. The concerts were a high, a reward for the mundane, slogging work and yet it was that same work that fulfilled them. There had been a feeling that, with Joel ill, even that would be gone. This reprieve was a gift.

The first couple of days were tentative. Joel dealt the best he could with the anxious glances that were turned on him. He flubbed his solo and looked up in frustration only to find Dixie chewing worriedly on her bottom lip.

"Kay, that's it. Break time," he hollered. The sound died down. "I catch you bums again and I'm not going to say anything - I'll just haul off and belt you. This is the last warning."

"What," Alix asked, a guilty flush staining her cheeks.

"Precisely," he replied. "I'm fine. I've made mistakes before on solos and it hasn't killed me so you can bet it isn't going to now. When I'm tired, I'll lay down. We won't get anything done if you don't concentrate." He turned to

Dixie. "And if you don't stop having lunch on that lip there isn't going to be any left for the poor sap you're dating right now to kiss."

Without thinking, she tossed a tape at him.

"That's more like it. Now, let's get back to work so we have something to take into the studio next week. I want to be at least halfway through by the end of August."

Joel spent a couple of hours with Alix in the basement each morning. The two had put together a surprising number of songs since his hospitalization. They hadn't had the luxury of this amount of time to collaborate since their early days together and, as usual, they worked quickly. Then came a break for lunch. Meals were still important, despite the fact that he had regained the lost weight, and both approached them with satisfaction. It was a time for discussion and planning and they found a new appreciation for a habit that had previously been a chore necessary for recharging. With staying in and not indulging in the string of bars and clubs that had been their passion before the fan harassment started, both developed an interest in films. Their living room became a hub for friends and there was a comfort and cosiness sitting around as summer passed and the nights grew colder.

Joel had a rest after lunch and the afternoon saw the arrival of the other band members. The work was concentrated as the new album began to take shape. Alix and Dixie were also writing together again. As the songs fleshed out all felt the familiar stir of excitement.

Bear sat back at the end of one session, laughing and uncapping a beer. "It's a good thing we're going into the studio Monday. We got enough material here for two goddamn albums."

"I think we should record it all," Dixie said, "then sift it like we always do. But Bear's right. Brad and Jack are going to be shocked when they see what we've been up to. This disc is going to get down in record time."

"You know, I wish I hadn't been so stubborn when Ash first suggested I buy a house," Joel said. "This set-up is working better than even I thought it would. Think of all the time we could've saved messing around in here instead of the studio." He grinned wickedly, leering. "I could've had me a whole lot more senoritas."

"You've had enough to reset world records, Mr. Hormone," Dixie retaliated, starting an argument that had gone on for years.

"You're just jealous," he retorted smugly. "I'm the one with the stud rep."

"Somebody save me."

"That's enough, you two," Leo said firmly, putting his bass down. "I think we're pretty well done for the day. Anyone interested in heading to the Alley View for a drink or a dozen?"

A chorus of yeas greeted him. Joel put his guitar aside. "You going to be there a while, pal?"

"Sure, why?"

"I think I'll lay down for an hour or so before I wander over. Sometimes I feel like an old man – all these naps and crap."

He looked drawn and tired. Alix put her guitar away and walked over to sit beside him. "You all right?"

"Course I am, girl; I'm just not used to hard work. I'll be there in a while. Later."

The four watched him go in silence. "Sometimes he seems so normal," Dixie said quietly, "and I forget. Then he gets that strain on his face and has to go rest and the whole nightmare comes home."

"We're lucky with what we've got now," Alix pointed out. "A few years ago we wouldn't have this much."

"I know. Once in a while it just hits me bad."

"We all feel that way," Leo assured her, "but Alix is right. We have to take what we're given and we're lucky right now. Buck up, Dix; it isn't the end of the world."

"And you're glad I didn't say this in front of him."

"Yes but he'd shoot me for saying so. I have to admit though; he's fighting better than I would've guessed. He's really positive."

"I know it sounds crazy," Alix said, "but he seems to have found a new lease on life."

"He's still secretive. Ash wants him to go down to the Centre and get into the counselling sessions but he won't budge. He doesn't want anyone to know."

"That's his choice. Ash should know better than to pester him."

"I'll talk to him." Leo walked over and put his arm around her. "Come on, let's go have some beers."

Bear shouldered him out of the way and scooped her up, depositing her across his shoulders like a sack of grain. He took Dixie and Leo by the hand and hauled them up the stairs, ignoring Alix's squeals. "I've heard enough discussion from you bunch. I'm thirsty and I'm doing something about it."

They piled into his van and drove to the Alley View. As promised, Joel joined them a couple of hours later, looking much better after his rest.

The group didn't stay long at the club. As happened when they so infrequently got together, people interrupted their fun. An additional problem had cropped up, as Brad told them on a bright August morning, their first day back in the studio in almost ten months.

"I gotta hassle you hombres right away. I'm getting a lot of calls and questions about why the Mask ain't on a European tour. It's been a stretch since you and Dixie were in sick bay, Durango" – this with a nod to Joel – "and nobody's yakking about it. We got to hold a press confab or something. Any bright ideas?"

Jack had left the sound booth and the group was alone. "What do you suggest?"

"I say we get a conference room and invite 'em all over to fire away. You get a story going you agree on and let them get it outa their systems."

"That's a good idea," Alix said.

"Course, babe, you oughta know by now I have only the best."

"And you're modest with it too," Dixie commented.

"You want my kick on this, I think you should stick to what you said before. You need a year off. And I'd add that you been working on new angles. It'd sell, hombres. Your last disc was a lot richer and more complex. This one heading down the same trail?"

"Yep," Joel said. "You know, that would work. It wouldn't be an outright lie and it sounds reasonable."

"Want me to arrange it?"

"Sure, go ahead."

"I'll dial you when it's a done deal." With a wave of his hand he headed out the door.

Joel spent mornings at home and afternoons at the studio. If Jack had any suspicions about the early day absences he kept them to himself. The others assembled on time to work on individual parts and harmonies and when Joel arrived, he was note perfect and in need of very little rehearsal or retaping. His work had become more concentrated, honed to a keen degree as he harboured his energy and released it to its best advantage. Halfway through the scheduled session most of the tracks were recorded.

When Jack came down with food poisoning, the Blue Mask elected to take a few days off to wait for his recovery rather than push on.

Robin took the opportunity to work in the first video shoot for the new album. Joel and Alix had done the storyboard. The Alley View was again engaged and Robin raided the theatrical costumers. The title track, 'Mad as a Hatter,' was like many of the songs that the pair had written lately: light and full of fun. It offset the brooding pieces that darker moments inspired and also reflected Joel's offbeat approach to his own life. Typically, the video had their twisted sense of humour.

The band came out in full make-up and costumes that morning howling with laughter. Bear was again the brunt of the jokes but it had become a tradition to lumber him with roles he didn't want and it was a mark of their affection. He'd be hurt if he wasn't cast as the comic.

The stage was tuned into Alice in Wonderland's tea party. Alix donned the host role as the Mad Hatter, Joel the March Hare, Leo the Cheshire Cat, Dixie the Door Mouse and Bear, grumbling, was Alice, complete with a fright wig of tumbling blonde curls. Work was regularly interrupted and Robin pleaded with them to try to get a grip on themselves so that they could wrap everything up by the next day. When the band got to the press room Brad had arranged, the mood of lighthearted banter carried with them. The conference was fun and breezy and all questions were answered with a minimum of fuss. No notice was taken of little inconsistencies; the explanations were accepted.

Joel had rested that afternoon and looked healthy and much like his old self. The members of the press remarked that all of them looked better for their time off. The last tour had revealed five haggard faces at interviews and photo shoots.

The manic energy subsided as Alix and Joel drove home later and she dropped into depression.

"What's up, girl? You got awful quiet awful fast."

"Everything went well, didn't it?"

"Like a clock."

"They bought that lark about postponing the European tour for a while."

"An indefinite while."

"It all seemed so normal."

"It was." His heart sunk. He knew what was coming.

"Oh, Joel," she cried, her voice thick, "I wish it was all the way it used to be." The tears fell and she struggled to get control of herself. "I'm sorry."

"No need to be," he replied, swallowing the lump of misery that had risen in him. "It's all right - go ahead and cry. I wish it could be that way too but it can't. We're in alien land, remember?"

'Yeah," she whispered. "At least we're together, right?"

He squeezed her hand. "Right." He dropped her off at the front door. "Go order us a big pizza and light the fire. Fuck summer heat."

"Where are you going?"

"To get a video."

The two settled in and the misery burned off as they watched a comedy he had purposely picked out. By the time they went to bed, equilibrium was restored.

CHAPTER 27

The band returned the next day to finish the video shoot, still erupting with laughter at Bear. Robin pushed them on; despite the goofing off work was completed. Word came through that Jack would be back by the following Monday. Everyone relaxed for the remainder of the week, visiting with each other and immensely enjoying the unexpected break.

Near the end of the weekend a call came through summoning Joel to the clinic immediately. He drove over, turning down Alix's plea to go with him. She was waiting when he returned.

"What," she asked quietly once he'd settled beside her on the couch.

He took her hand. "No need for alarm, girl. The doc warned us about AZT, remember? It causes bone marrow suppression. He put me on a low dose and he's been monitoring my white blood counts every few days to keep ahead. Well, the counts are down so I have to go off it for a while to give them a chance to rise. He said there was a drug I could take to offset the bone marrow suppression but I don't want any more damn drugs. I don't feel too bad and there's already a drugstore in the bathroom cabinet.

Eventually we'll have to go to transfusions, but that's in the future for now."

"Are you sure you shouldn't take those other pills?"

He shrugged. "I got a 'script anyway. I might as well get Ash to pick it up. I'll probably change my mind; I'm worse that a woman lately."

She let the barb slide past her. Normally he said these things to rile her, to veer away from whatever discussion he didn't want to continue, but it had no effect this time. "How long are you off AZT?"

"A few days. Until then, I have to be careful. I'm in a good position for opportunistic infections to set in. It's the white blood cells that fight them. I'll lay low for a while, record my stuff here and you can take it to the studio." In a sudden, frustrated rage, he knocked the coffee table over. "Dammit, Alix, it's not fair! I feel fine but I have to be extra careful 'cos I can't really fight anything that comes my way. I want to go to work. I don't want to stay home hiding from germs I can't even see!"

She reached over to squeeze his arm, then slowly righted the table. When she turned back it was to find that Joel's rage had given way to sorrow.

He brushed impatiently at the tears. "I don't want to die."

Gently, she pulled him to his feet and hugged him. "I'm here and we're going to fight until we beat this. Come on, I think a rest will do you some good."

Upstairs, he stripped down to his underwear and crawled into bed. Alix got in beside him, holding him until he fell asleep. She curled up against his warmth, listening to the steady sound of his breathing and then got up to phone Ash.

Joel didn't want any hint of suspicion to touch him so Ash had been picking up his prescriptions, a job he often did for other people at the Centre. She was waiting when he got back, a glass of Scotch and two bottles of beer in front of her. Ash handed over the medication and sat down at the kitchen table, opening a beer.

"Is this bad?"

"No. Dr. Marlowe wouldn't lead Joel down any garden path. He's in the early stages here. The AZT interruption is common, believe me. He just has to take it easy until his blood counts go up and then he's back in battle."

"It drives me crazy sometimes – he looks so good."

"Yeah, well that's a plus, isn't it? You wouldn't want him looking like shit."

"Course not. How long?"

"Probably a week or so." Ash took a long gulp from the bottle. "He's probably not going to feel too washed out or anything so see if you can keep away from the studio. He's got to be real careful for a few days."

"He said as much. Don't worry, he won't do anything stupid. He's a lot more patient than he used to be and he's scared. He'll follow Dr. Marlowe's directions."

"Good. You going to let the band know?"

"I'll phone them tonight. Joel said something about having a tape ready for Jack and it was already squared. I'm not sure what he meant."

Ash was but it was Joel's secret and he would tell her himself when the time was right. "I'd better shift," he said, finishing his beer. "I've got a lot to do before I fly to London at the end of the week."

"That's kind of sudden, isn't it?"

A big smile split his handsome face. "Not really. Morris got me a couple of contracts for album covers for two other bands and I'm going to deliver my smart designs in person."

"Would that be good business or just an excuse to see Morris?"

"If I said good business, would you believe me?"

"Not a chance," she responded, laughing. "Give our love to Roger and the lady Eleanor."

"I will." He rose, pulling her up with him so that he could hug her. "You take care of our pal. And of yourself too. I'll arrange with Robin to pick up any medicine you might need. She does that at the Centre too. I think it's best if you don't go yourself for the same reason Joel shouldn't."

"Thanks, Ash. I don't like this secrecy sometimes but I think I'd hate the publicity more."

"Who wouldn't?" He released her and headed for the door.

She made calls and everyone agreed that Joel was busy with a project at home. Early the next morning she collected the tape and went to work, leaving him in the basement.

Jack accepted the explanation without question. "Ah, the infamous magnum opus."

Alix stared back, puzzled. "You know about this?"

"The secret project? Sure. Joel told me about it ages ago."

She lit a cigarette and sat down beside him at the mixing board. "No kidding. I just found out."

"He had to bring me into it but I promised to keep quiet."

"I don't get it."

"Joel came to me one day and asked a lot of technical questions about equipment, recording and sound. He told me he wanted to work on solo material. When he acquired the house I advised him on what he needed and he brought in test tapes until he got the quality right. You and Dixie and Leo do vocals and back-ups and we don't need him here for that. This way he can spend his free time productively."

He touched her arm as he saw her frown. "It has nothing personally to do with the band. He's not leaving or anything. He just wants to explore his own trails. He warned me I might not hear the whole thing. He's still experimenting and not sure this will be commercially viable but he wants it done in case he can use it in the future."

"I'll just bet he does. Thanks, Jack. I'd better get down to work."

A lot of things started to make sense. Alix had always known Joel to go off by himself to work on guitar intricacies but his frequent retreats into the basement, coupled with the amount of tape she had seen filed away in a new cabinet near his work desk, were now clear. The little monster was stockpiling! She grinned in spite of herself. Devious was the only word for him.

She arrived home later that afternoon and found him in the basement. He put his guitar aside, switched off the power on one of the recording consoles and went over to the fridge to get her a beer and him a juice.

"Hard day at the office, honey?"

"Have you been down here all day?"

"Nope. I've had lots of rest, lots to eat and I've taken my vitamins. Do I get a reward?"

Alix strolled over to the open cabinet. "I've been meaning to ask about these tapes. They look just like the one I gave Jack this morning."

The lop-sided grin appeared and the sea green eyes sparkled with mischief. "He told you, huh?"

"He told me what he thinks we both know but we're talking about something very different, aren't we?"

"Maybe."

"Don't be coy."

"I wanted some info out of Jack so I lied a little."

"Why not tell me?"

"I didn't think you could take it at the time. Recording everything I can now so there's something left for the band after I'm dead is a bit bald even for you, Alix. Could I have told you that a few weeks ago?"

"I guess not. How long have you been doing this?"

"Since I got out of the hospital."

"There's a fair amount of material here."

Joel went over to his desk and opened the deep bottom drawer. There were more tapes.

She looked at him in shock. "When the hell did you find the time?"

"I'm pretty organized and I've been down here a lot."

"I guess I didn't realize how much. You are one devious bastard, Stark."

"Leo called me that too. And you have to admit, I'm clever as well. Jack doesn't suspect a thing."

"Is this healthy?"

"What, preparing for the end? I sure as hell think so. At least I'm doing something constructive. Don't worry, I ran it by the doc and got full marks for originality."

"I'm glad about that." She lit a cigarette. "Sherri coming over tonight?"

"No. I called her to let her know what's going on so we'll just talk on the phone until I'm back on my elixir."

"She hasn't been around much. Everything all right?"

"She needs time away when it gets too much for her. She hasn't been through the wars like me and you. She's just visiting alien land, remember?"

"Is it over between you two?"

"I wonder if it ever got a chance to really start. I told her I didn't mind if she saw other guys and she started to cry 'cos she thought I was dumping her." He shook his head in amazement. "I was trying to let her off the hook. She made me feel guilty; said she'd try to be better and spend more time with me."

"Poor Joel. Your good intentions get misread as your typical pig ones. Well that's what you get when you work most of your life for a bad reputation."

He grinned. "At least I'm trying. Think I'll make sainthood?"

Alix stood up. "Not a chance. I'm going upstairs to start dinner. You coming?"

"Yeah, I'll just shut everything down here first."

"You and your tapes." She laughed. "Will there ever be a time when you cease to amaze me, Mr. Stark?"

"Hope not." The smile stayed in place until she was out of sight. The truth was that he found the guitar sessions both fulfilling and daunting. Each tape carried its own pain and a reminder that the clock was running down. He worked steadily and would do so as long as the creative juices flowed – and flowing they were. Nothing like oncoming death to stir up ideas. But he wanted to leave something of himself behind, for his own sake as well as theirs.

Sherri was another matter. He'd wanted to give her a way out but had also been trying to get clarification as to where things stood between them. She wasn't close enough to be an intimate friend – they hadn't known each other that long – and yet she was no longer a girlfriend in any real sense of the word. She was less equipped to handle the situation than his friends. Her sympathy became pity in unguarded moments and her fears exhausted him, but he didn't have the guts to cut her off completely, this last reminder of the man he had been. Not that he believed all the press had written about his macho stud status but it was comforting to have some version of his salad days, like a scrapbook he could go through when older. "I'm not going to get older though," he said softly. He threw the power switches on his equipment and packed his guitar away.

He fought to calm himself, knowing this anger wasn't healthy. It led to self-pity and 'Why me?' and that was a road he was loathe to go too far down. He was trying hard to come to terms with having AIDS. If his friends thought it was no picnic for them they should spend a day inside his head. He seesawed constantly, from a nightmare of fear to a lifetime of regret to a sunny thankfulness for small things. He was starting to see trees instead of forests and as his scope narrowed his pleasure grew at the trivial details in a way he had never experienced before.

He put Alix's empty bottle in one of the cases near the fridge and went upstairs.

The two ate a quiet meal in front of the television. There'd been phone calls from friends but no one dropped by and the lingering loneliness of the morning had dogged him all day. Alix was in her room getting ready for bed when he knocked on the door. Her smile wavered at the look on his face. "What's wrong?"

"I..." He shook his head, struggling to find the right words. "Alix, will you sleep with me tonight?"

"What?"

"Not sex," he said awkwardly, "just sleep. I just can't face being by myself. I need a friend."

She hugged him. "Of course. Let me finish here and I'll be right in."

"I don't want to make you uncomfortable. If you'd rather not..."

"I know what it took you to ask and I'm not uncomfortable. I want to. Honest."

The light was off and he was in bed when she joined him. He turned to her. "Thanks."

She snuggled up against him. "Shut up. It does me good too. You think you're the only one who gets lonely?"

He laughed softly, relaxing. "Touché." But he was glad he'd found the courage to ask. It had been a test, though he hadn't known it until he realized how much was hanging on her answer. Ash often talked of people who were afraid of close proximity to AIDS patients because they knew so little about the disease. He occasionally experienced this with Sherri but Alix had shown no fear and he needed to know that her support was all encompassing.

The dragon side of his emotions retreated back into their cave and he settled down to let the healing sleep overtake him. There would be no nightmares tonight.

CHAPTER 28

Autumn 1993

By the end of the week Joel was back on AZT. He swallowed his pills, rested a day and then headed back to join the working world. The band happily welcomed him back into the fold. Jack took him aside with a wink and asked how the work was going.

"Fine."

"The tapes you sent along were perfect."

"How we coming on the tracks?"

"We're close to wrap up and so far ahead of schedule Mr. Davis ought to give us all a fat bonus."

"No protest from me, Jack. A bonus sounds great."

"Let's get this in the can before we get too cocky."

Down in the studio he signalled for attention. "Seeing as we're ahead, I'd like to work on a new song – well, not really new 'cos I wrote it while I was in the hospital and thinking of nicer things." He looked at Alix. "You ready, girl?" She nodded.

He started with a series of upbeat, flamenco-type pulses that stirred the blood, then drew back to a cheeky up-tempo back beat. Alix danced around him crooning out the words he had played with in those first days after

PCP had set in. He had been dreaming of their holiday in Mexico. The end result was a light comic chant that Alix giggled at when he played it for her. They decided it was a suitable partner to 'Mad as a Hatter' and resolved to play it for the other band members when the album was almost complete. That was a time when they always did light songs. It somehow seemed easier - a nice diversion when everyone was tired of spending hours in the filtered, recirculated air.

The song was called 'Get a Suntan on the Yucatan' and the two had already worked up a storyboard for the video. By the end the rest of the group were in stitches.

Bear wiped his eyes. "I got the perfect costume for you. We paint you up as a sun-darkened gringo, complete with poncho and sombrero and make you dance in the sand. It's your turn to be the village idiot!"

That brought fresh laughs and it was some time before they settled down to work out the rest of the song. Joel left to go home and when he returned the next afternoon, most of the details were ironed out so recording went swiftly.

Joel's other friends avoided disturbing him during recording but by mid-September, with work completed, they began dropping by the house again. There were a few bands still together that had gotten their start at the same time as the Blue Mask and most of them had kept in touch in a haphazard way over the years. The jam sessions and talks over drinks, though infrequent, were still an ongoing thing. He enjoyed playing with other guitarists. No one was allowed to know the truth about his illness and the visitors accepted that with the added fame he was finding it harder to go out in public undisturbed. If any had questions about this retreat, they kept them to themselves.

Amid the flurry of visitations and jamming, Alix tried to make sure Joel got enough rest, took over when he had to go lie down, and kept him regularly fed. Sherri was over occasionally, mostly to provide cover. A lot of these acquaintances knew her by sight and were good about making themselves scarce when she put in an appearance and Joel broadly hinted that he had things to do. It was a farce that made Alix want to cry sometimes and laugh at others. There was an unreality about this double life they all lead, knowing that Joel was fatally ill and acting like things were chugging along at a normal pace.

Sherri was increasingly absent for longer periods. Alix pulled her aside on day. Joel was taking one of his power naps so that he had the energy for a dinner Dixie planned for that evening.

"Are you all right? Is there anything I can do?"

The tears fell and she wiped at them impatiently. "I'm not good at this, Alix. I see him feeling sick or touch him and he's feverish again and he just seems fragile sometimes. I want so much, for him and me, but I can't tell him that. It's like there's a wall between us."

"Are you the one putting it there?"

"Probably. I know he watches what he says to me and I'm glad. Some of the jokes he makes –I can't laugh at them. It doesn't help if I'm crying when I'm around but I can't always stop. I don't know how to behave."

"Joel makes jokes 'cos it's his way of coping. I know they're pretty morbid but that's his sense of humour. He's been like that since I've known him."

"It doesn't bother you?"

"Sometimes I'm as warped as he is. It's one of the things we have in common."

The ghost of a smile flickered and was gone. "I know I haven't been around much but I'm having a difficult time.

I have to get away when it comes too close. I don't know if I'm going to be of any use when..."

"He understands."

"How does he know?"

"He sees more than you think."

"I wish it could have been different. I've wanted him a long time. I've been half in love with him since I first saw the band together, when Mark was still alive. But Elaine was in the picture and he took drugs and I couldn't seem to find a way to get close. When this started between us I was so happy. It sure didn't last long."

"I'm sorry too, for all our sakes. But there's no use cursing fate. There's nothing we can do except be together."

"I'll be back tomorrow. Thanks for the ear."

"Anytime. Sherri, you haven't told anyone, have you?"

"No but it's hard. Sometimes I need someone to share the misery with."

"Then share it with me."

Joel got up for Dixie's party and the two set off in good spirits but, as the evening progressed, he grew very quiet, picking at his food and excusing himself from the table. Alix followed him to the bathroom the second time, concerned. She heard him retching and was waiting when he came out.

"Why didn't you tell me you weren't feeling well?"

"It's just a bug. I figured I could work around it."

She put a hand to his forehead. "You've got a fever. We'd better go home."

His face fell. "I'm sorry, girl. I tried but I'm not up to this. You stay and enjoy yourself. I'll be all right; I just need some sleep."

"You're stuck with me. How can you expect me to have any fun without my partner in crime to help shit-disturb?"

The answering grin was weak but firmly in place. "That's true. 'Kay, you can come along. Just don't make a pass. I'm not in the mood."

"In your dreams, pal."

"You did once," he teased. "You just won't admit it."

"I was sleeping."

"Yeah but you still made a pass and it still counts."

"Don't tell anyone. You'll ruin my reputation. They all think I'm cold and aloof."

He rolled his eyes. "Little do they know." He took her arm. "Thanks. Cards on the table, I didn't want to go home on my own. I feel like shit."

Dixie and the others were not surprised by the announcement. She cleared the dishes and served coffee and liqueurs but no one seemed inclined to linger and soon the rest of the gang went home as well. She went to bed in tears. Joel seemed fine and then something like this would happen; something small and nondescript. It didn't take much to put any of them off balance these days, despite their quick efforts to recover and get on with things.

Joel stripped down and got into bed. Alix brought him some juice and sat on the side of the bed. "Should I call Dr. Marlowe?"

"I'm fine," he replied, exasperation creeping in. "I can't be right and then wrong suddenly."

"Do you mind if I at least check up on you?"

"No."

"Here, take these aspirins. Dr. Marlowe said they'll bring your fever down. He recommended them specifically."

"He had to. The only pills we knew how to buy were little white ones that kept us up for days."

"And we don't even know where to get them anymore."

He laughed. "I sure could use some once in a while. It drives me nuts when I don't have the energy to keep going flat out."

"I feel like that too. But at least we're into good health habits now. You know, not burning the candle at both ends."

"Yeah, well my candle sometimes doesn't even burn at one end."

"That's disgusting."

"Get your mind out of the gutter, girl."

"Sorry. And you did warn me not to make a pass."

"Goodnight, Alix."

She kissed him, turned out the light and left the room to go downstairs. Turning on the TV she poured a Scotch and flicked through the channels but there was nothing interesting on. Settling for silence, she sipped her drink and tried to steer around the depression that often crept in at this time of night. Tired, she shut out the lights and climbed the stairs. When she checked Joel was bathed in sweat. The fever had broken.

He woke up enough to let her change the sheets and wipe a damp cloth over his chest and back, sighing with pleasure at the coolness of the material against his skin. "Thanks," he said, giving her a brief kiss and burrowing in.

Feeling lost, she took her clothes off and slid in beside him, curling up against him for comfort. "Do you mind?"

"Nope."

Companionably, the two drifted off to sleep.

CHAPTER 29

Neither of them heard Sherri the next morning until she walked into the room and woke them with a loud gasp of surprise. As she turned to leave, Alix struggled up. "Wait, please. It really isn't what it looks like."

She came slowly back into the room. Alix sat up, reached for her shirt and put it on. "We do this every once in a while when we need company. It's just comfort."

"And I'm not here to give it. Is that what you mean?"

"No, girl," Joel cut in. "We've done this occasionally over the years."

She sat down on the edge of the bed, flushing guiltily. "You make me feel ashamed, both of you. I should be here. That's part of what you sign on for when you become someone's girlfriend - the good or bad times."

"I never asked for that."

Alix shifted awkwardly. "I'll go make us some coffee."

"No," Sherri said quickly, "I want you here. You see, Joel, I came to apologize for a number of things. One is for not being around much. But you haven't seemed to need me except for cover. You've been busy working or with your friends or resting and I'm in the way. I know it's selfish, considering what's going on, but I need more than that. I feel like a fifth wheel most of the time."

"I think I should leave," Alix blurted out, very uncomfortable.

"No. Joel, I think we should put an end to this relationship the way it is. I could cope with us better as friends. The way things stand, it hurts now."

"And you need time in bed, which I can't give you. I decided to tell you pretty much the same thing. I want you to see other men. You need to be held and seen to and I won't do it. I refuse to put anyone in that position. It's too dangerous, even with precautions. That's why we haven't made it since my stay in hospital. I know you were willing to try but I wasn't. HIV is one thing; AIDS is another. To me anyway." He shook his head in frustration. "I'm saying this all wrong. Promise me one thing though. When the next guy comes along, tell me. We're still friends, right?"

"I want that more than anything." She turned to Alix. "I wanted you to hear this because I didn't want you to see me with someone else and not understand why. I think of you as a friend."

"I get it. Now can I go make coffee? You two have stuff to say to each other." She swung out of bed, pulled on her jeans and darted quickly downstairs.

Joel was laughing. "Alix hates shit like this. Did you see her squirming?"

"Are you sure you're all right with this? Can I still come round?"

"Course you can. I'd miss you if you didn't."

"Me too," she whispered.

"Come here," he said, gathering her against him, letting her cry for what could not be. He swallowed hard. He wished he was better at letting misery out like this but mostly he did his crying alone late at night when no one could hear him. Some nights he didn't think the tears would ever stop.

Sherri pushed herself away eventually. Alix arrived tentatively with a carafe and cups on a tray. He patted the other side of the bed and she sat down.

"Everything's worked out; you can relax."

"Sorry but you know I'm no good at this emotion stuff, especially if it's someone else's emotion."

"You just felt left out 'cos you were the third and that made you the crowd."

"Shut up or I'll put salt in your coffee."

Sherri cleared her throat. "I just want to warn you. Hal Mason, Silver Bird's bass player, has been chasing me for the last few weeks. I'm going to go out with him next time he asks. He's sweet and fun and I like him but I was staying away for you, Joel."

"What a slime ball," he joked.

"It was never like that, not with him. Others though, you wouldn't believe it. I became a hot commodity when we got together. I got a lot of unasked for attention because I was Joel Stark's woman."

"Typical male territory challenge," Alix said. "Makes you sick, doesn't it?"

Joel was laughing. "I had no idea I was so popular."

"It's that fearsome reputation you've been working on for years."

"Yeah, well I'd still like to keep that piece of fiction up." He glanced at Sherri. "You won't spill my secret in the heat of passion, will you?"

"How dare you even ask?"

"Look, let's be honest. You're a very physical lady, as I've had the entirely enjoyable pleasure of discovering, so let's assume you're going to end up in the sack with Mason. Is that far wrong?"

"I do need sex, I admit it, but if you think I'm going to tell..."

"I think," he cut in, "that it could come out post-coital, when secrets often get spilled."

"You don't pull any punches do you?"

"No. Look, people are eventually going to figure out what's wrong with me but I'd rather wait till it's obvious if you don't mind."

She heard the underlying plea and brightened as a solution occurred to her. "I'll say that you dumped me after I got mad for catching you in bed with another woman. I did, after all, just catch you in bed with Alix."

"Don't bring me into it. I'll never get any peace," Alix said. "I'm the mystery, remember? I sure as hell don't want anyone thinking I've been having it off with Joel over the years."

"Wouldn't be far from the truth," he muttered.

She hit him.

Sherri watched them, the question again rising in her mind. So far she'd never had the courage to ask.

"This is going to leak to the press at some stage of the game. You know how they love to follow your conquests and we've kept that rolling all along."

"I won't say who it was," Sherri said. "That should solve everything perfectly. Joel keeps his reputation, the secret stays secret and it's a good reason why, after putting up with absences and work and everything else, I finally had enough."

"It fits the bill."

"Then that's what we'll do." Her words came true at the end of the week when she was reported out with the bassist. Interest in the now reclusive band, always simmering, erupted, along with questions as to why they weren't touring and why they were no longer seen closing down bars in the wee hours of the morning.

Sherri left shortly afterwards. Joel saw her out and came back into the kitchen where Alix was scrambling eggs. "I'm glad we got this worked out. I didn't have it in me to keep that thread active. I hope she's all right."

"You sound pretty happy."

"It's a relief, like a weight's been lifted. She's right though – it will get out. We both know what'll happen then. More speculation and more camouflage."

"The one thing she did was cut down the groupie pursuit."

"Don't think it hasn't crossed my mind. Shit, now they'll be knocking the door down again, looking to be my next lay. What the fuck have things come to? I can't be anybody's next lay! I'm beginning to feel like they just want me as another notch on their bedposts. They drove me nuts when we were in the studio, hanging around like sex-starved vultures."

"Serves you right," she countered, laughing. "For years that's all they were to you – notches."

"You're all heart, girl, you know that? And it's as black as your hair."

The phone rang and he went into the living room to answer it. He was gone quite a while and then she heard the receiver slammed down hard. He strode into the room, furious.

"Is Ash back from England?"

"What's wrong?"

"He's been telling tales."

"He wouldn't."

"He sure as hell would. That was Eleanor on the phone and she knows. Who else would she get it from?"

"What did she say?"

"Nothing outright. But she phones out of the blue, tells me she's coming over again on her next batch of holidays 'cos she had so much fun last time and then starts bawling. You got any other explanation? Where is he?"

"He flew in last night. He called but you were asleep and I didn't want to wake you."

"Why didn't you tell me this morning?"

"I haven't had a chance."

He didn't respond to the grin. "Will you phone him and ask him to come over right away? I need a chance to calm down. If I talk to him now, I'll hit him when he gets here." His face was grim. "Shit, I bet Rog knows. I want to tell people when I'm ready to. How dare he take that choice away!"

"You're jumping to conclusions."

"Eleanor, Roger and Morris are close. They have been for years. Shit, Eleanor is the godmother to Roger's daughter. You don't think she'll spill it to him?"

Her heart sank. Ash was one of Joel's oldest and closest friends and he needed him more now than ever. Though he refused to widen the circle of people who knew he had AIDS he relied heavily on those who did. Shutting Ash out would be cutting off someone that gave him the sane comfort he needed.

"I'll call but you calm down. This won't do anybody any good."

He started up the stairs, not answering.

"What about breakfast?"

"Fuck breakfast."

She heard the bedroom door slam and reached for the phone. Whatever the reason, Ash, she thought sadly, it had better be good.

CHAPTER 30

Joel sat in the living room, withdrawn and seething, his expression icy. The one thing he could not take right now was Eleanor coming over on a mercy mission to say good-bye. The only thing that could be worse was Roger coming too. And Ash, with a slip of the tongue, had started the whole ball rolling.

Alix came into the room, Ash behind her. He took a chair opposite his friend but couldn't meet the cold green eyes. A guilty flush stained his face and he stared resolutely at the floor.

"How the fuck could you? Eleanor was blubbering like a baby."

"I'm sorry," Ash whispered. "I couldn't help it."

"You couldn't help it? What the fuck kind of explanation is that?"

Ash's eyes met his friend's, pleading. "I can't tell you not to die. It's not fair. I've tried to support in every way I can but I have my own misery to face too and sometimes I need to talk. You've got Alix."

"What about Robin? Why the hell didn't you pick someone who already knew?"

"Robin 's away from me now busy playing house with Brad. My friend is Morris and we're in touch all the time. He's my outlet when things get crazy."

"Wasn't there anyone else?"

His eyes filled with tears. "We got drunk one night. Morris had just come from the funeral of one of his best friends and he was a mess. We talked, cried a lot and I spilled my guts. I knew he would understand. I swore him to secrecy but he said he'd have to tell Eleanor. She knew about you being HIV positive. He promised she'd keep it to herself, but she knows how close you and Roger are and he's no stranger to his friends getting AIDS either. Don't forget, he was close to Freddie Mercury. He helped his friend, kept his secret and had to watch him die. Believe me, it won't go any further."

"You've got one hell of a nerve. I can't take pity, Ash, ever – and especially not now. You should have heard her. She just lost it. If I have to put up with that kind of bullshit I`m better off dead." The green eyes wavered. "I can't deal. Don't you understand? What the hell have you started? She comes over here like that and it'll be the end of me."

After all they'd been through, Joel was finally letting his protective wall down and Ash saw the vulnerability, fear and suffering behind it. Oblivious to the tears spilling down his face, he knelt in front of his friend. "I'll straighten it out. You won't have to put up with any of that shit. I promise. You just stay strong and keep fighting. We'll beat this thing together, all of us. We're not letting you go."

The harsh face crumbled and Ash got up to sit beside him, holding him. "I'm terrified sometimes. I don't want to die."

Alix abruptly left the room. A ball of pain was caught in her chest and she reached blindly for the Scotch in the cupboard, uncapping it and swigging from the bottle. The harsh liquid was biting and she choked. Moments like this almost destroyed them. The fantasy they painstakingly built of normalcy could be shattered so easily by the reality of Joel's illness. A cough that made her pause, night sweats that left him weak and depressed, nausea, the Pentamidine treatments that flattened him for a day, the on again/off again interruptions of AZT – they were all reminders that brought their work down with a flash and the steady rebuilding would have to start all over again. That amid keeping Joel's weight even, making sure he got enough fluids so that his body wasn't dehydrated by the night sweats, keeping his spirits up and plugging away on songs and things he wanted to get accomplished. She could only guess at the panorama of emotions and reactions he went through. How many times could your heart break?

When she finally went back into the living room the crying jag had burned itself out and they were talking quietly. Dr. Marlowe had warned them that there were times when the poison had to come out – drain the misery and you would feel better. She placed the bottle of Scotch on the coffee table and went to fetch ice and three glasses. Joel's drink she watered heavily. "Bit like the old days," he said with a glimmer of a smile. "Drinking in the morning to take away last night's binge."

"I remember when your idea of breakfast was coffee laced with Scotch."

"Yeah, well we've all come a long way down that road and I, for one, am glad. I can't count the number of times I spent heaving over the toilet."

"That's for sure. But who of us admitted it at the time? It wasn't cool and that was so important to us."

"Among other things," Ash put in. "I also wanted to have me a ton of men and I sure didn't get too far."

"I wanted women and they kept falling into my lap."

"You were some slut," Alix agreed. "I could never figure out how you had the energy. Were you trying to set some kind of world record?"

"You never know."

The thought remained unspoken that that was what would kill him.

"I'm hungry. There are a bunch of rubbery eggs in the pan. I say we dump it and start again. Ash, you staying for breakfast?"

"Love to. Come on, let's teach Joel to cook."

"That'll be the day. He can't even boil water. I think he does it on purpose to get out of helping."

"Works every time too."

The three retired to the kitchen, harmony restored.

Joel disappeared that afternoon to lie down, Ash went to his office and Alix hit the basement to work on songs. Though they had finished recording it was not unusual for her and Joel to keep writing. The habit was never long interrupted and the material produced when they had time assured them of a choice on the next album rather than a shortage. There was always something left over. Joel had jokingly suggested that, when the band decided to retire, they should assemble what was left, put it on as many albums as they needed, wrap it up as a box CD and call it 'Pot Luck.'

Alix came back upstairs late and wandered into the living room, thinking about dinner. The phone rang and she answered it absently.

"Alix, love, how the bloody hell are you?"

The voice brought a smile to her face. Roger March was blessed with a light-hearted soul and people responded to it instinctively. "I'm fine, Roger, you old devil. How about you?"

"Sound as a pound, flower."

"What's up?"

"You must be due for some kind of European jaunt so come visit us. It's your turn. There's a benefit being done in London in November for AIDS and I want you lot in it. You've had enough bloody rest. You're all turning into right layabouts. How long does it take Joel and Dixie to get over a cold and a sore throat?" He roared at his understatement.

"I'd hardly call pneumonia and tonsillitis a cold and a sore throat. We've also put another album in the bag so you can't call us layabouts."

"I'm not having that as an excuse. When can you make it here?"

Joel was standing in the doorway, listening to her part of the conversation. She looked at him and with a resigned sigh he held out his hand for the phone.

"Hold on, here's Joel."

Roger launched into his spiel again but was cut off in midstream. "'Kay, pal, no more bullshit. Fess up. I know you know. I got it out of Ash."

"I'm sorry, old son, you don't know how much. You think you could manage a visit?"

"I know how it sounds but I don't want to chance going so far away. As for a concert, you already know the answer to that."

"A set, mate, maybe fifteen or twenty minutes. You could sit on a chair, make it like recording."

Joel winced at the pleading in his voice. "Sorry, Rog."

Alix left the room, giving him privacy. Telling people face to face was one thing but giving out that sort of news on the telephone, where contact was a disembodied voice, was quite another. She took some food out of the fridge and set about making dinner.

Joel walked into the kitchen twenty minutes later, his mouth a thin, grim line. "I don't want to tell anybody else about this. It's like reliving the nightmare every fucking time. And not, ever again, on the phone."

"What did he say?"

"He's got some time off after Christmas and wanted to know if it was all right to come for a visit."

"And?"

"What could I say? This friendship has taken both of us by surprise and I want to see him. I wonder if that's when Eleanor will come."

She poured meat sauce over the spaghetti she had drained and dumped it onto two plates. "Let's eat."

"I'm not hungry."

"Please don't argue."

"If you force it down it'll just come up again. Truth is I want to get drunk." He grabbed her hand. "Come on, Alix, how about it? Get drunk with me, like we used to."

"I don't think it's a good idea."

"I don't care. It can't all be good health and three squares a day. I lost my girl today and I've had two overseas phone calls from close friends who want to come and say good-bye. Do I need another reason to convince you? My best friend is in front of me and I want to get drunk with her. Any questions or objections, stupid or otherwise?"

"Like old times, huh?"

"Yeah, only you never needed to be talked into going to a bar."

"You eat dinner with me and I'll go drinking with you." She held out her hand. "Pact?"

He shook it. "Pact. You're as devious, in your own way, as me."

"I have a good teacher."

"'Kay, let's get this slop down and get out of here."

The evening had none of the edges of their past binges. The two stayed away from the rowdy bars they used to frequent, content to wander in and out of places where they weren't recognized. Though not drunk, both had had more than enough when they mutually decided to call it a night and go home.

"I'm beat," Alix said in disbelief, "and it's not even late."

Joel laughed. "These good health habits have screwed us up royally."

"I'm sure glad nobody knows."

"It would pretty much blow our reps as wild partiers."

"Leaving a bar before dawn," she said in disgust. "We're getting old, my friend."

The two ambled home amicably. The light on the answering machine was blinking. Alix pushed the play button and waited while the tape rewound.

Joel fidgeted beside her. "It better not be negative shit. I've had about all I can take today."

Brad's voice floated up to them. "Hey, hombres, where you hanging out? We got a confab in my office tomorrow. Robin wants to set up a shoot for 'Get a Suntan' too. Noon, dudes."

The beep went and Dr. Marlowe followed. "Can you get into the office tomorrow, Joel? I'd like to see you. Also, we'll have to interrupt the AZT again so don't take your next dose."

The calm tones took the top spin off the night. "When is enough too much?" He kissed Alix. "Thanks for the company. I'm going to bed."

She watched as he climbed the stairs, shoulders rounded in defeat. She locked up, shut the lights off and went to her room. Joel would probably be sick during the night and she decided to stay awake for a while in case he needed her. The drinking hadn't been a good idea but it had bolstered his spirits. She just wished they'd left the answering machine until morning.

CHAPTER 31

Winter 1993

Alix heard Joel throwing up in the middle of the night, as she'd expected. He rarely drank these days and his body had little tolerance for alcohol. She knocked on the bathroom door. "You okay?"

"Fine, girl, go back to bed."

She collected a jug of juice and a clean glass from the kitchen and placed them on his night table. The sheets were stained and she changed them quickly. Joel's bouts with diarrhea were infrequent – he was lucky not to be troubled too often with them as they could be quite debilitating – but he hated when it happened and usually didn't tell her. It made him feel awkward and helpless. She went down to the laundry room off the kitchen, put the sheets in the washer and started the cycle.

He was waiting when she got back upstairs. "I wish you hadn't done that, Alix. I can take care of myself, you know."

"Leave it, Joel." She got a couple of pills from the bathroom. "These should settle your stomach."

"They're for nausea, not excessive drinking."

"Stop fighting me."

He heard the exhaustion in her voice and backed off. "Sorry, I just..."

"I know. Now come back to bed. Call me if you need anything."

He slid beneath the clean sheets and accepted the pills with a glass of juice. "At least there's no fever tonight."

"That I'm glad about. See you tomorrow."

He slept through the night and was fine by morning.

The two made their way to the doctor's office after breakfast. Alix waited in the car, parked discreetly near the back door. Joel returned half an hour later. "Well?"

"I'm a slave to the numbers game. Other than that, I'm cruising. My weight's down a bit but all systems appear to be go. I have to take it easy though and I've got some more pills to swallow."

"Will you be off for a week again?"

"Probably. Eventually it'll have to be transfusions. That will get me back in action faster."

"Do you have to go that route?"

"The doc told me patients on long-term AZT become blood transfusion dependent. He said I'd feel a lot better. Perks some people up for days."

"How can you make a joke about this," she asked, seeing a grin lift his mouth.

"You got to laugh or cry, girl. The sun is shining, the leaves are turning awesome colours and I'm here seeing it. Today we laugh. Let's go home for lunch and then see what Brad wants."

Joel positioned himself away from the others, a habit he'd developed during AZT interruptions. Alix refrained from lighting up, though she needed a cigarette badly, and sat fidgeting near him. Dixie, Bear and Leo were perched around Brad who was seated behind his desk.

"Okay, hombres, let's get down to it. Robin's working on a shoot for 'Suntan'. Any probs?"

"Not till the end of the week. I'm in confinement again."

"You phone her, Durango, and set it up. Everyone good with that?" All heads nodded.

"When's our treasure due out," Bear asked.

"End of October. We'll do a party to launch it. You realize it's the last one in your contract."

"I think that's something we've all been wondering about," Dixie said. "It's not like Dome to leave things up in the air. Doesn't Mr. Davis like us anymore?"

"Chill, babe, he loves you all like he'd love his brats, if he had any. He dialled me before your last tour and made a whopper offer but we put it off till you flew home."

"And then things started to happen," Joel said dryly. "So why haven't you said anything?"

"I am now, Durango."

"Didn't Davis press it," Leo asked, puzzled.

"He knows the Mask is cruising happy and figured you'd be apeshit over the new contract, but Dix and Joel got sick and he left it with me. He's been on the horn but, like I said, he's got no worries."

"He's confident we'll sign." Joel craned his neck towards the pile of documents beside Brad's arm. "That it?"

"Yep. Here, copies for all but I'll recap the highlights." He outlined the basics contained in the neatly typed pages everyone held. There was silence at the end.

"Jumping frog legs, Bradman," Bear said with a whistle. "He sure does like us."

"He's made a ton off you bums and you been skimming even better cream. What's the verdict?"

All of them tensed. Brad had known this would be a dicey meeting. The commitment was for three more albums and the prognosis for finishing intact was not good. Alix looked at the others in turn, her brows raised. As each nodded, she sat back, relieved and satisfied. "We sort of discussed this, Joel."

"Yeah, behind my back. I figured you might."

"We're all agreed. We go with any decision you want to make."

"Okay, Durango, how you want to handle this? You wanna tell 'em?"

"No way."

"But can we sign it in good faith," Dixie asked. "It's three albums."

"Why not? Hell, Dix, I'm only one fifth of this band. Besides, I'm not dead yet, you know."

"I didn't mean it like that."

"Yeah, you did and it's all right. You brought up a good point." He eyed them sternly. "Three albums take time and we don't know how much I have."

"So let's sign for one."

"We're not talking about me, Leo; we're talking about the Blue Mask." Joel swallowed hard. He'd already thought about this. "You all going to be quitters? Come on, chicken shits, let's sign. If I don't make it all the way you'll just have to carry on without me. We're a damn good band – maybe even a great one. You want to go out with a fizzle like a sick fire or you want to keep burning big for as long as we can?"

Alix groaned. "Where the hell do you get these speeches from? Honestly, Joel, you've had a constant supply of this shit since the day I met you. You buy it in bulk or something from a bad comic?"

They all started laughing. The bubble of dispirited tension burst, as she knew it would. She had thought about this too, and it was important to go on for Joel's sake. Their faith in him being around for three albums might just help him do exactly that. And he was right – this was about the band as a unit, not them as individuals. The Blue Mask was healthy and going merrily along, despite them. Brad passed out pens and the five signed their lives away for the time it would take for three more albums – and a great deal of money.

Joel rested and was careful, as always during these breaks. Alix took more time with cleaning, going on disinfecting binges but eventually pulled up one day in frustration. They'd been working on songs for the next album and she was finding it hard to concentrate.

"I called Ash and he can set us up with a housekeeper through the Centre who isn't freaked to come and clean."

"No."

"I can't keep up, not with work and spending time with you. It's too much. Ash guaranteed that whoever we get will keep their mouth shut. Trust him."

"He's real good at keeping his mouth shut, isn't he?" He had been out of sorts all day, moody and sullen.

"Dammit, Joel, it's not like you to hold a grudge, or to be so selfish. I can't do it all; I need some help. Don't make this impossible."

"I'm the one who's sick, Alix, or have you forgotten? It's my secret and I'm keeping it. If you can't deal you know where the door is."

The cutting reply was a slap in the face. Her anger rose to meet his and she stomped up the stairs, getting away before she said something she'd regret.

"Where do you think you're going," he yelled.

"Even slaves get rest breaks," she countered, slamming her bedroom door.

He slumped down in the chair, suddenly exhausted. He'd blown it again. He was good much of the time and then this rising fury would flood him and if he wasn't alone, as he usually tried to be, he lashed out at whoever was with him. Ash and Alix had both been targets before.

He breathed slowly, trying to dampen the rage then went up to her room and entered to find her sitting on the bed. "I'm sorry."

"Why do you do that to me? I'm trying to help, you know."

"I know. Sometimes I just can't stop it. I've tried to explain."

"I understand, but sometimes it's hard to take."

He sat down and reached over to tug her hair. "I know, girl, and I really am sorry. You're the last person in the world I want to hurt. I need to lay down now. These tiffs take all the stuffing out of me. Friends again?"

There were tears in the big eyes. "Yeah, friends."

"Call Ash and get someone in. But I want a vow of silence or there'll be murder."

"I'll take care of it."

She contacted Ash and by the end of the week he'd found a woman who could come in daily. The load immediately lightened and Alix was grateful. She still cooked meals; it was something her and Joel did together, he seated at the island chatting and passing her things.

Mildred, their new housekeeper, was a motherly woman in her fifties, a widow who had lost her only son to AIDS. She'd signed on with the Centre, partly for company and partly to help others who had gone through what her son had. She was friendly, warm and the three melded happily together.

Joel had asked Robin to book the Alley View for the end of the following week. He got a call shortly after summoning him in and was back on AZT. The night sweats were getting worse but his weight was holding and he didn't feel too bad. He drank a lot of fluids to counteract what was lost at night with the fever/sweat pattern and, after a suggestion from Mildred to put towels under him instead of having to change the sheets constantly, found his sleep wasn't as disturbed.

The gang assembled to shoot their next video in good spirits. As planned, Joel was the village idiot and crowed along with Alix in dark make-up, a sombrero and a garish poncho. His blonde hair was hidden beneath the straw monstrosity and a thick, black mustache had been fixed to his upper lip. He cavorted like a maniac, drawing laughter from cast and crew while breaking up constantly himself. Robin chose to leave a lot of the hilarity in. They settled down to await the release of their next album and the party planned to launch it. There was a lot of speculation in the press about an upcoming tour and the group held strategy meetings to see just how they could justify no tour announcement. There was also excited talk about their next project.

As October rolled by tentative preparation sessions started in Joel's basement, experimental times often interrupted by discussions and fun. The work was haphazard at best as they waited for the album to be released. The schedule was always like that – none of them could concentrate totally on something new until the previous piece was in circulation.

Joel's cough was developing again but it wasn't much different from the one he'd had for months. Dr. Marlowe advised him to monitor his symptoms and check in if things got worse.

All were in fine form the afternoon of the launch party for 'Mad as a Hatter'. Ash had outdone himself on the cover design and there were raves over the richer production. There was an easy, playful camaraderie between the band and the reporters and reviewers assembled. Though there were new faces in the crowd, many had been around a long time. As the session went on and the alcohol flowed, the questions acquired a more rapid-fire delivery. One persistent soul, a reporter who had dogged Joel's trail for years, was bent on unravelling the mystery Sherri had started when asked why she was no longer with him.

"No one's seen you out on the town in ages and suddenly we hear about a mysterious lady your ex caught you in the sack with. What's the drill?"

"You just answered your own question."

"So who is she?"

"It's Alix actually. But I'm thinking of adding Dix for variety. I'm keeping it in the band 'cos they're used to me. No hassles."

Both women cuffed him.

The man continued. "Come on, Joel, seriously."

"Seriously, you know better than to ask these questions, Marv. You know I'm not going to answer them."

"Usually you call these little get-togethers to announce a new tour," one of the newcomers broke in. "I believe that's what we're expecting, especially since the last one was never completed."

Alix's smile froze. That was all they needed – a perceptive greenhorn nosing around trying to make her reputation with a big story. "We all needed a rest at the time Joel and Dix got sick. Doctor's orders. It was easier on us to go back in the studio and work on new material."

"When can we expect the next tour," she pressed.

A flurry of similar questions erupted.

"There won't be one," Dixie said.

Joel groaned inwardly. That kind of direct answer was just what he had been trying to avoid. "Look," he cut in above the noise. The room settled. "We decided not to tour this album 'cos we're working on more intricate material. We're going in a different direction and want to explore it while the momentum's rolling."

Alix jumped in. "We want to take a year off to work. We've been on the road for the last six years and it's too much when we're trying new angles. There's no time to experiment. This break will give us a chance. We're already plotting our next project."

Joel smiled as voices broke out again, feigning an easy confidence he was far from feeling. "We've just signed with Dome for three more albums. The Blue Mask will tour again in the future – it's just going to be a while." What he didn't add was that he wouldn't be with them when that tour started.

The afternoon ploughed on into early evening. The press consumed the remaining liquor and food and departed. Grateful, the band followed suit.

Joel went to lie down as soon as he got home. The conference had completely worn him out. When Alix went to wake him later to take his pills she found him restless and mumbling, his brow dry and on fire. She pressed a cool cloth to his forehead and sat with him, waiting for the fever to break. His body was racked by coughing fits. How had it gotten so bad so quickly? He'd seemed fine that afternoon, a little tired and irritated with the barrage of questions he didn't want to answer, yet holding. But the uneasy balance sitting on the fence between infection and health was as light as dust and as capricious as fate. Now he had suddenly fallen off and she was terrified.

"Joel," she whispered. A groan let her know he was listening. "I'm going to take you to the hospital. Can you get up?"

He tried to fight his way through the waves of fever but fell back on the bed, exhausted. She phoned Ash and begged him to come and help, then called Dr. Marlowe to say they were on their way in.

Ash's arrival triggered a flood of desperate tears. He wrapped a blanket around Joel, picked him up and carried him down to the car. Alix followed with a bag into which she had thrown pajamas and a robe. He'd left the car running and bundled his friend in, slamming the door against the cold air circulating outside. Alix wedged herself in and told him to hurry.

Forewarned, the hospital staff was ready. Joel was put on a gurney and wheeled away into the confines of examining rooms behind the double doors. Calls were placed to the band members and Robin and Brad but there was nothing any of them could do. They promised to keep their friends posted. Everyone would meet at the hospital the next day.

Alix and Ash settled in the television room for the long wait for test results. The diagnosis was no surprise to either of them.

"We conducted a bronchoscopy," Dr. Marlowe said.

He had explained this test to Alix before. A flexible tube is inserted into the lung for a specimen of tissue. PCP is an interstitial infection, meaning it invades the narrow crevices between the lung sacs. The test sounded simple but Joel told her it was gruelling. He'd been given an anesthetic and the pulmonary team had put an oxygen mask over his mouth and nose until it wore off. He had woken with a bruising, hacking cough, in real discomfort. When it finally abated he was limp and flattened out. Hence the sedative that left him sleeping while his tortured body dealt with the pain.

"Is it PCP," Alix asked.

"I'm afraid so. I thought we'd have more time. Has he been overdoing things?"

"It's hard to tell. I can't always watch him like a hawk."

"Don't worry. We have him on Pentamidine and there is no reason why he shouldn't recover."

But the honeymoon was over.

CHAPTER 32

Having been through this before, Alix knew what to expect when she entered Joel`s room. He lay on his back, face drawn and white with pain. An IV unit had been hooked up and the Pentamidine was dripping into his veins. Dr. Marlowe had prescribed some other drugs to help with the fever and a sedative to ease general anxiety and he languished in a somnolent word of shadows and muted noises. She sat down and took his hand. "It's all right. I'm here and I'm not going anywhere."

He sighed softly, whether in reply or not she wasn't sure. Ash ducked in briefly to say he was off to get some rest and would be back to relieve her later. She must have dozed. When she woke up her neck was stiff and she blinked uncertainly in the morning light.

Joel's eyes were open and he smiled as she turned to him. "I think I had a little blip in my recovery."

"Just a little one."

"What's the doc say?"

"You're going to be fine."

"Eventually and for a while, right?"

"Just concentrate on getting better."

"Must have been all that second-hand smoke at the conference."

"Sure."

He frowned. "There was no warning, Alix. I didn't even suspect it until I went to bed."

"I don't know what to say, Joel. You were coughing a lot more but I figured it was just the strain of the whole day."

"That's what screws me up about this damn disease. You don't get any warnings, like I thought I would. I've phoned the doc other times when I've had diarrhea or fevers and stuff he warned me about and he always says to wait it out. It could mean something or nothing. But you'd think for the big one I'd have some hint. But there wasn't any – not even a shot in the fucking dark. I hate this roller-coaster ride. Can you get me off?"

"I wish I could."

"No visas from alien land?"

"At least we're together."

His harsh face softened. "Yeah, well that's true, girl. And I'm grateful. I don't think I could deal without you."

"You're stuck with me, whether you like it or not. I'm not budging. You got that?"

"Yeah." He rolled his head back to stare up at the ceiling. "Se we just cruise and wait."

"We'll do stuff, just like last time. It wasn't so bad after a while."

"Except that each time will get worse till it comes to the last time. Have you thought about that, Alix? Sometimes I spend hours thinking about it. I'll keep going up and down, but always down more, till I hit bottom. Then that's it."

"You quit that right now, Stark," she replied, alarmed. "You're going to get better, not give up. What's the matter with you? You called us chicken shits when we questioned signing for three more albums. You going to be a hypocrite? Or are you going to fight this every step of the way – the same way we've fought everything else?"

"I'm tired."

"Yeah, and that going to make one hell of an obit."

His gaze swung sharply back. "Nice words."

"Make me eat them."

The sea green eyes searched her face; his own was a mask. She knew a fight was being conducted so she stayed calm and waited him out. He sighed wearily. "You're right; I couldn't live with myself if I just gave up, even if it's not going to be forever."

She let out the breath she'd been holding. "Nobody gets forever. You might have more time than any of us. Who knows? The important thing, the bottom line, is us. That's all that ever mattered or ever will."

"'Kay. I need to sleep some more. I'll be around in a while."

"I'll be here."

Ash came back as promised and handed Alix the keys to his car. "Home now and get some rest."

"Thanks," she said gratefully.

"You look done in."

"Joel's been on a downer again."

"You can't have him happy all the time. He's the one who has to work through this. Sometimes he needs to share a little misery."

"Misery, yeah, but not giving up."

"I hear you. I'll take good care of him."

She squeezed his arm and made her way home. A few hours rest restored her equilibrium and she returned to the hospital to find Ash, Leo and Bear gathered around Joel's bed telling bad jokes.

"We're bonding," Bear cracked. "Hey, should we let a woman in on this?"

"That's no woman, that's Alix," Joel said.

"Yeah, yeah, enough with the bullshit. You guys are regular comedians."

"I'm just enjoying the heavy artillery you called in."

The group didn't stay long. Joel tired easily and there were interruptions as nurses came and went, checking on their patient. During the afternoon, he visited with Robin, Brad and Dixie in between naps. Ash returned in the evening to keep Alix company. Joel would sleep a great deal during the next few days as the drugs cleared his lungs. His cough got less harsh and racking and the labour disappeared from his breathing. Determined, he ate around nausea. He had dropped some weight and knew how important it was to build that back up. Weight and fluids were all too easy to lose if vigilance was not kept up and they could debilitate a patient with amazing swiftness. She left a message for Sherri who came clattering down the hall near the end of the week, nerves jangling. Alix was at the nurse's station.

"You can't see him in this state."

"I feel so guilty. I phoned Ash and he told me how long Joel's been in here. Hal and I went away for a few days. I wouldn't have gone if..."

"How the hell could you know? Look, things have changed for both of you. Stop beating yourself up for being with Mason."

"I feel like I'm deserting."

"You're here, aren't you? That doesn't look like desertion to me."

Sherri brushed her fingers through her hair and took several deep breaths. "Do I get the nod to go in?"

"Absolutely."

Alix stayed outside, sitting in the hall chatting with patients that passed by and stopped to visit. She was on a first name basis with many of them and could be found in their rooms when Joel was sleeping. If the others knew why he was there, no one said anything and she was grateful.

Sherri came out half an hour later, composure holding. "He says he's going to be fine."

"He knows better than any of us. Did you tell Mason where you were going?"

"Just to the hospital to see a friend. Don't worry, if he finds out it won't be from me."

Alix watched her disappear down the hall. Joel was staring at the ceiling, lost in thought, when she went into his room. "You okay?"

"I was just thinking about Sherri."

"Thinking what?"

"Speculating really. If this hadn't happened to me, what would it be like? I don't think we'd have made the grade. She would've been history eventually, like Elaine. Is it all my fault or do you want some of the blame too? You deserve it."

"Me and John wouldn't have survived either, once you were back on the scene. Same deal, isn't it? We're more than just best friends; we're on some weird line of communication that goes deep. It's spooky and it's ruined us. We couldn't share the whole relationship deal – my fault I know – but what fucked me up wasn't my fault. I didn't ask a couple of monsters to rake me over the coals.

"But you and me, we have this bond we can't find with anyone else. Every other relationship was probably doomed from day one. Look at Elaine. If we hadn't met all those years ago you'd still be with her." She smiled. "I guess I can take half the blame."

"We would've met, Alix. It was fate, karma, destiny, whatever you want to call it. And you're wrong about us. We would've had the whole deal eventually. You were so fucked up you needed a lot of time to heal. Our bad luck is that we just ran out of time. But we got some left and we had a taste of what could've been. I'm glad."

"You have faith in me, huh? You don't think I'll end up a sexless old maid?"

"Not a chance. And sick or not, I'll help all I can." He reached for her. "Now come here."

Joel had a strong grip on her arm and jerked it hard, toppling Alix onto the bed. "Watch it, you asshole, you're going to yank that IV right out of your arm, all for a roll in the sack."

"Wouldn't the nurses love that," Dr. Marlowe said from the doorway. "Actually, I think you could get away with it, Joel. You seemed to have charmed the lot of them."

Alix disentangled herself and got up, face red. "That's his main talent. You'd think it was the guitar but you should see him in action."

"I have, even with an IV in his arm."

"I'm not in that category; I'm just a friendly romp when there are no senoritas around."

"And she's sticking to that story," Joel finished, winking lewdly. "What's up, Doc?"

"I just came to check on my patient. How are you feeling?"

"My energy's back and I'm getting restless. I want out."

"Not yet I'm afraid." He turned to Alix. "Can you excuse us?"

"Everybody wants to be alone with me."

"Can you put a muzzle on him?"

Dr. Marlowe laughed. "I'll see what I can do."

Brad strolled in one afternoon by himself and with a book in hand. "Hi, Durango, how's it hanging?" He tossed the book on the bed and took a seat. "I found this in a store and thought it might while away some time in between penning songs with Alix."

"What makes you think we're doing that?"

"I know you. When you're not flirting with the angels in white you're scribbling with your partner in crime. And if you're not then there's something real wrong with you."

Laughing, he had a quick look at the book. It was a beautifully photographed history of the Yucatan Peninsula. "Brings back memories. We had a riot on that trip."

"The video for that track is one of the funniest things you dudes've done. Me and Robin were watching it last night and splitting a gut."

"Thanks."

"No sweat."

"I get so bored in here."

"When they cutting you loose? You look almost normal now – a hell of a lot better than last week."

"I don't know. The doc says a few more days but nothing definite." He paused. "Any chance of getting into the studio soon? I got some stuff to work on."

"Heal up first. There's time for that later."

"No there's not. This is my second bout with PCP and next time will be faster. Shit, haven't you been listening to me? I'm not going to get better."

"What's brought this on?"

"Alix is hedging about work. She's backing off."

"She wants you back on your feet, Joel; we all do. Then we'll talk studio time."

"She's concentrating on me instead of work. She's letting it go and I don't want it to be permanent. Alix, more than anyone, is going to need something after I'm gone. Hard work with the band will help her cope. Left on her own she'll get into trouble."

"She ain't gonna be on her own. And, like you bitched to Dix, you're not dead yet."

"A ward like this gives you lots of time to think. Some people will get out but those of us in for PCP will be back. And one of those times we're not going to walk out; we'll be wheeled out in a body bag – me included."

"What do you want me to say?"

"Promise you won't let Alix break up the band. Her and Dix are coming up with some good stuff. I've got a lot of tapes to help with the transition to a new guitarist and I'll keep working as long as I can. If she stays, the band will. She'll eventually agree but you'll have to push her."

Brad looked at him for a long time. "You're an asshole, you know that? You also got more guts than any dude I know. It takes balls to look that kind of thing in the face and spit at it."

"I don't have much of a choice. You either lay back and waste or get up and fight. I try to make the fight good when I can. What do you say?"

"You got my word, Durango. I'll keep on her but I might get roughed up in the process."

"You can take it, partner, you're a man."

Both laughed and Joel quickly changed the subject.

Brad departed when Alix returned, making no mention of the agreement. She and Joel settled in for the remainder of the day in companionable harmony, talking, reading and tossing scraps of lyrics and melodies back and forth. Dinner was served, consumed and removed before evening visiting commenced. For once, there was no one to interrupt their time together. Alix had brought the cribbage board and cards from the tour bus. They were in the middle of a match, competing amid insults and jeers, when a man drifted into the doorway, clearing his throat for attention.

Hal Mason, Sherri's current lover, stood awkwardly half in the hall and half in the room. "Hi, Joel."

He froze, the cards dropping onto the sheets. "What are you doing here?"

"I thought I'd come see how you're doing. Sherri told me where to find you."

"Alix, go outside for a cigarette please."

She rose slowly. "You sure?"

"Positive, girl."

"Okay." She pulled her leather jacket on and walked slowly past the man, black eyes glittering. "Don't mess him up."

Mason nodded. Everyone knew what Alix's temper was like and few crossed her. "I just came to visit."

CHAPTER 33

Mason took one step closer and halted abruptly. "How are you?"

"You can't get sick from me breathing on you so sit down. I'm not shouting across the fucking room."

He moved to a chair and perched on it, ready for flight. He didn't remove his coat.

"How did you find out from Sherri and how much do you know?"

"I know this is a lung ward and you've got pneumonia again. The repeating one that has something to do with AIDS. It wasn't the normal kind you had last spring, was it?"

"Would you believe me if I said yes?"

Mason jumped as a coughing spell hit Joel. Embarrassed, he offered the box of tissues on the bedside table. "Sorry."

"Sherri promised to keep this to herself. You mind telling me why the hell she told you?"

"We were pals once, Joel; we jammed and had some good times. Don't get mad. I'm sorry I stole your girl but I'm not hurting her."

"That's not what I'm mad about. I wanted her to see other people."

"It all makes sense now. The story about finding someone else with you – that was a smokescreen, right?"

"Maybe."

"Well it worked. Don't blame her. She's been upset lately and since she visited her mysterious friend in the hospital this week she's been crying. I fed her too much wine last night and when she was just about to pass out I started asking questions. I wanted to help, that's all, and she wouldn't let me unless I got it out of her." He glanced around the room, his eyes running over the medication on the table, the IV unit in the corner, the signs of a longish occupancy. "I won't breathe a word. Nobody suspects a thing yet; I haven't heard any rumours."

"This gets out and I'll have no peace."

Mason looked at him then. "I hear you. Anything I can do?"

"Keep your mouth shut."

He rose to leave. "Don't get mad at Sherri. It's my fault not hers. I'll take good care of her. I'm glad to know what's eating her up. Maybe now I can help."

"She's a great lady, Hal. Don't forget that."

"I'm sorry, man; I really am."

Embarrassed, uncomfortable, scared, he scuttled out of the room. Joel groaned and rolled over onto his back. Alix found him like that when she returned.

"What's going on? Sherri spill the beans?"

"He got her drunk and started asking questions."

"So it's out."

"He said he'd keep quiet."

"He's one of the biggest gossips in town, Joel. Hal Mason couldn't keep his mouth shut if it was sewn up." She paused, trying to read his mood. "Maybe we should beat him to the punch?"

"What?"

"Maybe we should tell. We can get Brad to issue a statement. That way it's out in the open. We can have someone around to make sure you don't get hassled when we go out but we're home most of the time anyway. All this secrecy can stop."

"No!"

"How many young studs listen to our music – guys who follow your example? How many see sex as a conquest and think it's not macho to protect themselves? More people are going to get sick and die. The teens are the ones getting this disease now 'cos they don't think they will. If you can influence them, why not? You're someone they'd listen to. Hell, a lot of them want to be just like you. If you're a role model for aspiring Don Juans, why not help?"

He looked tired, defeated and ashamed. "Don't think it hasn't crossed my mind but the answer for now is no. I'm still trying to cope and it's a day to day thing. You know that. I live in the public. We all do. But I'm not sure I've got the strength or the guts to die in it."

"I never thought of it like that."

"If what you say about Mason is true, it'll get out soon enough. I'll deal then. Not before, please. I just can't yet."

She hugged him. "I'm sorry; I'm just not thinking today."

"It's been a long one, girl. Let's forget it. I've got to get some sleep now. Why don't you go home and grab some zzz's yourself. You look beat."

She nodded and got ready to leave. His voice stopped her at the door. "Don't forget to eat. We know how important food is, don't we?"

She laughed. "Touché. See you tomorrow."

Dr. Marlowe announced the next day that Joel could go home by the end of the week. He and Alix were overjoyed. They had been putting off making plans for Christmas, unsure that he would be available.

Alix told Mildred and the two spent a happy afternoon getting everything ready for the homecoming patient.

The house was sparkling, clean and disinfected and the refrigerator was groaning under the weight of the food brought in. As Mildred pointed out when Joel teased them, "You're as skinny as a rail. We're going to fatten you up like a Christmas goose."

Still tired and reacting to the drugs, he ate around nausea and every morsel kept down was a gain. Alix paraded him into the bathroom each morning for a weigh-in and gradually the lost pounds started to creep back. Dr. Marlowe encouraged him to fight to regain his stamina and the nightly walks commenced again, both bundled up against the cold and any possible infections. Alix was more on guard than ever against germs and anyone visiting who looked or sounded sick was discreetly placed out of Joel's range.

He tossed off excuses about being rundown and a returning cold as the reason for his hospitalization to friends and acquaintances not in the know but suspected that Mason had given him away. Oblique, doubtful glances, which he refused to acknowledge, were directed his way, although no one had the nerve to come right out and ask questions. Joel wasn't about to satisfy anyone's curiosity, particularly if they weren't man or woman enough to voice it. But he knew that speculation was increasing and it was only a matter of time before he would have to come clean. Until then he made no comment.

Plans went ahead for Christmas. Mildred went to see her sister in Saskatchewan for a week so the friends shared out the chores. For years they'd celebrated together, their family being each other and, by mutual consent, this party would be at Joel's.

It was a riotous affair with people dropping by on Christmas Eve and then assembling for dinner the next day. Joel came and went during the festivities, excusing himself when he needed to lie down and rest. Everyone pitched in with cleaning up before departing. They were getting older and the all night, raucous drinking binges were history.

Alix sat alone in the living room drinking coffee, pleased with the way things had gone. The smile on Joel's face had been constant and he'd thoroughly enjoyed himself. When the phone rang, she picked the receiver up quickly, not wanting the bell to wake him.

"Happy Christmas!"

"Eleanor, how are you?"

Roger barged in on an extension line. "Sound as a pound, flower, sound as a bloody pound."

"You're pissed."

"As a proverbial newt."

"Get off the line, you old reprobate," Eleanor scolded, laughing. There was a distinct click. "His wife just hauled him away. In case you haven't gathered, I'm over at the March abode for what was to be dinner and has turned into a bash. We're all assembled."

"Joel's in bed. He'll be sorry he missed you."

"Well he's not going to, is he? That's why I'm ringing. Roger and I are on our way over. We're having our New Year's Eve here and then taking to the skies to come your way. Is that all right?"

"It won't be much of a free-for-all. Joel's been in the hospital."

"I know. We got the news via Ash through Morris. This is about our only chance though. Mayday is due on the road soon and I'm up to my ears in tour promotions. It seems I am the gateway to Europe."

"That could be taken the wrong way."

"Probably bloody well is but it's a fabulous line for getting a laugh at parties."

"You're staying with us, of course."

"I'd love to if you're sure it's no trouble. Roger is another story. He's booked into the best hotel in Vancouver. You know how he likes his creature comforts."

"As in the creatures that comfort him on lonely nights away from home –his dolly birds?"

"I'm saying nothing," Eleanor chirped, giggling.

"Where you're calling from, I don't blame you. It's okay, his secret's safe with me."

"I daresay, with all of us."

"Joel will be so glad to see you. Me too. I can't wait."

"Then we can put all the wheels in motion?"

"Of course."

Eleanor hesitated. "Are you sure this won't wear him out? How is he really?"

"I think it'll do him the world of good. He's shaky but improving and his spirits are up. He's just been through his second bout of PCP though, Eleanor, and it hit pretty hard. He needs a lot of rest and is still fighting for energy."

"So no all night romps around town?"

"That seems so long ago. He hardly drinks anymore; it makes him too sick. We haven't gone out and gotten wild in months. But things are good. We've all slowed down and this new lifestyle suits us. We've discovered we want time to smell the roses, or coffee, or whatever the hell that saying is."

"I think that is part of the maturing process, darling. Your priorities change. Look at Mayday. In their salad days they were the biggest party band going. They can still stage a fracas when the whim takes them but, outside of the odd one on tour, most of the time you'll find them being stayabouts at home playing with the children."

"I guess so. I'm glad all of us have eased up. It helps cover Joel."

"Is he still obsessive about this being kept a secret?"

"He doesn't want the press finding out and hounding him. A lot of people drop by or come to jam and there's never a lack of company if he wants it but I think most of them are starting to suspect something's up since his last hospital stay. Before then, it was a novelty, him being around and people took advantage of it 'cos they thought it wouldn't last, that we'd be heading out on the road again. Now it looks like a more permanent thing and I'm sure people are wondering why."

"It's only a matter of time then."

"As far as I can see. We don't talk about it much."

In the background the music was suddenly turned up. "I think that's my cue to ring off, darling," Eleanor said brightly. "I'll be with you both soon."

"We'll have your room ready."

Alix hung up smiling. She and Joel would be glad to see Eleanor and Roger, but there was a sadness in the visit that wouldn't escape any of them.

The next day over breakfast she told him the news. He brightened at the prospect of seeing his friends again. Alix excused herself halfway through the meal and returned with a secretive smile.

"What are you up to," he asked suspiciously.

"I put a present in your room."

He grinned. "Then we're even 'cos I smuggled yours in while you were burning breakfast."

Like excited children, they abandoned their food and raced upstairs. Alix squealed with pleasure at the electric guitar lying on her bed. It had been specially designed for her and was painted the same black and electric blue as the logo that Ash had designed for the band. She hugged Joel tightly. "When did you get this?"

"I ordered it weeks ago. You like it?"

"It's gorgeous. I suppose this is a not so subtle hint to get off my ass and work, huh?"

"No flies on you, girl." He moved to the door. "My turn."

She nodded and followed him to his room. By the window stood a partner to the carousel horse that she had bought the previous year. Joel looked at her in wonder.

"I figured he looked lonely so I went hunting to find him a pal."

The green eyes glowed. "Now we've both got pals," he said, kissing her. "It's perfect."

She kissed him back and they went downstairs to finish breakfast.

CHAPTER 34

For Alix and Joel, New Year's Eve passed quietly, at home and in front of the television watching movies. The band members, Robin, Ash and Brad had all dropped by to say brief hellos, enroute to various parties. The two nestled together under a blanket, chomping on popcorn, sipping orange juice, with a bottle of champagne chilling for the turn of the year, content to be with each other and not whooping it up with their friends. Joel made it to midnight, kissed Alix and retired to bed.

She sat quietly in the dim room, tears running down her face, not seeing the film playing in front of her. She was glad to have Joel, grateful for another year together, but the misery would creep in when her defenses were down and the lonely future spun ahead of her. Finally, spent, she crept upstairs and crawled into bed with him. He sighed and rolled over toward her, settling in deeper. Comforted, Alix drifted off.

A couple of days later she was in the kitchen starting breakfast when the doorbell rang. Eleanor stood shivering on the front steps, armed with two suitcases and a big smile. Alix helped her inside as a cab pulled away.

"Why the hell didn't you let us know? I could've picked you up at the airport."

"This seemed easier." She enfolded her friend in a wave of perfume and clattering bangles. "How are you, darling? It's so wonderful to be here."

Alix squeezed her tightly. "I'm fine. It's great to have you back. Did Roger come in on the same flight?"

"He was booked to but his daughter came down with a cold over the new year so he opted to stay home a bit longer. He should be arriving the day after tomorrow if all goes well."

"Nothing serious I hope."

"No but when you're little you feel better having Mummy and Daddy there and that big smile just melts Roger's old heart. He can't say no, much to his wife's disgust. He spoils her and then goes on tour and Pam ends up having to sort out the monster from the delightful poppet."

"Somehow that doesn't surprise me. Want some coffee or are you ready for something stronger?"

Eleanor eyed her in mock disgust. "Some things never change. Scotch for breakfast?"

Alix laughed. "Not for a long time. Actually I'm just making food. Hungry?"

"Famished. I didn't get much sleep before I left so I napped all the way over. You're turning into quite the house mouse, if I may say so."

"We have a housekeeper. I'm just the cook and general gofer."

"It's one way to keep Joel eating and plugging along," Eleanor said quietly, understanding.

Alix nodded. "And it's fun. We usually make it an event. As long as he stays interested I'm happy."

"Is he still sleeping?"

"Yeah." She grinned. "Why don't you go wake him up? He'd love the surprise."

"Would it be all right? I don't want to interrupt his rest."

"Relax," Alix assured her. "Really, things aren't dire in this house."

"Done then." With a coquettish toss of her head, she disappeared up the stairs.

Alix continued cooking in the kitchen. When everything was ready she went upstairs to get Joel and Eleanor, only to find his door still closed and a series of giggles going on behind it. She knocked loudly. "Should I hold breakfast?"

"Down in a minute," Eleanor called out.

Laughing, she went back downstairs for more coffee and another cigarette.

Eleanor put in an appearance a short while later. "Joel says he'll be a time yet. He wants a wash and a shave." She sat down at the table. "I got in for a kiss and a cuddle. You don't mind, do you?"

"Why should I?"

"Well to be honest, I know you and Joel were an item and I wondered if you still harboured those kinds of feelings. It was just friendly between us, believe me."

Alix stared at her open-mouthed. "Joel and I have never been an item. I know you're friends and I'm glad, not jealous. Where did you get an idea like that?"

"You've been together before," she said firmly.

"I know Joel didn't tell you that – he's a clam – so how did you find out?"

"I could tell. I still can. Perhaps you weren't lovers officially but there is something terribly intimate about your friendship so I knew that you had been."

"Not even the rest of the band knows. We never said anything and nothing ever came of it. It was comfort mostly."

"That makes sense then. I knew it was something but I couldn't put my finger on it. It's pretty much why I held back, among other reasons. After all, one can't be hopping into bed with one's clients, can one?"

"I had no idea you'd even thought along those lines."

"It's my stiff upper lip, don't you know. But seriously, I fancied him like mad the first time I met him. I can tell you I had some quite delicious dreams. I still do on occasion." She winked at her friend. "I must say it's a damn good thing that Sherri was not here to witness my little reunion with Joel or to overhear this conversation."

"There's a lot to update you on. Sherri's history. Joel figured it was best. She was messing herself up with guilt pretty bad and he couldn't deal with half a relationship anymore." Alix giggled. "She caught us one day. We often sleep together and she walked in. It all came out that morning and they decided to just be friends."

Eleanor's eyes lit with delight. "Oh I love gossip. What happened?"

Alix briefly repeated the conversation and what Joel had told her afterwards.

"It never would have made the grade anyway. You were in the way. Not that you meant to be but you and Joel are so close, I think it would be very hard to get past that. But it's all a study in speculation now, isn't it?"

"Yeah, it is."

"Yet he seems fine. I would say he looks tired, a little rough around the edges, but that would be the last stay in hospital."

"He's holding his own. We just cruise along one day at a time."

"Then I shall cruise with you."

Joel came downstairs clad in trousers and a loose shirt. Eleanor sauntered up to him, flirting. "Nice clobber. You look marvelous. I love the new image."

He eyed Alix smugly. "I thought it was time to get out of the black muscle shirt and tight jeans and join the GQ set. I'm not outdated, like some people."

"I like being outdated."

"You can tell."

"Well if you want my opinion," Eleanor cut in, "I think you look good enough to eat."

"That's enough you two; breakfast is getting cold."

"She's getting bossy in her old age," Joel said with a wink.

Eleanor laughed. "Would you have it any other way? Let's nosh up. I'm ravenous."

It was the start of a wonderful visit. The three of them spent time walking along the sea wall, going out for the odd dinner and just hanging around. When Roger arrived it became a foursome. Gone were the riotous parties and all night clambers around the bars. Roger seemed content to fall in with whatever plans Joel wanted to make. The two often disappeared downstairs, closing the door firmly behind them and Eleanor and Alix left them to it. Occasionally a jam would ensue with other members of the Blue Mask, but for the most part the friends kept to themselves.

Joel paced himself and rested during the afternoons, joining the others when he could. With Roger and Eleanor's schedules piling up for the next few months, all were aware that this might be their last visit together but the impression was never fostered and the time sat lightly on them.

The ten days soon passed and Roger arrived in a limousine early one afternoon to fetch Eleanor. They were flying back to London together. Once the suitcases were loaded, he asked the driver to wait and came back inside, armed with a bottle of champagne. Alix brought out glasses while he opened it and the four sat down at the kitchen table toasting each other.

"I don't know when I can get back, old mate," Roger said to Joel. "We got one bloody gruelling tour coming up at the end of January. Six months around the bloody world. I'm getting too old for this. We're having the whole of next year off. Piss on the record company and the lot of them. I'm in for some weeks sunning in Ibiza."

"Sounds like paradise."

"Come along."

"You got a deal. It's something to shoot for, right?"

Roger grinned and reached across to hug his friend. "Too right, Joel, old son, too bloody right!"

Eleanor choked down her champagne and stood up. "I don't think they'll hold the plane, Roger, not even for you. We'd better get along."

The four struggled to the front door, arms around each other.

"I've had a marvelous time," Eleanor said, fighting back tears.

"You and Rog head back when the tour's done. Fall is a nice time here. We'll whirlwind you." Joel was struggling to keep his voice level.

"You got my nod," Roger said. "We got a date for autumn guaranteed. You take care of yourself and wait for me. I'll be back."

"I'll be here."

Eleanor hugged him tightly. "I'll be in touch. Thanks for everything."

He tugged her hair. "Come wake me up again soon."

"I will."

Both left quickly, hiding tears. Alix was biting her lip, trying not to cry, but the misery overflowed and she turned to Joel, seeking comfort. He held her for a while then gently let her go. "I have to lay down, girl. I'll be up in a bit."

She knew he wouldn't sleep; she could see the effort it was costing him not to sob in front of her.

CHAPTER 35

Joel got a call at the end of January to go off AZT immediately and get himself in for tests. Frustrated and angry at the interruption, he asked Alix to drive him over. Mildred insisted that it was merely a cautionary measure and gave him a comforting hug.

"I know but it drives me nuts. Just when I get something going my body jerks me around."

"Your body is taking care of itself the only way it can," she scolded gently, "and you'd best help it along."

"How come we're so lucky to have you?"

"We're all lucky here."

He kissed her cheek and left. Tests completed, the two were back in the afternoon. Joel went to lie down while Alix got on the phone to Brad to delay the studio booking. When he called back to confirm, Joel answered. Hanging up, he turned on her.

"How could you put off studio time?"

She looked at him, bewildered. "You know why. You can't go in till your counts come back up. Dr. Marlowe said you were to be extra careful or he'd stick you in isolation. Why are you being so dim?"

"I'm not," he said tightly, "and you know how important this is. Dammit, Alix, you guys can at least make a start.

Why the hell do you think I've been knocking myself out laying down bed and solo tapes? It sure isn't for the good of my health! I did it specifically for these times. Now I want you to get our studio back and haul your skinny ass in there with the others and do some fucking work. I'll be in as soon as I can. We've got to get this finished!"

The anger had turned to frustration and then to desperation and then to tears. He sat down abruptly, defeated. Alix gathered him to her, cradling his head against her chest.

"Let it go," she whispered. "The studio will always be there."

He pushed back slightly to look at her but did not break the embrace. "I won't. Don't you see? It's all I got left of the other life and I need to do it 'cos it means I'm still here and functioning. If you take that away from me you might as well let me go."

"I get it," she answered softly, "finally. I'll call the others. Just promise me you won't overdo things trying to keep up. Believing you can is fine, but please keep a grip on reality. If you're not careful you'll get sick and then you'll be stuck in the damn hospital again."

"That'll come soon enough anyway. 'Kay, girl, I promise I'll go easy."

"Come on, let's go lay down."

"I'm not tired."

"I am. Don't leave me alone."

He stood up and took her hand. "I'll give you a back rub."

"Just hold on to me for a while."

Joel's fevers started in earnest during this time. He worked when he could in the basement while Alix went off to the studio, coming home in the early afternoons often to find him wilting with a temperature, more than ready to be packed off to bed. She phoned Dr. Marlowe, anxious and worried, but there was little that could be done. Aspirin brought the fever down for now. It was one of the grey areas that had to be watched but they found it frightening – it could be nothing or a sign of some kind of infection..

Work at the studio went slowly. Mistakes were made because the band members weren't concentrating. Joel was on their minds constantly and they felt unfinished without him but until he was on AZT he was at risk. Alix came in each day armed with work he sent. Much to everyone's surprise, recording was actually getting done.

The interim period passed and the treatments started again. Joel rested a couple of days before going back into the studio. His temperature would soar without warning and often by noon he had to go home with Alix, needing bed and rest. His appetite waned and the two had frequent fights as she tried to cram food down him.

"If you make me eat it'll only come back up," he kept telling her but she persisted, panicked that he would lose weight.

The accompanying sweats as his fever broke soaked him. Dr. Marlowe warned him specifically to make sure he drank a lot of fluids to ensure that his body didn't get dehydrated. Alix pounced on this like a tiger and the fight became two-fisted: food on one hand; liquids on the other. Joel teased her when she got too intense and they would dissolve into laughter. As long as there was humour they were doing fine.

As thing got heavier, Joel felt more bowled under. He knew his friends couldn't help it but he had enough on his plate fighting his own depression without having to handle theirs, as well as Alix's manias about nourishment.

He came into the studio one day with two songs he had been toying with. The fever from the night before had broken, leaving him refreshed and, for once, with some energy to spare and he took full advantage of it. As soon as they were assembled, he called for attention.

"I got a couple of tracks to work on. Most of the melody is written and I did the lyrics for one. Alix will take care of hers first."

It was a song the pair had tossed around when he was in the hospital, a light, joking satire on his over-mythed romantic life called 'Lover Boy' and it set the rest of the band laughing. They went over it, adding and experimenting as Alix hammed it up.

Just before the lunch break Joel introduced his other song. He taught Alix the chords so that she could get the rhythm down and outlined breaks and solos. "I'll leave you guys to work out the flesh and blood of this track. I already know what I want to do on the solo."

"What about lyrics," Dixie asked.

"Oh, right, I'll sing it out so you know. It's written down here." They understood that he wouldn't be back in the afternoon.

He sat down and signalled Alix to start playing. He did the song himself, talking and croaking his way through it. When he'd finished he sat back, waiting for reactions.

Leo was smirking and Bear, not even trying to hold his laughter in, was hanging on to his sides. Dixie joined in with a fit of the giggles.

"I know you have a bad voice, Joel, but you've outdone yourself this time. You sound like a crow with a cold."

That sent them off again. Alix wiped her eyes. "What are you calling this prime piece?"

"'My Song'," he said in mock affront.

"How the hell do you want me to handle it?"

"You don't have to worry, girl, 'cos I'm doing the vocals. It's my debut."

More laughter erupted and the session finished on a light note.

By mutual agreement, no one worked on the weekend and when they assembled Monday everyone was ready. Joel's song was deliberately simple and he didn't want it marred by the intricacies that had become a trademark for the band. When the track was completed to the satisfaction of all, he asked if they could set up a shoot for the following weekend. It was an unusual request. The band usually did their videos after each album was complete, choosing two or three songs that stood out. The one exception had been when Jack was off sick for a week. Now they weren't even halfway through and he wanted to change the format.

"I don't get it," Bear protested after Joel had gone home. "Why is he in such a hurry? Is he getting sick with something, Alix?"

She shook her head. "The fevers are part of the disease but for now he's in a holding pattern."

Leo cleared his throat. "I think we ought to do it."

"But why this turnabout," Dixie asked.

Leo looked at Alix. "He's lost weight, hasn't he?"

"Only a few pounds. We're working on it."

"Did any of you think that maybe he wants to be shot on film while he still looks like himself? I don't mean to be a downer but as long as these fevers last he'll probably have a hard time eating. He wants to do it now in case he loses more weight and I think we should. What's a weekend shoot for us anyway? We used to be on a pretty rough schedule and you pups are whining because we have to put in a little overtime? Let's call Robin and get things in gear. I like Joel's idea for the video and it won't take long."

No one disagreed or crossed the sudden authority Leo had assumed. The shoot was set for the following Saturday and would be done in the studio.

Joel arrived dressed in his old trademark black muscle shirt and jeans. The group looked at him in shock. The trendy, baggy outfits he had been sporting for months had hidden a great deal but these tight clothes left little to the imagination and showed just how much weight he had lost. The severe colour highlighted his pallor and the strain in his face. He looked ill.

"Don't you think you should go with softer colours," Dixie asked carefully.

"I tried to tell him that," Alix said. "He won't budge."

"Stop dancing around it, Dix. I know I look like shit but I don't think I'll be doing any more videos and if this is going to be my swan song, I'm going out the way I came in. Robin, can you get a soft light on me?"

"No problem."

"What do you mean your last video," Dixie snapped. "So much for thinking positive. You're being hypocritical, Joel. You've been a lot of things before, but you've never been that."

She was on the verge of tears. He put a comforting arm around her and faced the rest of the group. "Look, I'm feeling not too bad and I'm still positive but let's deal with some facts. Nothing about the way I look is going to improve. Fact. As I get worse, I sure as hell don't want to be on film. Fact. So let's make the most of it and we can cover me up any way you like with the other videos. For this one, I want reality. Understood?" Nods all around. "Then let's have some fun. Believe me, once I start the vocals the atmosphere around here will definitely lighten."

It did. As planned, Joel was isolated in a small booth, crooning away, seemingly unaware that the other band members were sporting various types of ear gear in an attempt to shut out the sound of his voice. The final effect was hilarious, as he knew it would be with hams like Bear and Dixie in full form. The isolation worked; he was able to shoot his part separately and in a few takes and then could go home.

By Sunday night he was down with a fever again. Alix put him to bed and kept watch. By the next day it still hadn't broken and she could get little response. There was an infinite weariness about him. Mildred arrived and came upstairs to have a look.

"I think you should take him to the hospital. My son went through these fevers too and we found that he was merely dehydrated. Call his doctor, dear."

Dr. Marlowe agreed so Alix and Mildred bundled him up and drove over. He was admitted and whisked away for tests. Alix sent Mildred home, called the others and settled in for the long wait for results. The initial problem was severe dehydration. Joel was hooked up to an IV and Alix grew more worried as he continued to sleep, still weary beyond words and largely unresponsive.

As the test results came in negative each time, Dr. Marlowe assured her that the only problem was dehydration. The fever would eventually abate and Joel would start on the road to recovery again.

By the second night, Alix was frantic. She talked almost constantly, urging him to answer. She didn't care if he got mad and said things to hurt her – she would've welcomed it as something at least – but he deserted her. On the third day the fever broke, followed by a drenching sweat. She stayed late with him, talking quietly, changing his sweat-soaked gown as often as he needed it. The two climbed back aboard life and recovery.

She urged the band to stay in the studio and promised she would work to catch up when Joel got better. It was important to him that things continue and it gave him something to shoot for. By the end of the week, he was allowed to go home. He was to take it easy and not push himself but the studio was an option he didn't have shut down yet and that was all that counted for the time being.

Alix reluctantly headed back in to work on vocals and harmonies with Leo and Dixie and another track was completed.

"We're getting there," Leo assured her.

She nodded, fretting, anxious to get home. "Joel has something he wants to work on. He's been hinting about it all week. If all goes well he'll be in here tomorrow to talk about it."

"Any idea what it is?"

"No but he's real determined to get this recorded."

"Then record it we will."

"You're being awfully cooperative lately. Do you know something the rest of us don't?"

Leo put his arm around her. "No, I'd tell you if I did. I just think we should follow Joel's lead. There was never anything wrong with his instincts before and there's nothing wrong with them now. If he thinks a song will fly, it'll fly. Come on, Alix, stop being paranoid."

"Sorry Leo; the pressure gets to me sometimes."

"It gets to us all." He hesitated. "Look, I'm going to level with you. I think Hal Mason has said something. Remember that greenhorn reporter who bugged Joel during our conference last summer? She stopped me on the way in here today and asked point blank what was wrong with him. She's heard rumours about another hospital stay."

"What? He just got out. How the hell could someone find out so fast?"

"It's a matter of public record. All you have to do is phone admissions and ask."

"But who would know to do it?"

"Mason. I don't know if it was him, but word is getting out among our friends and acquaintances. Someone has opened their mouth to the press and I think Joel should know."

"Thank corporate wisdom the house title is buried in one of his holding companies. At least no one has tracked down where he lives yet."

"I think that's only a matter of time. It's best if he takes it public."

"We've had this talk before, Leo, and he's resisted every time. He wants his privacy and he's determined to keep it as long as he can."

"Just let him know."

CHAPTER 36

Spring 1994

Joel was resting when Alix came in but got up as soon as he heard her moving around. She was in the kitchen, standing in front of the fridge contemplating dinner, when he came up behind her.

"I got the song fleshed out. You want to work on it tomorrow?"

She spun around. "Sure."

"Sorry," he said, grinning, "didn't mean to scare you. You off in la la land?"

"Guess so."

"What's wrong? Someone upset you?"

She took a deep breath. "Leo got stopped by a reporter on his way into the studio who asked what's wrong with you. Someone put the wind up about your last hospital visit."

The grin abruptly disappeared. "Shit."

"I think it's time, Joel. Maybe if you answer their questions they'll leave you in peace."

"Not yet, Alix. I'll know when the time is and I'll do something about it then. I want to get this damn album in the can before anything breaks over my head."

"We're getting there, slowly but steadily."

"And you thought I'd get behind. Those tapes came in real handy. I'm glad I got Jack to educate me."

"Yeah, yeah, if you're finished giving yourself pats on the back you want to help me sort out dinner? I'm starved."

The two cooked their meal and ate in front of the television, watching a video. The evening passed quietly and both were in bed early.

Joel took Alix downstairs the next day, handed her a lyric sheet and briefly outlined the song he'd been working on. It was a soft, lovely ballad called 'The Forever Room'. At first it sounded like a love song but as she went over the lyrics she realized it wasn't. He was talking about them. The room was a place where time stood still, where they were always young and healthy and together. It was a moment frozen where they could hide and stay safe. It was Joel's swan song, though they didn't know it at the time. Both worked most of the morning and then separated, Joel to rest before lunch with Mildred, Alix to the studio.

"I'm coming in tomorrow so take the sheets and the tape we made with you and get the others going. I'd like to make a start on this."

The band spent the afternoon producing a rich softness that brought the song out. Like his last one, it was simply constructed, with delicate touches strewn throughout. As a solo piece it was one of the best things he'd done in a long time.

Alix returned home early to work on vocals. Her guitar wasn't needed for the recording; Joel wanted to take care of that himself. She sat downstairs, going over the song, strumming softly to accompany herself. The words whispered in the still room, gentle and with a haunting sweetness to them. Halfway through another variation she put her guitar aside and started to cry. Joel found her a few minutes later.

He sat down and took her in his arms. She pressed herself against him, the misery pouring down her cheeks. "Don't leave me, please."

"Stop it," he said, voice straining. "You can't ask me not to die. I don't have a choice."

"I'm sorry."

"At least we got a warning, girl. Look at the time we're getting in – time that means something. I love you, Alix, and I'll always be around in one way or another."

"I love you too. I just wish things were different."

"Wishing won't make it happen. All we can do is get the best out of it. 'Kay?" He pushed her away and gently wiped the tears from her eyes. "I had a good time and I lived long enough to see my dreams come true. A lot of people aren't that lucky. And who says it's over? We have time left. It's not going to go up in a puff of smoke tomorrow, you know."

"I know. I'm sorry. And I should be comforting you."

"We don't apologize in alien land. I'll get my comfort some other time. This time it's your turn."

"Seems like it always is. Who comforts you, Joel?"

He smiled. "You do. When you fuss over dinner or wake me up in the middle of the night with a glass of juice 'cos I'm sweating or when you sleep beside me or when you do any of the dozens of things you do for me. I'm not alone in this. It's you and me. That's a lot of comfort." He stood up. "Now come on. I think you've worked long enough. Let's go upstairs and get some grub."

Joel came down with another fever after dinner and went to bed. Alix pressed him to drink liquids and got up frequently to check on him. It broke sometime in the early hours before dawn. She went in to find the sheets soaked and woke him up to change them. The heavy sweats left him feeling refreshed and he was ready to go into the studio the following morning.

Everyone had done their homework and work went speedily along. When Alix sat down to do the vocals, she choked halfway through the first attempt, her eyes wet with unshed tears. Joel called a halt and went to sit beside her.

He kissed her gently. "Come on, girl, don't let me down. You can do it and it's going to be a smash. "Kay?"

She nodded. He moved his stool back behind her, signalled to Jack for the playback and they started again.

It took five more tries but she finally got it right and the effort was worth the trouble. Jack sat up in the booth, silent and grieving. If he had suspicions about Joel before, all had just been confirmed by the scene that had gone on down below. The weight loss and frequent absences, the lack of energy, the pallor and strain – he hadn't wanted to believe but this reality left him no choice. Bear and Leo sat stoically throughout the session and Dixie had twice gone off to the bathroom to pull herself together. When they broke for lunch it was with hugs among the band members.

The five left the studio together. Leo groaned loudly when they got outside. There were a handful of reporters waiting by the main door. Bear moved in close to Joel. A woman separated herself from the group and zeroed in, tape recorder in hand.

"Sue Downey, the Echo. Remember me, Joel?"

The rookie with a nose for a story. "Yeah."

"I have some questions about your recent visit to the hospital. That's three times since last spring. What were you in for this time?"

The harsh face closed, the green eyes glittered and the cruel mouth was a thin, fine line. "No comment."

"The band hasn't toured in a year and we've had all sorts of snow thrown at us. Just what is the truth, Joel? What's wrong with you?"

"I said no comment. Now leave me alone."

Bear moved to intercept the others crowding in. Leo and Dixie each took a side and Alix grabbed Joel's arm, propelling him towards the car.

"That's enough," Bear shouted, the booming voice momentarily stilling all action.

Car doors unlocked, Alix and Joel piled in. She gunned the motor and slid into gear but not before Sue Downey called out one more question. "There are rumours of AIDS, Joel. Is it true?"

The tires squealed as Alix wheeled out of the parking lot. Unseen, the reporter detached herself from the others, sprung into her car and followed the pair home.

CHAPTER 37

Alix immediately started in once they were safely in the garage but Joel held up a restraining hand. "I don't want to hear it and I don't want to talk about it."

"We have to do something."

"Not now," he bit out. "When I have a plan I'll let you know. Until then, shut up."

She understood that his anger was not directed at her. Both were too shaken up to think rationally and Joel was exhausted. He went inside and straight to his room. In the days that followed, nothing more was said.

Joel's cough was developing again but he put it down to strain and took a few days off. He lolled about on the couch, watching TV with Mildred or rested in bed and, when he felt energized enough, would disappear to the basement, shutting the door behind him. Anyone who happened to turn up wanting to jam was intercepted by Mildred and sent on their way. That was his only concession to the press incident.

When Ash called one morning wanting to drop by, Joel asked Mildred to let him in. Ash grinned as he stepped across the threshold and she quickly bolted the door behind him. "I hear you've become a smart warden."

She smiled, patting him on the shoulder. "And I'm keeping my prisoner out of sight and free from company?"

"Pretty much."

"Good, because that is precisely what he asked me to do. Though I must admit, some of them get very insistent."

"Keep up the good work, Mildred. You're doing a fine job and don't let anyone tell you differently."

"I won't dear, you can be sure of that. Joel is in the basement. I've made some tea and biscuits and I'll bring them right along."

He went down to find his friend just finishing a recording. "You want a beer?"

"Mildred's bringing tea and biscuits."

He laughed. "She would. I'm glad you got her for us, Ash; I don't know what we'd do without her. It's not just the difference she's made in the work Alix has to do, it's her whole personality. I can't imagine her not being here. She's a gem."

"I told you. I've known her about four years now and she just keeps surprising me. She was a mess when she first came to the Centre for help, when her son was sick, but we did what we could and she's given it back in waves. We miss her not being around so much but she drops by sometimes on her way home. It's people like her that really make the grade."

The door opened and Mildred came in with a loaded tray. Joel helped her set it down on a nearby table and kissed her cheek. "Thanks, sunshine."

She laid a gentle hand on his cheek. "You're welcome, charmer, anytime, as long as you call me sweet names." With a wink at Ash, she headed back upstairs.

Joel took a seat. "She cracks me up. You know, sometimes she makes me feel like a kid. Wish my mother had been like that." He poured a cup of tea and took a drink from the glass of juice on the tray.

Ash laughed. "Still a two-fisted drinker, I see."

"Yeah, but it sure as hell is a change from Scotch and beer. I don't drink much alcohol these days but Alix and Mildred have me downing everything else all the time. I'm always pissing."

Ash took the cup Joel offered. "It's important with these fever/sweat cycles. Are you doing okay?"

"I'm holding. For now, that's as okay as it gets." He regarded his friend levelly. "We talk on the phone all the time, Ash, and you visit but you usually don't make an appointment. So what's up? I have a funny feeling this isn't exactly a social call."

"Straight to the point as usual."

"Quickest way to get things done."

He took a deep breath. "The Centre, in conjunction with some other agencies, is doing an educational video package for high schools. It's sort of an all-points type of thing with music, interviews and information. I'm helping to set it up and I want to know if you'll let someone interview you."

"Did you tell them about me?"

"Of course not. Look, I know you've been helping out on the sly, so will you come out and do it publicly?"

Joel's face went blank. "What are you talking about?"

"I was in the office when a cheque arrived and Tisha told me this company has been making donations every month for over two years. I was around when you set your holding companies up, remember? I even helped you think up a name or two so don't try to snow me. I saw the cheque."

"So what if I want to donate?"

"I think it's great. And as for the interview, I'm the only one asking. It targets mid to late teens – the ones just starting to get sexually active."

"And the ones getting sick," he finished.

"A lot of them listen to your music and want to have your rep. I think it would help a lot. There's a big difference between having someone cool talk to you and a doctor giving you health advice."

"I know. Well I guess people have to know sometime and too many have already figured it out. Did you hear what happened outside the studio the other day?"

"Leo told me. What are you going to do?"

"I'm still working on it."

"I've had a lot of questions asked that I can't answer too. People will always believe what they want. This is a chance to set the record straight your way."

"'Kay, Ash, set it up."

"Thanks." He relaxed, glad the hard part was over and surprised at how easy it had been. Alix warned him that he'd have a fight on his hands. "Now we can have a visit."

"Had you going, didn't I," Joel said with a wicked smirk. "I still got the power, sick or not."

"Yeah, and as Alix is so fond of saying, eat ratshit. Now, what are you working on?"

He launched into his latest projects and Ash talked about his designs. He stayed for lunch but, seeing his friend start to flag, finished quickly and said good-bye, promising to call when things were ready. Ash drove home quietly, thinking about the years they had been friends. It saddened him at the turn things had taken and yet, since the diagnosis, not only had the friendship been forged in a new and closer way, its richness had ripened.

Joel was up when Alix came home. He grinned and gave her a hug but, before he could ask about the studio progress, a racking cough shook him. She froze. "How long has it been this bad?"

"Just since this afternoon."

"It's been getting worse over the last couple of days. I think we should call Dr. Marlowe."

"Already done, girl. I'm to watch and if it gets worse go to the hospital for tests. Relax, I'm on the job."

His half-hearted attempt at a joke fell flat. She started dinner.

"What happened today?"

"We got most of the stuff done for 'Broken Glass' but we need you to redo the solo break before the last verse. Me and Dix made some changes and it's longer than you recorded."

"You bring me a tape?"

She nodded. "Don't overdo it. Promise me. We can wait."

He eyed her with mock impatience. "Oh yeah, right. Come on, no bullshit. We're only halfway through the album. I'll listen tonight and if I can I'll do it tomorrow. If it's just adding on and blending I can work with Jack and probably be done by lunch."

"There's no panic, honest."

"Shut up. This is important. You and Dix are coming up with some good stuff and you should be encouraged."

She laughed. "You pompous son of a bitch."

"Just call me guru."

"I like idiot better."

He smacked her good-naturedly and went to sit on one of the stools at the island where she was chopping vegetables. Without thinking, she poured him a glass of juice and slid it across, then picked up her knife and carried on. Joel obligingly took a sip. The two looked at each other suddenly and started to giggle.

"It's second nature now."

"Seems to be."

"At least we're still on the same wavelength."

"That's a given. Always was."

"Yeah. You want a Scotch?"

"I wouldn't say no."

He poured her one, added ice and clinked his glass against hers before drinking. "Here's to wavelengths."

After dinner, Joel put the tape on and they spent an hour discussing it. Satisfied that he could work quickly, he went to bed earlier than usual so he would be energized for the morning session. Alix got up regularly during the night to check on him. The cycle of fevers and sweats was increasing and sometimes he would lie chilling in soaking pajamas with no energy to get up and change. She was also vigilant about getting as much fluid down him as possible to replace what he lost. His stay in hospital for dehydration had terrified her, especially when he had withdrawn into himself, and she did not want a repeat of that. But the process was exhausting and when she stumbled into his room at three a.m. he regarded her with concern.

She poured him a glass of juice and held his head up so he could drink. His forehead was very hot. The fever would soon break. "I want you to get hold of Ash tomorrow."

"Shhh. Just lay back. I'll stay here a while."

"I want a night nurse."

"Fuck off."

"You look like shit, Alix, and you're beat most of the time. You can't do it all on your own."

"We'll discuss it tomorrow. Get some rest."

She pressed a damp cloth over his face and chest and he sighed with pleasure. No one could give him her particular brand of care but he was determined. The fever broke soon afterwards. Alix changed everything, gave him another drink, and went off to get a couple of hours of sleep.

The two of them were up early and had breakfast before heading into the studio. He seemed frail today and his cough hadn't gotten any better but he persevered with Jack, ignoring his friends' concerned pleas to take it easy. The track was completed before noon. With five tracks still left to do, Joel began making plans for 'The Forever Room' video but Alix forestalled him. There would be time enough later. She dropped him off at home and went back out to buy groceries.

He seized the opportunity and called Ash. "Can you find me a night nurse?"

"You must have read my mind. I just got off the phone with Leo. He figured we should start searching for one and I said we shouldn't wait. The last time I saw Alix she looked like death warmed over."

"She's burning the candle at both ends. I need someone to be around but it can't always be her. She gets piss all for sleep now anyway."

"You all right?"

"For now but the sooner we can get someone in the better. Can you take care of it?"

"Sure. You want me to tell Alix?"

He laughed. "Are you nuts? You want to get yourself hurt? No, pal, I'll tell her. She won't charge me like a mad bull. Let's face it – I'm the only one who can get away with pulling a fast one."

"You're an asshole."

"So people keep telling me."

"I'll get on it right away. You sure you're okay?"

"Still holding." He hung up and the cough hit him again.

Mildred came in from the kitchen, frowning. "I don't like the sound of that, young man. Up to bed with you and if it's no better by the end of your nap you're going to the doctor."

He headed wearily for the stairs. "Ash is right. You are a smart warden."

"And aren't you the lucky one?"

"I wouldn't have it any other way."

"I'll be right up with a fresh jug of juice. You have a drink before you head off to the land of nod."

"Yes, ma'am."

She took some oranges out of the fridge, very worried. That cough sounded like trouble.

CHAPTER 38

The housekeeper caught Alix as soon as she walked through the door. "His cough is much worse, dear."

"I'll call."

"He's already done that. Don't worry, he won't do anything to endanger his health. You don't fret, dear. Between the two of us we'll see him right."

She smiled as Mildred donned her coat and went home for the day, but her blood turned cold at the thought that Joel might be sickening again. Brave face or not, he was terrified that each time he went into the hospital he wouldn't come out alive. So was she.

She cooked dinner and they ate in front of the television with a video.

Halfway through the screening the phone rang and he jumped up to answer it before Alix could move. The conversation was brief and when he retook his seat, he gently took the VCR control away from her and laid it aside. "That was Ash."

"What's wrong?"

"Nothing. Look, I know you're knocking yourself out for me and I appreciate it but..."

"Leave it, Joel. I want to take care of you."

"You do and still will, but I called Ash this afternoon and asked him to find a nurse who'll come for a few hours during the night. You need some rest, girl. I can't have you getting sick on me now. If you won't agree for your sake, then do it for mine. She's only available three times a week but at least you'll get some sleep. We'll find someone to take up the slack for the other nights and you won't have to get up every hour to make sure I'm all right. It's the same situation with us having Mildred – it gives us more time to be with each other."

She knew that a nurse was the last thing he wanted because it meant he was getting worse and his concern for her touched her deeply. She had to admit she was bone tired and sometimes resented having to get up when her eyes felt gritty and her head pounded from lack of sleep. Occasionally, in the dead of night, she wondered if she would ever get a full night's rest again and guilt would wash over her in sickening waves as she thought about what that meant. It could only happen when Joel no longer needed looking after. For now, he was offering a reprieve.

"You must see the sense in it," he carried on, seeing the gamut of emotions travelling across her worn face. "Don't make this any harder."

She turned to him with a sigh. "I won't. Thanks for thinking of me. I know it isn't easy and I don't like the idea of a stranger in here but you're right. I'm tired. I accept and I won't make a fuss." She held out her hand. "Pact?"

He took it and pulled her to him, hugging her tightly. "Pact."

"Now can we finish watching the movie?"

He laughed and released her. "I guess so. Then bed for you, young lady."

"When will she be here?"

"Tomorrow night. It'll be fine - you'll see."

Harriet checked in the next day. She was a semi-retired nurse with a no nonsense attitude who set herself up in the spare room and took over the medical side of things. Ash had warned them that she was quite martial but she'd come highly recommended and Joel would get excellent care. If her distance was a way to avoid getting involved with her patients, then that was to be accepted. Joel seemed happy. She was friendly, brisk and efficient and threatened Alix in no way at all. She checked on him, did what had to be done, monitored temperatures, dispensed medication and then was gone. If Alix happened to be awake and came in to give Joel a back rub or to just sit with him, she was not put out in any way. Their midnight moments continued without too much interruption.

Joel came downstairs early one morning to find Mildred engaged in an argument with someone at the front door. Angry, he broke his privacy rule and hurried to her side. "What's going on?"

"Sue Downey, Joel. I have some questions."

"That's enough, off you go," Mildred insisted.

"I'll handle this." He waited until she had reluctantly retreated into the kitchen and turned on the reporter. "How the hell did you get this address?"

She smiled smugly. "I usually don't reveal my sources but this time it won't hurt. I followed you home from the studio last week. Now will you answer some questions?"

"Get off my property."

"If it's not me, it'll be someone else."

"Well it's not going to be you so clear off. Otherwise I'll get the heat and have you charged with trespassing." She started to protest but he held up his hand to forestall her. "I mean it. Ring that damn bell again and I won't be responsible." He slammed the door, bolted it and leaned back, trembling.

Mildred moved in quickly. "Are you all right, dear?"

"I have a feeling hell is going to break loose."

"We'll cope. Why don't you ask that nice Bear to give us a hand?"

He kissed her cheek. "I think I'll do just that."

"Then come in before your breakfast gets cold."

"'Kay, Mildred, my angel, you got yourself a deal."

He went into the living room and made two calls, then joined her in the kitchen.

Ash got in touch at the end of the week. "I got the taping set up. Okay to pick you up tomorrow morning?"

"Sure thing."

He paused. "Look, word has gotten around about what you're doing. We have some press promoting this thing and they're bound to make a nuisance of themselves."

"One already has. The bitch that pegged me outside the studio followed us home and was ringing the damn doorbell yesterday."

"It was only a matter of time."

"I know." A tremor of dread ran through him. "I phoned Marv over at the Express office. I've dealt with him for years and I trust him. I agreed to an interview if he'd let me do things my way and then that's it – no more dealing with the fourth estate. I'm holing up and I don't want any trouble. Me and Alix talked it over and she thinks it's a good thing this is coming out into the open."

"I agree, but you have to be ready for hassles. You can't just make a statement and then sit back and expect no one to want more information. There's fans and well-wishers to consider too."

"I know. That's why I asked Bear to keep me company when I go out from now on. I have a funny feeling that between him and Alix no one will bug me. Can you imagine trying to get past those two in a bad mood?"

"I'd like to see someone try. It sure would be a laugh."

"For us, maybe, but no picnic for them. You got one vicious streak there, my friend."

"Just a tabloid reader's thirst for blood, same as you. My smart sports car only holds two so do you want to meet me at the taping?"

"No, I like to ride in that bombed out wreck. Things are cleared with Alix and Bear. They'll follow along and then the four of us can come back here for lunch. Mildred offered to whip us up a home-cooked feast."

"When's your other interview?"

"Day after. Marv's coming here in the a.m."

"Sounds like a plan. You sure you're okay for this?"

"I'm holding and to be honest I'm getting kind of sick of answering that question. A few of you don't seem to believe me but, straight up, if anything is happening I'll let you know. Now stop nagging."

"I am not, nor ever was, a nag," he said indignantly.

"Fair enough. See you tomorrow."

Ash got in touch with the video people confirming filming the next day and then sat back behind the desk in his office, staring vacantly at the wall. There was a lot of work to do but, for once, his creativity had deserted him. Why was Joel suddenly so anxious to come clean when he'd been hiding behind a wall of silence for months? Speculation about that didn't bear the light of day right now. Locking up, he drove over to a bar and spent the afternoon getting methodically, depressingly drunk.

Bleary-eyed and hungover the following morning, he drove his friend as arranged, Alix and Bear in tow. They were ushered into a small room by the cameraman. The interviewer shook hands with Joel, saw him comfortably seated and invited Ash, Alix and Bear to help themselves to coffee and donuts in another room before politely closing the door. Joel was closeted in for an hour. He emerged with a shaky smile and a resigned air but seemed upbeat enough. The interviewer thanked him, bid everyone good-bye and saw them out the back door with a minimum of fuss. He understood the need for privacy and no one had been alerted as to the time of the appointment. The four stepped into a deserted street, got into their vehicles and proceeded home to lunch.

Joel related how the man had led him through a series of questions designed to provide a framework for discussion and added that the work had been neither hard nor taxing.

"He's a big wig in some mag rag apparently," Ash explained.

"He sure as hell knows his stuff. Talk about manipulation. Even me and you could learn from him and you know how good at head games we are."

"Were," Ash corrected. "We haven't been playing them the last couple years."

"Don't tell me that you two have finally grown up," Alix teased.

Bear poured himself a beer. "The guy was like some kind of machine. Too cold for my tastes."

"I didn't know they ran that way," Ash said dryly.

"Keep talking and you'll be the one running," Bear responded good-naturedly.

"Now children, no fighting," Mildred cut in, laughing.

"Thanks, sunshine," Joel said brightly. "Sorry about these guys but, you know, sometimes you just can't pick your friends. Honest, they're really a good bunch when they're sleeping."

"They're a good bunch awake too. Who's for cake?"

CHAPTER 39

Joel spent a bad night, tossing with fever, vomiting dinner up and generally finding consciousness a misery. Harriet had her hands full. Alix stayed with the nurse, trying to help but it was after two a.m. before they finally got him settled.

He came down the next morning weary and shaky. Alix couldn't coax him into having breakfast but she managed to get him to swallow three glasses of juice and his morning pills.

"Cancel this interview," she begged.

"Leave me alone, please. I promise to do whatever you want after but I have to get this over with."

She couldn't convince him to change his mind and he disappeared downstairs when the doorbell rang. Mildred followed with a tray of coffee and juices and came back up shaking her head. He was determined.

Marv stood awkwardly at the door when Alix opened it, alone and armed with a tape recorder and notebook. "Hello, beautiful morning for April. No rain in sight."

"Yeah, it is, Marv. Joel's in the basement. I'll show you down but listen, do me a favour and don't tell him I asked. You know why you're here?"

He nodded sadly. "Joel didn't go into details when he called. He just said he wanted to give me an interview."

"He's not doing well today so go easy and don't tire him out. Say you have another appointment or something but, please, don't push him."

"I won't." He stepped inside. "For what it's worth, I'll keep this address to myself. The one thing I'm sure the poor bugger needs more than anything now is his privacy."

"Thanks, Marv. We've already been tracked down but there haven't been a lot of hassles yet. Once this gets out I have a feeling the roof will blow."

"You have my word; I'll do what I can to help."

She took him to the downstairs door and closed it gently behind him. The phone rang. Dr. Marlowe got straight to the point.

"Joel should come in for a transfusion, Alix. It will make him feel much better. Will you bring him in tomorrow?"

"Can we make it today? He had a bad night and I really think you should see him."

"No improvement on the cough and general fatigue?"

"I think he's feeling worse but he can be a clam when he wants and he insists he's fine. He'll listen to you though."

"I'll have everything ready by three p.m."

She hung up, fighting tears. Mildred found her a few minutes later and enfolded her in a wave of perfume and flour. She was baking. Alix explained what the doctor wanted and the older woman nodded firmly.

"It's best, dear. I've been very worried. I'm sure it's nothing serious so let's leave this to the good doctor. Come in to the kitchen. We'll have a nice cup of coffee and a hot biscuit. They're just out of the oven."

Marv looked around him in awe. "This place is a veritable studio. You've outdone yourself."

"I had a lot of help. You want a coffee?"

"Sure, top up my caffeine level." He sat down opposite the guitarist and sorted out the tools of his trade, glancing curiously at Joel. The man was a shadow of the mercurial figure that had treaded hundreds of stages. Even the tailored, loose clothing didn't hide the weight loss. His skin was a sickly grey colour, his face lined and drawn. The blonde hair was threaded with white. Though prepared for a change, this was a shock.

Joel smiled. "I know, I look like hell."

"You've been in the wars and you've got battle scars."

"Start your tape recorder, Marv. I'll tell you what's been going on and then you can ask any questions you want. Make it good 'cos this is a one-off."

He smiled in spite of himself. "This is the first time in years you've given me that kind of freedom."

"Who would've guessed, huh?"

The recorder light came on. "How long have you been sick?"

"It's April now, so that means I tested positive almost two years ago in England."

"'The Fast Track' tour, right?"

"Yeah. I broke through to full-blown AIDS last May."

"So the 'Raising Hell' tour was cancelled for you, not Dixie Adler."

"At the time it was both of us but, yeah, it would've been for me if Dix hadn't gotten sick. We used it as a cover."

"I checked the hospital records; you've been in three times – last May, November and this year in February."

"Twice for PCP –AIDS-related pneumonia – and this last one for dehydration."

"Now that the dates are cleared up, let's get down to you."

The interview wound on and Marv found himself working against the clock. Joel was visibly tiring and the racking cough was becoming more frequent. After an hour and a half he had the base of what he needed.

"Anything to add?"

"Yeah. I'd like the groupies to get themselves tested. I'm sorry I was careless but I haven't been with anyone since I got sick. Better late than never. And, for fuck's sake, tell everyone to use a condom. Star-fucking seems to be a popular past-time for some people but it can kill you."

Marv packed up and extended his hand. "I don't know what to say, Joel, but thanks for letting me be the one to do this. I'm sorry, more than I can tell you, for what's happened. You're a great talent and you've been a lot of fun for me over the years."

The guitarist shook hands. "Thanks, Marv, the feeling's mutual."

The reporter climbed the stairs, solemn and poker-faced. Alix saw him to the door. "I got my story but I sure as hell don't relish writing it." He swallowed hard. "I'll do my best by him, Alix, and that's a promise."

"That's why he asked for you, Marv."

She bolted the door behind him and headed downstairs. Joel sat dejectedly, depressed and tired. She perched on the chair and put her arm around him.

"Well, I guess it's official now," he whispered.

He turned, pressing his face against her chest. She hugged him gently, stroking his hair. "He'll do it right."

"I know."

She took a deep breath. "Dr. Marlowe called. He wants you in the hospital this afternoon for a transfusion. He says it'll make you feel a lot better."

"'Kay. I don't want any lunch. I'm going to bed. Wake me when it's time to go." He got up slowly and headed for the stairs. The look he shot her was full of fear and a kind of resignation. "Will you lay down with me for a while?"

"I'll be right up."

Alix drove them to the hospital later and, having delivered Joel into the hands of the waiting nurses, retreated with a book to wait. Dr. Marlowe had warned her that the procedure would take quite a bit of time. She tried to concentrate on what she was reading but the words kept blurring on the page and she finally gave up. Going outside, she smoked several cigarettes and wandered around the grounds.

Once inside again, she waited another hour before a nurse came to announce that she could see her friend. Puzzled, she followed her down the hall to a private room. Joel sat on the edge of the bed, head down, face flushed and rosy from the infusion of new blood.

"What's going on?"

He raised lacklustre eyes to her face and in a dull, almost bored voice said, "They're admitting me. You might as well go home. I'll see you in the morning."

"What the hell is wrong?"

"It's PCP. They wanted to do a bronc but I'm not going through that bullshit again. The doc is sure anyway, so they're hooking me up to a drip. I guess I'll be here a while."

She sat beside him, putting an arm around his bowed shoulders. "We'll get through it like we did the last two..."

He cut her off. "It doesn't matter anymore. It's okay, girl. I don't need a pep talk. Just leave me alone. I'm tired; I want to sleep."

He turned away. Alarmed, she sought out Dr. Marlowe.

"He'll come around, Alix," he said reassuringly. "He's tired and dispirited. You go get some rest. We'll take good care of him. I'll see he gets something to help him sleep and that should take care of this despondency. He'll be up and fighting in the morning."

She headed home and phoned Ash. The two talked for an hour, going over his previous symptoms, consoling each other and then, exhausted by worry, strain and the previous night, she went gratefully to bed.

Joel didn't come around in the next couple of days. Hooked up to the IV, medicine dripped into his veins, working its wonders. The cough abated and his breathing improved but the depression and withdrawal persisted. Friends could not draw him out and Alix was running out of things to say. A grunt or a simple answer were almost beyond him and often he just stared at the wall, ignoring her altogether.

By the fifth day she was panicking. Dr. Marlowe was worried but at a loss as to what to do. Joel's spirit had been sucked into a mud of apathy and he didn't care enough to break free.

She had spent the morning trying desperately to get some response but he merely turned a blind eye to her attempts. Finally, losing her temper, she abandoned the pleading, gentle tones and started to yell. He continued to ignore her. She turned away, feeling in her pockets for something to throw at him and came across some loose Xanax pills. Joel had been on them for months for anxiety. She occasionally took them herself, usually at dawn to relieve the stress of a night of constantly interrupted sleep. The pill had been invaluable to both of them. Joel had ceased to question the medication because there was so much of it: the AZT, the amino acid supplement because his body no longer produced it, the pills to help offset the AZT side effects, the endless vitamins she pumped into him, the aspirin for fevers and a host of others Dr. Marlowe would introduce for a time to relieve a passing infection. And the Xanax. Alix was careful when dispensing pills but Joel never took much notice.

She pulled out the four left in her pocket and waved them in front of his face – the little pills that so resembled the speed tabs they used to take.

"Look, Joel," she bit out. "I got some speed."

"I don't care."

"Me either so let's do these. Fuck the medication, the food, the fluids – fuck the whole fight. Let's get high and go get drunk and drive off Lion's Gate Bridge. You don't give a damn anymore? Well I don't either. Remember what Ash used to tell us? Live fast, die young and make a beautiful corpse. I'll unhook you and get you dressed and we'll blow this thing out."

She moved around while she hissed at him and he watched her intently, his green eyes narrowing. "Come on, asshole!" With a sudden cackle, she tossed the pills into her mouth.

He sat bolt upright. "Are you fucking nuts?!"

She turned away quickly and headed for the door, spitting the tablets into her palm.

"Don't you walk out on me," he yelled. "Where the hell do you think you're going?"

"I thought you didn't care. I'm going to get your stuff. You checking out? Burrard Inlet is waiting for us."

"Alix, stay here, I'll call a nurse. You got to get that shit out of your system right now. We didn't even do that many when we were speeding every day."

Slowly she walked back to his bed, eyes burning into his. When she reached his side she opened her hand. Taking a tissue out of the box beside her, she deposited the pills, wrapped them tightly and threw them in the garbage. She continued to stare at him, her face hard, not saying anything.

The anger cleared slowly and he nodded once. "A trick."

"At least it got a reaction."

"I couldn't, Alix; it all seemed so useless."

"I can't help you fight if you won't let me and I can't do it alone."

"I just feel like I'm going down."

"Then we might as well get some speed and take it. If you go down then I'm going too. We're in this together. I'll leave that on your conscience."

Tears welled up suddenly and spilled down his thin face. "I can't take it sometimes. I don't want to die. Help me."

She hugged him fiercely. Gasping sobs racked the battered form and he cried harshly, hanging on to her for dear life. She had never seen him sob like this. She thought of all the times she had poured out the poison in tears and wondered at what he'd built up inside, trying to be a rock for all of them. She wanted to take his pain away and she held on, letting him know that she was now the rock.

After a long while, his tears were spent and he drew back from her, blindly taking the tissue she offered. Her shoulder was damp. She would never tell him that once, late at night, she had considered that solution. It seemed so simple in the lonely, cold hours – a suicide to take them to where life stopped hurting, where he didn't have to suffer and she didn't have to stand helplessly by and watch. But it was never the answer and her other self – the survivor – had called her back from that road before she'd gone too far down it.

"Don't ever go away from me again, Joel, please. Pact. I can't take it when you're here and I can't reach you."

"'Kay, girl, I won't run inside anymore. Pact."

Dr. Marlowe was delighted with his patient's re-emergence from the cocoon he had woven himself into and, though he'd heard about the yelling that upset the nurses, he never let on. He simply accepted that Joel was back in the ring to fight with his usual determination.

CHAPTER 40

Alix hadn't laid eyes on Sherri in three weeks. She finally phoned to let her know what was going on. There hadn't been time before. She was too panicked by her friend's state of mind.

"I'm wrapped up with a closing."

"What's really going on?"

There was a long pause. "I can't do it," she said slowly. "Things weren't so bad when Joel looked well but the last time I saw him he was so thin and beaten. I can't deal with it; I'm afraid to even touch him."

'He won't break."

"It isn't that. I'm afraid..."

"Of what," Alix said tersely, suspecting the reply.

"He's sick."

"He's dying, Sherri. Don't you think he deserves your support? It's out in the press and he needs you now more than ever."

"I can't..."

"You're scared, aren't you?" The woman didn't answer and Alix fought to control her temper. "You read the information. You can't get AIDS from being around him. What the fuck are you up to?"

"I'm busy; I have to go."

"He figured you wouldn't be able to take the pressure and he understands. That's a laugh, huh? He knew this would happen. I wonder if he'll get any satisfaction out of being right. You make me sick. You're there for the fun but when things get messy you're off. So you won't go see him?"

"I'm sorry. Tell him I'll call when he gets home."

"Fuck off," she said acidly. "He doesn't need this shit. Just leave him alone." She slammed the phone down.

She decided not to tell Joel and yet, she figured he was probably more aware of the snubs than she was. This had become the norm as he got visibly weaker and more ill. Acquaintances no longer dropped by. Many felt safe enough to phone and he enjoyed the gab sessions but fewer and fewer were putting in appearances. It was something he had warned her about months ago and she'd merely laughed at his paranoia. He didn't seem to mind and he was grateful for what people could offer. Not Alix. She was furious at the desertion. So far, he'd been in the hospital almost a week and his only visitors had been the core of them that had been in on things from the start.

Frustrated, she headed into the basement to thrash on her guitar. Once Joel was out he'd be pressing for a return to the studio. They still had an album to finish.

By the end of the second week, though he'd lost weight and still looked frail, he was his old self. Fighting to regain his stamina he took to walking the halls visiting other patients or showing his pals around. No mention was made of Sherri.

Brad sat with him for most of one morning, going over the album and bringing him up to date on gossip, plans and everything else that he had missed.

"Do me a favour and keep Alix occupied for most of this afternoon," Joel asked just before his friend got up to leave.

"Sure, Durango. Any particular reason for the snowstorm?"

"I'm seeing our lawyer and I don't want her in the way."

"Anything wrong, hombre?"

"I have to take care of some stuff."

"That's no way to talk."

"I'm being realistic. There are a lot of things I need to get straight and I want to do it now, while I'm not feeling too bad."

Brad looked at him for a long time before nodding. "If it's what you gotta do, then it's what you gotta do. I'll head her off at the pass and keep her busy but don't be too long. She's pretty spirited and she can be kinda hard to rein in when she's feeling skittish."

"Don't I know it," he said, grinning. "Thanks."

"Anytime. I'll be in tomorrow."

He called Robin in to help and they persuaded Alix to come to their house to discuss the next video shoot. He claimed that Joel had been running ideas by him and he was going to do the storyboard with her so that the guitarist wouldn't be troubled with details.

"He wants the shoot as soon as he can and it's an interest he hasn't shown lately," Robin pointed out. "I think we should encourage that. It shows he's getting well and it's better than having him stare at walls."

Robin, reasoning that Joel would want complete privacy, decided to make the fiction fact and called in the rest of the Blue Mask for the same purpose. Brad applauded her foresight and the six of them spent an enjoyable and productive afternoon.

Alix didn't have a clue that anything was going on until she went to see Joel later. On her way in she ran into their lawyer. He greeted her gravely but did not stop to chat and she entered her friend's room with deepening suspicion. His face bore a look of guilty relief.

"That does it. I've been set up, haven't I? Why was he here?"

He set aside a sheaf of legal papers. "I had some things to do and I asked Brad to waylay you."

"Him and Robin did you one better – they waylaid all of us."

"I never even thought of that."

"Nice of Grayson to come to you."

"I phoned him yesterday. He knows the situation, has from the first and he's been advising me to do what I've just done."

"And what the hell have you just done?"

She was still angry and he didn't blame her. "Don't get mad, girl, it's for the best. I was trying to spare you the hassle of knowing beforehand."

She looked at the face of the friend she had loved for so long, now ravaged by pain and illness and smiled, coming over to sit on his bed. "All right; I'm listening."

"I just made out my will. Not much has changed from before but there are other things to consider now. I made you the executrix of my estate, which is a fancy way of saying I want you to manage everything.

"I've left some money to various places that help people living with AIDS, some to the Centre – you get my general drift. It's all in the will and I want you to make sure it gets to them." She nodded so he continued.

"I also signed something over to you called an enduring power of attorney. It means you can act for me if I'm not in a position to act for myself."

"What are you talking about?"

"Do you know what a living will is, Alix? It was in those info sheets I gave you."

"I remember."

"It's basically the same thing. Grayson will make sure everyone knows about it who has to. Dr. Marlowe's been told and the head of the nurses' station on this floor." He paused.

"Come on," she said unsteadily, fighting tears. "I know we have to so let's get this over with."

He swallowed hard. "I've got no family but you and our friends. Take care of me when I'm gone. I want to be burned and scattered to the sea."

"Joel..."

"You know what I mean, Alix. Don't put me in the damn ground. And...if anything happens...if I go into a coma or something...no life support..." She started to cry and he struggled to hold onto his composure. "I don't want to be a vegetable living 'cos I'm hooked up to a machine. I couldn't take that. Will you do that for me, girl? You're the only one who can now. That's what I had to take care of. Will you?"

She reached for him and whispered softly, between sobs, "Of course I will."

The two sat entwined in misery. Voices sounded outside in the corridor and then a burst of laughter from Leo. Alix sat back, wiping her eyes.

Leo and Ash sauntered into the room, carrying a flat box. "Dr. Marlowe said we could feed you some real food," Ash said.

Joel bumped shoulders with Alix. "Gourmets, that's what we have here."

"Sticks out a mile."

The two pulled up chairs, unpacked paper plates and napkins and proceeded to dish out pizza.

Joel wanted an early night and asked Ash to take Alix off his hands. She took the joke lightly and kissed him before leaving with the other two. Leo declined an invitation to join them, saying he had a date, his first in weeks. Ash and Alix drove over to the Alley View and settled at a table in a dark back corner.

"It seems like months since I've been here," she said, lighting a cigarette and nodding thanks at the Scotch and two bottles of beer he placed in front of her. He had three gins for himself.

"It has been."

She eyed all the alcohol and shook her head. "Like old times."

"We drank enough to pickle this bar."

"We sure had some good times. Bad ones too, but they're not what I really remember."

"Ditto for me." He sipped his drink. "Robin and Joel should be here to make our little family complete."

"There hasn't been a meeting for a long time. Too many other things going on."

"Do you ever think if we hadn't met here and got started – you know, the band and everything – that maybe Joel wouldn't have gotten sick?"

"That's a lame question, Ash, and you know it. He was a slut long before that. He would've been even if the Blue Mask was never formed."

"You have to admit though, the exposure helped him along."

"Yeah, but you can't blame the band."

"I'm not."

"Joel wanted it all: the fame, the fortune, the women laying themselves at his feet like slaves or doormats or whatever. We were all the same then – greedy and hungry."

"Yeah, but he paid one hell of a price for his share. More than any of us. What he got cost him big."

"We can't think about that now. Like he said, it's too late for regrets and that's pointless anyway. All we can do is go on."

"I realize it's pointless but that doesn't stop me from thinking about alternatives or what ifs or what could've beens."

"Don't waste your energy. Joel's had a good time; had his dreams come true. He told me that. And he's not dead yet."

"I know." He leaned over and kissed her. "No more of the morbids. Let's drink and reminisce about the good old days when we didn't have to be home by midnight because we were getting old."

She laughed. "Who would've thought we'd make thirty?"

"Joel hasn't yet."

"He will. A month isn't so long to go." She raised her glass. "To all of us."

"Forever young."

The two clinked glasses and proceeded to drink the evening away, for old time's sake.

CHAPTER 41

The day Joel checked out of the hospital was a nightmare. Leo came in with the bad news, followed by a grim and determined Bear. Ash, Brad, Robin and Dixie brought up the rear.

"There's a bunch of reporters downstairs," Leo said flatly. "One of them must have called record information to find out when you'd be free. I bet it was that bitch Downey."

Alix's heart sunk; Joel was not up to this. "What are we going to do?"

"I called the police and explained the situation. I'll go wait for them and see what they can do."

"The heat, that's all I need."

"They'll be a big help," Bear said. "I'll take one side of you and Brad'll be on the other. The rest of you surround and we'll go out in a gang." He laid a hand on the guitarist's shoulder. "Don't you worry; I'm a good bodyguard. No one will mess with you."

"Give me your keys, Alix," Ash said. "I'll bring the car right up to the door. It'll be a cakewalk. We'll bundle you and Joel in and I'll take off like greased lightning. We'll be Starsky and Hutch and friend."

"Which one is Alix," Joel asked jokingly. "I'd vote her in as Starsky but she's got no balls."

"Very funny." Alix handed Ash the suitcase she'd packed. "Take Hutch's stuff down with you, please. And if there's a muzzle in the back seat, you'd better get it ready. We're going to need it if he keeps up this shit."

The joking faded quickly as they made their way through the lobby and out the main doors. There were at least a dozen reporters, complete with photographers, ready to catch a snap of the dying man. As the automatic doors shot open, the crowd surged forward. Four policemen were in front, trying to keep them in check.

Alix pushed her way forward, seeing Ash pull up to the curb. A woman broke free and moved in fast, pulling a man with a camera in her wake.

"Sue Downey, Joel, the Echo. What is your current status?"

The man started to snap off photos at an alarming rate. Alix pushed the reporter aside, her face a hard, cruel mask, the black eyes glittering. "Leave us alone," she screeched, grabbing the camera and smashing it on the pavement.

"You bitch," the photographer cried. "I'll sue you."

"Get out of my way, you fucking piece of scum." She looked psychotic.

He halted, stung by the flickering acid and she darted in, fist clenched and already swinging. An iron grip locked onto her wrist; she twisted and kicked hard behind her. The cop went down like he'd been pole-axed. The heel of her leather boot had connected with his knee.

While everyone's attention was diverted, Leo propelled Joel into the back seat of the car and dived in after him. Ash had the front door open and was yelling for Alix. Bear had a grip on three reporters; Brad was helping the remaining policemen keep the rest in place.

A shrill whistle blew, freezing all action. The cop who held it yelled for order. He looked at his partner. "You all right, Fielding?"

The man nodded and got up slowly to face the singer. She watched defiantly, breathing hard, rage still seething through her.

"Considering the circumstances, I won't charge you lady, but count yourself lucky."

"I thought you were supposed to serve and protect, asshole. This fucking mob is attacking a sick man."

"That's enough," the other cop boomed. "Back off now or we'll get the wagon here and charge all of you."

"What about my camera," the photographer whined.

The snap of a shutter sounded in the air and Alix whirled around. "Anyone takes another fucking shot and I'll break everything in sight."

"That's enough!" Fielding approached her, limping. "I understand the situation, Miss Lane, but don't push it. What do you want to do about the camera?"

She turned slowly, eying both policeman and photographer. "Contact Easton Management. I'll pay for the damage."

"Is that acceptable," he asked the man from the Echo.

Her eyes were searing into him and he turned away with a short nod. "I guess so."

"Then let's clear out."

The group started to disperse when Sue Downey jumped in again, tape recorder rolling. "How long do they give you, Joel?"

Alix snarled and charged like a mad bull and the seething crowd erupted. Brad grabbed her and threw her into the front seat of the car, slamming the door as Ash sped away with screeching tires.

Joel collapsed in the back seat, moaning. "Stop it, Alix, I can't take anymore!"

The desperate voice pierced the red haze and she sat back limply, shaking. "Oh fuck, I'm sorry!" Tears poured down her face, harsh and acrid. "I lost it when the pictures started. They're like a pack of fucking vultures."

"Marv wasn't in there," Leo said quietly. "You picked right, Joel."

He didn't reply and the ride back was conducted in silence. Leo and Ash helped him in and got him settled in bed. Mildred brought a wave of soothing care and he submitted gratefully to her ministrations.

He heard the motor revving on Alix's car and winced as she wheeled away. He knew she was in pain and would seek the peace of her precious water. Grieving, worried, he retreated into sleep, knowing it would be a while before she came back. He would've done anything to spare her.

She woke him up a couple of hours later. The madness had gone from her face but her eyes were bloodshot and the small frame was sagging in defeat and remorse. "I'm sorry."

He struggled through the fatigue and sat up, patting a place beside him. She came immediately and he hugged her. "I've decided not to get sick anymore, girl. It's the only way to keep you out of jail."

She laid her head on his shoulder. "I can't let anyone hurt you and when they try it makes me crazy."

He laughed softly. "I noticed."

"I'm so tired."

He shifted her over enough to pull the covers back. "Come on, we both could use some sleep."

She slid in beside him, kicking her boots off. "I love you, Joel."

He gathered her against his chest. "Me too."

"You forgive me?"

"It's just us in alien land; there's nothing to forgive."

They drifted off together, pain, anger and loss forgotten.

Joel worked with determination, gearing himself for the steady uphill climb that was the recovery from PCP. He spent a lot of the day on the couch in the living room, making plans. Meals he insisted on eating in the kitchen and only at night would he go up to his room. Alix asked if he wanted a television put there but he adamantly refused.

"What are you trying to turn me into, girl, an old man with a box of chocolates by my bed and a channel changer in my covers?"

"Just as long as you eat the chocolates."

By the end of the first week he had managed to get to the basement and was actually getting work done but she made sure he didn't overtax himself. Visitors were his chief pleasure. His closest friends would drop by and he would sit on the couch holding court, dressed in an array of pajamas spanning the gamut from unusual to goofy. For those friends who didn't want to come over there was the telephone, which he used like a lifeline. Hours of conversations took place day in and day out. No mention was made of the studio or the unfinished album.

Alix and Mildred worked happily around him, perked up by his high spirits. And yet Alix noticed that Joel had somehow, in all that boisterousness and positivity, become remote; distant. He still drew his friends' problems, anxieties and feelings out, listened and comforted when they tried to comfort him, joked and laughed and enriched as he had been doing, told them how much he loved them – which he did on a regular basis – but something had changed. The top and bottom ends of his emotional scale were gone; the anger and depression but the elation as well. He had come through some sort of minefield. The end was coming and all he could do was to face it with courage. The change was easier on him and his friends responded to this new calm without realizing what it was.

For Alix, that realization came only after he was gone. It was then that she saw just how brave he had been. Knowing he could do nothing for himself, he had turned all his efforts to helping the people he loved most.

The fevers and sweats were a constant now and his pajamas often had to be changed three or four times a night. Harriet found another nurse to fill in when she could not work and Joel had all the attention he needed. Though his appetite frequently deserted him he pressed on and every meal he could keep down was a victory. There were no longer any fights about food. Alix knew he was trying and that was the best she could hope for. While he didn't regain any weight, at least he didn't lose any more.

She had updated Eleanor who was in touch on a regular basis, as was Roger, now on tour and phoning from various ports of call.

Joel would often commandeer one of the friends to take Alix out for a while to give her a break. She came in early one evening to find the VCR on and the controls sitting beside a jug of apple juice. She announced that she was home and he said he was in the bathroom and would be right out.

After pouring a Scotch, she pressed the 'PLAY' button on the controls to see what movie was on. Her face filled the screen and the camera swung away to pan across the stage. It was the live show that the band had recorded in London. Alix's heart constricted and silent tears coursed down her face. Joel looked so young and energetic.

She felt him sit beside her. "Eleanor called me tonight and we were talking about that show so I decided to watch it after I got off the phone. You know it's funny, you see your face in a mirror every day and you don't see the changes as suddenly. I watch this video and you look pretty much the same. I look at me and I see an old man. I went forward in time and you guys stayed where you were. None of you have changed much, except Bear is fatter now. Was it only two years ago?"

"It seems like ten sometimes, doesn't it?"

"Yeah."

Her eyes searched his face sadly. The blonde hair was heavily streaked with white and there was a greyness and pallor to features that were finely drawn and strained, a fragility about the once muscular body. And yet the sea green eyes still had the same mischievous glint of the troublemaker, the risk-taker.

"Let's watch something else," she said, pressing the 'REWIND' button. "We keep walking down memory lane and you'll want Brad to book us into Vegas doing our greatest hits."

"Rog told me he figures there are three phases in rock history. The first started in the morning when it was young, the second in the early evening when the party started and the third is at midnight when it's payback time."

"What do you think?"

"I say the last one starts at three a.m. when you're by yourself. A lot of musicians died during phase two but they died fast. They were the lucky ones. At least they didn't have to walk through a wasteland for months until they reached a cliff and fell into a black, bottomless pit that's cold and silent. That's for us in the third phase."

"Is that how you see the future?"

"Only when I look at it at three a.m. alone in a dark room. And I don't do that anymore."

"I'll spend tonight with you, Joel. Then neither of us will have to be alone."

There was understanding and patience in his smile. "Sure. You have a nice time with Ash?"

"Yeah, you would've loved it. We talked about you."

CHAPTER 42

May 1994

Brad phoned the next day to say that they were way behind schedule and he wanted the band back in the studio, with the exception of Joel. "He's the only one done his homework, babe. We got enough on tape to get moving."

"He's really pressing for a video shoot for 'The Forever Room'. He called a meeting here this afternoon so we can go over the storyboard."

"I'll round them up."

Joel was in bed when everyone arrived and begged Alix to make his apologies. His temperature was soaring and he couldn't think straight.

She went downstairs to relay the message.

"I booked tentatively for the shoot," Robin said quietly. "Should we cancel or what?"

"These fever/sweat cycles are revolving like crazy now but hopefully they'll settle. How long have we got? Can we wait it out?"

"We're set for the thirtieth of May. That gives us two weeks. You want me to change it?"

"We should be fine by then. Leave it for now."

"What did you guys finally decide on anyway?"

Leo spoke up. "Joel wants just us sitting on bar stools in a white room, leaning against a counter playing whatever instruments we feel like or sipping drinks. It's a pretty laid back song and he wants the video intimate."

"That'll work fine. It won't take long to shoot and it shouldn't tire him out too much. I'll set it up in the Alley View with partitions and a long, high table. We can do it simply and cheaply."

"Cheap is what I like," Brad said with a grin. "Less take off the cream."

"What a shark," Dixie groaned.

When the meeting finally broke up, Alix went to check on Joel. The fever still hadn't released its grip and he lay back limply, his breathing shallow, trying to fight the heat washing over him.

"Everything hurts, Alix."

It wasn't like him to complain. She reached for the bottle of painkillers Dr. Marlowe had prescribed. "Can you swallow some juice?"

He struggled to get his head up and took two pills with half a glass of liquid.

"I'll stay with you a while."

He nodded and closed his eyes. She did what she could but it was up to his body to throw off the fever. Mildred looked in and spoke to Harriet before going home.

The nurse ascended the stairs with compressed lips. "How long has this been going on," she asked after she'd taken Joel's temperature.

"All afternoon."

"You get some rest. I'll call you when it breaks."

The moon was high when she awoke after a distorted dream. Harriet was heading for the linen closet.

"What's going on?"

"He's had some diarrhea. It's all right, I'll change the sheets."

"I'll do it."

"He told me not to wake you. It makes him feel ashamed. I think it's easier for him when I do it because I'm more removed. Let me take care of this and then you can go in."

"Has the fever broken yet?"

"No but I'm sure it will."

She sat with Joel for a while but he was still hot and tossing fitfully in a troubled sleep. Weary beyond words, she went back to bed. Harriet woke her just after dawn.

"I think we should take him to the hospital right away. He's burning up and vomiting and that cough is getting bad. I don't like this at all. We need to get help."

Alix struggled out of bed, threw some clothes on and raced downstairs to bring the car around. Between them, she and Harriet managed to get Joel downstairs and into the front seat. Alix drove like a maniac. The nurse had called ahead and there was a gurney waiting at Emergency. He was put on it and wheeled away.

Harriet took the car keys, parked the vehicle in a lot and returned to the waiting room. "Can I call someone for you?"

Alix shook her head. "I'll be all right. Thanks for your help."

"You'll phone me?"

"As soon as we know something."

"I'll call the other nurse and let her know she won't be needed. They'll probably keep him in overnight."

Dr. Marlowe came out an hour later. "It's PCP again."

"How did it happen so fast?"

"I don't know, Alix. We've moved him upstairs. Why don't you go to the ward?"

He gave her the room number and she went up in the elevator like a zombie. How had things turned so bad so suddenly? Joel had seemed to be holding. He'd had a slight fever the day before and spent most of it on the couch. He had been sleeping a lot but he'd just been through a bout of PCP. And how long had that cough been racking? It had been with him so long that sometimes she didn't really notice it. Certainly it hadn't gotten worse until too late.

Joel was in his room when she arrived and she sat with him for most of the morning. His chest rose and fell in the slow rhythm of the heavily sedated. She wasn't sure he was aware of her, but she held his hand and stayed by his side.

Ash put in an appearance during the afternoon; Dr. Marlowe had phoned to warn him of the situation. He pried her gently away and took her down to the cafeteria. She hadn't eaten all day.

"He's in good hands, Alix."

"Is this it, Ash? Am I going to lose him?"

"I don't know. I wish I did."

The waiting lasted throughout the rest of the day and into the evening. Alix refused to leave but she was flagging fast as exhaustion took its toll and Ash called the others for help. Robin's efforts to persuade her to go home were fruitless but she did agree to walk to the coffee machine at the end of the hall for a drink. Robin talked quietly, trying to allay her fears.

When the pair returned Dr. Marlowe was waiting at the door. "I'm sorry," he said sadly. "We couldn't help him this time."

"Did he wake up," Alix asked anxiously.

"No, but he didn't suffer either. That's something you should remember."

The rest of the night was a blur.

CHAPTER 43

Robin finally got Alix home. "We didn't get the album done," she said on an angry sob, "and there's the video shoot. He was pushing himself so hard. Why couldn't we have more time? He wanted this and he's been through hell. Was a couple more months too much to ask?"

Robin saw the gathering hysteria and gave her a Xanax, then packed her off to bed.

"Don't leave me please."

"I'm not going anywhere. Come on, honey, you need to sleep."

The crying continued and, in the end, she finally crawled into bed with her friend and held her until the medication did its work.

Mildred took charge the next day, trying to help her through the initial stages of grief. Alix accepted this with the understanding that they were both scarred. "Do you want some help clearing everything up, dear?"

"Not yet. You're not leaving too, are you?"

The housekeeper hugged her. 'No, my girl."

Reporters gathered outside the house. Mildred refused to answer the door and Alix called the police, asking for Fielding and requesting help. Understanding, he agreed to clear them away, assuring her that he would have the area patrolled for the next few days.

Brad called a press conference and read a brief statement. "Joel Stark, lead guitarist and co-founder of the Blue Mask, died peacefully in his sleep of AIDS-related pneumonia at ten p.m. on May fifteenth. He was thirty years old. A private memorial will be held. Anyone wishing to remember him is asked to make a donation to the Persons with AIDS Centre. He is much loved and will be missed."

Questions started but he waved his hand in dismissal and left.

Mr. Grayson arrived the next day with the will. Outside of a few personal bequests and the AIDS endowments, Joel had left everything to his best friend. There was a substantial amount of money set aside for various societies and centers assisting people with HIV/AIDS. Alix suspected that he had spread things around to not only help as many as possible, but to keep her too busy to dwell on his death. He had already arranged and paid for his cremation and somehow she got through the red tape. She would be notified when his ashes were available.

Mildred went home at the end of the day and Alix wandered through the house, footsteps echoing. The silence was oppressive and she felt it as a physical force pushing down on her. She ended up in the basement. The overhead light felt bright and brittle. She found a list of Joel's recordings with a long letter to her about keeping up what they had started. He'd left a wealth of material as his legacy to both her and the Blue Mask. She lifted his guitar from its stand and sat, plucking the strings. How the hell was she supposed to carry on? It was too much to ask on top of everything else. She didn't want any more responsibility and he was piling it on her with the will and now this. He'd left her alone, stranded in alien land with no idea of how to get back to everyone else. "You asshole, Joel," she whispered. "Why did you leave me?" Angry and lost, she took the Scotch bottle from the top of the fridge and filled a glass, swallowing quickly and refilling it, trying to dull her senses.

Mildred found her the next morning on the couch, the lights still on and the studio door wide open. Worried, she called Ash.

Alix remained in the basement. Mildred came down at noon with some tea and a sandwich on a tray. "You need to eat something, dear."

"Thanks but I'm not hungry. Leave me alone, please."

She nodded and went back upstairs. Alix stayed there for the rest of the day, silent and uncommunicative. Once the housekeeper left that afternoon, she headed over to the Alley View. The owner had reserved a table near the stage for the Blue Mask; the bouncers made sure that it was available when the band and their friends came in and did what they could to limit any harassment. Alix sat alone, smoking and drinking steadily, ignoring anyone who approached her. Ash and Leo had gone to the house but it was dark and locked so they made their way to the club. She was drunk when they got there.

Leo sat down beside her. "What's going on?"

"I'm toasting my partner in crime, my soul mate, my kindred spirit or whatever the fuck you want to call him. He left me a will with lots of bequests, a list of recordings and a fucking letter."

"He gave us all that list."

"Yeah but I got a letter to go with mine."

"And?"

"I got more jobs and instructions to not break up the band. It all falls on me, Leo."

"It falls on all of us. Last time I checked, we all were in the band. Didn't know you were the only member now."

"You don't know what it was like, being the one there all the time. I'm supposed to carry on and now he asks for more? I can't start on any of this shit - I just lost my best friend."

Ash leaned over, tears in his eyes. "He was my best friend too, Alix. Before you were even on the scene. You're not the only one mourning."

"So what are you doing here, Ash? I'm doing my thing – how come you're not doing yours?"

"We're all in this together. Don't you think we should be helping each other?"

"I don't want any help right now. I can't even think straight. I need to get out of here." She stood up and headed to the door. Once outside, she hailed a cab and gave the driver the address of the Afterhours club.

Leo called a meeting in Brad's office the next day, asking Bear, Dixie, Ash, and Robin to join him.

"Joel wanted to keep Alix busy but he's overloaded her. There's too much pressure right now and she's cracking under it. Her way of dealing is to ignore everything and go on a tear," he said quietly. "I think we need to tag team her. Once Mildred leaves at the end of the day, she's on her own. When she had Joel to take care of she was safe. But she's alone now and he was scared she'd do something really stupid if it all got to be too much. I think we're there."

They came up with a schedule to make sure she wasn't alone in the evenings. Her forays to the Alley View continued and she was drunk most nights, often needing help to get home. Leo showed up at the house at the end of the week when he knew Mildred would be there.

"Do you have Joel's house key?"

"Yes," she said. "I am so worried about Alix. Every morning when I get here she is sleeping off the night before – and not always in her bed. She let me take care of Joel's medications but she won't let any of his things be packed up. It's not healthy. I don't know what to do - she's stopped talking and she's shutting me out." Tears welled in her eyes. "My sister in Saskatchewan has the flu and I need to go there to help out for the week. I'm so scared that little girl will get into serious trouble when I'm gone. She doesn't seem to care about herself anymore."

Leo kissed her on the cheek. "I don't know what we would've done without you, Mildred. Joel loved you a lot. Give me his key. I'll move in for a while and make sure Alix is safe. And try to make her see some sense."

"Thank you, dear."

Mildred explained her sister's situation to Alix, who nodded and hugged her. She was hungover and sick and said little.

Alix headed back to the Alley View that night. Leo and Ash had let everyone else know what was going on and she arrived to find all of them at the table.

"What's this? "

The look Brad gave her was challenging. "What you talking about, babe? We're here supporting each other."

"Looks like I have a bunch of fucking watchers."

His mouth thinned. "Looks like you need them."

"Stay or go, it makes no difference to me. Just leave me alone and save the lectures."

Alix continued to drink and was a mess by the end of the night. Leo took her to the bathroom, holding her head while she was sick. He wetted a paper towel and wiped her face, then helped her to his car and drove to the house. She was beyond protesting when he unlocked the door and took her up to bed. He went back downstairs, got a suitcase out of his car and hauled it up to the spare room.

CHAPTER 44

Alix said nothing about Leo moving in. When the call came that Joel's ashes were ready to be picked up they went together. She put the bronze urn in her bedroom and made no comment about any other plans.

The Alley View outings continued throughout the next week. Leo made sure that Alix got home safely. He often heard her getting sick in the night but did not go help her. He was at a loss as to how to handle her breakdown. He was mourning too and his resentment at her self-indulgence and self-absorption was reaching a breaking point.

Alix was paranoid at the constant attention and focus on her. So she wanted to drink herself into oblivion – what was the problem? She started early one day at the Alley View but knew the others would be arriving soon. Still relatively sober, she wandered around the West End, looking for a new place to drink. Finding one she'd never been to before she wandered in, took a seat at the bar and ordered a double Scotch. She had lit a cigarette and was sipping her drink when the woman who had been following her entered.

The reporter had been harassing Alix since Joel's death, trying to get comments or a story, and had gotten banned from the Alley View for her troubles. But she knew that the singer was drowning her sorrows in alcohol and waited for a chance to catch her alone. Confident that she could get a scoop without interference she sat down, tape recorder in hand.

"Sue Downey, the Echo. Joel's been dead two weeks and we haven't heard anything from the Blue Mask. The full interview he did with Marv Stentson has been released and the revelations in it are causing quite a stir. What's your take on this?"

Alix had been wallowing in self-pity but this woman called up an anger that had been boiling since she had started dogging Joel's footsteps. "Leave me the fuck alone! I've told you I have no comment. You stalking me now that you can't hassle me in the Alley View? Get out or I won't be responsible."

The reply was condescending and laced with sarcasm. "The Blue Mask is public and the public has a right to know. You signed up for that – it's the price of fame. And lately you've been seen out drinking yourself into a stupor. You've made yourself available so stop whining and answer the question."

Alix was about to throw her drink in the woman's face when a man came up to the bar. He stepped between her and the reporter.

"The lady said to leave her alone."

Sue Downey turned on him. "Mind your own business. I'm a reporter."

"And I'm a cop. You have been told to stop. You need to do that."

The woman turned to the bartender, ignoring the intruder. She would wait him out. "I'll have a beer."

He shook his head. "Not serving you."

The cop turned back to her. "Are you going voluntarily or do I need to help you?"

Her mouth twisted and she glared at both him and Alix. "This isn't done, not by a long shot." She stormed out.

Alix looked at the man who had helped her, a thank you on her lips, when she recognized him. Tall, dark-haired and dark-eyed, he had the same hard set to his features that he had after she'd kicked him when they had taken Joel out of the hospital the last time.

"Fielding?"

"Miss Lane."

"Alix. What are you doing here?"

"That would be my question."

"I needed to get away from everyone, find a new hangout."

"Didn't you notice the name of the bar before you came in?"

"No, why?"

He smiled. "It's called The Precinct. The man who owns it is a retired policeman. It's a cop bar."

"Fuck – I'm surrounded by the heat and didn't realize it? I must be drunker than I thought. Thanks for the save but I should probably get out of here."

"I'm heading out too. I'll take you home so that you don't get harassed again – it's on my way."

She looked at him with narrowed eyes. "How do you know where I live?"

"You asked me to help clear the reporters away after Joel Stark's death."

"Yeah, I did and I never really thanked you for that. Can I buy you a beer?"

CHAPTER 45

Alix was in Joel's room. Mildred had cleaned thoroughly and stripped the house of all his medications, taking the unused ones to the AIDS Centre to be given to patients who could not afford them. But Alix had refused her offer to pack up Joel's belongings. "I can't right now. I just can't deal with anymore stuff," she'd said quietly. She had moved the carousel horses to her room and left everything else as it was.

She ran her fingers over the things on his dresser – a wallet containing cash, credit cards and driver's license, some loose change, a cigarette lighter and a receipt from the video rental store. Opening the closet, she leaned in and breathed deeply. His scent was still on his clothes and her heart constricted. Would the pain and the heaviness ever ease?

Leo found her on Joel's bed, fast asleep. She was wearing his leather jacket.

She woke up late the next afternoon to an empty house. Grabbing her car keys, she headed out, driving around aimless and unfettered. Since Joel's death she had not sought the healing ocean, opting instead to drown her sorrows. Restless and edgy she took the road to Lion's Gate Bridge and drove across. She parked and got out, watching the water ripple in Burrard Inlet. It was a grey day with rain in the air and the wind buffeted against her. She stood for a long time, eyes on the waves, mind empty. On a sigh, she returned to her car, drove back across the bridge and parked near the Alley View. It was early and no one was around. She sat smoking and drinking double Scotches but this time they failed to ease the emptiness. Her head swimming, she realized that she'd overdone it and needed to get home before she passed out at the table. She slipped in behind the wheel, closing one eye so that there was only a single lane to drive in.

Leo showed up at the Alley View but Alix was nowhere in sight. Disgusted, tired and heart-sore he headed back to the house. Her car was parked the wrong way on the street – two wheels up on the curb with the rear end sticking out at an acute angle. His face hardened. All of them had tried to help her but enough was enough. They'd always had a gentle friendship and he was not a man given to violent emotions but he could feel the anger rising in him.

She was in the bathroom on her knees, head over the toilet bowl. The acrid bile burned her throat; the Scotch a vile taste as it came up. She stayed on the floor afterwards, chest heaving, sick and shaking.

He helped her up and over to the sink so she could splash cold water on her face. In the mirror, she watched as he put his hands on either side of her head. His voice was low but there was a hardness in it that made her flinch.

"He was scared of this. You were so strong when he was here but now you're falling apart. Do you think he'd want to see you like this? You need to get yourself together, Alix. You're not the only one grieving or suffering or who loved him. You made a pact with Joel that you wouldn't do anything stupid. But he knew how sneaky you could be. You wouldn't deliberately kill yourself but he didn't rule out you drinking yourself senseless and driving off Lion's Gate Bridge by accident. Is that what you're working up to? I never thought of you as a coward - so fucking prove to me that you're not. Are you the tough survivor or are you taking the easy way out? What do you think that'll do to the rest of us? How would you feel if I did that to you? Think about it." He turned and walked out.

Early the next day he went down to the basement. They had five tracks left to record and he gathered together the labelled tapes Joel had done – the base work and solos - putting them in a pile by the door. Then he went back upstairs, woke Alix and asked her to join him.

She watched warily as he picked up the small trash can by the fridge where they put beer bottle caps. He took it to the desk drawer that held Joel's latest tapes, scooped them into it and set it on the low table in front of where she sat on the coach. Taking the Scotch bottle from the top of the fridge, he put it beside the can and removed the cap. Then he picked up the box of matches on top of her cigarettes and handed it to her.

"Go ahead. Douse these and light them. Fuck how it affects the rest of us – it's all about you.

"Is this how you're going to deal with his work? How you're going to handle the pain he put himself through so we could have a couple of albums in the works while we look for someone to replace him? Because he wanted the Blue Mask to carry on. This is his legacy too. If you're done soak it and set it on fire. You may be our voice but you aren't the whole band. The rest of us will have to figure out how to go on. But we will."

She stood up slowly, tears streaking down the thin cheeks. "I'm sorry, Leo."

"I know you are. But that's not enough. We have an album to finish. I'm bringing the tapes to the studio tomorrow so we can get back to recording. But we need vocals and you have to decide if you can do that. We'll be there in the morning."

"Let's go together."

Leo shook his head. "I'm going home. It's time for you to stand on your own, to show up or not. Your choice, Alix." He wrapped his arms around her, hugging her close, this friend of so many years who meant so much to him. "My money's on you, my love." He kissed her and let her go, then picked up the tapes and left the house.

Alix sat quietly for a long time, staring at the bottle. It would be so easy to tip the Scotch down her throat and block everything out; disappear into a fog where she didn't have to think or feel. She'd seen the car; hadn't even remembered driving home. Was she working up to a trip to the bridge? Had she gone so far down the path to destruction that she didn't care anymore? She remembered the look of the water – cold and uninviting, a place that would suck her down into its depths without hesitation. Where the pain would be gone. Where she would be gone.

"Please help me, Joel." She could feel him in this room where he had spent so much time, working against the clock. There was a peace here that could stave off the loneliness and emptiness if she let it. She'd been spending a lot of time here lately, trying to get grounded. Sighing, she recapped the Scotch and put the bottle back on top of the fridge, then placed the tapes from the trash can back in the drawer. Turning off the lights, she closed the door and headed back upstairs.

CHAPTER 46

Leo faced the band the next morning. "I gave Alix what she probably saw as an ultimatum. I'm done with the soft approach; I had to do something harsher. I am so pissed at her right now."

Bear nodded. "I think we're all there, little buddy. What did you say?"

"I told her to set fire to Joel's tapes if she was done but that she wasn't the only member of the Blue Mask. That we would go on without her if we had to. And I moved back home; left her alone. I just hope I did the right thing."

Dixie put her arm around him. "You've been so good with her, Leo. The rest of us just don't know how to deal with her right now."

Jack came into the studio and they discussed the recording for the last tracks. Work went steadily as they started on the music for the first song. Though they were glad to be back, each of them kept looking at the door. By the afternoon all were depressed and exhausted.

The door opened suddenly and Alix walked in. She looked terrible – thin and strained, pale with dark circles under her eyes. But she was sober.

"Sorry I'm late." She walked over to the seat she usually occupied. "Where are we at?"

Leo pulled up a chair beside her, face blank. "Made your choice?"

She shrugged. "Looks like it. What are we working on?"

"'Down the Rabbit Hole'."

"I thought we were leaving the title track till last."

"Change of plan. You in?"

She gave him a long searching look. "Yeah. Let's get going."

Alix had called Brad and requested he set up a meeting after the session. He made arrangements for the band, Ash and Robin to meet in the Alley View. She arrived first and ordered a round. Drinks were waiting when they came in and sat down.

"I got a few things to say," she began, lighting a cigarette. No one smiled or said a word. Tears welled up in her dark eyes. "First, thanks for the support. I know I've been an asshole - haven't been here for anyone and been really busy feeling sorry for myself. Leo asked me a bunch of questions that made me think about a lot of things. His fucking pep talk helped too. He's right: this is Joel's legacy as well as ours. I thought about driving off a bridge with Joel when he was still alive. I've made a couple of passes since then and it scared the shit out of me. So I'm done with that.

"I booked a boat for next Friday for Joel's final wishes and called Eleanor and Morris and Mildred. Everyone good with that?"

Though they nodded, no one spoke.

"Can you come to the house tomorrow so we can pack up Joel's stuff? You all should take something of his that you want, that means something."

Again, they all nodded.

She drew nervously on her cigarette and continued in a quiet voice. "Mildred made a good point when she was trying to get me to do this - there are a lot of people at the AIDS Centre who could use his clothes and shoes and stuff. I couldn't deal with it before and I've been pissed at him for loading all this crap on me. For a great guitarist, his timing really sucked."

No comment.

She picked up the glass of Scotch in front of her. "So a toast – to Joel and to our future. 'Cos we have one."

They all drank. The silence pushed at her. "Am I forgiven?"

Brad looked at the others, waiting until each of them signalled agreement, then leaned over and put his arm around her, pulling her to him. "We're all pretty pissed at you, babe. That was a nice speech but you not getting off that easy. You've been a real pain in the ass, especially for Leo. So rounds are on you for the rest of the night. And if you bitch about it I'm gonna tell Dome to cancel the metal chick look and put you in fucking dresses.

"You also better get your skinny ass back in the studio. Our first album in the new contract and it's weeks behind. Joel did his homework. He'd be disgusted with you."

"I know. I'll be there, promise. And eat ratshit, Brad."

She hugged him fiercely and got up. The rest of the group followed suit, each of them holding her close. They were still a family. Forgiveness was a gift she would never take for granted again.

CHAPTER 47

Morris and Eleanor flew in near the end of the week. Roger, on tour in Australia with Mayday, had been on the phone almost every day since Joel's death but could not join them. Eleanor enfolded her friend, offering what love and support she could. The singer seemed vulnerable, like a deep winter had invaded her soul. But there was a determination and strength about her too, as if she had come through the wars and survived, battered but still standing.

When the final parting came it was a bleak morning.

Alix stood on the deck of the small boat. Waves were tossing and the sky was grey, the air cold. With her were the Blue Mask, Brad, Robin, Ash, Morris, Mildred and Eleanor. Roger had sent a single red rose. The bronze urn that held Joel's ashes was heavy and she gathered it to her chest, seeking comfort. She finally stirred and removed the lid. Crying quietly, she let the ashes spill out onto the water. Eleanor tossed the rose on them and the wind took him.

"Bye, Joel," Alix whispered hoarsely.

Everyone said their farewells. After letting the boat drift in his wake, the captain turned and headed back to shore.

It was a warm morning when the package arrived in the mail. All participants in the video project had been tagged to receive a complimentary copy of the finished piece and some idiot had sent Joel's, despite the fact that he was no longer around to see it.

Alix fed it into the VCR and fast forwarded to his interview. His face appeared on the screen, drawn, strained and so thin.

"Sticking a needle in your arm is no way to reach a ripe old age..."